CROWNS

BLOOD KING
PART II

NICOLA TYCHE

COLUMBIA RIVER
PUBLISHING

COLUMBIA RIVER PUBLISHING
Vancouver, WA 98685

ISBN: PB: 978-1-959615-18-7; eBook: 978-1-959615-16-3
HC: 978-1-959615-17-0; Audio: 978-1-959615-19-4

Cover design by Saint Jupiter Graphic
3D art created by Harry Osborn Art
Edited by Kate Studer
Edited by Hanna Richards
Proofread by Kate Studer

For Kaylin

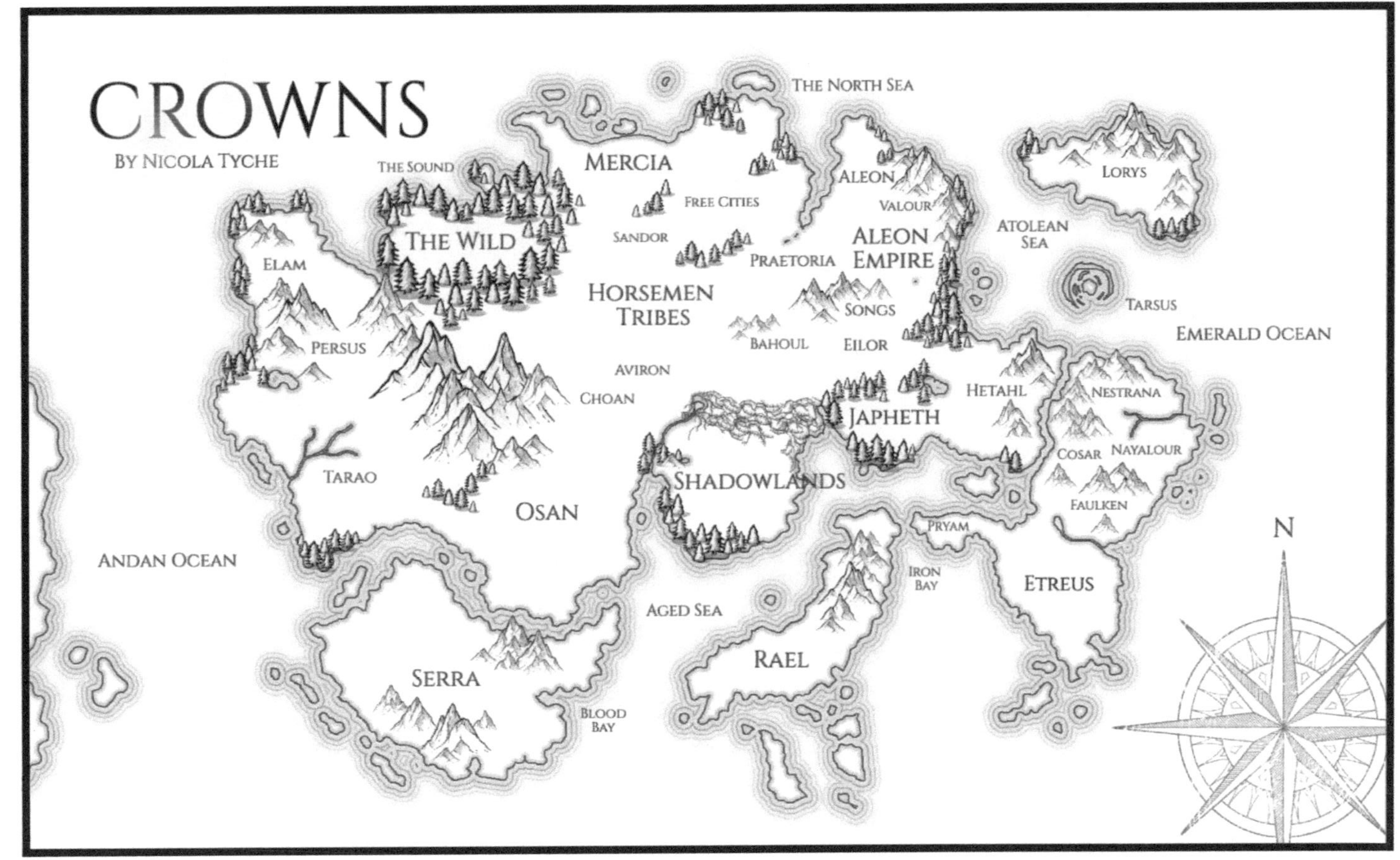

CROWNS
BY NICOLA TYCHE
THE NORTH SEA
THE SOUND
MERCIA
ALEON
VALOUR
FREE CITIES
SANDOR
PRAETORIA
ALEON EMPIRE
SONGS
LORYS
ATOLEAN SEA
TARSUS
EMERALD OCEAN
THE WILD
ELAM
PERSUS
HORSEMEN TRIBES
BAHOUL
EILOR
AVIRON
CHOAN
TARAO
OSAN
JAPHETH
HETAHL
NESTRANA
COSAR
NAYALOUR
FAULKEN
SHADOWLANDS
PRYAM
IRON BAY
ETREUS
ANDAN OCEAN
SERRA
BLOOD BAY
AGED SEA
RAEL
N

Blood King
Part II

CHAPTER ONE

Cyrus had said he wouldn't use assassins.

Now he was sending one to kill his brother. And the Shadow Queen.

It didn't feel right—not to go himself, not to do it with his own hands. It felt cowardly. Worse, it felt like a betrayal to his past self, a denial of the vengeance he was owed. But his closest friends Kord and Everan had made points he couldn't ignore. Cyrus was king. It wasn't practical for him to go. And more—Essandra had asked him to stay.

The assassin stood with a smirk on his face.

"This task will likely see you all dead," Cyrus told him. Let him smirk at that. *Bastard.*

They'd all gathered in Essandra's workroom as she prepared a mixture for the bonding spell. This was a different kind of bond than the normal blood bond. It would allow Cyrus to see through the assassins' eyes, hear through them, speak through them.

"We accept the risk." Orion cocked his head. "It's a mission against the Shadow King. Who do you think sold us to the Jackals?"

Cyrus knew. Essandra had told him. But he needed to be very clear—"This isn't a mission to kill the king," he said. "It's a mission to kill his queen."

"Whose death will crumble his alliance and kingdom," Orion added.

Cyrus didn't lift his icy stare. "It's also a mission to kill my brother."

Orion shrugged. "A gift. Because my lady asked." He glanced at Essandra, who stood beside Everan and Kord, and flashed her a smooth smile.

She pursed her lips, but Cyrus caught the hint of a smile in return.

The heat of jealousy rippled under his skin. This man was a breath away from a sword through his throat.

"You won't have control of their bodies," Essandra told Cyrus as she finished her mixture, "but you can talk to one another, and you'll be able to see, hear, and—if they allow it—speak through them."

Cyrus shot a daggered gaze at Orion.

"We'll allow it," Orion said begrudgingly.

"I don't know how long it will hold," she told them. To Orion, she said, "It's best if you also take a few vials of blood in case the bond breaks, then you can still contact us through the normal bond."

Orion snorted. "Just what I wanted—to keep carrying around a vial with the blood of another man."

"I could give you some of your own blood to carry around," Cyrus said.

The assassin's smirk faded, and he quieted.

"Get sketches if you can," Everan said. "Of the capital and of the castle, like you did in Serra." He rocked off the wall he'd been leaning against with his arms crossed.

The sketches Orion had drawn while scouting the slaving kingdom of Serra were extremely well done, as much as Cyrus loathed to admit it, and they'd been very useful in their war planning. Sketches of the Shadow capital and castle would be invaluable.

Orion shot Everan a caustic gaze. "Anything else you'd like? Should I do some market shopping, maybe?"

Everan ignored the jab.

They made short work of the remaining logistics. Orion and his men would sail across the Aged Sea and up the inlet on Japheth's west side, which would put them just above the labyrinth of the Canyonlands. Then, with the help of Cyrus and his sight through the birds, they'd weave their way through into the Shadowlands and make their way to the capital city.

Teron stood with Essandra as Cyrus and the assassins gathered around her, and she handed them each a cup with a dark liquid.

"Are we going to need him?" Orion asked, eyeing the healer.

"I do need to make some cuts. He's here to fix you up after." Essandra took the assassin's hand. "I need to join you together through a vein of lifeblood. I'll do it here," she said as she drew her finger across his wrist, just above the base of his thumb. "Then you'll clasp hands like this," she added, demonstrating, "and press the cuts together."

"Cozy," Orion said.

She didn't let go of Orion's hand right away, and Cyrus wondered if they'd still be able to do the mission if he were to cut that hand off. Instead, he drank down the bitter mixture in his cup.

"The two of you first," Essandra said as she had Orion and Cyrus face each other. She took their empty cups and put them on the table.

They both offered their right hands, palms up. She made quick slices as she whispered foreign words into the air. Orion's stare stayed locked on Cyrus, but he wasn't wearing his usual insufferable smirk. Was he nervous? *Good.*

Essandra continued her chanting. Cyrus didn't understand the words, but she repeated the same ones over and over. Then she pressed their wrists together. They clasped each other's arms just as she'd demonstrated.

The rush of the bond was immediate. It wasn't like the normal blood bond; there wasn't a mental pull. Instead, it filled Cyrus with a total sense of possession. Of *possessing.* It was like he'd been given an empty sea, and he filled it with the ocean of his being.

Orion jerked back as he twisted against him. "No, fuck this, get him out." He ripped his arm from Cyrus. "Get him out, get out!"

Essandra grabbed his arm, trying to calm him. "It will feel intensely invasive at first. Just give it a moment to pass."

Cyrus let the bond pull him in, exploring what he could do. He could see, he could hear, but he couldn't *feel* anything. He possessed the body but couldn't control it. It didn't keep him from trying, though.

Orion clawed at his head and chest. "Get him out!"

"Cyrus!" Essandra hissed.

Cyrus relented, pulling back.

Orion stumbled to the side of the room and vomited, and Cyrus let himself enjoy the small wave of satisfaction that came from seeing the assassin doubled over.

But that satisfaction quickly evaporated as Essandra put a hand on Orion's back. "You can push him out," she told him. "*You* control the bond. Just close yourself to him."

And the bond Cyrus felt disappeared.

Teron moved to Cyrus, but Cyrus waved for him to pause. "I'll wait until after we've done the others," he said.

"It has to be a new cut with each bond," Essandra responded shortly.

He narrowed his eyes at her. "I think you just like cutting me."

She pursed her lips. "Maybe I do. Right now, anyway."

Was she angry at him? She didn't give him time to think about it as she turned to the rest of the assassins.

"All right, who's next?" She looked at Cyrus. "It can't be everyone. It'll be too much, and you'll risk the stability of the entire bond. I suggest only three more, then just use the regular blood bond with the vials for everyone else."

"Thane, Raze," Orion said, slightly recovered now. "When we split, that will give eyes in each team."

"And one more?"

Orion considered for a moment. "Feran."

The three chosen assassins looked at Cyrus warily, then at Orion, before finally stepping forward.

Essandra created the bond for each of them, and the process went much like the bond with Orion had, with each man having a visceral reaction.

"Why is it making us sick?" Feran asked after, as he leaned against the table.

"Your body is trying to purge the cohabitation, like it's an intrusion," Essandra said. "It will be easier next time."

"It *is* an intrusion," Orion snapped. "And there won't be a next time." He eyed Cyrus angrily. "Make this one count."

They spent the next hour getting used to the bond. It took Cyrus a few tries, but he was surprised to find that it was easier to learn than the blood bond had been. It felt like a dance—he could lean in and lean out, step in and step out, provided the assassins opened themselves to him. Essandra had said it wasn't a physical bond, but it felt physical. Perhaps that was what made it an easier ability to wield.

It also wasn't as overwhelming as the blood bond. He didn't see their memories; he wasn't besieged with their pasts. He simply saw what they saw and heard what they heard. He could silently speak to them, and with a push, he could speak *through* them. It was as if they were sharing one body.

Yes. This would work nicely.

"All right," Orion told his men once they'd gotten comfortable with it, or, rather, as comfortable as they could. "It's late. Get some sleep. We sail out with the sun."

The men filtered out.

"I'm turning in as well," Essandra said. Then to Orion, she added, "I'll see you off in the morning."

"I wouldn't leave otherwise," he said.

She shook her head with stern lips, but there was a smile underneath. "Good night," she said, and she slipped out of the room.

Cyrus's eyes fell back on Orion. He should have asked Essandra if killing one of them would break the integrity of the bond with the others.

Orion chuckled. "I'm starting to get the impression that you don't like me."

"Were you *taught* your skills of observation, or do they come naturally?" Cyrus replied dryly.

Orion snorted. "I'm not trying to take your woman, if that's what you're worried about."

The fact this man thought he could talk to him about Essandra flamed the fire hotter, but Cyrus held his anger. "There's nothing about you that worries me. And she's not my woman." Cyrus had never had anyone who belonged to him. Whom he belonged to...

Orion chuckled again. "Yeah, okay." He grew more serious. "You know, she could have changed our marks of ownership to you, or to herself. But she didn't. She severed them completely. For that, I'm forever in her debt, and I'll always consider her a friend. But you don't have anything to worry about." He pulled a folded paper from his pocket and held it out to Cyrus.

Cyrus eyed it suspiciously but took it and opened it.

Orion smiled. "That's my woman," he said.

The sketch was so real, it felt lifelike. A young woman. Despite it being drawn in charcoal, Cyrus could tell her long hair was blond, probably similar to his own. She had a square face, although still very feminine and very beautiful.

"She has green eyes too," Orion said. "Like gems."

"You drew this?"

The assassin nodded. "The guild wouldn't let us keep personal effects. We couldn't have anything on us when we went to make a kill. Before every job, I would burn it, and after, I'd draw it again."

Cyrus refolded the paper carefully and handed it back to him. "Where is she?" he asked.

Orion shook his head. "I don't know. She was a slave in Elam. I met her when I had a job there. I was younger then. It went poorly, and she helped me escape." He stared at the folded parchment. "I took every job I could in Elam after. The next three years were the happiest of my life." He tucked the paper back into his pocket, and his smile fell. "Then she was sent to Japheth," he said. "But Japheth doesn't keep slaves, and from what I've learned, she's no longer there. I haven't been able to track where she might have gone." He paused, his breath uneven. "Or if she's even still alive," he added.

Orion spoke quieter now, so quietly that Cyrus had to strain to hear him. "Assuming she *is* alive, I like to think she'd come here, to Rael—that she'd hear of your promise and come." He cast his gaze to the ground. "It's the reason I stay."

Cyrus didn't have words.

"Essandra tried to help me find her," Orion said.

He leaned back on his heel in surprise. She hadn't said anything. "She knows?"

The assassin nodded. "But I don't have anything that belonged to her. There's nothing Essandra can do."

Cyrus stood quietly, now feeling very much like a fool. "What's her name?" he asked.

"Vitalia." Orion smiled, but it was a sad smile. "It's been a long time. She probably thinks I'm dead."

That might be all too true in the next few days. "Well, try not to let that happen," Cyrus said, "and I promise you, if you're successful, when you get back, I'll do what I can to help you find her as well."

Orion's surprised eyes locked on Cyrus. "Do you mean it?"

Cyrus nodded.

"That alone would make all of this worth it," Orion said. "Thank you."

Cyrus nodded again. It was the least he could do for a man who was about to help him destroy the Shadowlands. A man who still had something to live for.

CHAPTER TWO

It didn't take long for the assassins to cross the Aged Sea. They anchored a fair distance from the inlet, to keep from being seen, and dropped two rowboats that would take them through the narrow waters more discreetly. As they made their way up, they found Japheth's coast lackadaisically patrolled and had to use only the smallest of efforts to keep hidden.

"This is what happens when you employ mercenaries instead of citizens," Orion said as Cyrus watched through his eyes, as if Cyrus needed more reason to think less of Gregor.

When they reached the Canyonlands, Cyrus could see how quickly men could become lost in the twisted labyrinth. Despite the crippling headache that came from using the eyes of the birds, he was able to navigate the assassins through, helping them avoid the Shadowmen who guarded the pass as well. Only a few times they hit dead ends, with Cyrus receiving some colorful words from Orion, but by the next morning, they found themselves well within the Shadowlands.

They also found abundant hunting opportunities. The terraced rice fields drew endless numbers of ducks and geese. The men ate better than they ate in Rael, and while they stewed broth and meat over their campfires, Cyrus stewed even greater contempt that the gods would bless such a wicked kingdom.

Two days later, they reached the capital. Orion and his men set camp in the outer reaches and settled to run through their plan again and wait for the deep dark of night.

It came too quickly and took too long at the same time, and Cyrus found himself in his study, sweat beading his brow as Essandra, Kord, and Everan stared back at him. He watched through Orion's eyes as the assassins entered the city and slunk through the shadows.

It was the largest city he'd ever seen, larger than Carn, the capital of Rael. Orion and his men moved from building to building, cover to cover, making their way toward the massive black castle that sat slightly higher than the rest of the city and was covered in torchlight like a beacon.

Their progress was slow. Guards were abundant through the city, and high-hanging pole lanterns lit the streets a little too well.

It was well into the dark hours of the morning by the time they reached the castle. Servants rising early for morning chores were out and about, adding to the challenge.

The assassins split into three teams of four to spread out and look for a way in. Raze took three men to approach from the east side, Feran and Thane took another two west, and Orion led the third team around the back on the south side.

"We don't have much time before the sun's up," Cyrus said as they silently moved from street to street, drawing closer. *"We need to find a way inside, and soon."*

"Why don't you sit back and trust us to do our job, yeah?" Orion cut back through the bond.

"I would if you—"

"Found it," Feran said through the bond to Cyrus. *"West side. It looks like there's a servants' door that goes into the kitchen."*

Cyrus relayed the message, and Orion pivoted and led his team west, cutting back a few streets until women's laughs made his team fall back into the shadows, out of sight. Cyrus still watched through Orion's eyes. He couldn't see the women from the alcove the assassin pressed himself into, but one of the women chatting helped place them.

"If you like fabrics, you'd love Mercia," she said as they drew nearer. "The patterns you can get are incredible."

"A Northern accent," Orion said. *"Queen's maid, maybe."* Cyrus recognized it. It had been a long time since he'd heard it.

A door with a bell opened.

"There's one shop," she continued. "It's the oldest shop on the isle. They get everything from Tarsus..."

Her voice cut off with the closing of the door as they stepped inside the building. Orion peeked around the corner and glanced up at the sign—a seamstress shop.

"Tell the men we need to hurry things up," Orion said through the bond. *"We have early-morning maids out. If we're planning on going through the kitchens, we probably won't be able to if we wait much longer."*

"Cyrus," Raze called. *"I think I see the Shadow King. He's leaving the castle."*

Orion said something else, but Cyrus wasn't paying attention to him now. *"Are you sure?"* he asked Raze.

"He looks like the Shadow King. There's someone with him... who... also looks... like a Shadow King."

Cyrus traveled the bond to see for himself. Two large men moved through the dark, the street lanterns casting monstrous shadows as they made their way toward what looked like the stables. One wore a horned helm: the Shadow King. Fire lit through Cyrus's veins—the fire of bloodlust—but he watched quietly.

The other man... Cyrus had seen him before. Even with his face covered, even in the shadows, there was no mistaking him. This was the Shadowman he'd seen in his vision with the Mercian queen in Aleon.

"*The Shadow King is leaving the castle,*" Cyrus relayed to them all. "*And there's another beast of a man with him. Does anyone know who that is?*"

"*Probably his Destroyer,*" Orion said.

Cyrus snorted. "*His what?*" That was the stupidest title he'd ever heard.

"*The Shadow commander,*" Orion told him. "*He's no joke. We need to steer clear of him.*"

"*Looks like fortune's on our side today,*" Raze said. "*They're riding out. One less thing to worry about.*"

Cyrus watched through Raze's eyes as the Shadow King disappeared into the night. It was everything he could do not to tell the assassins to change course after him.

"*As much as I want to, that's not what we're here for,*" Orion said.

Cyrus snapped back. "*What?*"

"*The thousand ways you're thinking of killing him—that's what you're showing us right now. Not that we don't enjoy it. Just reminding you of the mission.*"

Cyrus quickly pulled back his mind. The mission. He pushed himself to refocus.

The men managed to slip through the side doors and into the kitchens, using the morning's dark hours and the dimly lit castle to hide themselves. Once inside, they split up into teams, with each man dotting his skin with blood from a vial in case they needed to fall back on the blood bond.

Feran and Thane took their team down one hall, and Raze led his down another, both in search of the queen, while Orion took three men to look for Alexander.

Cyrus stayed with Orion.

"*What does your brother look like?*" Orion asked, moving stealthily from hall to hall.

Cyrus paused for a moment, then said, "*We're twins.*"

"*Ah, exactly like you then.*" Orion chuckled. "*So, you're telling me I might enjoy this.*"

"*I was starting to like you—don't ruin it.*"

Orion chuckled again.

"*I think we found the queen's chamber,*" Thane called.

Cyrus peeled himself from Orion and dropped into Thane. Two Shadow warriors stood guard at the end of a long hall in front of a private chamber. They wore nothing over their chests and arms, displaying markings not entirely unlike his own. Their faces were covered.

"*They're different from others we've seen,*" Feran said. "*More markings. Royal guards, I think.*"

Royal guards. Guarding a royal.

Thane and Feran stepped from the shadows and sent two flying daggers that buried themselves in the chests of the warriors. Both Shadowmen fell back against the wall, trying to use it to hold themselves. But the daggers had been aimed to kill, and the men slumped to the ground.

The assassins pulled the bodies out of sight, then Thane slipped into the chamber.

The sun hadn't yet risen, but the approaching dawn lit the room enough for him to make out the Shadow Queen under a layer of quilts.

"*She's asleep*," Thane said.

Cyrus wondered how she could sleep so easily. Was her mind quiet? Was her heart at ease?

Thane drew his dagger.

"*Not yet*," Cyrus told him. "*I need to find my brother first.*" Alexander needed to know as Cyrus brought his whole world down.

"*If we have the chance now, we need to take it,*" Thane warned.

"*Find my brother first,*" he said again.

"*The queen is more important.*"

"*I said we find Alexander!*"

Thane stood, staring at the sleeping Shadow Queen for another moment before he finally sheathed his dagger.

"*He'll be close,*" Cyrus told him.

Thane slipped back out into the hall and motioned another assassin in. "*Silva will stay with the queen in case she wakes. If she does, we have to kill her.*"

Silva was bonded only with the blood, but it was fine—Cyrus didn't need to see or hear the sleeping queen. He did need to find Alexander, though. Quickly.

"*Fine,*" he said.

"*We found the queen,*" Cyrus said through the bond to Orion.

"*Good. Have Raze bring his team to join them.*"

Cyrus relayed the message.

"*On our way,*" Raze answered.

"*Keep searching the lower level,*" Cyrus told Orion, "*in case Alexander is already up and at the day.*"

Thane and Feran split, each taking a hall, checking chamber by chamber. Cyrus stayed with Thane. The potential behind every door made his pulse race, but every empty room served a dagger of disappointment. One after another.

"*Shit,*" Raze called through the bond. "*We've been spotted. Top landing of the stairs.*"

"*How many are there?*" Cyrus asked him.

"*Just one. A Northman.*"

"*Looks like we might be in for a bit of trouble,*" Cyrus told Orion. "*Raze was spotted by a Northman.*"

"*Tell them to manage it.*"

"*Deal with him,*" Cyrus said to Raze through the bond.

Thane and Cyrus moved down another hall. Still, there was no sign of Alexander.

"*She's awake,*" came Silva's voice. "*The queen—she's awake.*"

Cyrus cursed under his breath. He'd desperately wanted to wait until he found Alexander, but they couldn't risk losing their chance. "*Kill her.*"

They were running out of time.

"*Anything?*" he asked Orion.

"*Not yet. I'm going to check the east side.*"

"*Cyrus!*" Raze called. "*We need help! We have two men down!*"

"*From the one Northman?*"

"*He's a big fucking Northman!*"

Cyrus swore again. *"This Northman is causing problems,"* he told Orion.

"Tell Raze to fucking deal with it!" Orion snapped back.

"Guys, I'm out." Silva came through the bond again. *"She got me with a dagger."*

"The queen?" What the fuck was even happening right now? *"Silva?"*

Only silence.

"Is something wrong with Silva?" Thane asked.

"Silva?" Cyrus called again. But there was no bond. Nothing. *"Get back to the queen's chamber!"* he ordered Thane.

Thane barreled back toward the queen's quarters, Cyrus with him. *"Feran!"* Cyrus bellowed through the bond.

"On my way," came Feran's reply.

Thane reached the queen's hall. She stood just outside her chamber, staring at a smear of blood on the wall where her guards had been. Sensing Thane behind her, she whipped around to face him.

"Impressive," Cyrus said through Thane's voice to her. "You surprise me, Queen Norah." He hadn't expected her to be skilled with a knife.

Confusion rippled across her face as she glanced toward the bedchamber, then back to him. "Who are you?" she demanded.

Understandable question, but not one he was willing to answer just yet. "Let's say, a very old friend."

"Friends don't kill each other," she snapped.

"No, I suppose that's what family's for."

She shook her head again, her brows dipping, her breaths quick. "What do you want?"

"Is it not obvious?" he said as he stalked toward her. "You."

She bared her teeth. "Well, then, I'll have to disappoint." She spun and raced back toward her chamber.

"*Kill her*," he told Thane.

She reached the chamber in only a few steps, but Thane was close behind. She slipped in and tried to swing the door closed. Thane stopped it with his arm. Cyrus didn't feel the pain, but Thane's bellow rang loud in his head as she threw her weight behind the door, crushing his forearm. Thane surged forward, throwing her back. She lunged to a dead body on the ground—Silva—and pulled the dagger from him. Then she spun back to face him.

Thane swung his short sword, and she jumped back. His blade caught the fabric of her gown and sliced it open. He swung again, high this time, and she ducked. It hit the post of the bed and lodged itself into the wood. Thane and Cyrus cursed in unison as she jumped forward, slicing the dagger into his forearm.

Cyrus cursed again.

Thane released the sword and staggered back.

The queen seized the opportunity to jerk the sword free, and she launched an attack of her own.

And there was nothing Cyrus could do to help him.

She brought the sword down hard. Thane reached up to shield himself and the blade cut into his arm, partly severing it. He bellowed again as she whipped forward with the dagger in her other hand and plunged it into his gut. The last thing Cyrus saw was a blade arcing for Thane's neck.

Then the bond went dark.

CHAPTER THREE

Cyrus roared. He fumbled for another bond. *"Feran!"*

"I'm here; where are you?" came Feran's call, and Cyrus dropped into him.

"Where's Thane?" Feran asked.

"We lost him."

Suddenly, Raze appeared, joining them. Alone.

"Where were you?" Cyrus snapped at him. *"And where are the rest of the men?"*

"I told you—the Northman."

Cyrus was confused. *"You lost three men to one Northman?"*

"We're not bloodsport fighters. We're men of stealth—we get in, we kill, we get out."

As they turned the corner to her hall, they nearly ran into the queen. She held both a sword and dagger now.

Time to finish this.

"You keep surprising me," Cyrus told her.

"Who are you?" she yelled at him.

"As I said, an old friend. But not a friendly one."

She shook her head. She was confused. *Good.*

"*Don't play,*" he told Raze and Feran. "*She's dangerous.*"

Feran, to her left, attacked first. She jumped back and swung a counter, then turned and broke past, fleeing down the staircase.

Fuck the gods. If they lost this woman...

Feran and Raze both tore after her. Raze caught her at the bottom. She wrenched free but didn't run again. Instead, she clenched her blades and faced them.

"*I don't think your brother's here,*" Orion's voice cut through.

"*He is! His blood touched her.*" He'd felt the bond with the queen. He'd seen her. Only with his brother's blood would that have been possible. Alexander was here with her. "*Keep searching.*"

Feran and Raze were now both fully engaged with the queen. She stood with her back toward the wall, her eyes darting back and forth between them. He could see her panic creeping in.

And he couldn't resist.

"*Salara,*" he said through Raze on her right. "Not queen of Aleon. Even I didn't realize the vision of you on the Shadow throne meant a marriage to the Shadow King."

"You're from Aleon?" she asked bitterly. "You're here for revenge?"

"I'm most certainly here for revenge," he said through Feran now. "But I'm not from Aleon."

Her eyes darted between the assassins again, then they narrowed. "How are you doing that?"

Her lip quivered, and her nostrils flared, and she attacked. The assassins faltered. This woman was fast, he'd give her that, faster than both of them, and she sliced her sword across Raze's side. He fell to his knees, but it wasn't a fatal wound.

She spun to meet Feran, and their swords clanged as he delivered a counter.

"Why?" she shouted as she fell back a few steps. "Why have you come?"

For blood. For Rael. But most of all, Cyrus had come for revenge.

"They'll suffer, as I have suffered," he seethed. "Especially Alexander."

Her eyes flashed, and she bared her teeth. "You won't find him here. He's gone."

She smiled. She was lying. Rage rippled through him.

"He's here!" he snarled back at her. "His blood touched your skin."

Raze was on his feet again and moved together with Feran toward her. She lunged forward, throwing her dagger at Raze, hitting him squarely in the shoulder, then swung her sword with full force at Feran. He met her with his own blade in a counter, and she slipped to the side. He heaved another swing, and she dodged, knocking his shoulder and using his momentum to drive him sideways.

Then she bolted into the dining hall. Feran followed her.

"*Cyrus,*" Orion called again. "*I'm telling you, I don't think your brother's here, and we have a bigger problem. The Shadow King is back. We need to get out of here.*"

Fuck the gods. All of them. All the fucking gods.

"*Where is she?*" he snapped at Raze, who had finally managed to get back onto his feet again. He didn't need to wait on an answer as the queen tore back out of the dining hall. She slid to a stop when she saw Raze.

Feran stumbled back out into the main hall behind her, blood streaming from a cut across his temple. She darted down another side hall.

What was even happening? *"Finish it!"* he snarled at them both. *"We're out of time. We have to go."*

Feran and Raze chased her down the side hall to a single chamber at the end, and she ducked inside. Finally. There wasn't an outlet here. She was trapped.

"Be quick," Cyrus told them.

Feran pushed open the door, and both men stepped inside, closing it behind them.

The queen stood in the center of the room, backed against a large bed, facing them. There was no escaping now.

But the fear that had been in her eyes before was gone.

"Cusco! Cavaatsa!" she hissed.

Feran chuckled. "Do you call for your gods?"

"I call for your blood!"

And before the assassins could react, two giant beasts jumped from where they'd been crouching on the sides of the bed, tackling the men.

All went dark in Cyrus's mind, and he bellowed into the void.

"What's going on?" came Orion's voice.

Cyrus was nearly shaking with rage now. *"Get out of there,"* he snarled at him. He followed the bond to see where Orion was and caught a glimpse out the window of the Shadow King entering the castle. *"Get out!"*

"I'm working on it. Did we get the queen?"

"No," Cyrus gritted out. *"How many are still with you?"*

"Still four of us," Orion said. *"Where is everyone else?"*

"There is no one else."

Orion's silence was deafening.

"If they're coming in through the side, maybe you can slip out of the front," Cyrus told him.

"I know how to get out of this fucking castle," Orion snapped back, not bothering to hide his own anger.

"Are you all together?" Cyrus asked.

"Shut up. I'm trying to concentrate."

Cyrus quieted and tried to simply watch through Orion's eyes.

Shadowmen ran past the alcove he was tucked in with his men.

"Watch out," Cyrus said.

"I said shut up."

More Shadowmen swarmed the halls. In mere moments, they'd find the assassins.

Cyrus's pulse raced faster. *"Can you make it back to the—"*

He lost his vision.

"Orion!"

No answer came.

"Orion!"

He searched for the bond but couldn't feel it.

"Orion!"

Cyrus tore open his eyes to find himself in his study again. Kord, Everan, and Essandra scrambled to their feet. They'd been sitting silently the entire time, not sure what was happening but still there, waiting anxiously to see if the mission was a success.

"What happened?" Everan asked.

Essandra wrung her hands. "Are they out?"

But Cyrus was so angry, he couldn't speak. He paced the floor, his chest heaving.

"Cyrus," Everan said.

Still, he couldn't answer.

Essandra stepped closer. "Cyrus?" Her voice was thick with worry. Then came a pull.

Cyrus flung open his mind, desperately searching.

"*I'm here,*" Orion said, but his tone was short. "*We're out.*"

A breath of relief escaped him. He felt like he needed to sit down. "*Where the fuck were you?!*"

"*You were going to get us killed, distracting me. Probably like you did the others.*"

Cyrus put his head in his hand, digging his fingers into his temples until it hurt.

"*We're on our way back,*" Orion said coldly. Then the bond went dark again.

He opened his eyes back to his study.

"Cyrus," Everan prompted.

What an absolute fucking failure.

His throat was dry and raw. He picked up a chalice from the sideboard, but he couldn't bring himself to drink.

"Did they get the queen?" Everan asked.

Slowly, Cyrus shook his head.

"What about your brother?"

Again, he shook his head. In a flash of anger, he flung his chalice against the wall, and it clanged to the ground.

He'd lost.

He'd lost eight men, and he'd lost his chance.

Cyrus leaned his weight over his desk in silence. He'd been so sure about this. So confident.

So wrong.

"Orion has a couple men left," he said finally. "They're out. They're headed back."

Essandra gave a breath of relief.

Another pull tugged his mind. Not Orion.

He opened his mind. It was Jaem, who was still keeping an eye on Bravat, the troublesome bloodsport fighter that refused to return from the Mercian outer reaches.

"*What?*" he said shortly. He wasn't in the mind to hear updates. He certainly wasn't in the mind to hear about whatever Bravat was up to.

"*Hey, I just thought you'd want to know—a Mercian company passed through the Free Cities today, coming home. Guess who was with them.*"

If this was news about Alexander, Cyrus was going to absolutely lose his mind.

"*The Mercian lord justice,*" Jaem said.

Cyrus roared as he swept an arm across his desk, scattering books and parchments to the floor.

Fuck Alexander. Cyrus would kill him. And when the opportunity came again, he'd do it himself.

CHAPTER FOUR

Cyrus sat heavily in the leather wingback chair of his study, alone. He'd even sent the dogs away. The burn in his blood had turned from the fire of fight to the blister of defeat. He let himself slide lower, both in the chair and in his mind.

At first, he'd blamed the assassins.

But this wasn't their fault.

Cyrus had no one to blame but himself. It hadn't been enough for him to *tell* Alexander that he'd killed his queen. He'd wanted him to know as it was happening.

But Alexander wasn't there.

And this queen—she wasn't what he'd expected. She wasn't a helpless victim. She was strong. They'd lost two men before they'd realized just how strong she was.

He sank even lower into the chair, his elbows on the armrests. He tented his hands against his forehead with his eyes closed.

Another attempt would be near impossible. The element of surprise was gone. The Shadowlands would have increased their guard; Cyrus doubted he'd even be able to enter the kingdom now. Not to mention that his council was beside themselves—first for casting aside his focus on Serra and taking on such a rash mission; second, for risking Rael; third, for not telling them... He didn't even know why he was bothering to number the reasons; there were too many to count.

Without the active compulsion of bloodlust, he saw it now—the irrationality. The madness.

Everan carried the weight of defeat on his shoulders. He blamed himself for not being able to dissuade Cyrus, but Cyrus alone was to blame. It had been his idea—he was the only one manic enough to think this effort had been possible, and he'd refused all reason to the contrary. No one could have stopped him. And Cyrus wished he could say that they should have never gone at all. That was what he *should* say.

It was the right thing to say.

It was the right thing to believe.

But the truth was, if he had missed this opportunity, he would have hated himself even more than he did now. He should have gone himself. He should have—

He felt the pull of a blood bond, and he bolted upright.

His breath caught, and his chest tightened.

It wasn't Orion. It wasn't his men. It wasn't Jaem.

The Shadow Queen.

It couldn't be. She'd need his blood, and Alexander wasn't there.

But the pull...

He should ignore it. It didn't matter. He couldn't do anything now anyway.

But it clawed and it scratched at his mind. *What if Alexander was there? What if she'd lied?*

No—Jaem had confirmed he'd passed through the Free Cities on the way back to Mercia.

What if he'd been wrong?

Cyrus shook his head against the pull. He shouldn't open himself to it. It would only bring back the madness, potentially fuel it more, given that there was nothing he could do about it.

But the pull, the pull, the pull...

He closed his eyes.

And surrendered to it.

The pathway wasn't clear. The bond wasn't strong. It was either a little bit of blood, perhaps diluted, or old blood, or... He wasn't quite sure. It could be any number of things.

But he found her.

Only, just as he connected, the bond broke, and she disappeared.

He staggered up, his heart racing. For a moment, he questioned if it really had been her.

No, he was certain of it. It was the Shadow Queen.

He also felt the madness returning. He paced the room, trying to push it down. Even if Alexander was still there, there was nothing Cyrus could do. Knowing would only make him obsess—take over every thought and every dream. Make him do something foolish. He'd get his brother, he assured himself, and he'd bring down the Shadowlands eventually, just as he was planning to bring down Serra.

Serra.

He needed to focus on Serra and push Alexander from his mind. His council had pressed him into making a public address, to share the progress in building their army and assure the people that he had a plan against the slavers' kingdom. It had been well received by the masses.

Cyrus had put Kord in charge of the basic-combat regimens, and each arriving refugee ship brought a new wave of men to start training. It wouldn't be long before he had a healthy-size army.

But his mind drifted back...

If Alexander was in the Shadowlands...

Cyrus's heart beat faster.

If Alexander was in the Shadowlands...

He had to find out.

His eyes settled on the iron birdcage in the corner.

Three days it should take a bird to reach the Shadowlands.

It had been only a day and a half, and the bird Cyrus had sent had almost reached the castle. He tried not to push the animal nonstop—it would do him little good if it died of exhaustion before reaching its destination, but it was all Cyrus could think about.

He should have sent two birds. He should have sent them all.

"Cyrus?" Everan prompted.

He looked up to find his council staring back at him from around the table and tried to refocus through the relentless throbbing in his head.

"Is everything all right, Sire?" Fatim asked.

"Of course," he replied, blinking back the pain behind his eyes. He certainly wasn't going to tell his council about the bird he'd sent to the Shadowlands. He hadn't even told Everan and Essandra.

"You'll meet with the nobles, then?" Turin asked. Turin had joined as his new master of law, after Murius had been killed in the nobles' first attack.

Cyrus cupped his fist as he leaned forward on his elbows, trying to focus his mind on their conversation. Three harvest wagons had been taken in another strike by the nobles. Fortunately, no one had been killed, but the nobles were now formally requesting a meeting. They'd sent a letter the night prior. The audacity fired his blood. And he hadn't forgotten about the pyre that had been lit in his courtyard—a threat against the witches.

His council had been pushing heavily for him to meet with them, as had Kord, but Cyrus hadn't wanted to commit then. And he didn't want to commit now.

He tucked his chin and pinched the bridge of his nose between his eyes, briefly closing them. He checked on the bird again.

It was almost to the Shadow castle.

His pulse quickened. He needed to leave—he needed to find somewhere private, somewhere he could focus.

He stood abruptly.

"Sire?" Turin pushed.

"Fine," he said quickly. "Arrange it."

Kord straightened in his chair. "Really?"

"I said do it," he snapped back, sharper than he'd intended. He settled himself. "Set it up," he said, cooler this time. He pushed his chair back. "If that's all, there's something I need to tend to."

The councilmen nodded, perhaps not wanting to push their good fortune, and he turned and strode from the council room.

"Cyrus?" Essandra caught him in the hall.

He paused and looked back.

"Are you all right?" she asked. "Do you need help with something?"

He shook his head. "No, we'll talk later."

"Cyrus—"

"I'm fine," he assured her. Then he quickly made his way to his chamber.

As soon as the door closed behind him, he dropped to his knees and sat back on his heels, closing his eyes and letting his mind race the pathway.

The bird had reached the castle and sat perched on top of the tower. The animal was weak, its vision blurry, and the connection was fading in and out. The bond would break soon, if the bird didn't break first.

He pushed it off the tower, willing the small animal to carry itself on exhausted wings through the outdoor open galleries that ran the walls of the castle. Under the high-arched walkways, it flew from window to window, with Cyrus searching for any sign of Alexander through its eyes.

He found nothing. A deep ache pierced his mind, but he pushed through it.

Through a colonnaded forecourt, across an expansive garden, and down another covered walkway, he flew. Up, up. Window after window after window.

Until moonspun hair caught his eye.

The Shadow Queen.

He let the bird pause and rest on the railing of the outside balcony. He recognized this room—where he'd tried to kill her only days ago.

She sat across a settee, a cup of steaming drink in her hand. A book lay open in her lap, but she wasn't reading it. There was someone else in the room, just out of view—a maid, perhaps—but the queen paid them no mind, and neither did he.

Her eyes were blank as she stared through the window.

Blank as they looked at the sky.

Blank as they landed on him.

She straightened. Her lips moved, but he couldn't hear her.

Then she stood abruptly.

A sinking feeling pitted his stomach, but he barely had time to form a thought before she flung her teacup at him. The windowpane shattered, and the bird took flight.

Cyrus's connection broke. He threw his mind back into the chaos of the Aether, searching desperately, but the pathway wasn't there. He wasn't sure if it was the bird or just the bond.

Either way, it was gone.

Cyrus opened his eyes. He was once again in his chamber, hunched forward and panting. Sweat beaded his brow and trickled down his temple. He breathed heavily on his knees.

Until his heart slowed. Until his breaths quieted.

Then he rose to his feet. He swayed slightly before catching himself. Pain throbbed in his head, but he ignored it. Wiping his face roughly with his hand, he lumbered toward the sideboard where a pitcher of water and a chalice sat. He drank straight from the pitcher.

His control was slipping. He could feel it. Slipping right through his fingers.

What was he doing? He needed to get back on track, he needed to rebuild Rael and bring down Serra.

He needed to meet with the nobles, like he'd committed.

Nobles who were just like Pyro.

Nobles who had killed Essandra's witches.

Nobles who threatened her still.

Fire rippled under his skin. And that control he was so desperately trying to hold on to slipped a little bit more.

All around him was darkness.

Not the natural darkness of night—a darkness with weight. It pressed into him from every side. Cold. Merciless.

And there was something in the darkness.

Fear surged through him. His body screamed to run. And he tried—

Blind. Breathless. But he couldn't.

The darkness wrapped around him. Desperately, he pushed himself harder, but it tightened. And tightened more. Binding him. He fought against it. He couldn't move, and he struggled harder.

A scream ripped from his lips. "No! Please!"

But it wasn't his voice that cried out.

It was hers.

Essandra.

Drenched in sweat, Cyrus snapped up in his bed, his lungs heaving. The dream clung to him—still vivid, still visceral.

Another nightmare.

He threw off his sheet and tore down the hall, not thinking, just moving, the dogs at his heels. He needed to be sure...

When he reached her door, Aaron was there.

The guard straightened as Cyrus approached, holding up a calming hand. "She's all right," he said quickly. "She just opened the door a moment ago. Asked for water. I've sent a man to fetch it."

Cyrus's eyes moved to the closed door. His racing heart slowed. He wanted to knock, wanted to see her. But she wouldn't like that. She didn't want comfort. She wanted control. She wanted power against what was after her.

She hadn't said a name in the nightmare, but she didn't need to. He already knew who haunted her.

Soroya—the high witch of the coven Essandra had escaped.

The dogs whined at his side. Cyrus put a hand on One's head, calming himself as well.

Essandra was safe. There was nothing he needed to do. Nothing he could do. At least, not right now. He sighed, giving a short nod to Aaron. Then he turned and padded quietly back to his chamber, carrying the weight of her fear with him.

Chapter Five

"You look pretty," Kord said.

Cyrus ignored him.

They sat on their horses on the ridge just outside the capital, Kord on his right, Everan on his left. Essandra and the rest of his men were just behind him.

They'd come to meet the nobles. Cyrus shifted in his armor—the armor Essandra had made him wear. She was concerned that perhaps the nobles' intentions weren't ones of goodwill. Cyrus wasn't sure his own were either.

"Are you wearing silk braies underneath?" Kord jested.

Cyrus snorted. "I'm wearing no braies at all, so you don't want to be around when I take it all off." He hadn't told Kord about how the forge witch had imbued the armor with magic. Maybe because it sounded silly. Maybe because he wasn't sure if he believed it himself. Or maybe it was the needle of guilt that he was the only one with it. He should ask for armor for his men, although he knew they wouldn't wear it.

"What will you say to them?" Kord asked, finally turning serious.

Cyrus cut him a quick glance. "It depends on what they say to me."

The nobles sat on their horses a distance away. There were quite a few of them—more than Cyrus had thought still remained. They didn't have their army with them—a poor decision—but they had more than the number of men Cyrus had brought. They were obviously committed to *some* show of force. Cyrus wagered these were all the instigators.

He waited for them to make the first advance.

They didn't.

"They're waiting," Everan said.

Cyrus snorted. "They're the ones who wanted to talk."

"They're probably trying to figure out if you've come to play nice."

He chuckled. *The nobles were nervous.* He reached up and unbuckled the clasps of his breastplate, then dropped his armor to the ground.

"Cyrus!" Essandra hissed. "Put that back on."

He glanced over his shoulder at her. "I look like I'm here to fight," he said as he took off the remaining pieces, dropping them as well.

She pursed her lips.

"I'll go alone," he told his men, and urged his mount forward.

He drew closer to the group of nobles, and a man in front urged his horse forward to meet him. Cyrus recognized him. Alric. A friend of Pyro's.

They met in the middle.

Alric slid down from his horse.

Cyrus did as well.

"King Cyrus," Alric greeted him.

Cyrus didn't greet him back.

They warily closed the space between them, coming to stand face-to-face.

"Thank you for agreeing to meet with us," the noble said.

Cyrus still didn't reply. He had nothing to say. While he had agreed to meet them, the nobles certainly weren't welcome here.

Alric shifted uncomfortably. *Good*—he should be uncomfortable.

"We want to negotiate a truce," the noble said. "We'll accept the terms of your rule. In return, we ask for our homes back. Our land."

That land was now being used for farming to feed the people of Rael. Cyrus would *not* be giving it back.

"We also want ten percent of storehouse rations," Alric added.

Cyrus almost snorted. Did this man really think he was in a position to negotiate? Anger heated his core. This man was too bold.

"And"—Alric's gaze moved behind Cyrus, to where Essandra waited—"you will expel the witches."

Faster than the wind, Cyrus drew his sword and had it to the noble's throat.

Alric's eyes widened. "You gave your word that this was a meeting of peace."

Cyrus frowned. "I don't even know what peace is." And he pushed the blade through his neck.

Bellows rang down the line of mounted nobles, and they kicked their horses forward in a charge. Alric sank to his knees, choking as blood spilled down the front of his jacket, the blade still piercing him.

Behind Cyrus came the roar of his men as they charged in a counterattack. But Cyrus didn't take his eyes from the nobleman. He reached down and grabbed the top of his hair, holding his head as he severed it from the rest of the man's body.

Horses thundered around him as both sides clashed in blood, but he paid them no mind. He turned, severed head in hand, and walked to where Essandra held back her own mount from the fight.

He tossed the head to the ground in front of her. "Reparation," he said. "For your witches."

Then he turned to see his men finishing the remainder of the nobles. It didn't matter that his men were outnumbered. The nobles didn't stand a chance. They hadn't come with their army, and it was over as fast as it had started.

Cyrus walked back and mounted his horse again. He didn't even wait for his men to finish off the injured before he motioned Essandra back toward the capital.

Eventually, Kord and Everan caught up with them.

"You planned for that to happen all along," Kord said, anger hitching his voice. "They were willing to submit to your rule. Was that not enough?"

"No," Cyrus said. "It wasn't. They wanted land, food from our storehouses." He paused, glancing at Essandra. "Among other things."

Kord's nostrils flared. "It's called negotiating! You could have countered."

But Cyrus hadn't come to negotiate.

Kord snorted angrily and shook his head, then urged his horse forward. Everan followed.

Cyrus watched them go. "Something is wrong with him," he said to Essandra.

She sighed. "People grow weary of death."

"The nobles didn't deserve to live."

"You should have told me that was your plan."

"I didn't have a plan." He cocked his head. "But did you really think I would meet them in peace? After what they've done?"

There could be no peace.

Chapter Six

The dining room was quiet. Not everyone was there. Brant and Bash were in Pryam, and Jaem in Mercia, but still, it was too quiet. Cyrus could hear the dogs breathing under the table.

He put down his fork and let his eyes travel the hall. When he'd first moved into the palace, before Visa had pulled them together, he'd felt alone. Now, under the weight of everyone's disappointment, he felt alone again.

Cyrus took a sip of mead from his chalice. "It had to be done," he said, finally breaking the silence. He wanted this to be over; he needed them to be able to move past the incident with the nobles.

"I think that's a matter of opinion," Kord said.

What wasn't a matter of opinion was that he couldn't go back and change things now. Not that he would if he could. "What's done is done," he said. "And it's over."

"And what if it's not?" Kord cut back. "What if that wasn't all of them? What if there are more nobles?"

Cyrus shrugged with a feigned frown. "Ask them if they want to meet to talk."

Kord dropped his fork onto his plate and pushed back in his chair.

Apparently, Cyrus's humor wasn't appreciated.

Kord's eyes were cutting. "What if we'd lost another man? What if Everan had taken a blade?"

Cyrus snorted. "A Raelean noble wouldn't have been able to take Everan down."

"Accidents happen, mistakes happen. What about our men who weren't gold-tier fighters? What about Ram and Sergen?" His voice grew louder with each word. "What about Hephain?"

"Kord," Everan warned.

"No!" Kord snapped at him. "They had upward of a hundred men. We came with thirty." He shot his icy gaze back to Cyrus. "If your plan all along was a fight, we should have brought more men! It's a gods-damned fucking miracle we all walked away from that!"

"That's enough," Everan said firmly, putting a hand on the table.

"You know it's true," Kord told him.

"Calm down," Everan said. "Eat."

"I've lost my appetite." He shoved himself up from the table but stood a moment as he turned his angry eyes back on Cyrus. "When you deal in blood, you pay in blood." Then he turned and strode from the dining hall.

Hephain sighed, setting his fork down, and moved to rise and go after him.

"I'll go," Cyrus said, stopping him. He stood, emptied his chalice of the rest of the mead, then followed after Kord.

He wasn't offended at Kord's anger, maybe because he knew he deserved it. Maybe because he'd come to accept that there would be people who wouldn't understand him and what he needed to do. He'd just never thought Kord would be one of those people.

His friend wasn't in the practice field, leaving one other place for him to most likely be—where Cyrus did find him—on the outdoor armory pad, polishing his vambraces, the only armor Kord wore. Polishing armor was pointless, but it was a good activity to do while mad.

Cyrus sat on the low work stool beside him. "I know you're angry with me," he said. Sometimes stating the obvious was the best way to start a conversation.

Kord scooped more polishing paste onto his rag and started working it into the metal. "I'm angry with myself," he replied. "I've known you for ten years, Cyrus. I don't know why I expected that meeting with the nobles to go any differently."

"Why do you care so much about the nobles?"

"It's not just the nobles. It's fucking everything. You're relentless."

Cyrus watched him work the paste across the metal, applying pressure, building the heat of friction—heat made with anger. That was why polishing was an excellent task to do when mad.

"I know you hope for a different life," Cyrus said quietly.

Kord paused and looked up at him. "You don't?"

He never thought about a different life, let alone hoped for one. "I can't," he said. "This is who I am. It will be who I am until I kill my brother. Until I kill the Shadow King."

"And what if you never do?"

He didn't say the answer they both knew to be true—that he'd die trying.

Kord dropped his rag in the caddy and set down the armor piece. "I was never scared before."

Cyrus didn't know what to say to that.

"In the arena," Kord continued, "I accepted my fate and my life. I wasn't afraid to die, because I thought a bloodsport fighter was all I'd ever be. I had nothing to lose. But now, now that the arena's gone, now that there's a life to live, for the first time—I'm scared. To have come this far..." He sighed. "It's not that I'm afraid to die, but I'm afraid to die without having lived." His face was full of sorrow. "I want this to stop. There's so much more that I dream for, but right now, I just want this to stop."

Cyrus understood, but... "I can't," he whispered.

Kord nodded. "I know."

And then what else could Cyrus say? Where did this leave them? He tried to swallow the hard lump forming in his throat. What else could he do?

There was only one thing—

"If you want to go, you have my blessing," Cyrus told him.

Kord's mouth opened. He stood.

Cyrus stood too.

His friend didn't answer, only stared at him in disbelief.

Cyrus reached out and hooked an affectionate hand around the nape of Kord's neck. "My blessing and my love," he added. "I want you to be happy, brother. And if you need to leave to do that, then you can."

Kord's eyes teared.

Cyrus gripped his shoulder tightly.

His friend looked to the ground, then back up at Cyrus. "There are people I love here."

Cyrus nodded.

"But I can't stay," he added.

His words cut. Cyrus stared at him. He'd meant it when he'd offered; he just hadn't expected Kord to accept. He nodded again as his heart broke.

Chapter Seven

The smells of the port brought back thoughts of Pryam, but Cyrus wasn't headed to Pryam. He'd put off Japheth for as long as he could, and despite having replied to Gregor that he'd visit several weeks after his last letter, it had now been over a month and a half.

That could still be considered *several weeks* to some. To Cyrus.

But the council pushed him not to wait any longer, and Essandra wouldn't let him wait any longer. He was still building an army to move against Serra, and despite it growing quickly, they weren't ready to act yet. In the meantime, he needed to continue to move Rael's future forward. And although he'd delayed a trip to Japheth, he wasn't particularly disgruntled about going. He'd come to see that forming an alliance with Gregor might also serve his own interests. If he could break Japheth's alliance with the Shadowlands, it would be one less ally to come to the Shadow King's aid.

The ship was nearly ready as he boarded, and he joined Everan and Ram on the bow. It was strange not to have Kord beside him. Out of all his brothers, Kord had been in his life the longest. They'd fought together, survived together, wept together, grown together. Kord knew him better than he knew himself. Now he was gone. He'd said he would travel the world, and Cyrus had given him the means to see everything he wanted and more. He desperately hoped their paths would cross again, but he also knew he'd have to come to terms with the fact that they likely wouldn't, and that left an aching hole in his chest. He tried not to think about it, but it had been on his mind since they'd said goodbye two days ago.

Another brother gone from his life—

And this one hurt the worst.

Essandra stood on the docks, her dark hair blowing in the sea breeze. She'd contemplated coming with him to Japheth but decided not to. He was glad. He didn't like the idea of bringing her to a place he hadn't first visited, a place he didn't know was safe. And he didn't trust Gregor. He didn't like him.

Gregor was not a friend.

Apparently, she felt the same. Earlier that morning, she'd worked a spell over him. He recognized it—it was the spell she'd used when they had traveled through the Aether to the stone circle.

"This just lets me know if something goes wrong, if something happens to you," she'd told him.

Cyrus wasn't worried about what would happen to him in Japheth so much as he was about what would happen in Rael while he was gone. The times he'd left before, the nobles had tried to retake the capital, but the past three weeks had been quiet. Cyrus wasn't foolish enough to truly believe they'd killed the entire resistance with the last encounter, but they'd likely killed the leadership. They'd cut the head from the snake.

But the thing about decapitated snakes—they could still be dangerous.

Cyrus knew Essandra could take care of herself, and she had her guards. Hephain and the palace guard would remain with her, as would the dogs. Still, he didn't like leaving her.

Footfalls came behind him, and Cyrus turned to see Sergen.

"The horses are loaded," Sergen said.

"Good." It had been Kord's idea to bring the animals, so that Cyrus wouldn't be pressed into accepting an offered carriage. He'd mentioned it when they'd visited Pryam, and it was a good idea. Kord had a lot of good ideas. Cyrus wished he'd listened to him more.

"Are you all right?" Everan asked.

Cyrus looked up to find his friend staring back at him with a trenched brow. "I'm fine," he said.

They both turned and started toward the shipmaster's room. They needed to review navigation plans one last time. The weather wasn't expected to be favorable. Cyrus was hoping that expectation had changed.

"Have you seen Orion?" he asked Everan.

"I know he boarded, but I don't know where he's at now."

Cyrus hadn't been sure if the assassin would come, given he was still angry about the Shadowlands. Cyrus had hoped he would—not because he needed anything from the assassin but because it was the last known place of the woman Orion had been searching for, Vitalia. Despite the devastating failure in the Shadowlands, Cyrus still felt obligated to help find her. He didn't expect the offer to make Orion any less angry at him, but it was still the right thing to do.

"Are all the men ready?" he asked as they took the stairs down from the top level of the bow.

"They are," Everan said. "I also checked supplies. I'm assuming we can restock in Japheth, but if for some reason we can't, we have enough to get us there and back."

Cyrus nodded. "Good. I also want—"

He stopped abruptly.

And he stared at Kord walking up the gangway.

His friend carried a pack over his shoulder and dropped it on the deck when he reached them.

"I don't want to talk about it," Kord said before Cyrus could even find words.

Cyrus shook his head, still in disbelief. "What are you—"

"I said I don't want to talk about it. I can't believe you think I'd let you go to Japheth by yourself, though." He jabbed a finger to Cyrus's chest. "But I swear to the fucking gods, if you start a war while we're there..."

Cyrus shook his head again, this time in reassurance. "I'm going to discuss an alliance—"

Kord's eyes narrowed. He glanced at Everan and then looked back at Cyrus.

Cyrus smiled. "You have my word, brother."

CHAPTER EIGHT

Sailing into Japheth was like sailing into another world. An abundance of greenery softened two towers that sat nestled just beyond the seawalls. Vines stretched across the rockface, blending green and brown with the bright sandstone. Seagulls sounded overhead. The port wasn't empty, like Pryam's, but it also didn't have the bustling trade Cyrus had expected. Maybe he shouldn't have expected it. He knew Japheth primarily traded with Tarsus, the small island kingdom in the heart of the Atolean Sea, as well as with the Shadowlands. The thought of seeing a ship from the Shadowlands made his whole body tense.

But none of the ships in the harbor bore black flags.

He did, however, notice Japheth's flag—a lion surrounded by six stars. "That's what you were talking about," he said to Everan as he nodded at it.

Everan snorted. "Yeah. He only holds Japheth and Hetahl, but he claims the four kingdoms of the Aleon Empire too."

As he had in his letters. Gregor insisted they were his birthright. Perhaps that was true, but then he should go to war and fight for them, not put them on his flag and pretend.

Kord joined them on the bow of the ship. His relief at the sight of land was palpable. The journey hadn't been an easy one. They'd hit a storm in the night that had made Cyrus wonder if they'd even make it to Japheth. It had left Kord heaving over the railing and cursing Cyrus even more. Cyrus had needed to use his blood to force the horses to calm. By morning, the sun had come out with no more than a balmy breeze. Compared to the heat of Rael, it felt like paradise. It looked like paradise. But it wasn't paradise.

Gregor wasn't at the docks to meet him, although, after gaining a little insight into royal visiting practices in Pryam and having been better prepped this time by his council, Cyrus had learned that was not unusual. However, unlike in Pryam, here there was a rather large group of people who did await him.

They looked to be primarily people to help with unloading, with the exception of a well-dressed dignitary of some sort in front.

As Cyrus walked down the gangway, the dignitary bowed low—lower than a man ought to be able to bow. Cyrus had never gotten comfortable with people bowing to him, although he'd at least grown somewhat used to it. However, this prostration brought a whole new level of discomfort.

"King Cyrus," the man said, still not rising. "Welcome to Valour. I am Moran Siefer, lord governor of Valour."

Cyrus paused. "Valour, as in the capital city of Aleon?" But this was Ivera, the capital of Japheth.

"Aleon belongs to King Gregor by birthright," said the man. "We've temporarily established Valour here as coterminal capital, until we can drive the usurper from our northern lands."

It amused him that they referred to Phillip, king of Aleon, as a usurper, as though his father hadn't granted him reign.

He glanced around. "But... this is still Ivera?"

"This is Valour," Moran corrected. "*Temporarily*, by coterminal trans-city establishment."

Cyrus narrowed his eyes. He wasn't sure what any of those words meant, but he got the gist of the message. Gregor was calling this the temporary capital of the empire—an empire that he claimed but did not actually hold.

"And how long does it *temporarily* stay Valour before it just becomes permanently Ivera?" he asked. Apparently longer than ten years, which was how long Gregor had been bickering with his brother.

Kord delivered a sharp poke to Cyrus's back.

"Thank you for the welcome," Cyrus said, moving on.

"King Gregor is very much looking forward to meeting you," Moran said, still holding himself low and not raising his eyes.

"Where is he?"

"In the throne room, Your Majesty. It would be my pleasure to take you there now."

Cyrus would be meeting the king right away, then. That was good. "Lead the way," he told the man.

"Of course, Your Majesty." Somehow, Moran bowed even lower before finally rising and starting down the dock toward the port city.

Cyrus and his men followed to where a large carriage waited.

Moran opened the door and bowed again. "After you, Your Majesty."

"We'll follow," Cyrus told him.

The man's head bobbed, but he still kept his eyes down. "It-it's a long way, Your Majesty," he stammered.

"I brought horses, and a ride would be nice after so long on the ship. We'll follow."

Moran had nothing to counter with. "As it pleases Your Majesty," he said finally, before climbing into the carriage himself.

Cyrus's men brought the horses for him, Everan, and Kord, who mounted and then followed the carriage deeper into the capital.

It really did prove to be a long way, and Cyrus found himself thankful for the horses instead of the carriage ride. He glanced back at his men marching behind him and was proud to see them smoothly keeping up.

As the streets grew more elaborate, the buildings more ornate, the greenery more carefully kept, Cyrus sensed them getting close. It wasn't much longer until a palace came into view, and when it did, Cyrus couldn't take his eyes off it.

Colorful mosaics of interlocking stone ornamented the outside walls. Greens, blues, and yellows wove patterns of delicate florals and winding vines in meticulous symmetry.

A congregation of people standing out front drew his attention—more specifically, a man who could be none other than King Gregor, as evidenced by the too-large crown that sat atop his head. He wore a thick embroidered doublet under an even thicker embroidered cloak, which was lined in furs that were *not* fitting of the climate. Japheth wasn't hot like Rael, but certainly no one should be wearing furs.

"I thought he was waiting in the throne room," Cyrus said as they drew nearer.

Kord shrugged. "Maybe he's excited."

"Or desperate," Everan added.

"Ah, King Cyrus!" Gregor said as they reached him. "Welcome to Valour!"

The capital name still needled Cyrus. He wasn't sure why he cared. It was Gregor's kingdom—he could name things whatever he wanted. But pretending one capital was actually another just seemed silly and petulant. Still, he forced a pursed smile and nodded before dismounting.

"King Gregor," he greeted him. "Thank you for the warm welcome."

"You must be travel-worn after your long journey."

It actually wasn't that long—only slightly longer than it took to get to Pryam. Gregor made no inquiry to *how* the journey had gone, which didn't bother Cyrus, as he wasn't one for small talk.

"I'll show you to your residence, where you can freshen up before dinner."

Upon entering the palace, Cyrus was first struck by the clash of culture. Old-world beauty mixed with... whatever Gregor considered his gaudy style. Golden tapestries covered much of the intricately sculpted reliefs along the walls. Under the beautifully mosaiced ceilings hung cast-iron chandeliers that Cyrus was fairly certain were not part of the original design. Waist-height pillars lined the hall between the tall arabesque-topped windows, each holding a tawdry bust of various men. Drawing closer, Cyrus realized they weren't various men. They were busts of Gregor. All Gregor. He almost chuckled—Gregor did *not* have shoulders like the muscled ones sculpted here. Cyrus was fairly certain not even in his youth, however long, long ago that was.

The route to Cyrus's chamber felt almost as tiresome as the ride from the ship, and circular, as Gregor boasted about various things throughout the palace. Cyrus was starting to wonder if they'd ever reach it.

Gregor swept into a large hall that was *not* a bedchamber. In fact, it was very much a throne room. Gregor strode quickly and seated himself on the throne.

"I added these beams," he called, waving to arched ceilings above them. "They were carved from the original battering rams that my grandfather, High King Mathias, used to take Japheth."

Great, an unsolicited history lesson to go with the unsolicited tour. Cyrus wasn't entirely sure what he'd been expecting for the first meeting with Gregor, but it wasn't this. Still, he obliged.

"Come, come," Gregor said, sliding off the throne. "I'll show you the rest."

"I can't wait," Cyrus said dryly.

Through two more halls they walked, under Gregor's grating voice, and Cyrus was just about to ask how much longer when they paused in front of a portrait. A king, not Gregor, posed with what appeared to be a young queen and three sons, one of which *was* Gregor.

"I would love to get rid of this," Gregor said, "but you see, it fuels me." Spittle had gathered in the corner of his mouth.

Cyrus was familiar with the history. Gregor had been set to inherit all six kingdoms that comprised the Aleon Empire, but his father, on his deathbed, had split the kingdoms between his three sons. Gregor, feeling robbed of his birthright, had killed his youngest brother and now was actively trying to kill the other to reunite everything under his singular rule.

Gregor pointed to the king in the painting. "My father, High King Horvath."

The woman looked younger than Gregor. "Is that your mother?"

The king snorted. "Gods no. My mother—may the gods hold her close—died in childbirth. My father remarried." He scowled at the painting. "To a lower noble woman." He pointed to the young man on the left. "That was Aston."

The brother he'd killed.

Gregor dropped his hand, but his bitter eyes moved to his other brother. "That is Phillip."

"Happy family," Cyrus said.

Gregor stiffened, and Kord poked Cyrus again.

Gregor looked back at the painting, frowning. "There were rumors that Phillip and Aston were bastards, that their father was a man in the guard. I would have believed them if we didn't look so much alike."

Everan's brows dipped, and Kord expertly held back a laugh. Cyrus stared at the painting. Phillip was a handsome man, and Gregor looked absolutely nothing like him.

"You know, it *has* been a long journey," Cyrus said. "I'll take that room now."

"Oh, of course!" Gregor said. "I almost forgot." And he led them back the way they'd come.

They reached an elaborate suite on the east side, and Gregor promised to send for them once it was time for dinner. Inside, Cyrus let out a long exhale after he'd closed the door.

"Seems like a friendly fellow so far," Kord said.

Cyrus frowned. "I don't like him."

"All things holy," Kord muttered.

"Relax. I'm not going to do anything," Cyrus assured him. "I'm just saying I don't like him."

"Me neither," Everan added.

Kord sighed. "Well, I don't either, if I'm honest, but we're going to go to dinner, and you need to pretend like you do."

Dinner was as royal dinners were—unnecessarily excessive in atmosphere, food, and time. However, Cyrus obliged. Kord and Everan had been seated on the far side of the room with the other men who'd accompanied them. Cyrus wanted to object, but he noticed Gregor placed his own men at a distance as well, leaving the two of them space for private conversation.

"Again, I can't tell you how happy I am that you finally made the trip," Gregor told him, despite having said it multiple times. He nudged Cyrus with his elbow, which meant he was sitting entirely too close. "And I'm very eager for us to explore the possibilities between our two kingdoms," he added.

Cyrus eyed him skeptically. "Tell me of what's between Japheth and the Shadowlands," he said. He couldn't bring himself to waste any more time if Gregor had no intention of severing his alliance with the Shadow King.

"Ah." Gregor smiled as he shifted uneasily in his chair. "As you may have gathered, relations are strained at the moment. Now that Kharav is allied with Mercia, who is allied with my brother, it either makes them all friends or all enemies. It is a devastating betrayal by Mikael."

Mikael. Was that his name? This Shadow King. So little was known about the Shadowlands.

"So, you severed your alliance?"

"Oh, no. Of course not." He shifted again. "In fact, I would prefer Mikael not know about this meeting of ours."

Cyrus frowned. This wouldn't work at all. "Then I'm not interested," he said.

Gregor pulled back, his mouth open in disbelief. He swallowed quickly. "Wh-what do you mean?"

"I cannot be a friend of the Shadow King. Nor a friend of a friend. And I need an ally of action. I'm sorry to have wasted your time." Cyrus moved to rise, but Gregor's thin fingers wrapped around his arm, stopping him.

"I'm sure you are aware of the situation that most recently occurred in Kharav," Gregor said. His voice grew even quieter. "An attack on the queen."

Cyrus stilled in his chair. "Do you know something?" he asked.

Gregor smiled at him. "I might."

Did Gregor know it was him? The odious man's eyes gleamed as his smile broadened. Was he trying to hold it over Cyrus's head? Was he threatening him with this knowledge?

Gregor's voice dropped to a whisper as he leaned closer. "Perhaps I might even have been *involved*," he said.

Cyrus let the breath of fight ease from his lungs as the fire across his skin cooled. This idiot had absolutely no idea. Cyrus's left eyelid twitched under the strain of a stone countenance. "Is that so?" he said finally.

"You say you need an ally of action," Gregor cooed. "Now, I admit it did miss the mark, but it was a temporary setback, I assure you."

"That's good," Cyrus found himself saying. "Did you go yourself?"

"I should have," Gregor said. "Perhaps the job might have gotten done, then."

Cyrus snorted and quickly covered it with a cough. This man was absolutely unbelievable.

"But we could accomplish great things together, I think," Gregor continued.

Cyrus settled back in his chair. "Perhaps we could."

The turn in conversation made the evening infinitely more interesting, and Cyrus tolerated the rest of the dinner without too much agony. However, he could barely contain himself by the time he got back to the suite, where he filled in Everan and Kord on everything Gregor had said.

"Why would he claim responsibility for a failed effort against the Mercian queen?" Kord asked.

"To get in Cyrus's good graces," Everan answered. "This is a good thing, though. Not only does it show Gregor's desperation, which I think means he *will* break with the Shadowlands, but it also means no one knows who is responsible for our attempt, including the Shadow King."

Cyrus had already surmised the same. He still held somewhat of a benefit of surprise for whenever he chose to move against the Shadow King again.

"Agree to an accord," Everan pressed.

Kord frowned. "An accord on what?"

"It doesn't matter," Cyrus said. "I think he'll take anything that remotely looks like an alliance."

"What will you offer him?" Everan asked.

"He's a bitter man; I'll offer him the promise of war. And trade."

Kord snorted. "Trade what? We don't have anything."

"He doesn't know that. I'll keep it vague."

And that was precisely what Cyrus did as he and Gregor met the next morning. It was easy to do, since Gregor asked him nothing more about Cyrus, or Rael, or their trade. Gregor did, however, take the opportunity to boast everything Japheth had to offer.

"We have plants that can't be found anywhere else in the world," he gloated as they strolled through a stained-glass ambulatory after breakfast. "Morander, serium, encanthus..."

Cyrus paused in his step. "Did you say *serium*?"

The plant Essandra had been searching for.

"Ah, finally, a man with appreciation of the rare herbs of this world." Gregor grinned. "I will give you some clippings to take back if you wish. Each leaf is worth a small fortune."

"You'll give me a bush, with intact roots."

Gregor paused. "Serium cannot survive in Rael."

"You'll give me a bush, and we'll have an accord."

Gregor gaped at him.

Cyrus cocked his head. "You have more than one, presumably."

"Of-of course," Gregor stammered.

"So, this is hardly an ask at all," Cyrus said. Because it wasn't an ask. He wasn't leaving Japheth without that fucking bush.

"An-and we'll have an accord?"

Cyrus nodded. "That's right."

"There is still so much to work through."

"We'll work it through over the next several weeks."

Gregor was speechless. "I'll prepare a bush for you to take back."

"Excellent." Cyrus held out his hand. "My friend."

Chapter Nine

Sailing back to Rael felt longer than sailing to Japheth, and as the ship pulled into port, Cyrus couldn't help the smile that tugged at his lips. He couldn't wait to see Essandra's face when he gave her the serium—and not just a few dried leaves but a whole bush that she could grow and collect at her whim.

He'd watched the plant incessantly throughout the two days it took to sail back, worried that it would die before he got it there. It was coming from Japheth's humid climate, and he took care to mist it often within its linen-shaded glass house. Now it sat in the rear cabin. He would surprise her with it after settling.

Essandra was there to meet him at the docks. He was happy he'd hidden the bush away. One of the dogs was with her—Three.

"Welcome back," she said as he stepped off the gangway.

"It's good to be back. And good to see everything looks as I left it." No fighting, no destroyed buildings, no capital ablaze.

"It was mostly uneventful," she told him. "A letter arrived from Miriel."

Pryam's young queen still refused to communicate through the blood bond, despite becoming quite close with Cyrus. It was probably better she didn't use it. As much as he liked Miriel, he didn't want her voice incessantly in his head. And he liked her letters.

Three pushed his snout against Cyrus, wagging his hind, and Cyrus dropped his hand to scratch the animal behind the ear. Three had become partial to Essandra, often breaking from One and Two to follow her around.

Cyrus didn't blame him.

Her green eyes reflected the light like emeralds, and her dark hair swirled around her in the harbor breeze.

"What?" she asked with a wrinkled brow.

"What?" he asked back.

"Why are you smiling?"

"I'm not."

She eyed him suspiciously. Then she waved her hand and breathed, "Amana fasora," breaking the bonding spell. He'd forgotten it was even there. And it was strange she even bothered to break it. She should just leave it all the time. It seemed tedious to have to create and break over and over again. But he didn't care about the spell right now.

"I brought you something," he said. "A gift."

Her eyes traveled his face as her brow quirked. "What is it?"

"You'll have to wait until later."

"Why?"

He shrugged. "Because I want you to wonder about it for a while."

A smile lit her face, and he realized he didn't see it often. He liked it.

"But come with me now to the council room," he said, "and hear about everything that happened in Japheth."

"Did you reach an agreement?"

"Yes."

"Are you married?"

"No."

"Are you going to get married?"

"No." He eyed her. "Why do you care so much about my potential marriage?"

"I don't," she said quickly. "It was just a topic on the table, and I was curious. That's all."

"Well, it wasn't even discussed."

"Good—I mean, interesting." She clasped her hands in front of her.

"The whole trip was interesting. You'll want to hear."

In fact, everyone wanted to hear. They crowded the council room as Cyrus recounted the details—from the arrival, to the city's naming debacle, to the description of the capital and the palace, to the dinner where Gregor claimed responsibility for the attack on the Mercian queen, to them committing to work out the terms of their alliance over the coming weeks. He shared everything. Everything except for the serium bush, which he would surprise Essandra with later.

The council was gleeful, even seeming to forget about the confrontation with the nobles that they'd previously been so upset by. Cyrus was happy to learn things in Rael had been uneventful while he was gone, putting him in even higher spirits. All in all, it was the best he'd felt in a long time.

The sun hung well past its peak before Cyrus finally managed to steal away with Essandra to her workroom. He'd had his men move the glass house there while they were in the council meeting.

"Keep your eyes closed," he told her. But, not trusting her to keep them closed, he covered them with his hand as he pushed the door open and led her through. She stepped carefully.

"Keep them closed," he said again.

"I am!"

He positioned her in front of the glass house, which had a cloth draped over it.

"Keep them closed," he said yet again as he backed toward the house, watching that she followed his instruction.

She stood with her eyes squeezed shut as a grin spread across her face.

Carefully, he pulled the cloth from the glass. "You can look now," he told her.

Essandra opened her eyes and stood grinning as her gaze settled on the glass. Her expression changed to one of confused surprise. "How... cute. A miniature conservatory."

He waited.

She stepped nearer, nodding. "I'm sure... this will come in handy for—"

She stopped abruptly. The grin dropped from her face, and she just stared at the glass. *Through* the glass.

"Cyrus," she breathed.

He smiled.

"What is that?" she whispered.

"You said you needed serium."

"How did you even remember that, and"—her throat bobbed as her words caught—"where did you find it?" She didn't even give him time to answer before she gasped. "And it's a whole bush!"

"Gregor said it can't grow in Rael."

"It will grow," she said eagerly. "I can make it grow."

"I suspected you could. And now you have as much as you need, for however many spells you need it."

Her eyes welled.

"Will you be able to bring back your family with it?" he asked.

"It will let me build the missing pieces I need for the Amoran Cup spell."

He nodded. "Good."

A tear spilled down her cheek. "I don't even know what to say."

"Say nothing. Get started." And, giving her another smile, he left her to her work.

Orion's stare was cold and reserved. He'd barely said two words since returning from Japheth. Cyrus didn't know why Orion's being upset bothered him. It *didn't*, he told himself. So he wasn't sure what made him call the assassin to his study.

"Another job?" Orion said curtly. He didn't try very hard to hide his anger. He actually didn't try at all.

Cyrus shook his head. "No."

"What do you want, then?"

"I just wanted to see how your men were doing."

"What do you care? There are less of us now. What you wanted, no doubt."

"That's not true."

Orion snorted. "Yeah, okay."

Cyrus eyed him. He wasn't offended by his resentment. "I'm sorry about the Shadowlands," he said. He wasn't sure where the need to apologize came from, but it wasn't wrong. In fact, Cyrus probably should have apologized sooner.

Orion shifted slightly. "Oh."

"It's my fault we failed. I made them wait."

"I know." The assassin's voice was still bitter.

Cyrus straightened the inkwell on his desk. "Thane wanted to kill the queen while she was sleeping, but I wanted to find Alexander first. I..." He paused. "I wanted him to know what I was doing. I wanted to hurt him."

Orion's eyes narrowed. "But you were already going to kill him."

"Sometimes, death isn't enough."

The assassin moved to the window, looking out.

Cyrus sighed. This had been a mistake. Why did he care what Orion thought, anyway? He hadn't called him here to be judged. He should just dismiss him.

"You can't wait on a kill," Orion said. It wasn't said with malice. The assassin's gaze traveled the courtyard below. "I delayed once," he said. "It cost me someone very close to me." He turned back to Cyrus. "It's a lesson most everyone learns the hard way."

Was this forgiveness? Not that Cyrus needed forgiveness, not that he sought it. Or maybe he did. It would be nice to move forward. It would be nice to stop thinking about it.

"Did you find anything in Japeth about your woman?" Cyrus asked, testing.

Orion shook his head. "No," he said quietly. "No leads to where she might be, no information that she'd even been there at all."

A quiet sat between them.

"You know," Cyrus said finally, "I have a man who's good at getting information. I could have him look into things."

"You'd send him to Japheth?"

Cyrus shrugged. "I don't know if he'll be able to find anything that you couldn't, but—"

"It doesn't matter. I don't care. If he *can* find anything, anything at all..." His eyes pierced Cyrus in desperation. "You'd really do this?"

"Consider it done," Cyrus said. Jaem would be up for the challenge, and he really was good. He might even obtain some additional useful information on Gregor. "I'll send him the next time he calls through the bond."

Just then, Essandra burst in. "I'm ready," she said breathlessly.

She hadn't left her workroom in days. However, each time Cyrus had checked in on her, she was in high spirits and focused—chanting spells, mixing herbs, scribbling notes. He'd let her work, having meals delivered so she didn't need to stop to eat.

"I'm sorry," she said, suddenly noticing Orion. "I didn't mean to interrupt."

"No, no, it's fine," Orion said quickly. "I should go."

"It would be great if you could stay," she told him. "And help."

He glanced at Cyrus, then back to her. "Uh, all right. What do you need me to do?"

"I'm not sure," she said as she shook her head. "I mean, I don't know yet. Maybe nothing. Maybe something. This is a proxy spell for my sister, and there's no telling what will happen."

"Okay," he said. "Now?"

She nodded with a smile, still breathless. "Yes." Then her eyes found Cyrus again. "If now is all right?"

"Of course it is," he told her.

"Uh..." Orion eyed her. "Do you... want to look a certain way when you see your sister for the first time?"

Only then did Cyrus notice her wrinkled dress and the hair that had fallen wispily from where it had been pinned up.

"Well, I'm not going to actually see her tonight. This is just the first step of many. I'm creating a series of alternative spells, which I then hope to string together later for the final spell with the Amoran Cup."

"Ah, right," Orion said.

"Wait." She paused. "Is there something wrong with how I look now?"

"Absolutely not," Cyrus said quickly as Orion shook his head and said, "No, not at all."

Her smile returned.

Cyrus and Orion glanced at each other, then followed Essandra to her workroom.

She picked up a small copper bowl with a mixture of herbs that had already been finely ground, and she ground them some more.

"Have you figured out what you need me to do yet?" Orion asked.

"Just stand there and... catch him if he passes out. Or if..." Her words trailed off as she looked up from the herbs and paused. "I think we should get Teron too."

"I'll grab him," Orion said, and left the room.

"Why would we need Teron?" Cyrus asked. They hadn't needed him before. In fact, Teron's healing magic had never been able to help Cyrus with things like this before.

She still worked the herbs in the bowl. If she kept at it, there wouldn't be anything left of them. Was she nervous?

"Do you think Everan could come as well?" she asked.

Now she was making Cyrus nervous. "Why do you need Everan?"

Orion stepped back into the room, with Teron just behind him.

"Teron," Essandra said. "Thank you for coming."

"Why do we need Teron?" Cyrus asked again.

She clutched the bowl. "Well..." She bit her bottom lip. "I'm not sure if I'm bonding my sister to *you* and the living, or if I'm bonding you to *her* and the dying."

"What does that mean?"

"It means you might need Teron." She bit her lip again. "The bond might make you suffer the same injuries she did when she died."

Orion glanced back and forth between them. "An injury from what?"

She quieted, sobering. "From a blade."

"I'm not afraid of a blade," Cyrus said, but his light attempt at humor made no impression.

Worry blanketed her face, and she backed slightly. "You know what, I don't... I don't think I've thought this through all the way. I'm not sure exactly what will happen."

"Well, we're about to find out," Cyrus said.

She shook her head. "I-I don't even know if I'm doing it right, if I'm reading the spell right." She clutched the copper bowl in her hands, staring at it.

"Teron can check it."

She nodded nervously. "Right." She got the book and handed it to the healer.

Teron scanned the page and then looked at each of the ingredients laid out across her table. "Where is the myrna?"

"It's already mixed in. Here." She motioned to the bowl. "I only had two leaves, so I just used one."

He nodded. "That should be enough. It looks right to me. Just the serium now."

"You see?" Cyrus said. "It's all in order."

She swallowed. Slowly, she reached into the glass house the serium still sat in and plucked a leaf, then she tore it in half and dropped it into the bowl. She emptied the bowl into a small cup and poured in some steaming water, brewing it.

"You should sit," she told him.

He doubted that was necessary, but he took to a floor cushion.

She lowered herself in front of him and held out the cup for him. Her hands were shaking.

He took it, but as he lifted it to his lips, she grabbed his arm, stopping him.

"Wait," she said. "You don't have to do this."

"I know." He moved again to drink it.

"Actually, I don't want you to." She tried to take back the cup, but he pulled it away.

"No—we've gotten this far," he told her. "It's worth a try."

"This could hurt you."

"I get hurt all the time"—he cut her a smile—"mostly by you. Teron's here. It's worth trying to see if it works."

She shook her head. "No, I've changed my mind."

"This could bring your family back."

She stilled. Her eyes welled.

"Let me at least try," he said.

She shook her head again.

"Essandra," he said softly.

She rocked slightly. "Just... slowly," she whispered.

Cyrus drank down the warm tea, and as he did, she whispered words he didn't understand.

She stared at him, her breaths short and shallow, her eyes deep with worry.

He finished and handed the cup back to her. She took it but sat frozen, still staring.

"How long before we know if it worked?"

"I—" She rocked back and forth a little. "I don't know." She shook her head. "I don't know," she said again. "We might not know until the final spell, with the cup."

That was a long time to wait. But... "All right," he said.

They sat in silence, waiting.

"Am I going to pass out if I stand?" he asked.

"I don't... I don't think so."

He got to his feet. And felt fine.

Essandra scrambled up with him.

"I'm fine," he assured her. "I guess... you start working on the next step."

She said nothing, her eyes still wide and watching, but she nodded.

Suddenly, a searing pain cut through his stomach. Then another came across his chest. He stumbled back, looking down to see blood seeping through the front of his tunic.

His eyes found Essandra again as he swayed. Horror etched her face. His strength left him, and he sank to his knees.

"Teron!" Essandra screamed as she rushed forward.

Cyrus crumpled backward, but Orion caught him.

"I got you," Orion told him. "I got you."

Orion said something else, but the words weren't making sense to him.

"Cyrus!" Essandra cried. She cradled his head as they lowered him to the floor.

He felt Teron's healing warmth, but it wasn't enough. The darkness was closing in.

"Cyrus! Cyrus, stay with me." Essandra's voice was fading. She clasped the sides of his face. "No! No! Look at me."

He tried to focus his eyes on her, but he couldn't see. He couldn't breathe. *He couldn't breathe.*

"Cyrus, look at me!"

He tried again to focus on her face.

"Help him!" she screamed at Teron. "I'm so sorry," she cried. "I'm so sorry."

She didn't need to be sorry. He didn't want her to be sorry.

"Teron," she begged.

Teron said something, but Cyrus couldn't make sense of it.

His vision blurred and then went dark. He wasn't sure if his eyes were open or closed.

"Cyrus!"

Slowly, the pain subsided.

"Cyrus!"

Finally, he was able to suck in a breath, and he desperately gulped in air. The rush of dryness stung. Despite Teron's touch, a needling pain still snaked its way down his chest. Not pain of the body. Pain of the spirit.

He opened his eyes to find Essandra, Orion, and Teron leaning over him. He gave himself another moment. Slowly, his senses came back to him. "Does this mean it worked?" he was finally able to ask. His voice was hoarse.

"Who cares!" she practically shouted. "Are you all right?"

"Did it work?" he asked again.

She nodded as she wiped a tear from her cheek.

"What's next?" he asked.

"Gods, Cyrus," she breathed, shaking her head. "I can't even think about that right now. I just want to make sure you're all right."

"I'm all right." He pushed himself to sit, and Orion helped him. Cyrus's vision darkened for a moment, and he paused until the lightheadedness passed.

She clutched him tighter. "Easy."

"Help me stand."

"I think you should wait."

"Help me," he said again.

Orion looped his arms under Cyrus's and helped him to his feet as Essandra gripped him tightly.

Once standing, he felt even better. The lingering weakness seemed more in his mind than in his body.

Essandra's eyes dropped to his chest, and he looked down at his bloodstained tunic, which had been torn open.

Her eyes teared up again.

"I didn't like this tunic anyway," he said.

She shook her head. "This was a mistake. There's a reason this has never been done."

He gripped her shoulders, making her look at him. "You will do what no one else has ever done, because you are willing to try what no one else has ever tried. As am I. I promise you, you will see your family again."

CHAPTER TEN

"I've lost Bravat." Jaem didn't sound like his normal self.

"What?" That wasn't what Cyrus had expected to hear.

"I should have told you sooner. I'm sorry. I went to the Free Cities, and when I got back, he wasn't here."

Cyrus swore. It was bad enough that Bravat was running unchecked and razing Mercian temples with no regard for consequences to Rael. To completely lose eyes on him wasn't good.

"Don't worry," Jaem said. *"Sid is with me. We'll find him."*

Sid. Cyrus had to think for a moment but then remembered. Sid was a lower-tier fighter from House Akim. He'd been a thief as well, when he and Jaem had been caught together and sold to the arena. Good kid. Bad fighter. But, fortunately, Cyrus didn't need him to fight right now.

"We won't fail you on this," Jaem said.

"You're not failing me," Cyrus assured him. *"Have Sid keep on; give him a vial to call me when he finds Bravat. I have another job for you, though. I need you to go to Japheth and see what you can find about a woman."*

"A woman?"

"I promised someone help in finding her. Meet me at the stone circle. You'll sail from Rael."

"All right. I'll call to you when I'm close."

Cyrus rubbed his temples. He'd let Bravat go on too long. When Sid found him, Cyrus would have to take care of him.

He set his attention back on the parchments in front of him on the desk, but his eyes glazed over, and he tossed them back down. More problems. They just kept coming. It never stopped.

"What are you doing so glum in here?"

He looked up to find Essandra in the doorway. She wore a dark purple gown that showed off her shoulders and the length of her neck, but he was careful not to let his eyes linger too long. "Not glum," he said. "Just annoyed." Although slightly less annoyed now.

"Annoyed at what?" She stepped inside.

"We lost eyes on Bravat. Who knows what he's doing now. I'm going to have to do something about him when I find him, though. I can't just leave him in Mercia, doing as he pleases." He held up a stack of papers. "Then I have things like this."

"What's that?"

"A petition to change public irrigation as a result of land redistribution." He held up another stack of papers. "And a petition to keep it the same."

She smiled. "Well, I didn't come to annoy you further."

"You're not," he said quickly. "Did you need something, though?"

She shook her head as she moved to his desk. "I just wanted to see how you felt, after... you know. Everything."

After the spell.

"Completely back to normal," he said.

"Nothing hurts?" She'd been carrying a lot of guilt since nearly killing him.

He quirked the corner of his mouth. "Like it never happened," he assured her.

She nodded. "Good."

Cyrus watched her curiously as she stepped around the desk. He narrowed his eyes. "What are you doing?"

She pushed him back in his chair and climbed on top of him, straddling him. "I just thought I should properly thank you."

Not that he objected, but... "I didn't do it for your body."

"I know." She reached down between them, unlacing his leathers.

"And you don't have to feel obligated," he said.

"I don't." She paused. "But if you don't want my body—"

"I didn't say that."

She smiled and pulled him free. Then she positioned herself, ruffling her dress, and took him inside her.

Cyrus let his head fall back as her warmth engulfed him. He gripped the back of his chair. He didn't trust himself not to grab her hips, not to run his hands up her stomach and her breasts, up her neck and into her hair. He didn't trust himself not to pull her lips to his.

Their relationship was built on rules—the only rules he made sure he followed.

Essandra moved in rhythm over him as he thrust from underneath her. She fisted his tunic against his chest. He wanted to pull it off. He wanted to pull off all the clothing between them, to not just feel her but see her, but he forced restraint.

Suddenly, she pulled herself from him, and in a brief moment of surprise, he thought she might leave him wanting, but instead she pushed herself back onto his desk. Papers scattered to the floor. Glass shattered. He wasn't sure what had broken; he didn't care.

Essandra pulled him to follow. He did, standing quickly and moving back between her thighs. She guided him, and sinking into her a second time felt just as good as the first.

Better.

This woman. If he wasn't careful, he could lose himself in her.

She panted through open lips, lips he desperately wanted to kiss. He wanted her mouth more than he wanted her body—to taste her. His teeth begged to feel her flesh between them.

Her thighs tightened around him, and he moved faster. Deeper. Closer, and closer. But he waited for her. He waited as he felt her building. He chased her need. As she reached her peak, he let himself come as well. Over the edge she brought him—spiraling, falling, reeling—until she collapsed back onto the desk. He fell over her, barely able to hold himself up.

They stayed in the quiet, with only the sounds of their panting breaths.

This was the second time he'd had her on this desk, and it was now his favorite piece of furniture. But...

"We should probably stop doing this in here," he said, although he couldn't hide the disappointment in his voice at the thought. "Anyone could walk in."

The corners of her lips quirked up. "Does that not make it a little more exhilarating?"

He couldn't help his own smile. She stared up at him with her emerald eyes. She was so incredibly beautiful.

"I never know what to say after," he said softly. "Would a thank-you be inappropriate?"

She half snorted a laugh. "Well, I think that was *me* thanking *you*."

"You're going to have to let me know what else I can possibly do for you."

She laughed again.

The jesting faded, and he grew more serious. "I mean it, though. Regardless of"—his eyes traveled her underneath him—"this... I'll help you with whatever you need."

"I know," she whispered. "And I will need more from you."

"What's next?" Perhaps it was odd to be having a conversation while their bodies were joined, but he didn't want to pull away from her. Not yet.

She let her breaths calm a little more. "Well, the proxy spell worked, as far as we can tell, which means you can fulfill any requirement that would normally be needed from my sister."

"Like what?"

"The familial bond."

He wasn't understanding. "What does that mean?"

"You have a brother."

And?

"He can be the second anchor," she said.

He stiffened. "You want to use my brother?"

"Yes. I mean, no." She swayed her head. "I mean, kind of."

Did that mean Alexander would have to be alive?

"Both my sister and my mother need a familial anchor to the living, people with power. I can only be that for one of them. But now, with you bonded as a proxy for my sister, your brother could be the other anchor."

So, she was asking Cyrus to spare him... The air thinned in his lungs as a cold rippled over his skin. This wasn't a simple favor she was asking. He pulled himself from her.

"All I need is the blood," she said.

His chest tightened. He took a step back. "Alexander's blood," he repeated, the words sharp on his tongue.

She sat up. "That's the beauty of it," she told him. "I have *yours*. And if his blood can work in place of yours—which we've seen it can—then, hypothetically, your blood can work in place of his. That's just a natural version of a proxy bond anyway." She brought her fingers to her temple. "I know it's complicated, but this is... the brilliance of magic weaving. It can be layered and manipulated to where you can make anything possible." She wiped her face. "Look, I don't know if it will actually work. An anchored person can't be an anchor for someone else, which is why I can't use my sister to bring back my mother. I don't know if a proxied person can be a proxy for someone else. It has a high possibility of failure."

"And if it does fail, then you *would* need my brother. You would need him alive, and you would need his blood." He shook his head.

Her breath caught, and she bit her lip.

The cold under his skin turned to heat. "You would ask me not to kill him?"

Something he couldn't do...

"It would just be until I could do the spell," she said quickly. "And that's only if this fails."

"Which you said has a high possibility of doing just that." He fastened his clothing, his anger building. He turned away from her, then ran a rough hand through his hair. "I wish you would have talked to me before you did this."

A heavy pause sat between them.

"I'm-I'm sorry," she said. "I only had one shot at it, and it needed to be someone with power. You're the most powerful person I know. I-I didn't... I didn't think you would refuse."

"I wouldn't have!" he snapped. "But I wish you would have talked to me first."

She stared at him with her eyes wide and her lips parted.

A knock sounded on the door, and it swung open.

"We have a problem," Orion said as he stepped inside. He paused when he saw the mess of desk items on the floor. His eyes shifted to Cyrus, to Essandra, then back to Cyrus.

Cyrus was too angry to jest at Essandra for his earlier point being made. "What?" he asked, making no effort to hide the irritation in his voice.

Orion frowned. "You know how I used to be owned by a for-profit operative assassins' guild by which the only way one can leave is to die? Well, they found me. Us. Me and my men."

Essandra's eyes widened, and she stepped around the desk to him. "Did they send someone for you?"

He nodded. "A couple someones."

Her mouth dropped open and her eyes grew wider. "And? Is everyone all right?"

"For now." He shifted. "They have an ask."

Cyrus narrowed his eyes. "What kind of ask?"

"The same gift given to me. To release them from their bonds."

Even more anger rippled through him. "You made a bargain on behalf of Essandra?"

"I haven't guaranteed anything," Orion said quickly.

"I'll do it," Essandra interjected, "if that's what lets them go peacefully."

Had she lost her mind? "No." Cyrus shook his head. "You're not going to free every assassin who comes here. All that does is make you a target."

Orion's face fell as the implication hit him.

"I can take care of myself," she said.

"I said *no*. I don't want you getting involved in this."

She scoffed at him in disbelief. "What you *want* doesn't matter. I'll do as I please."

"Yes, you've made that clear," he said shortly.

Her eyes narrowed. "What's that supposed to mean?"

Cyrus cut his gaze back to Orion. "Where are they now?" he demanded.

Orion hesitated, his eyes on Essandra. "I didn't mean to put you in danger—"

"I'm about to take care of that," Cyrus snarled. "*Where are they?*"

He sighed. "In the workroom."

"You put assassins in her *workroom*?" Cyrus stormed out of the study and down the hall.

"Cyrus, wait!" Essandra called.

Orion raced alongside him. "They don't mean her harm! They won't tell anyone."

"You speak for them now? You speak for all assassins?"

Orion stammered. "No! I... They simply want the bond broken, the same as she did for me."

"Which she shouldn't have even done to begin with!" Cyrus growled.

"Cyrus!" Essandra called, her voice urgent now. "What are you going to do?"

He reached the hall to her workroom and drew his sword in a smooth, practiced motion.

"Cyrus, no!"

Orion stepped in front of him, pulling his own blades. "I can't let you do this," he said.

"Move," Cyrus warned.

"They just want out," Orion said. "That's all. They didn't choose this life any more than I did."

"They should have stayed away."

"They had no choice."

"Neither do I." Cyrus stepped forward.

Orion braced to meet him.

"Get out of my way," Cyrus said through his teeth.

"No."

"Cyrus, stop!" Essandra shouted. "Please!"

"Orion," he warned one last time.

"You'll have to go through me," the assassin said.

Then that was what he'd do. His muscles coiled, rage tightening in his throat. But as he surged to strike...

Pain hit him.

A searing jolt lit through his arm—burning him, disabling him. He dropped his sword. The blade clattered to the stone floor as he doubled over, clutching his arm to him.

Essandra.

Her power didn't just hurt; it nearly crippled him. He panted out agonizing breaths, trying to scrape back control.

She shoved past him and grabbed Orion, yanking him into her workroom. The door slammed behind them.

"Essandra!" Cyrus bellowed, his voice raw. He staggered to the door. "Essandra!" he roared. "Open this door!"

There was shuffling inside.

"Essandra! Open this gods-damned door!"

More scuffling. The fall of something heavy. A struggle?

He slammed his shoulder against the door. "Essandra!"

If she was harmed...

A fury swept through him. He'd kill every single one of them, including Orion.

Cyrus rammed the door again. It gave a little but still held.

Glass crashed to the ground.

He gave another roar as he shouldered into the door again, this time with all his strength, and it burst from its hinges. As he barreled inside, he found Essandra backed against the center table with her eyes wide.

Orion stood poised in defense against the far wall, breathing heavily, his blades drawn.

Cyrus scanned the room. There was no one else with them.

"They're gone," Essandra told him.

His eyes traveled the room again and landed on the open window. He lunged toward it and hung out, but he saw no one.

He whirled to face her, and she stumbled back. "You freed them?" he snapped

"I had to."

"And now more will come."

"And I'll free them too," she spat back defiantly.

His eyes blazed at Orion. "This is your doing," he said between his teeth. He'd kill him. He didn't have his sword, but it didn't matter. He'd pull him apart with his hands.

"Cyrus," a voice called from behind him. Kord stepped into the room, his eyes on the door hanging off its bent and broken hinges. His hand moved the hilt of his sword, but confusion snaked his brow. "What the fuck happened here?"

"Not now," Cyrus snapped.

"Uh, yeah now. You're going to want to come... Gregor's here."

CHAPTER ELEVEN

Cyrus sat at the dining table, his plate of food untouched and his eyes fixed on Gregor, who sat at the opposite end, chewing his food with his mouth open.

Cyrus didn't like unplanned visitors.

He didn't like visitors at all, especially when his mind kept turning back to Essandra.

But he was quickly finding he didn't so much mind this visit.

Gregor had sailed straight from the Shadowlands after meeting with the Shadow King, and he was furious.

Cyrus had let him rant at length in the throne room, where he'd greeted him, and continue on through the main hall, then throughout a walk of the palace grounds, where Cyrus didn't speak at all. And the man still hadn't exhausted himself as they took their evening meal alone together. The king of Japheth raged about how his nephew had met a suspicious and untimely end in the Shadowlands, for which the Shadow King had offered no retribution.

"Mikael has absolutely no regard for how one should treat an ally," Gregor said as he shoved another slice of meat into his mouth with his hand.

Of course he didn't. He was the Shadow King.

"And he just let that woman stand there and threaten me with war." He licked each finger on his hand. "Threaten me with my own brother!"

That woman. The Shadow Queen. Gregor had quite a lot to say about her.

"It's too bad your previous efforts weren't successful," Cyrus said.

Gregor's bushy brows drew together. "What do you mean *not successful*? What—oh!" He licked his lips. "Oh, yes, yes. Absolutely, too bad."

Cyrus forced down the smile forming on his lips. Perhaps the queen escaping his grasp wasn't an entire loss—it looked like she'd break the alliance between the Shadowlands and Japheth for him.

"All he had to do was give me the Destroyer," Gregor continued.

It was now the second time Cyrus had heard that ridiculous name. "This is his commander?"

Gregor gave a jerky nod. "He can't give me *one* man?"

"How many men does he have?" This was the real value of Gregor's visit.

"Who knows?" He waved a hand in irritation. "He shares *nothing*! Everything is hidden when I visit, everything's a secret. So-called allies."

And suddenly this man was worthless. Cyrus was now very much done with this visit.

But Gregor, in his exceptional ability to read a room, continued. "I'm in need of a good commander to oversee the various mercenary armies I employ. Do you have a man?"

Was he really asking Cyrus to give him one of his trusted men?

"You have a couple, I think," Gregor said. "The dark-skinned one is with you quite often. I'm assuming you'd like to keep him for yourself?"

Everan. Cyrus shifted, offense creeping over his skin. "Everan is a free man who makes his own choices."

"Of course, of course," Gregor said quickly. "What about the golden-haired one?"

Kord. Cyrus snorted. Kord didn't even want to fight for Cyrus; he certainly wouldn't fight for Gregor.

"I'll tell you what," Cyrus said. "You find a man who wants to take your job, and he can go with my blessing."

"Well, it can't just be anyone. I need someone with very specific talents. A dangerous man." He shook a long, knobbed finger. "Mikael's man is feared by everyone. A man of blood and death. This is the kind of man I want."

Bravat was the only man who came close to that, but Cyrus was going to kill Bravat, not send him on a job. Gregor wouldn't find another man like that here, even among the bloodsport fighters. In the arena, they'd fought because they had to. They'd fought to live, to survive. Cyrus was the only man with bloodlust now.

"Money is no object," Gregor said. "He can name his price. I'll pay him his weight in gold."

Gregor might not be a man who dealt in slaves, but he acted as though he could buy whatever he wanted, perhaps because he employed an entire mercenary army, who obviously had a price. But he didn't understand things like conviction and heart and loyalty. Gregor wouldn't get a man from Rael, but Cyrus would certainly get amusement from watching him try.

When Cyrus's tolerance was gone, he withdrew for the evening. He would meet Gregor again in the morning for breakfast, where he hoped to convince him to break with the Shadow King. His council had urged him to discuss joining against Serra, but if Gregor wouldn't break his alliance with the Shadowlands, there was no use discussing anything else with him. This was needed to allow their own alliance to progress. If one could call it an alliance.

He stopped by Essandra's chamber on the way to his, but there was no guard at her door and no answer when he knocked. He hadn't seen her since he'd left her workroom. It was probably better that way. They'd both been heated, and it would likely take her a little time before she was open to talking. He'd find her tomorrow.

For now—sleep. He closed the door to his chamber behind him. His annoyance sat coiled in his shoulders, and he reached back and gripped the nape of his neck, squeezing tightly. It wasn't terribly late into the evening, but he was tired. He stood at the edge of his bed and let his eyes close and his head fall back.

And he found himself in a kitchen.

It was a kitchen he recognized, one he'd been in before. A very, very long time ago.

The kitchen of the Mercian castle.

This vision wasn't like other visions. He wasn't merely an observing bystander. This was a memory, the same as the memories that he saw in others' minds when he traveled the blood bond.

But there wasn't a blood bond right now.

A bowl of figs sat on a wooden center table. He—or, rather, the host of his vision—grabbed one and cut it in half. Cyrus frowned. He didn't even like figs. No sooner had he pulled the halves apart than a young woman came barreling through.

She grinned when she saw him.

The Mercian queen.

She was younger here.

Her mouth spoke silent words, rattling through them faster than he'd be able to follow even if he could read her lips. Then she pulled him down a side hall and into a back pantry. Sunlight poured through the window of the small room, but they pressed back into a recess behind bags of grain.

He obviously said something, as her hand shot up over his mouth.

They were hiding from someone.

But her face was all smiles.

He held out the fig he still had, and she smiled wider and took a bite. Cyrus watched as his thumb traced her lower lip, and he leaned forward to kiss her.

When he pulled back, she was still smiling.

Cyrus let the vision drop. He'd seen the queen many times before, and the visions of her weren't particularly meaningful, especially a silly vision of young love. He was more interested in how blood-bond sight could come to him without a blood bond.

He'd ask Essandra.

Later.

He still felt anger from what had happened with Orion, and there was probably a little something left over from the conversation that had happened just before that. Cyrus had been with Gregor since he'd arrived, so he couldn't say for sure that she was avoiding him, but no doubt there was an argument coming. He wasn't willing to let Essandra continue to break the ownership bonds of assassins. The Jackals certainly weren't a group he wanted to catch the attention of. He had enough things to worry about, and with something like this, it wouldn't be Cyrus they'd come after—it would be Essandra. Which was worse.

His blood heated just thinking about it.

The Jackals would come after her.

They would come to kill her.

And Orion had brought this.

The thought lit a fire in him, and before he even thought about what he was doing, he strode out of his chamber and down the hall. Orion had opened a door that couldn't be closed now, with a danger that would linger. Essandra was already burdened with a powerful witch after her, and now to have an assassins' guild too... With each step, he grew angrier.

Cyrus didn't even bother to knock. He tore straight into Orion's room, his sword drawn.

The bed was empty.

The room was empty.

Behind him was not empty. And Cyrus spun.

The tip of his sword touched Orion's throat just as Orion's blades touched his.

They stood, each poised to deliver a lethal cut.

"You knew I was coming," Cyrus said.

"I thought you might. And you're not the quietest man in this castle."

"Do you really think you can kill me?" Cyrus challenged, leaning directly against the points of Orion's blades. Daring him to try.

"Oh, I'm a dead man, for sure," Orion said. "But I'd hoped you'd stop long enough for me to tell you that I never had any intention of putting Essandra in danger. I wasn't thinking. It was a mistake. I would never choose to hurt her."

"Your ignorance chose for you," Cyrus snarled back.

Orion nodded sullenly. "More men will come now, and I know that's because of me." He dropped his swords from Cyrus's neck, surrendering. "You never did strike me as a forgiving man, so I won't hold it against you if you do intend to kill me."

That was exactly what Cyrus intended.

"But if you find the grace to spare me, I'll make sure no one gets to her again."

Cyrus paused. Essandra wouldn't stop breaking the bonds simply because he told her to. But if Orion stopped the men before they even reached her...

He put more pressure on his blade against Orion's skin. A trickle of blood ran down the assassin's throat. "I can't bond you like the Jackals can," Cyrus said, his voice edged in warning. "Nor would I. But you'll consider yourself bound to me all the same. You'll kill every assassin that steps foot in Rael."

Slowly, Orion nodded.

"If something happens to her," Cyrus warned, "I'll carve my own mark into your flesh just before I flay your skin from your body."

Orion swallowed. "I'll take that as grace."

Gregor licked each finger on his hand, chewing his breakfast loudly in between. Cyrus had never been one to pay attention to anyone's table manners, much less be bothered by them, but he found his appetite quickly waning now. And his patience.

They'd spent the better part of the morning at an impasse. Gregor wanted to negotiate building alliances. Cyrus wanted to negotiate breaking them.

"I just don't know how you expect me to make up for the loss in trade from Mikael," Gregor said.

"Tarsus trades rice," Cyrus said. Tarsus was a premier island trading port situated in the middle of the Atolean Sea. It sat just off the coast of Hetahl, the kingdom Gregor had stolen from his youngest brother. Cyrus expected trading in Tarsus would be the same or less effort than dealing with the Shadowlands.

"At premium prices!" Gregor exclaimed.

"The same premium prices you'd charge for your own goods."

Gregor guzzled from his chalice, then thudded it down in front of him, sending droplets of wine splashing over the rim and onto the table. "I already rely too much on Tarsus. This would make me fully dependent."

Cyrus didn't care.

"Men, then," Gregor said. "Ten legions."

Ten legions. *Fifty thousand men.* That was three-quarters of Cyrus's current force. He wasn't giving Gregor that. However, he wasn't opposed to sending men. His numbers were growing fast, almost faster than he could feed and house them. Also, if he had men in Japheth, he wouldn't have to move as many across the Aged Sea when he was ready to march against the Shadow King.

"My people push me to move against Serra," Cyrus told him. "I need to see to this first. Then I can send all the legions you can hold."

Gregor nearly choked on his food. "Serra?"

"They are slavers of men. I can't let them remain."

"You can take Serra anytime. Did you not hear me about the Mercian wench? She's plotting with my brother now! We have to be prepared to respond when they act."

Cyrus didn't care about Mercia and Aleon, nor was he convinced a threat from them was imminent. And he couldn't put off Serra. The people of Rael were becoming restless.

"When Phillip moves against me, Mercia will stand with him," Gregor said. "And Mikael will join them. That cunt heels him like a dog."

"She controls the Shadow King?" He didn't believe that.

"By the balls. You know he annulled his wives for her?"

Cyrus sat back in his chair. "He had more than one wife?"

"Living every man's dream. She stripped it all from him. And he just let her."

Hardly every man's dream. One woman was enough as far as Cyrus was concerned.

"I heard she freed all his servants around the castle." Gregor chuckled. "I would have loved to have been there to see his face."

Cyrus leaned forward. "She did what?"

"And his Destroyer is sworn to her now." The king snorted. "I assume that means he'll be doing a little less *destroying*. I could have done so much with that man."

Cyrus sat back again and crossed his arms. Had he judged this queen wrong? No. And this couldn't be true. He'd seen the aftermath of her capture with his own eyes. How could she go from that to taking so much control? But it would explain the vision of the commander at the queen's side as she went to Aleon...

"Anyway, the bitch will call Mikael to her aid," Gregor said, "and I'll need you to handle him so I can focus on Phillip."

An opportunity at the Shadow King. That was what Gregor was offering him. But how likely was that? And how soon?

"When?" he asked. "When would we move?"

Gregor nodded smugly. "I'm just waiting for Phillip to tip his hand."

That wasn't good enough. "When?" he pressed.

"Soon!"

Cyrus's army was nearly ready to move against Serra. They had upward of seventy-five thousand men, with more joining training each week, although he didn't need them all—not for Serra—not even close. However, it was what he'd agreed to with his council.

"Break your alliance," he told Gregor. "Pull your trade from the Shadowlands and I'll send you three legions."

"*Three?* That's only fifteen thousand men!"

"To start."

"Seven," Gregor countered.

Cyrus didn't completely object to the notion. "Pull your trade from the Shadowlands and I'll send you seven legions."

"Send them first," Gregor insisted.

"After you pull your trade." And after he was certain the Shadow King was truly within reach.

Gregor scoffed. "You want me to act on good faith for our alliance, but you won't do the same?"

Cyrus took a drink from his chalice. His wine was the only part of his breakfast he'd had. "Fine," he said finally. "I'll send four legions now, three after. And you'll feed them." His council wouldn't like it, but it would force Gregor to act, and it would also take some burden off Rael's swelling ranks. And he still had more than enough for Serra.

Gregor clapped his hands together. "We have an accord! You see? We both move forward in good faith."

Good faith wasn't what Cyrus would have called it.

Chapter Twelve

A rooster crowed as the sun poured through his chamber window, and Cyrus found himself wondering when they'd gotten chickens. He couldn't remember the last time he'd seen a chicken.

As he opened the door to step out into the hall, he nearly collided with Visa, who was entering.

"I'm sorry," she said quickly as she stumbled back. "I thought you were already gone." Her eyes dropped to the frown on his face. "I was just bringing these by," she added, and held out a stack of folded tunics.

The dogs pushed by him to huddle around her, wiggling excitedly. They were always happy to see Visa.

Cyrus stared at her, still not sure exactly what was happening. "Why would you bring me tunics?"

"Um, because... you need them. And wear them. And mess them up. And need new ones. Often."

He still wasn't sure why Visa was bringing him tunics.

"I'm just going to put them in your dressing chamber," she said.

And then it hit him. "Wait, do you stock my clothes?"

Her brows twitched. "Of course I do."

"Regularly? This whole time?"

Her eyes narrowed. "Cyrus, who do you *think* stocks your dressing room?"

He'd actually never thought about it. There were lots of people employed around the castle to keep things up. His chamber was always clean, his clothing always pressed. "I had no idea," he confessed. Shame licked his cheeks. "You don't have to clean up after me."

Visa shook her head. "Oh, I don't clean up after you. We pay others very well to do that. I just see to buying your clothes and making sure they're here when you need them."

She slipped by him and into the side dressing chamber.

"Thank you," he said, "although you don't have to do that either."

She stepped back out after putting the tunics away. "I don't mind. I'm already doing the same for Everan." She smiled. "Plus, I think it's fun to shop for the king."

He chuckled.

They left his chamber and made their way down the halls to the mainway. The dogs followed.

Floral garlands hung from the side pillars.

"What's all this for?" he asked.

"For Heart's Harvest."

That couldn't be right. "We did away with all the old festivals," he said. They'd done away with everything of the past regime, putting new traditions in place, new holidays, new celebrations.

"Well, mostly, but not Heart's Harvest. We missed doing it last year because the rebellion had just happened."

He paused in his step. *It had been over a year since the rebellion.* He'd known this, but hearing it...

Over a year.

And what had he done in that year?

Nothing.

"Are you all right?" Visa asked.

"Of course." He straightened.

"Are you going this evening?"

"Why would I?"

Heart's Harvest was intended for those seeking a marriage match. Cyrus hated the name. There wasn't a harvest, only an overindulgence in food and wine, which they were already in short supply of. And there were no hearts involved—marriages were brokered to secure family status. At least, that was how it had been. It had started with nobility, but over the years became a festival that included common citizens as well. Eventually, it was even shared by slaves, who snuck one another small gifts to reveal their affections. Perhaps only for slaves— those who had no wealth to bargain and only their hearts to follow—was it truly a heart's celebration.

"I'm not looking for a match," he said.

She laughed. "Well, I already have one, but I'm still going. Everan has promised to dance as long as I want, and I'm going to take full advantage."

"Have fun."

"Essandra will be there."

His eyes darted back to her. "Why is *she* going?"

And this was exactly how Cyrus found himself standing in the overcrowded main hall as the sun dipped below the horizon, watching the festivities and drinking wine too quickly. It was awkward, but if he were honest with himself, it was also a reprieve from ruminating on

Gregor's visit. Gregor had sailed back to Japheth three days ago, and Cyrus hadn't been able to think about anything else since.

Until he saw her.

The most beautiful woman in the room.

Essandra had definitely been avoiding him; she was still distant from their situation with the assassins. And after his conversation with Orion, he thought she'd be doubly angry, but Orion had told Cyrus he'd kept that to himself.

So, she should only be regular amounts of angry. He expected her to still avoid him here, but when she saw him, she gave a visible sigh and—to his surprise—walked over.

His anger at her about using his brother for her spell had faded. He would have let her. It made sense for her to try to use Alexander as an anchor. She had everything she needed here, and Alexander would be none the wiser, provided it *worked*. But it would become complicated for Cyrus if it didn't.

He still hadn't been able to ask her about the blood-bond vision that had come to him without an *actual* blood bond. He needed to.

Her eyes held a scowl as she neared.

He'd probably wait a little longer on the vision.

"I'm glad to see you're trying not to have too much fun," he told her when she reached him.

"This isn't what I would call fun," she quipped.

"Why are you here?"

"Why are *you* here?"

He shrugged. "I'm king, I'm expected to be at these kinds of things."

"Since when have you cared about doing what's expected of you?" Her tone was curt and cold.

He didn't particularly think that was fair. He'd been trying hard. Lately.

He looked back out across the hall. "Are you looking for a match?"

She laughed, but it wasn't a merry laugh. "Maybe I am."

Of course she wasn't.

But it eased a little between them.

"What are you looking for, exactly?" He'd meant it as a jest, but as he said it, it sounded stupid, and he cursed himself.

She pursed her lips as she rocked on her heel. "He would have to be a powerful man." She cut him a side look. "Very powerful." Her eyes trailed down his body. "And a fine specimen of male physique."

He snorted. "Is that so?" He stepped closer.

"Tall," she added, looking up at him.

He was tall. He smiled.

"With dark hair, preferably black, and deep brown eyes," she said.

The air left his lungs. But he straightened and looked back out across the hall full of people.

"Will you keep an eye out for me?" she asked. Then she quirked her lips into a smile and slipped into the crowd.

Fire rippled across his skin. She'd had him for a moment, which made him feel even more sheepish. He wasn't even sure why he'd come. He didn't have to, regardless of what people expected. They knew him—they probably didn't expect anything.

He shouldn't have come.

Heart's Harvest was a stupid festival with a stupid name.

The room grew warmer. He needed air.

Cyrus pushed out of the side doors to the mezzanine outside. *This woman...*

Did she like making a fool of him? She probably—

He paused when he saw Hephain, who stood leaning against the railing and looking out over the lights of the dusky city.

Something wasn't quite right.

"Shouldn't you be inside... celebrating?" Cyrus asked.

Hephain jerked, not having heard Cyrus come outside, but when he saw Cyrus, his shoulders loosened. "I'm not in the mood for celebrating," he said as he turned back to the city.

Cyrus leaned his weight on his forearms against the railing beside Hephain. "No luck tonight?" he jested, trying to lighten the air. He knew Hephain was already with someone, although he hadn't met her yet.

But his ex-guard showed no amusement.

"What's wrong?" Cyrus asked him.

He shook his head and took a drink of wine from a chalice that Cyrus hadn't noticed until now. Cyrus also hadn't noticed his red-rimmed eyes.

Hephain drained the rest of his cup.

Cyrus looked out over the city too. He wasn't good at... emotional things. "How far do you think you can throw that?" he asked.

Hephain's brows drew together. "The cup?"

Cyrus shrugged.

Hephain snorted. Then he heaved the chalice as far as he could off the mezzanine.

It was impressive. Cyrus was glad he didn't also have a chalice to throw. He feared he might have been shown up.

They both leaned against the railing again.

"Have you ever had a broken heart?" Hephain asked finally.

Cyrus's heart had been broken many times, if betrayal counted. Not quite the same, but he could still empathize. "Women can do that."

"So can men."

Cyrus briefly lost his words. He hadn't even realized... And he didn't know what to say. "Fortunately, there are plenty more of those around here," he said, filling the void with another jest.

"I only want one," Hephain said.

And Cyrus suddenly regretted trying to jest at all. He quieted again for a moment. What did one even say after that? "He doesn't feel the same way?" he asked finally.

Hephain shrugged. "He does, but... he says he needs a traditional life—a wife and children. He said he needs to build his legacy—sons to carry on the name of his father, for that name to be respected in society, to be respected in history." He paused. "He had a family crest drawn for him. He's so proud of it." His eyes welled again, and he wiped his face. "I can't be angry with him, though. Before he was free, he couldn't dream. Our love was enough. Now, the world offers him more, and he wants it." He smiled sadly through his tears. "But I just want him."

Cyrus didn't have words for him.

Hephain snorted. "Clearly this has sent me on a path of self-destruction. I can't believe I'm sharing this." He shook his head. "But I guess I don't care if people see me as less. I'm not trying to build a legacy."

Cyrus looked back out across the city. "Who is this man?"

Hephain shook his head. "I can only tell my own secrets, not his."

Cyrus could respect that. He glanced back at the festivities continuing in the main hall. He didn't know what would make things better for Hephain, but he was pretty sure spiraling out here wasn't it. "Will you come back inside?" he asked.

Hephain shook his head. "I think I'm going to call it a night. I really don't want to watch him look for a wife in there."

Cyrus nodded. He wasn't sure what else to say, so he just cuffed Hephain on the shoulder and started back inside. Then he paused. "Hephain," he said, turning back. "I don't look at you as less. Nothing you've shared changes what I think of you, or the respect I have for you."

"Thank you for saying that," Hephain said hoarsely, and, with that, Cyrus left him to the evening.

As he stepped back inside, his eyes combed the room for Essandra again, but instead of finding her, they landed on another sad face. Sergen stood alone against the wall, his eyes traveling the room but not really seeing. Cyrus knew the look—the look of a ruminating mind.

Cyrus glanced around. Everan danced with Visa for what was probably the fifth song in a row. Kord danced as well, with a blond-haired woman Cyrus had never seen before. Everyone seemed caught up in the festivities, enjoying themselves. Everyone but Sergen.

The song ended in clapping and laughter, and Cyrus took the opportunity to slip across the hall to the other side. "Are you enjoying the evening?" he asked as he stepped beside Sergen.

He jolted, suddenly realizing Cyrus was beside him. He drew a breath in and nodded. "Everyone seems to be having a wonderful time."

Everyone but Sergen.

And Hephain.

"Are you all right?" Cyrus asked.

He nodded. "Of course," he said quickly.

Sergen had been a surprising addition to the bloodsport team. He wasn't like Pyro's usual purchases. He wasn't a large man, although he'd shown himself to be a decent fighter. He was fast and smart. That went a long way—many times further than strength—but he wasn't the kind of man one generally saw in the bloodsport.

Sergen was a gentle soul, soft and quiet and kind. And Hephain had always been a protector. Cyrus could see how things might have grown between them.

"You know what's great about the Heart's Harvest festival now?" Cyrus almost couldn't bring himself to say the stupid name. "Everyone is free to follow their heart, not what society puts on them."

"Not everyone," Sergen said quietly.

Cyrus didn't want to push him to admit something he wanted to keep private—something Cyrus wasn't even supposed to know. The only thing he could try to do was make him feel comfortable and safe. He clasped Sergen's shoulder. "I just want you to be happy."

Sergen's brows twitched, but he nodded.

Cyrus gave him a reassuring smile. "Any relationship you might pick has no bearing on what I think of you, or what your place or status will be here. You can build your legacy regardless."

Sergen nodded again, slowly this time. "Thanks."

Satisfied, Cyrus clapped him on the shoulder and passed back across the hall to where Visa and Everan had finally opted for a break in their fun.

"Trying to pull Sergen out of his slump, I see," Visa said. "He's really heartbroken."

His eyes darted to her. *She knew.* "I know. I talked to Hephain outside."

Her brows drew together. "Hephain?"

Cyrus stilled. Maybe she didn't know.

"What's going on?" Everan asked.

Visa cast her gaze across the floor at the downtrodden young man. "Sergen's been in love with Leti for months, but she's only got eyes for Kord."

Cyrus did a double take at her. Now he was thoroughly confused. "Who's Leti?"

Visa nodded to the woman Kord was dancing with.

And suddenly, he felt very foolish.

A lively song picked up through the hall.

"Ready to go again?" Visa grinned at Everan and pulled him back out into the twirling masses.

No doubt they were going to be at it for a while yet. Cyrus had no intention of dancing or trying to give any more relationship advice. He took his opportunity to slip out and away from the throngs of people.

"Making your escape?" Essandra's voice called from his right.

He turned. "I've been caught," he said.

She raised a brow.

"Looks like you are too," he said. "You didn't find a match, I take it."

She gave a cold laugh. "There's not a man who's a match for me here."

Cyrus swallowed. That one stung a bit. It shouldn't have. She was right.

Her face softened. "And you?"

"I have enough people trying to match me already."

She almost smiled. But not quite.

They stood in the silence for a moment.

"I don't like when you're upset with me," he said softly.

"And I don't like when you're upset with me. I'm sorry I did the proxy spell without really talking to you about it. I-I was just so caught up, and I honestly didn't even think because it didn't even occur to me that you wouldn't agree."

"I would have let you. It makes sense. It's just... you're so closed to me."

"I'm sorry," she said again. "I really am."

He nodded. He wholeheartedly accepted her apology.

She raised a brow. "Is there anything you're sorry about?" she asked.

Anything he was sorry about? Slowly, he shook his head. "No?"

She scoffed. "What about the assassins?"

"But I'm not sorry for that."

Her eyes blazed.

"I'll never be sorry for doing whatever I need to do to protect you," he said. "I'll never let anything happen to you."

The fire of fight in her eyes dimmed ever so slightly.

His voice dropped lower. "I'm doing the best that I can, Essandra. I hope you see that."

Her face softened, and a quiet settled between them again.

He sighed. "Where are you going now?"

She held up some fruit in her hand. "I'm going to go back to my chamber where no one will disturb me to enjoy these in the quiet of solitude."

His eyes caught on the fruit. *Figs.*

"What?" she asked him.

He shook off the hold that had grasped him. "Nothing. Those just reminded me of something I need to talk to you about. A vision. When you stop being angry with me."

"A vision about figs?"

"Of the Mercian queen. It was a strange one, though—a memory, like through a blood-bond vision, but there was no blood bond."

Her eyes narrowed. "Show me."

"It's not significant," he said. "It doesn't offer any information. But I do want to know *how* it happened."

"I want to see it."

"Let's go somewhere private."

They reached her workroom, and she promptly dropped the figs on the table. Essandra worked quickly, laying two cushions on the floor for them to sit on and pricking his finger for his blood. While they had the bond that allowed them to share power, she still needed his blood to share their minds.

With a small smear of blood on the back of her hand, she sat and closed her eyes.

Cyrus did the same. He brought her into his mind, setting a door in front of them. He opened it to the Mercian castle kitchen.

They both watched as hands cut the fig taken from the bowl on the center table and then as the Mercian queen came racing through.

"She's younger, for sure," Essandra said. "Maybe seventeen or eighteen here." Then she paused. "I see what you mean—about it being a memory. And you're sure you don't feel a bond?"

"There's no bond." But what had made it come to him? *How* had it come to him?

And this memory seemed so insignificant.

They watched as the young queen pulled whoever it was with her into the back pantry, her lips smiling through her silent words. She took a bite of the fig he offered to her.

"Oh, that's so sweet," Essandra said as the man traced his thumb over the queen's lower lip, then leaned forward to kiss her.

Cyrus glanced at Essandra, but her eyes were fixed on the vision.

"It looks like they really were in love, doesn't it?" she said.

He looked back at the queen.

And he froze as his chest tightened.

The words on her lips.

He hadn't paid much attention before. Cyrus stopped the vision, took it backward, then watched it again.

Then again.

And again.

"What are you doing?" Essandra asked.

But his eyes were on the queen's mouth.

On her words.

He'd never been skilled at reading lips, but he could read what he saw now. As sure as if he'd heard it.

Do you love me, Alec?

Alec.

Alec.

Alexander.

"It's my brother," he whispered. "This man is my brother." He puffed out an incredulous breath as he watched it again. "So not only is he her lord justice. He's in love with her."

"But this was a long time ago," she said.

He shook his head. "Look how clear it is. Every detail. It's something that still lives in his mind over and over again. He still loves her."

"And she's married to the Shadow King."

Cyrus nodded slowly. "Which makes things quite interesting."

Chapter Thirteen

Cyrus stood on the docks as the large ship from Pryam pulled into the harbor. The young Queen Miriel waved frantically from the bow with a grin that showed all her teeth.

Essandra laughed beside him. "She looks happy to see you," she said.

Yes, she did. This was her first visit to Rael. And Cyrus was happy to see her, but his mind was on a letter that had just come from Gregor. Cyrus had sent him four legions, which his council was still not aware of, but Gregor remained reluctant to pull his trade and break his alliance with the Shadow King. He said he needed to prepare, although Cyrus wasn't entirely sure what he was preparing for. He knew he should have waited.

The gangways were lowered to the dock, and Cyrus tried to push his frustration with Gregor aside as Miriel came rushing down.

"Cyrus!" She threw her arms around him. It was a nice distraction. He'd forgotten how much he liked her warmth. He smiled down at her. She was a sweet girl.

Miriel pulled back and gasped. Then her eyes moved to something behind him. "You must be Essandra!" She pushed past Cyrus and pulled Essandra into a hug, who laughed in uncomfortable surprise. "Cyrus has told me so much about you!"

"But not that much," Cyrus hurried to interject.

"Oh!" Essandra laughed again. "All good things, I hope."

"Wonderful things! Like how incredible you are."

Okay, that was a little much. "I don't think I put it like that," he said.

"And how beautiful!"

Essandra looked at him, and he shook his head, although he might have actually said that.

Miriel clutched Essandra's hands. "Oh, you're exactly as I'd imagined. I'm so honored to meet you."

Essandra smiled. A real one this time. "I'm honored to meet you too, Queen Miriel," she said.

"Call me Miriel!" The girl let out a squeal. "I can't believe I'm here!"

Cyrus couldn't help a smile of his own now. However, as happy as Miriel was to see him, she was just as happy to forget about him as she walked arm in arm with Essandra to the carriage. He was glad Essandra had told him to bring it. He had a hard time imagining Miriel riding a horse back to the palace.

Brant and Bash stepped off the ship and smiled when they saw Cyrus.

"It's good to be home," Brant said.

Cyrus cuffed him on the shoulder. "How was the sailing?" he asked.

"All right. That woman talked the entire way."

Bash chuckled as he clasped arms with Cyrus in a warm greeting. "She was just excited."

Cyrus could imagine. They mounted their horses and followed the carriage back. Brant took the opportunity to give him a very brief update on how things were faring, although Cyrus was eager to hear more.

When they reached the palace, Cyrus helped both Miriel and Essandra down from the carriage.

"You have to show me around!" Miriel said. "I have to see everything!"

"Brant and I have a few things to catch up on," Cyrus told her. "Maybe Essandra can show you how the schools are coming along, and then I'll take you around after."

Miriel clapped her hands together. "Yes! I have to see the schools!" It was an effort Miriel wanted to pursue for Pryam as well.

Essandra's face held a warm smile. It wasn't often she had someone as excited as she was about the schools. "They're not finished yet, but I'd love to show you."

Cyrus hadn't expected they'd go right away; he'd thought maybe Miriel would want to settle in first, but the two of them struck off immediately, and he watched them go in amusement.

Then he turned to Brant. "Shall we?"

Everan and Kord joined them in the council room, where Brant laid out records and reports. The Etrean Union, the collective of kingdoms surrounding Pryam, still wouldn't entertain a conversation with Miriel—wary of her witchcraft—but things seemed stable for now. Brant updated them on how the army was progressing. The training was proving effective at developing skills of warfare, despite many of the relocated refugees having no prior military experience.

Kord was pleased: it was his training regime being employed, the same one he'd crafted for the Raelean army.

Additional councilmen joined them throughout the afternoon, and they moved to an army office by the barracks, where there were more detailed table maps.

Brant walked them through his additional observations and recommendations and what he'd like to continue advising Miriel on. They discussed resource options, trade balances, and ways for those who couldn't join the army to still contribute to the community and economy. Cyrus watched him with pride. Brant had come a long way from their time together in the arena. Now he was a leader, a strategist, someone Cyrus depended on, the same as he did Everan and Kord.

His mind wandered back to Gregor, who still pressed him for a man he could trust to lead his mercenary armies. If Cyrus considered Gregor a true ally and friend, he'd send him someone like Brant.

But Gregor wasn't a true ally. Or a friend.

Cyrus would be sending Brant back with Miriel.

It was late into the evening by the time they finished. As Cyrus walked back into the palace, a sudden tiredness hit him.

"There you are!" Miriel called out as he passed the dining room. She and Essandra sat at the corner of the long carved table with hot cups of tea.

A pang of guilt stabbed at him. He'd entirely forgotten he'd told her that he'd take her around.

"I'm sorry, I lost track of time," he said.

"That's all right." She shrugged. "We can do it tomorrow."

"Of course. Tomorrow."

"Well, I guess I should turn in for the evening." Miriel stood and smiled at Essandra. "I had the best day."

Essandra smiled back and stood as well. "I did too. And it will be a great day tomorrow. Do you remember the way back to your chamber?"

Miriel nodded. She leaned in and gave Essandra a kiss on her cheek. "Thank you so much for everything. I'll see you tomorrow." Then she flitted to Cyrus and stood on her toes to give him a kiss on the cheek as well. "Good night!" And she toed out of the room and down the hall.

Cyrus sank into the chair Miriel had vacated and leaned his head forward in his hand.

"She just wants to spend time with you," Essandra told him.

"I know, and I don't mind. I'm just tired."

"Do you think you'll actually sleep tonight?"

He snorted. "Probably not."

She smiled sympathetically. "At least try."

He looked at her for a moment. Things were almost back to normal between them.

"I'll see you in the morning?" she said.

He nodded, but as she moved to leave, his eye caught on something, and he grabbed her wrist.

She tried to pull back, but he held her.

"What are you—"

"What is this?" he asked, and pushed her sleeve up to reveal inked markings that hadn't been there before.

"I just needed more power to try a few alternative spells."

"Dark magic?"

She finally pulled her wrist free. "It's nothing."

It wasn't nothing, now that he knew about it. Dark magic had destructive properties for the one who wielded it, and the markings served to protect against it.

"The markings are only a precaution," she said. "I'm perfectly fine."

He eyed her. "I don't like it."

She pursed her lips. "Noted." She pulled her sleeve back down. "Good night, Cyrus."

"Did using my brother as an anchor not work?"

She paused, and her eyes shifted to the ground. "I didn't do it."

He rose from the chair. "What?"

Still, she wouldn't look at him.

"Why not?" he asked. "Why didn't you try it?"

"Because it feels wrong."

"What about it is wrong? I told you I was fine with it."

"That's what's wrong!"

He shook his head. This didn't make any sense.

"I usurped your right to decide whether to use your brother," she said. "I chose for you, and I shouldn't have done that. But I told you I was sorry, and I've committed within myself not to do it again. You overrode a decision I made for myself, you *haven't* apologized, and I know you would absolutely do it again. So, accepting this agreement from you now and moving on..." She shook her head. "It feels like I'm accepting it as payment for your wrong. I'd be using him and allowing it to mend things between us, when, really, what should mend things is us agreeing to respect each other's right to decide for ourselves. So, you see, I can't do it."

"That's ridiculous," he said. "I told you I was fine with you using Alexander as an anchor before I even knew of the assassins."

"No, you didn't. Not really. "

"Essandra, please just use him."

"Do you not hear what I'm saying?"

"So, you're just going to waste this opportunity? Because I won't apologize for trying to keep the Jackals from coming after you?"

She closed her eyes, pushing out a breath. "Good night, Cyrus," she said again, then turned and walked away.

He watched her disappear around the corner. This woman was impossible sometimes. He sighed and struck out toward his own chamber.

As he walked, a pull came in his mind, and he was too tired, too defeated, to do anything other than lean against the wall and accept the bond.

Jaem entered his mind with a smile. He was way too cheery for Cyrus right now.

"*Did it,*" he said triumphantly. "*Got some information about that woman you're looking for.*"

All tiredness quickly left him. He'd almost forgotten about Orion's woman. "*Vitalia? Did you find her?*"

"*Well, not exactly. But there was a green-eyed dancer from Elam who was given as a gift to Gregor.*"

That matched the information Orion had given him, all except the dancer part. This was good news. "*So, she is there, then.*" He wished he would have known she'd been a gift to Gregor. He could have just asked Gregor for her while he was there. He'd write to him.

"*No, he lost her in a bet.*"

Damn. "*A bet with whom?*"

Jaem grew more serious now. "*The Shadow King.*"

This wasn't good news. In fact, it was the absolute worst. *"So, she's in the Shadowlands?"*

"It would appear so." He waited for a moment, then asked, *"Do you want me to go to the Shadowlands, see what else I can find?"*

"No," Cyrus said. *"It's not safe for you there."*

"I can keep a low profile."

"I said no," he said sharply. A little too sharply. Cyrus cursed and shook his head. *"I'm sorry. You've done well, and I'm grateful. This just isn't the news I'd hoped for."*

"That's all right," Jaem told him. *"Do you want me to head back?"*

He sighed as he raked a hand over his face. *"Yeah. Come on back."*

Cyrus lumbered down the hall, but he couldn't go back to his chamber. Not yet. He turned and made his way through the east wing and beat on the ironwood door at the end. It swung open.

Orion stared back at him. When he saw Cyrus, he rocked back on his heel. "No other assassins have come. My men have been—"

"That's not why I'm here." Cyrus pushed by him and stepped into the room. He let out a long breath. "I think Vitalia is in the Shadowlands."

Orion's face twisted, and his nostrils flared. He shook his head. "No. No, she can't be."

"Was she a dancer?" he asked.

Orion paled.

"Jaem said Gregor was gifted a green-eyed dancer from Elam. But he lost her in a bet with the Shadow King."

Orion turned from him, unsteady. He gripped the back of the chair by a small side table and leaned his weight against it. "She's in the

Shadowlands?" His voice was barely more than a whisper. "We were just there. I didn't even know."

"Even if you had, you wouldn't have been able to do anything." He likely wouldn't have made it out at all.

Orion straightened. "I have to go back."

"It's too great a risk." Especially when Orion was driven by desperation.

He shook his head. "I don't care."

Cyrus caught him. "She might already be free. Gregor told me the Mercian queen has been freeing slaves there. Vitalia could be one of them, perhaps she escaped and is on her way here to Rael."

"And if she's not? If the Shadow King still has her?"

"We'll be moving against him soon."

"When?"

"*Soon.* The Shadowlands *will* fall. We'll find her."

The sun peeked above the horizon before Cyrus could drift to sleep. He gave up and rose and washed his face in the water basin. He'd promised Miriel he'd take her around today. And it wasn't just showing her around. Like Essandra had said, Miriel wanted to spend time with him, and he was happy to do so. He'd escort her to breakfast, then show her the capital after.

Cyrus rapped on her door.

A shuffle sounded inside, and he waited. He was actually looking forward to taking her around. Rael was very different from Pryam in its style and culture. She'd enjoy seeing new things.

She was taking longer than he expected, and he knocked again. Another shuffle came.

"Miriel?" he called.

Another shuffle. Cold rippled through him.

Something didn't feel right.

Cyrus tried the door, but it was locked. "Miriel?"

Then came a small crash—something falling to the floor.

Worry lit through him, and he threw himself against the door, bursting into the room.

Miriel yelped as she stood at the end of the bed, clutching a sheet around her. "Cyrus!" she gasped.

He scanned the empty room, combing every corner with his hand on the hilt of his sword. "What's going on in here? Are you all right?"

"Nothing! And yes. I'm just... getting dressed." Her breaths were short and clipped as she nodded. "Perfectly all right. Never better. Great, actually."

He eyed her. Something was off.

She clutched the sheet nervously. "I-I would like to get some clothes on, if that's okay. Should I find you in the dining hall for breakfast?"

He looked back over the room. His eyes stopped on the lamp that had fallen off the small side table beside the bed—the side table relatively far from her right now.

A sinking suspicion weighted his stomach.

He grabbed her arm.

"Cyrus!" she cried, and the illusion fell.

Bash stood by the side table, stripped naked but holding his leather breeches as though he were about to put them on.

Fire lit Cyrus from the inside.

Bash forgot about the leathers and just clenched them in his hands as he backed against the wall. "Cyrus," he said nervously. He held up a hand. "This isn't what it looks like."

"Then what is it?" Cyrus snarled.

Bash glanced at Miriel, then nervously back to Cyrus. "Okay, maybe it's a little of what it looks like. But I haven't touched her, I swear—"

Cyrus bared his teeth and lunged at him.

Bash jumped onto the bed, fled across it, and off the other end to the door.

"Cyrus! Stop!" Miriel cried as she grabbed him.

But Cyrus was too caught in the rage of the moment. He ripped free and tore down the hall after Bash.

"Bash!" he thundered as he chased him down the side hall and into the mainway.

The fighter darted down another side hall but found it a dead end with only two closed doors that led to the dining room.

Cyrus pulled his sword as he stormed toward him. "I'm going to cut off your fucking balls."

Bash winced. "I'd really like to keep them."

Cyrus barreled forward, and Bash jumped—faster than Cyrus had ever seen him move—and bolted into the dining room.

Visa and Essandra were there, and they both gasped with a jerk.

Bash, still clutching his leathers, was out of escape options, and he put the table between them.

Cyrus pointed his sword at him. "How could you do this? She's a *child*!"

"She's only a year younger than I am!"

Cyrus paused. He was lying. "You're not... sixteen..." Or whatever the fuck age was a year older than Miriel.

Bash's brow creased. "How old do you think she is?"

"I'm eighteen, thank you very much," Miriel shouted as she burst in through the doors behind Cyrus in a misbuttoned robe with her hair disheveled.

"You are not!" he snapped back at her.

"I am! And he's nineteen!"

Cyrus gaped at Bash, a man taller and larger than himself. "He is not!"

"I am, actually," Bash said.

Cyrus stared at him. He didn't believe that. Bash was a man, and a big one at that. But his eyes caught on the boyishness of his face, and he thought about the innocence he so often saw in him—the innocence of youth.

But Bash wasn't innocent anymore. Cyrus glared at him. Boy or not... He pointed his sword at him again. "I put you in charge of her safety."

"And I've seen to it," Bash said quickly. "With my life. I would never let anything happen to her."

"You took advantage!" Cyrus thundered.

"I love her!"

"It's not his fault!" Miriel shouted. "I seduced him!"

"You are not seductive," Cyrus snapped at her.

She gasped in offense.

Essandra stepped forward. "Cyrus," she said cautiously as she reached out and touched his arm.

But Cyrus couldn't take his eyes off Bash. "I'm going to kill him."

"Or we can just take a break," she said, "and talk about this when we've all calmed down."

"I am calm."

Essandra pushed him back from the table, putting herself between them. "Bash, go get some clothes on," she said over her shoulder.

Bash sidled around the table cautiously, not taking his eyes from Cyrus as Essandra clutched him. Cyrus knew she would use power if she had to.

She might have to.

Bash quickly disappeared.

Essandra looked at Miriel. "You too. Go get dressed."

"And don't even think about speaking to him," Cyrus told her.

"You can't tell me what to do!" she snapped back. "I'm not your subject!"

"Bash is, and I will string him up in the fucking courtyard!" he thundered.

Her eyes widened, and she swallowed. Then she pursed her lips and whirled around with a huff, storming from the room.

"You need to cool down," Essandra told him. "Go... Go for a walk outside."

"It's fucking hot out there."

"It's cooler than you. Go. *Now.*"

Essandra followed him to the side doors, ensuring that he left, and he struck out toward the sparring field. Heat fumed off him.

He'd left Bash in Pryam to protect Miriel, not take advantage of her. He'd trusted him.

And Bash wasn't nineteen. That would mean he'd have been eighteen when Cyrus had toppled Rael. Seventeen in the arena. Sixteen when Cyrus had taken him under his wing. No. That couldn't be right. But if it was...

If he'd known Bash was younger, he would have tried to protect him from the horrors a little longer.

Regardless, Cyrus expected more when it came to Miriel. The anger returned. He pulled a spear from the weapons hold and heaved it down the field, launching it long. It struck the ground on the far side.

"Not bad," Kord called, coming up behind him.

Cyrus pulled another spear and sent it following the same trajectory. It landed within a hand's length of the first.

"I hear it's been an interesting morning," Kord said.

Cyrus paused. "Did you know Bash is only nineteen?" He turned for another spear, but Kord held one for him. He took it.

"I didn't. He does look older."

Cyrus hurled the spear Kord had just handed him, and it buried itself between the first two. Then he stopped. "That means he was just a boy in the arena. I gave him heavy roles. I put the responsibilities of a man on him, and he was just a boy."

"He's not a boy anymore. And Miriel's not a little girl."

"She's enough of a girl. And she's a queen. He's... a soldier."

"So?" Kord shrugged his shoulders. "What does that matter? Is that not what we fought for? To make our own life, to forge our own path? To be the masters of our own destiny?"

He wasn't wrong.

"And we're making history," Kord continued. "We should all be thinking about how our legacy will live on, you included. I know you dismiss it, but you should find a wife, have sons who will carry your name and be heirs to your throne. You're building something great here—we all are."

Cyrus didn't care about a legacy. And he didn't care about heirs to the throne.

Kord smiled. "Can I show you something?"

Cyrus quirked a brow.

His friend pulled a folded parchment from his pocket. "This is just a draft, but you can see the idea."

Cyrus unfolded it, and he froze as he saw the drawing of a sigil crest.

"Orion helped me come up with it," Kord told him. "I've just been thinking—our legacy is what still lives after we're gone. Before, I was a slave, a bloodsport fighter, a nobody. I knew that when I died in the arena, it would be as if I'd never even lived. But now, my name will be written in history. My father's name. I'll have sons and it will be their name. It will be a name said with respect. That's what I'm building now. Bash can build his name too. He can be worthy of a queen."

Cyrus stared at him, the realization sinking in.

Kord. It was *Kord*.

Kord's brows drew together. "What?"

He shook his head. "Nothing," he said quickly.

"Let him live his life, Cyrus." He took his parchment, folding it, and returned it to his pocket. Then he handed Cyrus another spear before turning and walking back to the castle.

Chapter Fourteen

They ate dinner in silence, with only the sound of silverware tapping their plates. Even the dogs were quiet. Visa had tried to start general conversation around the table, but it had quickly died, and she'd conceded to the quiet again. Miriel glared at Cyrus between her bites of food. He'd managed to make it through the day without killing Bash, although Bash wasn't at the table with them now.

And there was another absence.

Hephain.

It had been over two weeks since the festival, and Hephain hadn't joined the group for their regular dinners since. Each time he'd had a rational reason, but now, with a string of rational reasons piling up, Cyrus wondered if he planned to stop coming altogether.

Cyrus's gaze wandered to Kord. He appeared unfazed, although his eyes repeatedly caught on Hephain's empty chair across from him.

Cyrus wasn't normally bothered by uneasy air, but these were the people closest to him. Even Miriel.

"We'll go for a walk this evening," he said to her. Their day had been disrupted, and he hadn't yet taken her to see the capital. It would be light for a little longer, and Rael at dusk was quite beautiful. And they could talk.

"I might actually head to bed early," she replied. "I'm quite—"

"After we walk," he said firmly.

Miriel pursed her lips.

They finished dinner and stood.

"I need to change my shoes," she said shortly. "I'll meet you in the hall."

"If you don't, I'll come get you," he told her.

Her lips thinned, and she stalked from the room.

Cyrus glanced at Essandra to find her disapproving eyes on him. "What?" he said. "You think I should leave her alone?"

"I think you should start treating her with more respect. She's a queen. And an adult who can make her own decisions."

"To be fair, I didn't know she was an adult until today."

Everan, Kord, and the others stood awkwardly until Visa ushered them out, leaving Cyrus and Essandra alone.

"You should apologize to her," Essandra told him as the doors closed.

"She doesn't understand. I just need to—"

"Impose your company?" She shook her head. "*No.* Apologize."

"But I'm not—"

"Don't say you're not sorry! Be sorry! I know it came from a good place, but you were wrong, and you acted wrong." The strength of her voice grew with each word.

"I don't think it was wrong!"

"It was! And even if it wasn't, sometimes the apology isn't about you being wrong. It's about caring for the other person enough to show them that repairing the rift between you is more important than being right!"

He paused. Her green eyes were aflame, her lips parted and ready with more words.

"This isn't just about Miriel, is it?" he asked.

She scoffed. "Of course it's about Miriel."

"I'm sorry," he said softly.

Her breath hitched, and her eyes of fire shifted to eyes of surprise.

He stepped closer. "There's been a distance between us, and I know it's my fault." He took another step nearer, closing the space between them. "I'm sorry if I made you feel like you don't have your own agency. I know you make decisions for yourself."

She eased ever so slightly.

"These things aren't always clear to me," he said. "Sometimes I miss, but I'm trying my best."

She was quiet for a moment, then she said softly, "I know."

"I'm sorry," he said again. "For you, I'm sorry. And completely separate—I want you to use Alexander. It makes sense for you to, and I would have agreed. You don't have to use him in place of an apology, because I do apologize. I won't make decisions for you again. *I'm sorry.*"

"I'm sorry too," she whispered.

She stared up at him, her chest rising and falling. She looked like she wanted him even closer. His eyes moved to her lips, and he let his head drop ever so slightly.

She didn't move. He waited for her to lift her face, lift her chin, something—anything—the smallest of movements to invite him to kiss her.

So badly he wanted to kiss her.

Of course she wouldn't invite him. She'd never let him kiss her before. Now they'd been distant for weeks, and they were at odds over Miriel, not to mention he was in the midst of an apology.

Kissing her now would be peak failure of that apology.

It would be one more thing to apologize *for*.

But he was entirely prepared to apologize more. He dropped his head to her—

The door to the dining room opened, and Miriel stepped inside. "There you are. I was waiting in the hall."

For a moment, Cyrus's mind went blank.

"This walk I was threatened with?" she snipped.

Essandra stepped back from him. "Yes, your walk," she reminded him. "You should go." Then, she added, in a whisper just for him, "Behave and be nice."

Cyrus sighed. He waved the dogs to stay with Essandra and followed after Miriel.

The blazing heat of the afternoon had left with the sun, and he was grateful. Some last rays still lit the western sky, but torches started to speckle the city.

His attempts at conversation were met with minimal replies. Not that he was expecting her to be friendly after the events of the day, but he wanted to mend things between them, even though she showed no sign of feeling the same.

He led her up the tower, which boasted the best views of the capital. They stood on the terrace of the highest level. The sun sank even further, giving way to a rolling sea of torchlight.

"The best view of the city," he said, doing his best to fill the void. "There's another place I'd like to take you—a bluff overlooking the Aged Sea. It's my favorite in all of Rael. We can go there tomorrow." And now he was rambling. *Gods.*

She gave a stiff nod.

He sighed. "I'm sorry," he said finally. Although he wasn't sorry for going after Bash, but he managed to still his tongue on that.

Her head jerked up and her eyes widened. "You are?"

Sorry enough. *Damn it.* He fell back on Essandra's words. "You're a queen, and an adult, and can make your own decisions."

She gaped at him. "Do you really mean that?"

No. "Yes."

"And you're not angry at me?"

"No." That part was true.

A wide smile broke across her face but then faltered. "You can't be mad at Bash either."

Oh, he absolutely could.

"I was scared after you left Pryam," she said. "I thought that as soon as people saw you go, they would know I was all alone. I couldn't sleep. He stood outside my door constantly to make sure I was safe, and he coordinated all the men guarding me."

"Yes, that was his job."

"I was so stressed." Her fingers picked at the frill on the front of her dress. "I spent some time away from the capital to try to calm my nerves. He never left my side. On the way back, we stayed at Devry Castle, which is barely a castle, by the way. Hardly any accommodation."

His eyes blurred under a slow blink.

"Anyway," Miriel continued, "I told him he could share the bed. And he slept in the chair *by the door*." Her words became higher pitched, betraying her annoyance.

"Again," he said, "I'm glad to hear he was doing his job."

"We went for *months*, and he never kissed me, although I gave him plenty of opportunities to do so. He even averted his eyes when I got naked."

At this point, it was starting to sound like Miriel had taken advantage of Bash.

"I finally just told him that I really liked him," she said. Because apparently she hadn't been obvious enough. "He said he really liked me back. And he did end up letting me touch him, but he was so worried about you being mad at him that he couldn't... well..." Her cheeks flushed, and she shrugged. "*You know.* And then I cried, and it was the most terrible evening ever."

Cyrus shook his head. "You don't need to share any further."

"But that's how it's been," she continued. "He said we couldn't do anything until he had your blessing, and he's been planning to talk to you since we've arrived."

Maybe Bash had been telling the truth. "He really hasn't touched you?"

She rolled her eyes. "He refuses." Then she gave an unapologetic smile. "We do take off all our clothes and sleep beside each other, though."

"I didn't need to know that."

Her smile widened. "He's so handsome."

That was *not* what he wanted to hear. "I... Maybe you should talk to your friends who are girls about these kinds of things."

"I don't really have any."

No, she probably didn't. "Yes, well… um…" He trailed off as the final rays of the sun disappeared. *What to say…*

There was always the practical. "What happens if you decide to execute a marriage alliance?" he asked her.

"Are *you* saving your heart and staying chaste for a potential future political transaction?"

He snorted. *Fair.*

"So can I take Bash back to Pryam so we can be together?" she asked.

"You don't need my blessing."

"Bash does. He respects you more than anyone, and I think he'd rather fall on his sword than disappoint you."

He wanted to say no. He was still angry. But she looked so hopeful. This would make them both happy, and Cyrus did want them to be happy. He sighed. "You have my blessing, then."

She smiled, and before he could stop her, she threw her arms around him.

Miriel's hugs were soft and warm. Not just warm from her body, but warm from her spirit, and Cyrus didn't realize how much he needed that until he felt it. He let himself hold her in return. Touch was healing—not just any touch, but the touch of someone who cared for him and who he cared about.

When she pulled back, she smiled up at him. "You give good hugs."

"I don't think anyone else would agree with that."

She frowned. "Do you hug anyone else?"

"No."

She shrugged. "Maybe you should."

No. He wasn't going to do that.

Banners flapped wildly against their staffs, and the canopies that stretched across the market streets for shade billowed and pulled at their ties. These were the Winds—not a great feat of naming creativity—and the sand that came with them could scrape the skin off a man. Fortunately, they were rare, hitting once, maybe twice a year. Only once did Cyrus have to fight in the arena during the Winds. Bloodsport games were usually canceled to protect spectators, but the Winds had come in the middle of his fight. Although victorious, he and Ram had suffered severe sand burns. It had taken Teron two days to heal them.

Cyrus clutched the letter in his hand and waited for a small break before quickly crossing the courtyard toward the army office. He needed to find Everan. The coward king of Japheth had done it—he'd actually diverted trade intended for the Shadow King and sent it to the trading kingdom of Tarsus instead.

And now Cyrus needed to be ready.

Not that he thought one single refused trade shipment would send Japheth and the Shadowlands crashing into war, but it did show their alliance was breaking.

Cyrus stepped into the army office and was surprised to find Hephain. He sat at the desk, his hand gliding a pen across a parchment, and looked up when he heard the door open.

"Good morning," he greeted Cyrus as he stood. "I'm just finishing recording everyone who's registered to go to Pryam when Queen Miriel returns."

Cyrus nodded. Their approach was working well. Instead of choosing which refugees were to be relocated to Pryam, which could better support them, they'd asked for volunteers. These volunteers would be given a small piece of land and an opportunity to start a new life. He had been pleasantly surprised. Ten thousand people had already registered—mostly intact families. People still holding out hope that their enslaved loved ones would escape and come to Rael generally decided to stay to wait for them.

"Three thousand of them are soldiers who've completed their basic training," Hephain said. "About four hundred of those have completed advanced training."

That made sense. While they were part of the army, most soldiers had families, and if their family wanted to relocate, they would want to go too, which Cyrus fully supported. He'd committed to sending Miriel men to bolster her army; he'd just expected to have a harder time of it. This was good news. He might have to recall those soldiers if he moved to war, but he'd manage that when the time came.

"That's great," Cyrus said.

Hephain nodded. "I'll make sure you get the final tallies."

"Thank you. Have you seen Everan?"

"You just missed him. I think he might have been looking for you."

He was probably headed to Cyrus's study. Cyrus would meet him there. He looked out the window. The Winds had picked back up again. He waited by the door. "Don't mind me—I'm just waiting for the Winds. Don't let me keep you."

Hephain sat back down, dipping his pen in the inkwell.

Cyrus couldn't help himself. "You weren't at dinner again yesterday evening," he said.

Hephain nodded but kept his eyes on the parchments in front of him. "I've just been really busy. I've had—"

"Is it because of Kord?"

Hephain's hand stilled. His eyes darted up and locked with Cyrus's, and he swallowed. "You can't say anything. No one can know. He doesn't want anyone to know."

"I'm not going to say anything."

"Even to him."

Cyrus caught on those words.

"Even to him," Hephain begged.

"Even to him," Cyrus finally assured him.

Hephain sighed a long breath and closed his eyes. "And I don't want to talk about it anymore."

"We don't have to."

Silence hung heavy between them.

"There is something I would ask, though," Hephain said. "I'd like to go to Pryam with Queen Miriel, when she returns."

"Hephain—"

"I know I sit on the council and have duties here, and I don't know what I would say to Kord, but I..." His words waivered. "I..."

It was painful to watch a man break, especially when that man was a friend.

He couldn't help himself. Cyrus rocked off the doorframe he'd been leaning against. "Hey, I'm actually glad I found you here. I, uh, wanted to tell you that I think it would be prudent to have a member of our council in Pryam. Brant is doing an excellent job, but I want him to focus on the army. Miriel needs advisers too. She needs help assembling her own council. A man with experience. Is this a position you'd be willing to accept?"

Hephain's eyes welled. "I accept," he said hoarsely.

Cyrus nodded. "Good. I'll let everyone know that I'm sending you."

Then he stepped back out into the Winds.

Chapter Fifteen

Cyrus stood on the port wall, watching as ships sailed out of the harbor. This was the fourth day in a row he'd come to the port. A few days prior, Miriel had returned to Pryam. She'd taken Bash, who had continued to apologize profusely to Cyrus to the very end, all the way until the gangways were raised on the ship. Cyrus still wasn't sure he'd forgiven him, but in watching them both together, it was quite clear who controlled the relationship. And it wasn't Bash.

Now Cyrus was here again, seeing out yet another fleet of ships with the last of the three legions bound for Japheth. It was the second wave of what he'd committed to Gregor. He waited for news of how the Shadow King had taken the loss of his alliance. Cyrus didn't think this would actually spiral them into war, but an opportunity at the Shadow King was close now.

He could feel it.

And he would be ready.

"I'm surprised the council didn't come with one last effort to stop you," Kord said, appearing beside him.

Yes, they'd fought him quite valiantly with very compelling arguments when they'd learned he was sending nearly half the army to Japheth. Not compelling enough to sway him, though.

"Why do you even have a council?" Kord asked.

"Because they have ideas. And advice."

"But when do you listen?"

"Look at all the infrastructure changes I've approved."

"We were ready to take Serra," Kord said.

"We're still ready to take Serra."

Kord scoffed. "With half an army?"

"I don't even need an army." Cyrus felt like he was repeating the same things all over again. People weren't listening. He knew he could take Serra simply with the slaves from within. And keeping his men in Japheth under the guise of an alliance solved two problems for him: it kept pressure on Gregor, and it fed an army that he struggled to sustain. He'd also have his army on the mainland and be ready to move against the Shadow King.

He was planning a war.

A war that was close.

And he had to be ready.

Back at the palace and feeling energized, Cyrus took the mainway steps two at a time, heading toward his study. However, before he reached it, Orion caught him in the hall.

"There's something you need to see," the assassin told him.

And now the energy he'd been feeling was waning. Still, he followed Orion to the arena and through the corridors underneath, to a small holding room where three men lay on the floor.

Unfamiliar men.

Dead men.

"We caught them trying to get to Essandra," Orion said.

"They're assassins?"

Orion nodded but wouldn't meet his gaze.

"To break their bonds?" Cyrus didn't even need to ask the question. He already knew. He'd known this would happen. Anger flamed inside him.

Orion nodded again but still didn't look at him. "They were surprised to find me and my men. They thought we'd left, which means the guild probably thinks the same."

Cyrus wasn't sure if that increased the risk to Essandra or if it helped. He was a little concerned at how losing three more assassins in Rael might appear to the Jackals. "Is the guild able to distinguish between when an assassin's bond is broken by death and when it's broken by a witch?" he asked.

"Yes. They'll know these men are dead."

"Good." That was certainly better than them assuming more interference from Essandra. "Does Essandra know about these three?"

Orion shook his head.

"Good," he said again. "Get rid of them." Cyrus turned to leave.

"Do you know how I killed them so easily?" Orion said.

Cyrus paused.

"I let them think I was helping them." His voice was thick with guilt. "I let them trust me."

"You did the right thing."

"The right thing?" Orion snorted as he shook his head again. "All they wanted was their freedom. You think this is right?"

Their stares locked.

"This keeps Essandra safe," Cyrus said. "That makes it right."

Within the month, the first of the new schools was finished, and they celebrated with music and food and activities, which were somehow very different from the other stupid festivals with music and food and activities.

Cyrus stood in the central hall of the new three-level spired building with stained-glass windows, watching people make merry.

"Congratulations," he told Essandra as he handed her a chalice of wine.

She gave a smile. "Thank you." She took a sip. "I just wish Miriel could have seen this."

"She will. We'll have her back soon."

"I hope so."

"We will," he assured her. "I don't want her alone in Pryam all the time anyway. Rael's a short journey; she can spend part of her time here. Plus, it's better for her to be around you and the coven as much as possible, learn as much as possible."

Essandra smiled. "She's already worked through all the spells I sent back with her to practice."

Cyrus chuckled. "She wrote to you?" He'd gotten a letter too, where Miriel had told him the same.

"Are you jealous?" she teased.

"Of course not. She drew a flower on my letter."

"She drew two on mine."

Cyrus couldn't help another chuckle. He was glad to see Miriel and Essandra growing closer. He'd hoped as much. Miriel needed another woman in her life. She needed another witch. Essandra was the best of both.

"I have been thinking quite a lot about Miriel," he said. "Perhaps she could join your coven."

Essandra shook her head. "I don't think that would be a good move for her. She's a queen, which complicates things. She has to straddle both the ordinary and the magical world, and I don't think her being accountable to a high witch—especially a foreign high witch—is the right thing for her, even if that high witch has the best of intentions for her. And I don't think it will help her win favor with the Etrean Union. It could make things worse. They'd see my potential for control as a threat."

"Should she try to form her own coven?" he asked. "Build more powers that she could use?"

"It's actually not common for the witches of a coven to share power. My coven can because of me. Miriel would have to find a bond witch, and there aren't very many of us. It's why we're so valuable."

Cyrus cocked his head. "And here I recall you trying to convince me at one point that you didn't have any power," he joked.

"A bond witch is only as powerful as those who agree to bond with her. If she has no one who will share their power, she's power*less*. And bond witches are usually used to make *other* witches powerful, not themselves."

"Is this why you think Soroya will still come after you?" Soroya was the high witch that led the coven Essandra had been bound to before she broke free and got away. Just the thought of her coming after Essandra lit a fire in his veins.

"Soroya will come after me because I escaped her," she told him. "I'm sure she's found another bond witch by now, but she'll still come to punish me."

Cyrus dropped his voice. "You still have nightmares." He'd meant it as a question, even though it didn't sound like one. It had been a little while since he'd seen a nightmare from her, but with the new bond she'd created between them, Essandra didn't have to use his blood as much as she used to, which meant he didn't have access to her mind as often as he used to.

The faintest slip of her face answered for her.

He stepped closer. "I've told you this before, and I'll tell you again. I won't let anyone hurt you."

She shook her head. "Even you can't stand against Soroya."

"Both of us together?" he said. "Our power together?"

She shook her head again. "It doesn't matter. I told you—she drains people of their power. It doesn't matter how much you have. Even if she somehow didn't, Soroya is two hundred years old. Her skill, her spellwork—"

"Two hundred years old?" Tension pulled his brows. "Do all witches live that long?"

"They can, yes. Longer, even. Our power slows our aging."

"So, *you* can live that long?"

She grew quiet, then she said, "I'll live until Soroya finds me. It won't be two hundred years."

He stepped even closer. "Essandra—"

"Don't tell me you'll stop her. You'll make promises you can't keep. And I've already accepted my fate. I accepted it when I broke my bond and chose to leave, and I accept it over and over again each day that I choose to stay here."

She smiled, but it was a sad smile. And Cyrus didn't even know what he could say to all that.

Essandra looked back out across the floor full of people dancing, to Visa and Everan, who'd been at it song after song. "They're having fun."

Well, Visa was definitely having fun, but Cyrus was pretty sure Everan was just trying to survive.

He heard the call of his name and turned to see Kord walking toward him. On Kord's arm was a woman with long blond hair and a blue dress that matched the hue of her eyes.

"I want to introduce you to Leti," Kord said.

The woman made a low curtsey. "So pleased to meet you, Your Majesty."

This was the woman Kord had been dancing with at the festival over a month and a half ago—the woman Kord thought he needed to build his legacy and lead a respectable life. The woman who'd replaced Hephain in Kord's ambition.

"Cyrus, this is Leti," Kord said again, making another attempt at the introduction.

She swallowed and glanced at Kord, then curtsied again.

Essandra stepped forward, extending her hand. "It's a pleasure to meet you as well."

Leti clasped it, confused, but smiled and nodded respectfully. "And you, Lady Essandra." She gave another unnecessary curtsey.

Kord gently pulled at her. "Why don't you get us some wine?" he told her. "I'll be right there."

"Of course!" She smiled, gave yet another curtsy to both Cyrus and Essandra, then flitted away.

Kord's eyes bore into Cyrus. "What's the matter with you?"

"Nothing." Or nothing he could say.

"You can't even greet her? That's fucking bullshit."

"You can't tell me this is what you really want."

Kord shifted back on his heel with a snort, and his face twisted. "As opposed to what? War?" He shook his head. "Do you not want me to be happy?"

Cyrus snapped up his head, and their eyes locked. "That's *all* I want for you."

"Then why don't you act like it?"

Cyrus wished he had the words, but they wouldn't come.

Kord shook his head again, then turned and disappeared into the crowd to find Leti.

Essandra swatted his arm. "What was that?"

"He shouldn't be with that woman."

"Why not?"

He couldn't tell her. "He thinks she's what he wants. But she isn't."

Essandra sighed. "Not everyone wants war and blood and death. Most people want a person to share their life with. A family. Love."

"That's not what I..." He shook his head. "No."

Essandra stared at him, a deep sadness etching her brow. "You can't see it because it's not what you want." Then she, too, disappeared into the crowd, leaving Cyrus standing on his own.

In his mind, he felt the pull of the blood bond. *Sid.* Sid had stayed in Mercia, taking over Jaem's search for Bravat, and hopefully he'd found him, although hearing about Bravat was the last thing Cyrus really wanted to do right now. Still, he pushed out a long sigh and stepped back outside onto the empty mezzanine, letting his mind reach out.

"*Woah,*" Sid said as Cyrus entered his mind. It was the young fighter's first time using the blood, and Cyrus could hear his unease.

"*Did you find him?*" Cyrus asked.

"*Yeah.*"

"*Good. Good work.*" It was a relief he wouldn't have to send Jaem back to help. Jaem had just returned from Japheth, but Cyrus had other things planned for him than chasing down a wayward troublemaker.

"*There's a problem, though,*" Sid said.

"*What kind of problem?*"

"*Bravat's got himself an army.*"

Chapter Sixteen

A hundred and fifty men were not an army. However, they were a problem. Apparently Bravat had been picking up random vagabonds along his escapades. *Drifters*, Sid had called them. Not only did this complicate things for Cyrus, but it increased their risk of being caught in Mercia even more. Cyrus had let this carry on long enough. He pulled Essandra and Everan from the celebration activities, and they quickly made their way to Essandra's workroom. Kord came as well, although he made no effort to hide his continued anger at Cyrus over the interaction with Leti. Cyrus would talk to him about it, but later.

"What are you going to do?" Everan asked.

"What choice do I have but to go after him? He's going to bring war with a kingdom that we can't afford to be at war with."

"You can't go traipsing across Mercia," Kord said. "Not right now."

"I don't want to go, but what else can I do? I haven't had to concern myself with Mercia and Aleon, but Bravat will quickly make them my concern. I have to get to him."

"And do what?" Essandra asked. "He has a hundred and fifty men."

"Only thirty-three of them are fighters. The rest are these vagabonds."

"It's still a lot."

Kord looked at Essandra. "You could bond him. Like the assassins were bonded. Just do your"—he waved his hand—"magic stuff, and then Cyrus can call him back."

"It doesn't work like that," she said shortly. "And I don't bond people against their will."

A knock sounded on the door, and Ram pushed in his head. "Cyrus, a letter from Japheth just arrived." He held it out.

For a moment, Cyrus forgot about Bravat. He tore the letter open, his heart in his throat. This was what he'd been waiting for. He didn't want to get ahead of himself, hoping that it would be a call to march against the Shadow King—it was too soon for that. But just the thought had his heart racing.

Gregor's handwriting was nearly illegible, far different from the pompous script he usually used. He'd obviously been beside himself as he wrote it. But as Cyrus read the words, his shoulders dropped.

"What does it say?" Everan asked.

"He says Aleon has taken Tarsus," Cyrus told them.

Everan's brows stitched. "Tarsus—the island trading kingdom?"

Cyrus nodded. He gave a disbelieving scoff as he flipped the parchment over, scanning it for anything more. "Where..." He scoffed again. "Where's the rest of it? He says nothing about the Shadow King." He handed the letter to Everan and then turned and paced to the window. "How can he say *nothing* about the Shadow King?"

"Clearly he's frantic," Everan said, passing the letter to Kord. "With him breaking trade with the Shadowlands, he relies on Tarsus for everything now. If his brother has taken that away, everything has fallen apart for him. I think you'll hear more, and soon. This is just him reacting in the moment."

"All the more reason not to wing off to Mercia right now after Bravat," Kord added. "You need to be here. And be ready."

Cyrus pushed out a frustrated breath as he leaned against the windowsill. They were right. He just had to accept the risk with Bravat for the time being and hope for the best.

The torchlight danced shadows across the wall as Cyrus made his way toward Essandra's chamber. Two days in a row she'd missed dinner. She could have been caught up in her work, but he couldn't shake the feeling that something was wrong.

Neither Aaron nor Amiel was by her door, which didn't necessarily mean she wasn't there. She'd been sending them away lately, which Cyrus didn't like. He knocked lightly. She didn't answer, and he knocked again. He hadn't checked her workroom first. Perhaps he should have. If it was work that had tied her up, that was where she'd be. He was just about to leave when she finally opened the door.

He paused.

Her hair was pinned up, not exactly unusual, although the wisps falling down around her face were. She looked defeated. Or tired. Or both.

"You weren't at dinner," he said softly.

She stared at him blankly, looking at him but not quite seeing. "Dinner," she said in a voice little more than a whisper. "Oh."

"Are you all right?" he asked her.

She turned away from the door but left it open for him to enter.

He followed her in. "What's wrong?"

She turned to face him again and swallowed. "It didn't work."

"What didn't work?"

"The spell."

The realization hit him, and he shifted back slightly. "Alexander? The anchor? You tried it?"

"I can't figure it out. The only thing I can think of is that using your blood in place of your brother's is a natural proxy, and maybe you can't be both a natural proxy and a spelled proxy together. I just... I don't know." She put her head in her hands. "I keep going rounds with this, and I'm to the point that I'm confusing myself. I don't know how to make it work."

"How long have you been at it?"

"Four days."

He balked slightly before stepping closer. "Four days? Why didn't you tell me?"

She shook her head. "I... I couldn't."

"Why not?"

"I don't know. I-I just..."

"Essandra," he said gently.

"I was afraid it would lead to asking something of you beyond your limits," she said finally, "and I can't do that."

He knew exactly what she meant. "Now you need Alexander alive."

"I'm not going to ask that of you." She shook her head. "I should have used Perr and Fierra. They offered." Perr and Fierra were two witches in her coven. Brother and sister.

"You can't use them now?" he asked.

"I've already done the proxy spell on you. There's no reversing it. And I can't do it more than once." She crossed her arms over herself and rocked back and forth, shaking her head again. "I was worried they wouldn't be powerful enough, but I should have just used them. I should have tried."

"But if they weren't powerful enough, you wouldn't have been able to try again with me," he said.

"I'm just making a mess of all of this."

"So, what is it you need now?" he asked. "Alexander's blood? And you need him alive, at least long enough for you to do the spell?"

"I told you, I'm not going to ask that of you. I'm not going to be the one to stand between you and your brother for my own gain."

Good. Because that was the one thing he couldn't do. When an opportunity at Alexander came, he would have to take it, no matter what.

Commotion from outside drew his attention. He moved to the window and looked down below to see guards running toward the courtyard.

"What's happening?" Essandra asked.

"I don't know." But he needed to find out.

Quickly they moved out of Essandra's room and down the hall. When they reached the crossway, he saw Everan.

"There you are," Everan said, hurrying toward him. "I was looking for you."

"What's going on?"

"Protests at the palace gates."

Cyrus didn't ask why. He didn't need to. The people had been growing increasingly restless about the delay in moving against Serra. "I'll go talk to them."

"You can't go out there," Essandra told him. "People are angry. It could turn violent."

"That's exactly why I need to go—to keep that from happening." He looked at Everan. "Where's Kord?"

"Gathering the men."

"Have him hold them inside. I'll go on my own."

"Cyrus," Essandra said uneasily.

"That's a terrible idea," Everan added.

"If I go out with an army, it's only going to increase the tension. I'll go alone."

"At least take the dogs," Everan said.

"I'll go alone," he said again. He didn't give them the opportunity to argue further, as he struck out toward the front gates.

The number of people holding torches lit the palace entry like day. A thousand, perhaps more. Cyrus ordered the gates open and strode through them. The masses quieted, falling back in surprise.

He walked to the center of the crowd, his eyes traveling around him. No one spoke. "Am I not the one you came for?" he called out.

They fell back a little farther.

"Speak your minds," he told them.

Slowly, a man stepped forward. He was a little older than Cyrus. He wore a patch over one eye, and thick scars marred his arms. "We want to know when you'll take Serra," he said. "We have families suffering there. And all we do is wait."

Cyrus wasn't a stranger to that sentiment. He also felt like all he did was wait.

"Most of us have joined you to fight," another man called out. "But then you sent half our army to Japheth."

Cyrus nodded. He knew this was a point of contention, and not just for the people but for his council as well. It was because they didn't see the bigger picture. "The battle we wage has multiple fronts," he told them. "I am preparing us for them all."

"What's in Japheth?" another man asked.

"An opportunity against the Shadow King."

Murmurs rippled through the crowd. Now they would understand. They'd see why he had—

"We should be focusing on Serra first," a man shouted from the back. The murmurs grew louder in agreement.

"I hear you," Cyrus assured them. "I *do* hear you." This was the opinion of many, and while he didn't entirely disagree, he at least expected them to see the necessity of preparing a multipronged approach. "The Shadow King supports the slave trade—he fuels it," he explained. "If there's an opportunity to bring him down, we must be prepared to take it."

"But Serrans are the actual slave traders," the man with the eye patch said. "Serra is where our families are."

Cyrus couldn't argue with that. "We *will* take Serra. But I ask that you trust me and give me just a little more time."

"How many people are we losing in that time? We can't wait." The crowd rumbled their agreement. "We don't want the Shadow King," the man said, and the people grew louder behind him. "We don't want new schools." Louder still they sounded. "We want our families free." And the night flamed alive with their rally.

"And they will be!" Cyrus called out.

The crowd quieted.

"You think I don't know the pain of waiting?" Cyrus's gaze burned into them. "You think I don't know loss?"

Quieter still the crowd grew.

"You know where I came from!" He let his voice boom over them. "But look around!" He walked a large circle around the center. "Who else among you can bring down a kingdom?" he challenged.

Murmurs rippled through the masses again.

"I will destroy Serra!" he thundered. Shouts rang out in support. "I will get your families!" The shouts grew louder. "But I won't stop there. I won't stop until they all pay. Serra. The Shadowlands. All of them." Cheers rang between his sentences.

"I will bring down every kingdom who has ever made us suffer!"

The crowd roared.

"Go home!" he told them. "Eat. Sleep. Train. Grow strong. And when it's time, I will lead you to Serra myself."

A thousand sounded like ten thousand, and their voices rose high into the night. They cheered him all the way back to the palace.

Once inside, Cyrus watched the torchlight fade as the crowd finally dispersed.

"I can't believe you were able to settle them," Everan said as he and Kord moved to his side.

"Why not? I'll give them what they want."

Essandra shifted uneasily as she crossed her arms.

"So, we're really doing it?" Everan asked. "We're going after Serra?"

"Soon."

"Should I recall the army from Japheth?" Kord asked.

Cyrus shook his head. "No. When Gregor sends word, we need to be able to move." He wasn't going to lose his readiness against the Shadow King.

Kord's brows dipped. "You mean for us to go to Serra with only half an army?" He said something else, but his words were drowned by the call that pulled at Cyrus's mind.

It was Sid. Cyrus sighed, but he couldn't ignore it. He turned away from Kord and Everan and reached out his mind.

"*Cyrus,*" Sid said as they connected. "*You're going to have to do something. Things are getting bad.*"

"*Another village?*"

"*Worse. Bravat's taking captives.*"

Cyrus froze. "*For what?*"

Sid paused. "*He's taking women. For his own enjoyment.*"

A cold rippled through Cyrus. "*And if they refuse?*"

"*It doesn't matter.*"

That cold turned to a burn—a deep burn of building fury. "*Has anyone from the villages followed? Has anyone come for the captives?*"

"*There's no one to come. He's killed everyone.*"

His blood raged hot. This was what his lack of action had allowed.

"*Cyrus?*"

"Cyrus," came Everan's voice on his right. "What is it?"

"*I'm coming,*" Cyrus told Sid. Then he opened his eyes to Kord and Everan staring back at him.

"Get ready," he told them. "We're going after Bravat."

"Wait—what?" Kord asked.

Cyrus looked at Essandra. "I need to get men to the stone circle."

Kord swore. "Cyrus, you literally just had a mob at the gates calling for Serra, and a letter from Gregor is going to arrive any moment to call you against the Shadow King. You can't just leave."

"Bravat's taking captives. This is my fault. I've let him go too long." He put his hand on Kord's shoulder. "You don't have to go with me."

Kord swore again and shook his head. "Let me get my sword."

Cyrus took only nine: Orion and his team of four men, Everan, Kord, Essandra, and Jaem. He also brought the dogs. Everan had encouraged him to bring more men, but the more he had, the slower they'd travel. And he wasn't trying to match the numbers of Bravat's band of misfit followers. He expected the drifters to run at the first sign of trouble. In fact, he was counting on it. Cyrus was here for Bravat and Bravat's men only. There were thirty-three. With Essandra's power and the dogs, Cyrus was confident it wouldn't be a problem.

It required four trips through the portal to get them all to the stone circle, where Sid met them. Sid had run out of blood to be able to trail Bravat and navigate Cyrus to him. But he'd brought horses and held a small cage of half-feathered finches.

Cyrus eyed the birds. "Can they even fly?"

Sid shrugged. "The markets are sparse here. It was this or two chickens." He nodded back at the horses. "And I could only get six mounts. Some of us are going to have to double."

Cyrus led a horse to Essandra, and she crossed her arms.

"Are you all right sharing a horse?" he asked her. "Or would you rather ride alone?"

The sharp lines of her face softened ever so slightly. "I have the option?"

"You always have the option."

She tilted her head as she glanced at the animal, then she drew her gaze back to him. Her brow quirked. "You're sitting in front," she said.

He couldn't help a small smile.

They rode northwest. Time passed quickly. Despite their smooth-gaited horse, Essandra kept an arm wrapped around him. Her hand rested just above his belt, her fingers curled into his tunic. He tried not to read into it. Of course she had to hold on to him.

But she sat close against him.

Closer than she needed to.

Or maybe he was just imagining that. Still, her closeness felt good. Her warmth felt good. She smelled good. Cyrus reined in his wandering thoughts and forced himself to focus on the task ahead. He needed to find Bravat, then get back to Rael as quickly as possible.

They set a fast pace, stopping only to water and rest their mounts. Sid had said Bravat was about two days' ride from the stone circle, and Cyrus wanted to catch up to him before that distance became longer.

They pressed on even as darkness fell and the Northern night grew colder. Essandra still lacked the power of a fire witch to warm them. Cyrus unfastened his cloak and turned and swept it around her.

She leaned back in surprise. "You didn't need to do that."

"I know." Then he set his eyes forward again.

"Thank you," she said. Her breath dusted the back of his neck, sending a prickle over his shoulders. She shifted slightly, leaning more into him, and adjusted her grip. Her hand slipped up to his chest. Warm. Soft. His fingers tightened on the reins.

"You're tense," she murmured.

"Am I?"

"We'll find him," she assured him.

Bravat.

Right.

The stars hung hidden behind the heavy clouds that stretched across most of the blue-black sky. When they reached a quiet dell, Cyrus called them to stop for the night. They made a fire and sat close.

"You still feeling confident?" Cyrus asked Sid. The last thing they needed was to be traveling in the wrong direction.

"More so now, honestly," Sid answered. "We've passed a few familiar things."

That was good.

Cyrus would use the birds in the morning to scout ahead. If they could fly.

As the sun rose, he was pleased to find they could. Well, some of them. He sent two into the air, holding back the rest. The ache in his head came almost immediately, but he ignored it. It was a small price to pay for sight.

Cyrus pushed the group's pace hard again, sweeping the birds back and forth ahead of them in search of any sign of Bravat. Visibility was good. The Mercian outer reaches were rocky and mostly barren, like a winter high desert. Occasional pockets of trees scattered the landscape. They passed two villages, both untouched by Bravat's destructive tirade. Cyrus led them wide, taking care not to be seen.

By midafternoon, the ache in Cyrus's head had grown to a pulsing pain. He'd lost both his birds in the sky—he wasn't sure of the reason. Maybe he'd pushed them too hard; maybe the bond had somehow slipped.

"You should give yourself a break," Essandra said as he pulled two more birds from the small cage on Sid's saddleback. They all stood along a stream, letting their horses drink their fill of water.

They didn't have time for a break. He needed to find Bravat and get back to Rael. Cyrus marked the bird with blood and released it into the air. He hadn't actually expected to find Bravat yet, but he'd hoped. He pushed the bird higher for a greater view.

Suddenly, a flurry of wings flashed, and his sight went dark. "What—"

His eyes darted to the sky.

"What's wrong?" Essandra asked.

"I lost another bird." Confusion flooded him.

"There," Orion said, pointing, and Cyrus followed the line of sight to a white hawk dropping to the ground with the small bird in its clutches.

Anger blazed through him. *Fucking hawks.* He leaned and grabbed the crossbow behind Orion's saddle.

"Wait!" Orion said.

But Cyrus didn't wait, and he aimed and loosed an arrow, squarely hitting the hawk.

Orion threw up his hands as he shook his head. "Those are my mark arrows—don't waste them on birds."

Cyrus glanced at him. "Mark arrows?"

"You don't survive a hit from one of those. They also pierce metal."

Kord snorted. "Metal?"

Orion cut him a steely gaze. "Put on a breastplate. I'll show you."

Cyrus looked at the second bolt that sat pre-nocked in the double bow. His eyes traveled its sharp tip and barbed edges. He weighed the crossbow in his hand. "A nice bow too. Balanced."

"Yeah, it is," Orion said warily.

Cyrus didn't give it back.

Three more downed hawks and a half day later, Cyrus found Bravat outside the ruins of a Mercian town. Jaem had told him that Bravat was laying a path of destruction, but Cyrus hadn't understood the magnitude. Fires still burned across the southern quarter of the town, their embers casting a glow inside the charred remains of homes and market stalls. The stone temple at the town center was still standing, but its stained-glass windows had been broken, and smoke billowed out one side from within.

Cyrus's original plan had been for Orion and his small team to sneak in first, quietly taking down as many of Bravat's men as they could. Then Cyrus and the rest of them would follow as stealthily as possible in a second wave. The hope was to find Bravat before he even knew they were there.

But Cyrus didn't wait for the second wave.

Nor did he make any effort at stealth.

He strode down the center of the mainway, Orion's crossbow in hand. He also couldn't help the rich satisfaction in having Essandra, the goddess of destruction herself, walking beside him. He'd seen her level whole sections of the Raelean capital to the ground, and he was very interested to see what she might do with this band of miscreants.

Bravat's men drew back when they saw him—a wise choice, although it wouldn't save them. Every one of them was going to die. Just like Bravat. The drifters who'd joined the blighted band fled immediately, as he'd expected. Cyrus let them go. He wasn't here for them.

As he drew nearer to the burning temple, Bravat stepped out from inside. When the fighter saw Cyrus, he smiled.

"I didn't think you'd come," Bravat drawled out in a graveled voice. "Some balls, I'll give you that." He chuckled. "But I'm glad you did. Wait until you see—"

Cyrus drew up the bow and loosed an arrow, sending it beautifully through the hollow of Bravat's neck. Almost immediately, he released another, slightly higher, sending the second arrow right through the center.

The large fighter staggered back, the whites of his eyes thick and round. Sputtering, he grasped at his throat as he swayed before finally falling forward onto his knees.

Cyrus stalked to him, wrapping his hand around the shafts of the arrows and pulling them free. A large chunk of Bravat's throat came with them. He watched for a moment as the fighter fell back, writhing on the ground and drowning in the blood from the gaping hollow. Then Cyrus turned and strode back to Essandra.

Her own eyes were wide with surprise. "You didn't want to hear what he had to say?" she asked.

"No."

He handed the arrows to Orion, who stood just behind her. "Here," he told him. "I know you wanted to keep these." It was probably the first time he'd seen the assassin stunned.

Realizing their fated judgment, Bravat's men pulled their swords. Some of them scattered.

"Thirty-three!" Cyrus ordered. "I want every single body. And find the women!"

Cyrus's team was outnumbered, but it didn't matter. They swept after Bravat's men with ruthless abandon. Kord, Everan, and Jaem moved to meet those who tried to stand and fight, with Essandra making their work even easier. Orion and his team went after those who fled; Cyrus sent the dogs with him.

Cyrus coursed the village, looking for the captives Bravat had taken.

Essandra joined him. "Do you really think they're here?" she asked as they ducked in and out of buildings.

"Bravat likely brought them with him. Where else would he keep them?"

"Well, maybe it would have been good to ask him before you killed him," she said shortly.

He paused. "Are you angry with me?"

"It was a little sudden."

"But that's what I came here to do." And Orion had told him to take a kill when he had it.

She only stared back at him.

Suddenly, her eyes darted behind him, and before he could fully turn, she flicked her hand and summoned a fist-size rock, hurling it with her power over his shoulder and felling one of Bravat's men. The fighter staggered as the split above his brow poured blood down his face. He stumbled and fell backward, hitting the ground hard. His sword hand twitched for a moment, then stilled.

A second man leapt in attack from behind a stone hovel, but Cyrus twisted, ripping his blade along his midsection before slicing back for the kill.

Closer to the central temple, Kord and Everan had taken on a small group of men, dropping them one by one.

"Cyrus, here!" Jaem called out at the entrance to a thatch-roofed house, where he locked swords with another of Bravat's men. They both crashed inside.

Cyrus quickly followed. However, as he rushed in, he paused abruptly when he saw a group of women huddled in a corner. Their hands were bound.

Jaem still fought Bravat's man. Cyrus recognized the fighter—Bevin. Jaem wasn't strong enough to best him. Cyrus barreled through with a hard shoulder, slamming Bevin into the far wall. The fighter shoved off with his elbows, then launched a counter, but Cyrus caught him straight through the shoulder with his blade. Bevin fell back against the wall again and sank to the floor. It wasn't a mortal blow, but as Cyrus moved to finish him, he stopped abruptly as one of the women cried, "It's the lord justice!"

He whirled, and his stare locked with hers.

Before he knew what he was doing, he had the blade of his sword to her neck.

"Cyrus!" Essandra called out in alarm from where she stood in the doorway.

His breath shook. "I'm not your lord justice," he said to the woman.

Tears sprang from her eyes as she fervently shook her head.

"I don't want to hurt you," he said, "but I can't be known here."

"I'm sorry," she whispered shakily. "I've seen nothing! I don't know who you are; I've seen nothing!"

Cyrus cut his gaze across the rest of the women.

"You saw nothing," he said to the woman.

"I saw nothing," she repeated. "*We* saw nothing."

A shuffle sounded on his left.

"Cyrus!" Jaem shouted.

Cyrus spun just in time for the blade that Bevin had thrown to narrowly miss him. He whipped his own dagger from his belt and flung it, hitting Bevin squarely in the center of his chest and instantly killing him.

One more man down. Only twenty-something more to go.

"Cyrus," called Essandra. Her voice was barely a whisper.

When he turned, he froze.

She still stood in the doorway, staring down at Bevin's blade lodged in her lower abdomen as dark blood seeped through her dress.

CHAPTER SEVENTEEN

Essandra stumbled backward, and Cyrus lunged to catch her. She clutched her stomach around the blade as the wound poured blood.

"I'm all right," she said shakily. "It's not deep."

But it looked deep, just above her left hip, with the crimson stain spreading across her stomach and all down her front. She wrapped her hand around the narrow hilt.

"No—"

But before he could stop her, she pulled the blade out. It was hardly a blade at all, a stunted throwing knife, but still long enough to cause damage.

"I'm all right," she said again. She waved him off. "I just need a minute."

"Essandra—"

"I'm fine."

Only she wasn't fine. She wavered, and he caught her. "I got you," he said, scooping her into his arms. He needed to get her back to Teron. Immediately.

"Hey, what do I do with these women?" Jaem asked, following them outside.

Cyrus didn't care about the women anymore as he carried Essandra, looking for his horse. "Give them money. Send them home."

"I don't have any money."

Cyrus prayed to all things holy to save his patience, because he was quickly losing it. "Check Bravat's body. And his men." Where was his fucking horse?

Everan spotted him and came running. "What happened?"

"A knife to the stomach."

"I'll be fine," Essandra told him. "Honestly, being carried is worse than just walking," she added.

"I need to get her to Teron," Cyrus said.

"What happened?" Kord asked, suddenly appearing beside them.

"Bevin got her with a blade. I need a horse."

Kord found a mount and brought it. Cyrus lifted Essandra up into the saddle. She winced, holding her stomach tighter, and a rage swept through him. If he could kill Bravat all over again...

He looked at both Everan and Kord. "I need to take her back," he told them. "When you're done here, ride for the stone circle. I'll meet you all there to bring you through. You have blood?"

Kord nodded, then asked, "What do you want us to do with the bodies here?"

Cyrus glanced around the village. "Put them in a house and set it on fire. No one will know they weren't Mercian."

Kord nodded again.

"Cyrus!" Orion called, and Cyrus turned to see him riding toward them. He strode to meet him.

"We have a problem," Orion said as he reached him, and he slid down from his horse. "A Mercian company is headed our way, and there are Shadowmen with them."

Cyrus swore.

"There's something else," Orion added, but his words cut as his gaze landed on Essandra. His eyes widened. "What the fuck happened?"

Cyrus glanced back at her. "She caught a blade."

"She doesn't look good."

"She'll be all right if I can get her back to Teron."

Orion looked at him warily. "She'll need you in order to pass back through the portal."

"I'm taking her now. But what else were you going to say?"

Orion glanced at Essandra, then back to him.

"What is it?" Cyrus pressed.

Finally, he said quietly, "Your brother leads the company."

Cyrus froze. "Alexander?" That couldn't be.

"He's your spitting image," Orion told him. "There's no mistaking him."

His heart beat faster.

Alexander was coming.

And Cyrus was here. He had Kord. He had Everan. He had everything he needed to take him. Cyrus could kill him. He could kill Alexander. *Finally.*

"What do you want to do?" Orion asked him.

He wanted to stay and kill Alexander. When would another chance like this come? Perhaps never. He glanced back at Essandra. Orion was right—she needed Cyrus to pass back through the portal to Teron.

But he had *some* time. She'd said she was fine...

"Cyrus?" Orion said.

Alexander was coming...

Essandra had said the injury looked worse than it was. She was going to be all right. She could hold on until Cyrus dealt with Alexander.

But if she couldn't...

"Cyrus?" Orion prodded.

Cyrus swore again. Then he strode to his horse and swung up behind Essandra.

Alexander would have to wait.

"Finish up!" he barked out. "Thirty-three! Make sure we got them all!" He looked back at Orion. "I want you all gone before he gets here. Meet me back at the stone circle. And don't lose my dogs."

Orion gave a nod.

"Before who gets here?" Essandra asked Cyrus.

He hesitated. "Soldiers. They're on their way. We need to leave."

Cyrus spurred his horse out of the burning village and back toward the portal. He held Essandra close to keep her from being jostled. She let him, but he wasn't sure if it was because she was grateful or too weak to fight him. He'd worry about that later. For now, he focused on getting her to Teron.

Straight through the night and the following day he pushed his horse. He didn't stop. His mount grew slower, lathered and breathing heavily, but he pushed the animal on.

Essandra continued telling him she was fine. However, she didn't look fine. She grew paler in his arms, and she let her head rest back against him.

"I'm cold," she told him.

He adjusted his arms around her, holding her even closer. "Not much farther," he promised.

He stopped only when Essandra asked him to, for short breaks and necessities. On through the second night they rode, until his mount threatened to stop. Finally, the stone circle appeared on the horizon.

Essandra was asleep. He hated to wake her but...

"Essandra."

Her eyes fluttered open.

"You have to do the bond so I can take you through." It was ridiculous that she broke it after each pass through the portal. She should just leave them connected. He was fairly certain he could do the bond himself. He'd seen it done, he knew the words, but it was best not to risk it if she was able to do it now.

She brushed a small smear of her blood onto his lips and whispered the spell. Then he poured the mixture from the small sachet tied at her waist and, picking her up again, crossed the threshold back into Rael.

He went directly to Teron's chamber.

"I can walk," she said.

But he kept going, not putting her down.

Thank the fucking gods Teron was in his work chamber when he got there. Cyrus took her directly to the table and sat her down gently.

"Lady Essandra!" Teron said in surprise.

"It looks worse than it is," she said. "It's not deep at all." But her voice was faint, and she was the palest she'd ever been.

"It's dark blood," Cyrus told Teron.

"Stop hovering." She pushed Cyrus back.

"Can you open your gown?" Teron asked her.

She shot a prompting look to Cyrus, and he turned to give her privacy.

"How is it?" he asked Teron over his shoulder.

Teron was quiet, and Cyrus's heart beat faster.

"Teron?"

"It's fine; she'll be fine," the old man said finally.

A breath of relief escaped him. For what felt like the first time in two days, he let himself breathe. Cyrus moved to the pitcher of water on a side table and poured a glass, drinking deeply. He hadn't realized how thirsty he was. He poured another glass and drank it down. He'd done it—he'd taken care of Bravat. Finally. But there was no feeling of accomplishment. No satisfaction.

He'd lost his opportunity at Alexander.

Still, that wasn't what bothered him most right now.

Cyrus waited for Teron to finish, and as Essandra refastened the last few buttons on her bloodstained riding dress, he moved back to her. She looked much better, although still a little pale.

"I shouldn't have taken you to Mercia," he said. He hadn't even thought of the danger, and he cursed himself.

"You say that like it was your decision."

He eyed her seriously. "You could have died."

"You could have too."

"You're too important," he said.

"You're king!"

"So, it was my responsibility to go."

She pursed her lips.

A knock sounded on the door, and Sergen popped in his head. "I'm sorry to interrupt, but I just heard you were back," he said. He held up a letter in his hand. "This came for you yesterday."

Cyrus waved him in. He took the letter and turned it over to find Gregor's green seal, and his heart beat faster. But as he tore it open and read the words, a fury rose in his core.

The dogs followed him as he paced the room. Cyrus was glad to have them back. He dropped his hand to One's head to help calm himself as Everan read the letter. Cyrus hadn't given him or Kord even a moment to recover from their return before he thrust Gregor's letter at them. His anger flared hotter as Everan read the words aloud.

"*With Aleon taking Tarsus, I'm so glad I had the foresight to give Mikael the excuse of a failed crop.*"

It was all Cyrus could do to keep from snatching back the letter and crumpling it in his fist. Gregor hadn't told the Shadow King the real reason he'd stopped sending trade. He'd made excuses. "That fucking coward. He didn't break his accord, not really. He hid behind lies."

"And he admits it," Everan said in disbelief. "To you, of all people."

"He's as stupid as he is spineless," Cyrus said. Gregor had promised him they'd move against the Shadow King, and Cyrus felt stupid for having believed him. He'd sent Gregor half his fucking army.

"So, he pulled his trade from the Shadowlands but left himself an opening," Kord said. "Now he can pick back up with the Shadow King as if nothing happened." He shook his head. "Do we know yet why Aleon took Tarsus? Wealth?"

"Aleon is already one of the wealthiest kingdoms in the world," Cyrus told them, mulling. "I imagine it's because Tarsus was where Gregor did all of his trade. The king of Aleon is making a strike against his brother, and an impressive strike at that." He cast his gaze to the floor, and the room grew quiet.

Everan finally spoke. "Hey. Orion told us about Alexander."

Cyrus jerked his head up at his brother's name.

"You'll get your strike too," his friend assured him. "But for what it's worth, I think you made the right decision to come back. Essandra needed you."

Everan's words made him pause. Not because he needed to hear them. But because the thought that he might have made the wrong decision had never even crossed his mind. He held no regret.

And as if thoughts could summon her, she entered. She was the perfect picture of health again, unlike when he'd arrived with her two days prior, but a deep concern was written all over her face.

"Cyrus, you need to come see this," she told him.

Cyrus glanced at Kord and Everan, then they followed her out of the palace toward the school. When they reached it, an anger swelled within him. The sidewall of the outdoor walkway had been toppled, with the stained-glass windows broken all along the south side. Scripts of slander were painted across the stone.

Blood before books.

Swords, not scrolls.

Cyrus, where is your sword?

And there were names. So many names.

"What is all this?" Kord asked as his eyes traveled the marked stone.

Cyrus knew exactly what it was. "These are the names of people still in Serra," he said. "Names of the lost. Those still in chains." The people of Rael didn't want schools. They didn't want to rebuild.

They wanted their families free.

And Cyrus had waited too long. "Gather the men," he said. "We're going to Serra."

Kord gaped at him. "Wait, what?"

"We're going to Serra," Cyrus said again.

"Are we recalling our army from Japheth?" Everan asked.

"No." The Shadow King would be next—with or without Gregor. Cyrus needed to keep those legions of his army on the mainland and ready. Plus, he didn't need them. "We have almost fifty thousand men here in Rael, and I'll have the slaves in Serra."

"They'll be chained," Essandra said. "They can't fight if they're not free."

"I'll take Mal," he said. The forge witch had the power to break chains.

"I'm not risking another witch," she told him. "I'm going with you."

He shook his head. "No. It's too dangerous. Look at what happened in Mercia."

"I'm perfectly fine now—"

"I'm not taking you to Serra."

Her lips thinned. "That's not your decision."

"Give me the spells to manipulate metals," he said. "I'll do it myself." Through their bond, he could access the power of the coven. That included breaking chains.

"You've never used the power."

"Because you didn't want me to."

"And what if you get over there and can't?"

"I work well under pressure."

"Cyrus, I'm not joking."

He pushed out a frustrated exhale. "Everyone is looking at this like it needs to be some strategic takeover, which it would be if I wanted to keep Serra, but I have no intention of doing that. I merely intend to kill King Milar and inspire a rebellion. It will be easier than Rael."

"You're oversimplifying," she argued, "and it will be just as difficult as Rael, if not more. Men fought here because they were trained to fight. You had forty thousand bloodsport fighters behind you. The people in Serra are in servitude. They don't know how to fight."

"It doesn't matter. They still will. They just need hope."

"And you need the power of the coven."

"Which I have."

"Yet not the faintest understanding of how to use it." She shook her head. "No. I'm coming with you, whether you want me to or not."

Cyrus pursed his lips. "Fine."

She sighed, satisfied. "When are we leaving?"

"Three days."

She nodded. "I'll be ready."

He watched her disappear out of the room.

Once she was gone, Cyrus turned to Everan. "Do you think it's a foolish decision to go?" he asked.

"I'm a poor judge of what would be foolish or not."

"You've never been shy with your opinions before—"

"My mother died in Serra." Everan cast his gaze down and swallowed, before lifting it to meet Cyrus's again. "I would war against that wretched kingdom even if I had nothing but a stick in my hand and the wind at my back."

Cyrus stared at him. How had he not known this?

"So, three days?" Everan asked.

Cyrus shook his head. "No. We leave tonight."

"But you just told Essandra—"

"I know what I said. We leave tonight."

CHAPTER EIGHTEEN

It was challenging to move twenty thousand men out of the harbor in the dark of night.

Challenging, but not impossible.

They sailed with a thousand men to a ship, maximizing space by taking no supplies. They would stop at the southwest port and gather a few more ships, even out their numbers, and take on provisions. The urgency was in departing before the council could delay him.

And before Essandra noticed he was gone.

She'd be furious when she found out, but she was right—he couldn't stop her. He could only leave without her. He didn't anticipate that this would be a particularly perilous effort, but he wouldn't risk her safety, not again, especially since he also refused to take Teron. Both would stay in Rael, away from harm.

Cyrus took only half his men, leaving the other half to defend Rael. He regretted sending Hephain to Pryam so quickly. He would have felt better having him in Rael while he was gone. But the guards that protected the coven were some of the best fighters he had, especially Aaron and Amiel, Essandra's men. And she was stronger than all of them together. She also had open access to his power through the bloodline bond now, and she had the dogs. She'd be safe.

He didn't stop for long at the southwest port. Additional ships and provisions were waiting, and within a half day, they were on their way again. It would be at least three days more before they reached Serra.

Cyrus made his way to the bow of the lead ship as they hit the open sea. There was a hypnotic calm to standing where the hull split the tide.

Orion was already there, leaning against the rail. He'd been upset by the news they were moving on Serra. He'd desperately wanted to take action against the Shadowlands first. And Cyrus did too, but as long as both Serra and the Shadowlands fell, he wouldn't begrudge the order it happened.

Orion kept his eyes on the water as Cyrus stepped beside him.

"You know how our move against the Mercian queen was poorly planned and poorly executed?" Orion asked.

"How can I forget when you like to remind me so often?" Cyrus said dryly.

"Well, this is even worse. You're just planning to walk in and dismantle another kingdom with several thousand men who barely know how to fight?"

Cyrus didn't take his eyes off the horizon. "Twenty is a little more than several, and a few of us know how to fight."

The assassin groaned. "Cyrus, this isn't a fucking joke. The men in Serra are in chains. You can't count on them to be able to join us."

Cyrus spun and grabbed Orion by the metal clip and chain at his shoulder that fastened his cloak around him. It crumbled in Cyrus's hand, letting the wind snatch the cloak and carry it out across the sea.

Orion stumbled back, his eyes widening and his breaths coming quicker. "How did you do that?"

If he were honest with himself, Cyrus didn't know exactly *how*. Just before he left Rael, the coven's forge witch had given him the spell to focus his power to manipulate metal, but Cyrus found he didn't need to use the spell, he didn't need the focus. He could simply will it. However, he did need to touch the metal, which could prove a challenge when they reached Serra, but he'd worry about that when he got there.

"When we reach the port," Cyrus told him, "I want you focused on one thing: finding and killing King Milar. The Serrans will know there's a problem as soon as we sail into Slaver's Bay, so you won't have much time."

The assassin nodded. "I know where he'll be."

"And then you'll find the two heirs," Cyrus added.

Orion's head snapped to him. He swallowed. "They're young. Very young."

"Then make it quick and merciful."

Orion stared at him for a moment, then shook his head. "Not kids. I don't do that anymore."

This wasn't something Cyrus took pleasure in, but he couldn't allow the bloodline to continue. Supporters of the regime would put the Serran heirs on the throne and groom them to uphold the same values, perpetuating the same culture. This was a necessity. Surely, Orion saw that. But Cyrus wouldn't ask anyone to do something he wasn't willing to do himself.

"Then bring them to me," he said.

Orion said nothing. He only turned and left Cyrus alone again on the bow of the ship.

For three days, they sailed. Cyrus stood on the bow, resting his hand on his sword at his waist as he stared at the horizon. It was true that the wants of his people had pushed him into action against the slavers' kingdom, but he hardly needed the pressure. He wanted to destroy Serra—he *needed* to destroy it. He only regretted that it had taken him so long to go.

He glanced down at the intricate gold adornments on the hilt under his thumb. He hated gold—a weak metal—even if it was only in the hilt. But the forge witch had told him this sword was unlike any other. *Stronger than Mercian steel*, he'd said. Cyrus would be the judge of that. He pulled it from its scabbard, looking it over again. A red firestone was set between the base of the blade and the grip.

It was a light sword, much lighter than it should be for its size. He swung it easily with a single hand. Perhaps he should have asked for two.

He paused.

Maybe he could make it two.

He'd seen Essandra do it—turn one sword into two. He wasn't sure if it had been the power of the forge witch she'd used, but whoever's power it was, he had access to it.

He closed his eyes, holding the sword with both hands. "Two," he commanded.

Which did absolutely nothing.

Because, no, that was stupid.

Will it, Essandra always told him.

He held the sword in front of him again. And he concentrated. He imagined the feeling—the leather grip in his hand, the metal center adornment against his palm, the weight of the blade.

Hand over hand.

Then he pulled them apart.

And one sword became two.

He let out a disbelieving laugh in surprise. *He'd actually done it.* Two swords he held now—one in each hand.

"Sire, we're half a day out," a voice called from behind him.

Cyrus smashed them back into one and turned to find Nevin, his shipmaster, accompanied by Ram. He'd have to play with this newfound skill later.

"Should we slow and wait for the cover of night?" Nevin asked.

Cyrus slipped the sword into its scabbard and looked back out to the horizon. "No."

"They'll see us coming," Ram said.

Yes. Yes they would. "I want them to know I'm coming." He reached his mind through the blood bond to Everan and Kord, who were on separate ships. *"The shipmaster says we're half a day out."*

"We'll be ready," Everan replied.

"Is the plan still to just sail into the harbor and start killing Serrans?" Kord asked.

"Pretty much, although once they figure us out, I imagine it won't be quite that simple."

Serran ports weren't open trade ports. The slavers delivered their trade to other kingdoms, which meant their harbors held only their own ships. Cyrus's vessels didn't bother to carry Serran flags, and it wouldn't take the Serrans long to realize they weren't supposed to be there.

He and his men would likely face heavy opposition once they landed, but Cyrus wasn't unfamiliar with opposition. He positioned archers along the bow rail. They weren't good archers, unfortunately, but wildly launched arrows were better than none at all. The challenge would be for his archers not to hit his own men.

By late afternoon, land broke the stretch of sea in the distance.

"Serra!" came the bellows of men amid the ring of the upper deck bell.

Cyrus walked calmly to his cabin. He sighed as his gaze settled on the armor he'd promised to wear when he went into battle.

She wouldn't know. Essandra wouldn't know if he didn't wear it.

He groaned.

She would know. But what would she do?

He didn't want to find out, and he pulled on the metal plating.

The port of Slaver's Bay was massive. And busy. However, despite the large vessels that were already moored, there were enough open docks for Cyrus's ships.

Perfect.

They were ready.

On the top deck, Cyrus clutched his sword. As soon as the ships pulled in, they'd throw down the gangways and he'd lead the charge. One level below, his men formed lines at the portside doors, waiting.

They sailed quietly into the harbor. Serrans bustled along the docks, paying them little mind, more focused on the lines of chained men that they drove from their own ships up into pens like cattle. Cyrus was a little surprised they hadn't yet roused suspicion, but as his eyes traveled the harbor, he noted the Serran fleet was a motley one, comprised of various vessels likely stolen from around the world. As were Cyrus's.

A shout rang out in the Serran tongue, and men picked up toward the docks.

There it was. *They'd been discovered.*

"Well, that's interesting," Orion said.

Cyrus snapped a glance at him. "What is?" He gripped his sword tighter and prepared to launch himself forward as soon as the gangway touched down.

"That was a call for more men to help moor our ships coming in."

Cyrus paused, lowering his sword ever so slightly as he realized. "They think we're Serrans."

"Perhaps the gods favor us today." Orion was proving to be quite useful with his understanding of the Serran tongue.

Cyrus glanced back to where the men were prepping the docks. Was the goddess of fortune really with them? Well, Cyrus wasn't a man to miss an opportunity. He turned to Ram, who stood just behind him. "Tell the men below to hold and wait for my call." He reached his mind back out to Everan and Kord and the others. "*Hold. They think we're Serrans, and they're helping moor our ships.*"

"*That's convenient,*" came Everan's reply. "*We'll wait for your charge.*"

Two men trotted down the dock to where Cyrus's ship was coming in. One picked up the mooring line, the other waved the ship in.

Cyrus glanced at Orion. "This just keeps getting better."

The assassin's face was covered by his head wrap, but his eyes smiled.

Ram reappeared back on deck. "The men are holding."

Cyrus nodded. They just needed to wait long enough for all the ships to dock. Then there'd be no stopping them.

The ship came to a halt, and the two men on the dock quickly worked to secure it.

Cyrus's men dropped the gangway. He held out a hand to motion them to continue to hold, then he calmly walked down to the dock. Orion and his small team followed. They would slip into the city and head for the palace. With their newfound luck, they'd likely make it there before the men on the docks even realized what was happening.

The rest of Cyrus's ships moved into place and were secured by the Serran dockworkers. He couldn't have planned this better.

As he stepped onto the dock, the man closest to him called out something in the Serran tongue.

Orion chuckled behind him. "He makes fun of your pretty armor."

Cyrus would kill *that* man first.

Orion's small group of men skirted around them and disappeared as they took off toward the palace, but Orion lingered for a moment.

The Serran man jerked in surprise as the team slipped past. He looked back to the ship, and his brows drew together. His eyes drifted to Cyrus and narrowed. He spoke again.

"He asks if you have cargo," Orion said.

It was Cyrus's turn to chuckle. "Yes, I have cargo."

The man's brow trenched even deeper in hearing Cyrus's foreign words, and Cyrus couldn't help but smile as he watched the wave of realization hit him that something was wrong—very, very wrong.

The rest of Cyrus's fleet were docked.

The waiting was over.

Cyrus looked back at the man, then took his sword and pulled it into two.

"Okay, that was impressive," Orion muttered.

Cyrus's smile grew.

The man gaped at him, staggering back quickly, but not quickly enough, as Cyrus took his head in a single sweep.

The second man on the dock turned and fled, but Orion caught him with a knife thrown with absolute precision.

A shout rang out on the harbor wall, then more shouts.

"Took them long enough," Cyrus said as the Serrans finally started to catch on that this wasn't another regular delivery. "Get to the palace," he said to Orion, and Orion broke away after his men.

"*Now*," Cyrus called through the bond to Everan and the rest of his men.

And Slaver's Bay fell into chaos.

Chapter Nineteen

The plan was simple: kill Serrans, free slaves, rouse rebellion.

The doing was not simple.

Freed Serran slaves were not bloodsport fighters. Even when struck from their chains, they cowered in fear, reluctant to move against the people who'd beaten them into submission. Many simply fled. Almost none fought.

Cyrus knew that collective masses would fuel the slaves and give them strength, but he had to physically touch them to free them, and he couldn't do it fast enough. He tore through the wharves, shattering every chain he could grasp. His men moved quickly, physically breaking the chains, cutting ropes, prying open cages. Still, it wasn't enough.

And they found another challenge they hadn't expected: traps.

The Serrans were experienced with the desperation of men. Traps lay hidden throughout the port to capture runners, should a slave find themself free of their chains with ambitious thoughts of escape, and these traps were claiming Cyrus's own men. Most were harmless, netting and foot nooses, but impervious to Cyrus's manipulation of metal and time-consuming to free one from. He didn't have that time.

Although the Serrans were still unorganized by the surprise attack and their resistance was weak, Cyrus wasn't gaining the momentum he'd expected. Hardly any slaves had joined the fight—they were still fleeing.

More. He needed to free *more*. There was power in numbers, he just needed to get those numbers. He pushed harder, bellowing to his men to follow him. They did. Finally, they broke beyond the harbor front and spilled in between the rows of warehouses that stretched in nearly all directions.

But suddenly things shifted.

The Serrans started killing slaves, mercilessly firing arrows at them as they ran.

Cyrus snarled as he pushed even harder, even faster. He spotted a small group of Serran archers, and he ripped through them. His twin blades sang as they slashed through air and flesh, arcing sprays of blood around him.

Harder still, he fought. His armor slowed him, and he tore it off.

Ram fought beside him, and they settled into the kill combinations they'd used in the arena, working their opponents high and low.

Then the Serrans turned their attacks on the slaves not yet freed, brutally cutting down people bound with no means to defend themselves, with no ability to get away.

Ram staggered to a pause, horror etched across his brow. "What are they doing?"

Cyrus gritted his teeth as Slaver's Bay descended into slaughter. He knew exactly what they were doing. The Serrans were punishing them—killing them for being saved. It was only a matter of time before the slaves would turn on Cyrus and his men to stop it. Their fear would drive them to fight against their own freedom.

Cyrus had been counting on the slaves to join him. Now he was dangerously close to having to fight them as well.

The Serrans sensed it too and turned even more vicious. Screams cut through the air as whole groups of people were set on fire within their cages.

Cyrus pushed harder, grasping more chains, turning them to ash.

To the next and to the next.

But it wasn't fast enough.

And the slaves began to turn on those there to help them.

Chaos reigned around him.

"Cyrus!" Kord boomed to his right as he came crashing through. "We have to fall back!"

Cyrus staggered to a stop and raked his gaze around him, panting as he assessed the fight. *Fall back?* Blood blinded his right eye, and he swiped it away. He wasn't sure if it was his or someone else's.

"We have to fall back!" Kord yelled again.

"No! We just have to free more. If we can get mass—"

"They're fighting us! They don't want to be free!"

"They do! But they're afraid." Cyrus surged forward and dropped a Serran who had launched an attack from the left.

Suddenly, an arrow *sipped* by, burying itself into the wall of a warehouse just behind him. Kord grabbed Cyrus and pulled him behind the cover of a stack of crates.

"We have to fall back! We're losing too many men!"

Cyrus shoved him off. "Fall back to where? To the ships? To sail away?"

"If we wait much longer, we won't be able to!" Kord pointed to the harbor. "They're setting the ships on fire!"

Cyrus glanced back to see smoke billowing from several vessels. The bastards were trying to push him back toward the water.

It wouldn't work.

He shook his head. "We're not leaving."

"Cyrus," Ram interjected, "if they burn all—"

"I said we're not leaving," he snapped. "Where's Everan?"

"Still at the docks," Kord said. "Some of the Serran ships are loaded with slaves; he's working to free them."

Good. He looked north. He couldn't see the palace from where he was, but he expected Orion and his team had made it there by now. Cyrus needed to trust Orion with his task and just focus on freeing people. He motioned to his left to a series of warehouses. "Take men and start on that row," he said to Kord. Then he nodded to Ram. "You're with me." But as he started toward the center buildings, screams cut through the air, coming from the harbor. His gaze darted to a flaming ship back at the docks.

A Serran ship.

Horror hit Cyrus as he realized. "There are people on there."

Kord froze. "That's the ship Everan's on."

Everan.

No! All focus on their plan left him. Nothing else mattered. Not Serra. Not the warehouses. Not King Milar. He bolted back toward the docks.

"Cyrus!" Kord called from behind him, but the sound faded beneath the rush of blood in his ears. The Serrans had somewhat organized themselves now and were coming heavy in defense to the docks. He tore through them, taking arms, taking heads, taking lives. He'd kill every single one of them.

Thick black smoke poured from the burning vessel. The screams were no longer screams of fear but screams of agony. Flames licked across the portside, racing toward the mast. The sails burst like paper.

He was almost there.

His heart pounded. Everan was on that ship—

An arrow struck a bollard just to his right, and he ducked left, but as his foot hit the next plank, the wood gave way to net.

And he was falling.

He'd hit a trap. He knew it before he even crashed.

Someone roared his name. Kord, maybe?

His head hit something hard, stunning him. He dropped his swords. For a moment, things went dark, but sound still flooded him—yelling and footsteps.

Then they were on top of him.

Rope bit into his skin as it was pulled tight around him. He thrashed, but still it held.

He was caught.

Metal pinched around his wrists, and he wasn't prepared for the panic that rippled through him. As they jerked him to his feet, all Cyrus could do was stare down at the cuffs.

He was chained. Not just chained—manacled. The same kind used on him in Rael's arena.

His heart pounded against his chest. He couldn't get a breath.

Captured. Chained. Again.

He couldn't breathe.

Someone bellowed his name, but it was too far away.

The men around him shoved him forward as they jerked the chains.

"Cyrus!" Kord raged as he fought to reach him, but he was still too far. Too far away, too many men, too many screams.

"Cyrus! Fight!"

It brought him back.

Fire rippled under his skin.

Cyrus raised his eyes to those who held him. The man in front of him laughed.

Laughed.

The manacles around his wrists burned hot. And hotter still. They turned darker, then brighter, until they glowed orange. The man's eyes widened. Cyrus surged forward and looped the glowing chain around his neck.

The man let out a scream—a scream that was cut short as the searing metal cut through his flesh.

Others grabbed at him, and he felt the burn of ropes again. His anger swelled deeper. He let out a roar with a burst of power, shattering what was left of the chain and manacles and arcing a spray of molten death around him.

He was free.

He whirled back to the ship, and his heart seized in his chest when he found it completely engulfed in flames. His legs felt like they might buckle.

"Cyrus!"

Not Kord's voice this time.

Everan's.

Where?

Cyrus spun to see his friend on the next dock over. Everan stood soot-streaked and bloodied, but breathing and alive. Emotion tore through him. However, his attention was quickly pulled to where Everan pointed his sword. On another flaming ship, hundreds of slaves were leaping from the fiery bow into the waters of the harbor. The portside doors burst open, and amid the billows of smoke, more slaves jumped.

Their chains were gone. *All of them.* Just... gone.

Suddenly, a different kind of chaos swarmed them. Cyrus ripped around in confusion as hundreds of slaves rushed from everywhere they'd been held and joined them against the Serrans.

Not hundreds.

Thousands.

From the ships. From the cages along the docks. From the warehouses.

"Yeah!" Kord shouted, finally reaching him. "You did it! You freed them!"

Cyrus shook his head. "No, I couldn't have—I have to touch them."

"Their chains literally turned to ash—there's no other fucking person who could have done that but you." Kord's eyes scanned the port. "Look at them!"

They were all free.

"Here," Kord said, picking up Cyrus's sword—a single sword now—and holding it out for him.

Cyrus took it. He glanced back at Everan, who cut him a wide grin and charged back into the fight.

If it could even be called a fight anymore.

As soon as the slaves saw that their chains were gone, that they were *all* free, they fought. And they fought hard. They took the capital like a tide, destroying everything—the ports, the markets, the city.

Cyrus broke away and headed toward the palace.

He reached the palatial steps just as Orion was descending. Behind him, surrounded by his men, walked two boys. One held a sword nearly as large as himself.

Cyrus cut Orion and annoyed eye. "You let him keep a sword?"

Orion stopped at the foot of the stairs and shrugged. "That's how I found them. You just said to bring them to you."

"The king?" Cyrus asked.

"Dead. Step around the west side if you want to see. I hung him from his balcony."

As Cyrus's gaze moved back to the boys, his blood chilled.

They were twins.

Seven, maybe eight.

The one with the sword held it in front of him and clasped his brother tightly behind him. His brown eyes burned fiercely. The boy leveled his blade at Cyrus. "If you put a hand on my brother, you'll lose it!"

So fierce, so loyal as they both faced death. But Cyrus knew the loyalty of a blood brother—loyalty turned like the tide. Real loyalty came only from those bonded with the blood of battle. Blood of the womb meant nothing.

"Give me your brother, and I'll let you go," Cyrus told him. He wasn't sure why he'd said it; he wasn't one to taunt. But there was something in him that needed to prove how easy betrayal came.

"You can't have him!" The boy gripped the hilt of his sword tighter. His arms had started to shake. "Return to your ship and I'll let *you* go."

Interesting.

Cyrus stepped toward him, but the boy didn't cower. Instead, he lunged forward, arcing his blade in attack. Cyrus knocked it away with his own, sending the sword skittering across the cobblestone.

The child scrambled back, wrapping his arm around his brother's head and covering his eyes. "Don't look, Martine. And don't be afraid. When we wake, we'll play among the gods. Together."

Cyrus paused. He couldn't take his eyes from the young boy who clung to his brother, staring death down without fear. Choosing to leave this world together.

Pain clawed at his chest from the inside. *Mercy*, it whispered.

But a quick death *was* mercy.

Yet...

Cyrus swore under his breath. He couldn't let these boys go free. He couldn't leave them to be put back on the throne, to carry on what their father had built.

He had to kill them. Here. Now. He had to be done with it.

They had to die.

The boy's brown eyes bore into him.

Cyrus tried to lift his sword, but it was too heavy in his hand.

Too heavy in his chest.

Finally, he sighed. "Put them on my ship."

Six days it took for Serra to collapse—faster than Cyrus had expected, but longer than he'd wanted. The freed men had swept the rest of the kingdom like they'd swept the capital, and everything crumbled. Slaver's Bay became Blood Bay, for the red water that now filled the harbor.

This was where Cyrus stood, looking out over all the Serran ships they'd pulled together, so many that they butted against one another. On the bows, the flayed bodies of their crews were strung.

His eyes drifted down to his blood-smeared arms and the crusted crimson staining his skin. The slavers' deaths hadn't been enough. To feel their skin in his hands, their blood running down his arms—it wasn't enough.

Kord stepped beside him. "Is this really necessary?"

But Cyrus said nothing as he watched the remaining Serran slavers driven onto the ships. They'd be chained. As Cyrus had been. As everyone they'd stolen away from their homes had been.

He leaned heavily on the port wall as exhaustion started to set in. A pain needled his side. He hadn't realized he'd caught a blade across the ribs until after they'd taken the capital. It wasn't severe, but he'd need to keep it wrapped until he got back to Rael and Teron.

He'd depart for Rael with the morning tide. Until then, there were still a few last things to finish.

Cyrus motioned to the archers, who set their flaming arrows on the Serran ships, and the slavers chained to them.

Chapter Twenty

His footsteps echoed through the empty hall. Night still hid the sky, but it was good to be back in Rael. Cyrus had been gone less than two weeks, but it felt so much longer. Six days it took to sweep through Serra, although it required minimal effort after the capital had fallen. The freed slaves, empowered with their masses and the momentum of the capital victory, claimed the rest of the kingdom on their own, as he expected they would. Even though they'd praised him, it was their own work, their own doing. He'd merely been the catalyst.

Now that it was done, those who'd been freed could figure out for themselves what they wanted to do with Serra, and he could focus his attention back where it belonged: on Rael, on Alexander.

On the Shadow King.

And now the people were behind him. Victory over Serra had fueled them, and they were ready for more. The crowds that welcomed him home called for the Shadowlands next, and he was happy to oblige. He'd start planning immediately. Well, tomorrow. Now, sleep called to him. He thought his legs might not be able to carry him to his chamber.

"Cyrus!" Orion called from behind.

Cyrus groaned as he slowed. Exhaustion filled every fiber of his being, and all he wanted to do right now was get to his bed. He turned.

Orion caught up to him. "What are you going to do with the boys?"

He hadn't decided yet, and he didn't want to think about it now. He'd figure it out tomorrow. He'd figure everything out tomorrow.

"You can't kill them," Orion said.

"Can't I?"

"Cyrus—"

"I haven't decided," he said irritably.

Orion didn't protest more, but his eyes bore into him.

Cyrus sighed. "I'm not going to kill them." He'd decided that much, but now what to do with them—he had no idea.

Slowly, Orion nodded.

Cyrus moved to leave. He desperately needed sleep.

"There's one more thing," Orion said, stopping him again. "I'm leaving for the Shadowlands."

Wait... "Now? Tonight?"

"I can't wait."

Cyrus shook his head. "No. I can't jeopardize another chance at the Shadow King. We'll go together when I have a plan."

"I can't wait for a plan! Vitalia could be gone by then. She could be dead." The night hid his face, but his voice carried his desperation for this woman. "The Shadow King won't even know I'm there. I doubt I'll even see him."

If Orion was caught in the Shadowlands, that would complicate things even more. They'd been fortunate the first effort hadn't been traced back to Cyrus. He couldn't risk something else going poorly.

But he *had* committed to helping Orion. And he wanted to help him.

"Cyrus," Orion begged. "Please. I'll go alone—be in and out. No one will know I'm there. I promise. No one knows my face. I'm unmarked. I'll have nothing on me."

It was still too risky...

"You told me you would help me," Orion pressed. "You don't even have to do much; all I need is the birds to get through the Canyonlands."

Fuck the gods. Cyrus pinched the bridge of his nose. He was fairly certain he was going to regret this. "There are blood vials in my study—you know where they are."

Orion nodded eagerly.

"You get in, you get out," Cyrus told him. "No one knows you're there."

Orion let out a shaky exhale. "In and out," he promised.

With that, he disappeared into the darkness and finally let Cyrus continue to his chamber.

It was still a few hours before sunrise, too early to go see Essandra, and Cyrus needed those few hours to revive his mind and body before he faced her. If she wasn't still angry about him leaving without her, she'd certainly be angry about him losing his armor. All he'd been able to recover after taking the Serran capital was the breastplate and the left vambrace. He was tempted to tell her he'd at least kept the breastplate on, but the festering wound across his ribs would be quick to call him a liar. He'd need to see Teron about that in the morning too.

Cyrus turned the corner, and he was suddenly stripped of time to think of more excuses, as he found Essandra striding toward him.

She stopped when she saw him. The flame from the small lantern she held flickered shadows across her face, darkening her brow. He couldn't tell if it was anger he saw or only tricks of lantern light.

His tiredness evaporated, and he closed the distance between them. Stopping in front of her, he gave a small smile, although he wasn't sure she could see it.

"Essandra," he greeted her softly.

She answered with a sharp slap across his cheek.

So, it wasn't the shadows—she *was* angry. And she didn't even know about the armor yet.

"I can't believe you just left me," she seethed.

Yes, no doubt she'd see his secret leaving as betrayal, but it had been the only way to stop her from going.

"I told you that I didn't want you to go," he said.

"It doesn't matter what you want!" Her words were laced with venom. "You're not my king, you do not *command* me, you do not *own* me, you do not *decide* for me. I don't know how much clearer I can be."

She'd been pretty clear, but this was different. He hadn't had a choice—he couldn't have her hurt again. She wouldn't see it that way, though, and he was fairly certain he wouldn't be able to convince her. So, he simply said, "I'm sorry."

"You're not sorry," she countered. "If you were sorry, you wouldn't do it again, but I know for a fact you absolutely would."

Anger lapped at him now. "I'm protecting you!"

A surge of force hit him, knocking him against the wall. She grabbed him by the throat, using her power to pin him, and she leaned close.

Her face was shadowed, but he knew her eyes had changed from green to black.

"I am more powerful than you will ever be," she hissed. "There is nothing you can do for me that I can't do for myself. I decide where I go and what I do. I'm here because I *want* to be. I gave you access to my power because I *wanted* to."

He struggled against her hold, but he couldn't move. "And I gave you access to mine," he gritted back.

"You have no power!" She gripped him tighter, and he struggled for breath. "It doesn't belong to you! You're merely a gateway to the Aether's power—a power that could kill you without me. I give you markings to shield you; I give you armor to cover your weak human body."

This probably wasn't the best time for him to bring up that armor.

"*I* protect *you*!" she continued, her fingers still digging into his throat. "You're *nothing* without me, and you can do *nothing* for me. Am I clear now?"

Her words cut him, no doubt as she'd intended.

"Am I clear?" she hissed again.

"Very," he managed.

She released him, and he gasped, his lungs desperate for air. Then she turned, still with her lantern, and headed back the way she'd come.

Cyrus let the wall hold his weight. The blow of her power had hit him hard, and he pressed his palm against the ache in his side. Wetness seeped through the bandaging, blood with infection, but the injury wasn't the thing hurting him most right now.

That hadn't gone quite as he'd expected. Or hoped. Cyrus lumbered slowly to his room, a little worse for wear now, both in body and spirit. He'd known Essandra would be angry at his leaving. He thought it would have simmered in the time he'd been gone. Instead, it had festered. This was the angriest he'd seen her.

He would talk to her again tomorrow, although he knew this wasn't the kind of anger that waned overnight.

Her words echoed in his mind: *He was nothing without her. He could do nothing for her.* It was the anger talking, he told himself. Then he shook his head. Even if it was, that didn't make it any less true. He *was* nothing without her. But this wasn't what bothered him.

What if he was nothing *to* her?

Or maybe he had been something, and he'd just ruined it.

His chamber was quiet. The dogs weren't there, like he'd hoped they'd be. They were probably in Essandra's room.

He sank into his bed, not bothering to strip his clothing. With Essandra on his mind, he knew sleep wouldn't come now. Still, tiredness paralyzed him, and he closed his eyes.

To the vision of another woman.

He'd never seen her before. Color marked her face, black around her eyes with a strip of red across her cheeks—not blood. Her dark hair streamed behind her in the wind, long and woven with braids and feathers. He hadn't seen many Horsemen in his life, only a few, but they were very distinctive, and he recognized her as one. She rode a white horse with eyes of gold, her teeth bared in a silent scream. Even though he couldn't hear the cry, he knew what it was—a battle cry. She was interesting, this woman of war, but not interesting enough to keep him from the sleep that finally claimed him.

Cyrus sat absently as everyone filtered out of the council room. At this point, he wondered if there was anyone *not* upset with him.

Gregor was furious about Serra. Not that Cyrus cared—he was furious about Gregor being a fucking coward. Gregor feared that the Shadow King's close relationship with Serra might prompt a reaction from the Shadowlands, and that it would put pressure on Japheth to react as well. Cyrus hoped it would.

Still, he had to play nice. He expected the additional twenty thousand men he'd just sent to Japheth would appease Gregor. In a couple of months, Japheth would hold numbers that rivaled Aleon's great army. With Cyrus's sights now set on the Shadow King, he had also proposed a plan. It was no secret that trade negotiations between Japheth and the Shadowlands had been growing contentious. He suggested that Gregor invite the Shadow King to Japheth to finally settle them.

Where Cyrus would be waiting.

Of course, his council disagreed, as they had with Serra. They were upset at the plan and upset he'd taken action toward that plan without their involvement. They were also upset that he still held the two Serran princes, although Cyrus wasn't sure what they wanted him to do with them because they'd also been disturbed when they'd first learned he'd considered killing them.

Essandra, on the other hand, seemed quite relieved he'd spared the boys, although not enough to forgive him. It had been three weeks since he'd returned, and she'd spoken no more than a handful of words to him. When she learned he'd lost his armor, she'd said nothing. No chiding, no scolding. Nothing.

And she hadn't replaced it.

Her apathy worried him more than her anger.

He worried he'd ruined what was between them.

There was nothing between them, he corrected himself as he watched her during the council meeting.

Then he worried he'd ruined *the nothing* between them.

She ignored him—ignored his gaze, ignored his words—offering input directly to the council as if he never said anything at all.

As if he weren't there at all.

He noted a new marking on her arm. She was still using dark magic. He didn't like it, but he wasn't in a position to confront her. It wasn't his business or his concern. Except he *was* concerned. Now that she didn't see using Alexander as a viable option for bringing back her sister, no doubt she was searching for alternatives.

He'd thought a lot over the past few weeks—thought a lot about how he'd so easily passed the opportunity at his brother. And he came to a realization. Cyrus couldn't kill him. If Alexander's blood gave Essandra what she needed, if his life could be used as an anchor, Cyrus would give it to her. But he couldn't tell her that. Not yet. She'd see it as a gift given in an effort to dismiss her anger, and that wasn't what this was.

So, he said nothing and let her pass by him without a word.

After he had sat long enough, he finally rose and left the council room too. When he stepped into the hall, the first smile in weeks spread across his face.

"Hephain," he said as his newly appointed ambassador to Pryam strode toward him. Well, not quite *newly* appointed. Hephain had been in Pryam for over six months now, helping the young Queen Miriel under the guise of representing Rael.

Hephain grinned back but paused to bow. "King Cyrus. It's good to be back in Rael."

The dogs trotted over from where they'd been freely roaming about the halls and jumped around him, their hinds wagging. Hephain chuckled, giving them each an affectionate pat.

"How is Miriel?" Cyrus asked him.

"Very well." Hephain straightened and held out a letter. "She sends this."

He took it with a nod. It was thick, as if she didn't write to him weekly. He couldn't help another smile. "How long are you here for?"

"A week, maybe a little longer. I've come to consult with the masters of education and law for some projects back in Pryam, and, when convenient, update you on how things are going."

Cyrus nodded again. "Come to dinner. Essandra will want to hear too."

Hephain hesitated. "I'd love to, but I can't leave Corwin to fend for himself his first evening in Rael." He gave a small motion to a man behind him. Cyrus hadn't noticed him. He wore white and gold, the color of Pryam, with the signature beauty of the Pryamese people.

"Forgive me," Hephain said quickly. "Let me present Corwin Lewis of Pryam."

"Lord Corwin," Cyrus greeted him.

"Not *Lord*," the man said as he bowed. "Just Corwin, Sire."

Not a lord. If not court business, Cyrus wondered what had brought him to Rael.

Hephain swallowed. "Corwin is a friend. I invited him to accompany me. I hope that's all right."

Friend.

Cyrus nodded as it dawned on him. Words escaped him for a moment, then he said, "Well, if Corwin is a friend, he'll dine as a friend. Bring him to dinner as well." A conversation at dinner would be nice for a change. It had been quiet during the past weeks. Kord was busy with the army, so he wouldn't be there, and Essandra still wasn't speaking to him.

Corwin's mouth dropped open in surprise.

Hephain shook his head. "That's not necessary."

"Sire!" a voice called to his left. Cyrus turned. A page. "Lord Everan requests you join him in the throne room."

Cyrus had to go. He glanced back at Hephain. "I'll see you both this evening." And he struck out toward the throne room.

"What's this about?" he asked the page.

"I don't know, Sire. There are visitors. But Lord Everan and Lord Kord are already there."

Cyrus couldn't help a chuckle. *Lord Kord.* Everan and Kord had become lords in Rael after he'd taken the throne, although this was probably the first time he'd heard them called by their titles. *Lord Kord.* He chuckled again.

He made it to the throne room and strode in. Only a small group of men were there. Kord and Everan waited patiently by his throne, the signal he should sit on it. Cyrus stifled his previous amusement—he'd have to save his jesting of Kord's rhyming title for later. He turned his attention to the men now before him. There were four. They were nicely dressed, not as fine as most lords from other kingdoms but nice enough to show them as men of status. They all bowed, although only one stepped forward.

"King Cyrus," the man in front said. "I am Vin Atari." He was an older man, perhaps fifteen or twenty years Cyrus's senior. He continued, "I am by trade a teacher, by heart an artist, and now a public servant to the people of Serra."

These were freed men from Serra. *Interesting.* Cyrus hadn't expected to see anyone so soon.

"I've come to ask that you ratify the decision of the people," Vin said. He bowed again and held out a stack of parchments in his hands. "I've outlined my background, education, and history of service, which I submit to you for your consideration, so that you may decide if I am worthy of this position."

Cyrus frowned. "What position?"

"To lead the people of Serra."

Cyrus could only stare at him.

Vin motioned to the men behind him, who stepped forward holding a large leather-bound ledger. "These men lead the Independent Trust and oversee the voting," he said. "They have brought the sealed records for your review as well."

Cyrus cocked his head to the side. He couldn't have understood him correctly. "So, the freed people of Serra have chosen a man to lead them, *you*, and you want me to *approve* this?"

The man bowed his head again. "Yes, Sire."

"Why? I'm not king of Serra."

Vin leaned back on his heel with his mouth slightly agape. "Yes, you are."

Cyrus stood from his throne. "No, I'm not."

Vin glanced at the men who'd accompanied him, then back to Cyrus. They all shifted now. Clearly they hadn't expected this reaction.

"Sire," he said, "the people of Serra consider you our king. We've pledged our loyalty."

"Loyalty to what?"

"To your crown! The position I put before you is the position of viceroy. I would act as your hand, extending your reach across Serra."

But Cyrus didn't want to extend his reach across Serra.

"Sire, it's under your reign that Rael has risen again," Vin said.

More like despite his reign.

"Serra can rise again too. Better. Like Rael."

If this man knew Rael, Cyrus doubted he'd want Serra to be anything like it.

"And we're committed to your cause," Vin added. "You bring justice for our people; you right what has been wronged."

Cyrus glanced at Everan and Kord. They said nothing, but he read it in their eyes. He was barely running Rael; he couldn't take on Serra. And he'd already committed enough justice, if one could call it that. He had to turn this man away. If Serra was organized enough to vote, they were organized enough to take themselves on a different path. A better path.

"Eleven ships have accompanied me," Vin said. "And more are sailing as we speak. Regardless of whether you deem me fit for the position that I've shared with you, these men have come to join your army."

Cyrus paused.

Eleven ships.

Thousands of men.

And more to come.

"They would need training, of course," Vin acknowledged, "but they're men of heart."

More men to train, but they were still *more men.*

Kord leaned closer. "Cyrus," he warned quietly, so that only he could hear.

But Cyrus was focused on Vin. These men would join him against the Shadow King.

"We have to send them back," Kord whispered.

He couldn't send them back. He needed every man he could get. And if Aleon engaged in the war to come, as Gregor feared, he'd need even more.

"Cyrus," Kord pressed.

"I'll approve this position," Cyrus said. "Show me the records, let me see that it was a proper vote."

Vin bowed. "Of course, Sire."

"Get ready to receive these men," Cyrus said to Kord.

It was late by the time Cyrus made it to the dining room. Kord strode beside him, silent. He didn't approve of Cyrus accepting Serra. Neither did Everan, but they would help him. His brothers—he could count on them above all else, even if they didn't agree with him.

As they stepped into the dining room, Cyrus stopped when he saw Hephain... with the friend whose name he'd forgotten.

Just as he'd forgotten he'd invited them.

At the time, it had seemed like a good idea, but with Kord in rare attendance, it didn't seem quite as good of an idea now.

When he noticed Cyrus, Hephain stood from where he'd been sitting with Essandra and Visa, his face filled with warmth and laughter. Then he paled when his eyes caught Kord.

Hephain's friend wore a broad smile, completely unaware. "King Cyrus," he said, standing as well and giving a bow. "We were just hearing from Lady Essandra about the new schools."

"Who are you?" Kord asked him.

The man paused, humbling his smile. He swallowed as his eyes darted to Hephain, but Hephain's gaze was locked on Kord.

"I invited him," Cyrus said. "He's visiting from Pryam." Cyrus silently prayed Hephain would make an introduction and spare him from having to ask the name of his invitee, but Hephain stood frozen with his stare still on Kord.

In seeing he wouldn't be getting the introduction he'd also hoped for, the man quickly stepped forward. "Yes, of course, I'm so sorry. I'm Corwin Lewis." He gave another bow.

Corwin. Yes, that was his name.

"Corwin is a friend of mine," Hephain said, finally finding his voice.

Kord's eyes shifted to Hephain now, acknowledging him for the first time. As if he hadn't noticed him. As if he felt nothing. *Did* he feel nothing?

If only Hephain could do the same, or at least not be so obvious about it.

"Forgive us for being late," Cyrus said. "I'm starving." He motioned to the table. "Please."

Everan moved and greeted Visa with a warm kiss on her cheek, then everyone took their seats at the table. Hephain resumed his place next to Essandra, with Kord directly across from him, and Corwin next to Hephain.

Cyrus sat in his usual place, at the head of the table, with a full view of what would surely be an awkward dung fire of a dinner. It seemed time had mended no wounds with Hephain. Neither had a new *friend*.

Meanwhile, Kord sat completely unaffected.

Or perhaps not.

Cyrus caught his friend's stare on Corwin.

"So, Essandra was sharing how things were coming along with the schools," Visa said.

Thank the fucking gods *someone* knew how to start a conversation again.

Corwin's smile returned. "It sounds like things are going w—"

"I've spent a lot of time in Pryam," Kord interrupted. "I don't remember ever seeing you at court, Lord Corwin."

Corwin's smile faded slightly. "Not *Lord*," he said. "I'm not a man of court. My father is a mason, my mother a baker."

The table grew quiet.

Corwin swallowed again as he looked around.

"Well, we all used to be chattel," Cyrus said, trying to lighten the air.

No one laughed. Not that it was intended to be funny, but it was the lightest he'd ever been able to say it. Visa winced.

"Corwin makes music," Hephain said.

Essandra leaned forward in her chair. "Really?" she asked, with the first smile coming to her lips in weeks. "What do you play?"

"Pretty much anything."

"Anything?" Kord asked.

Corwin shrugged. "Yes, I've been playing instruments since before I could walk." He gave a light laugh as he glanced at Hephain. Hephain smiled back.

"A tempir?" Kord asked.

Corwin nodded. "Yes."

"A lyrar?"

"Uh, yes."

Kord's eyes narrowed. "I'd love to hear." He turned to a page. "Can you get us a lyrar?"

"That's not necessary," Hephain interjected.

"Kord," Cyrus said in a low voice.

"What? It would be nice to hear a tune with dinner." He looked around the table. "Do you not all agree?"

Hephain looked at Corwin. "You don't have—"

"No, it's fine," Corwin said quickly. "I'd love to play for you all."

Or make a fool of himself in front of them all. Cyrus didn't play any instruments, but back when they first took the palace, he and Everan and Kord had goofed off a bit in the adjoining room, where a number of instruments were stored. Kord could actually play a few of them half decently. Cyrus didn't know what a lyrar was, but he knew there was absolutely nothing in that room he could personally use to produce anything that remotely resembled a song. And, aside from Kord, he expected most people to be the same.

The page quickly brought the complicated stringed instrument to Corwin, who slid his chair back to allow it to lie across his lap. He paused and nervously looked up at them all. "The lyrar is typically played with two people, and it's been a long time since I've held one, but I'll try to do it some justice."

There it was—the disclaimer. Cyrus almost grimaced. Why did he feel nervous for this man?

But that nervousness evaporated as the most beautiful melody filled his ears.

Cyrus had never heard anything like it. He almost wouldn't have believed it was a sound that could be created by a man if he weren't watching it with his own eyes. Corwin's fingers danced across the multitude of strings, playing even faster. It was mesmerizing. They all sat in a trance, not eating, not drinking, simply listening.

Then the tune ended, releasing them all, and Cyrus laughed in amazement.

"That was beautiful," Essandra said, nearly breathless.

"Pure magic," Visa added. "You had us all absolutely under your spell."

Corwin laughed. "Sadly, it is my only talent."

"He's too humble," Hephain interjected. "He teaches music and is opening a proper school for music back in Pryam."

Visa clapped her hands. "How exciting!"

"Agreed," Essandra said. "You have to let me know if you need anything with the school. I'm happy to help however I can. If you're teaching others to do *that*, you're giving a gift to the world. I could listen all evening."

Corwin smiled. "Thank you, Lady Essandra. And I am happy to play anytime, anywhere, for whoever will listen."

"He should play for us tomorrow evening," Everan said, "for the dinner with the new leader of Serra."

Essandra's brows dipped. "The what?"

The table quieted.

"What did you say?" Essandra asked Everan again.

Everan took a drink from his chalice. A long drink.

"Serra has a new king?" she asked. "And he's here?"

Kord chuckled. "The irony," he said as his gaze settled on Cyrus. Kord wouldn't dare. Cyrus shook his head, warning him.

"Cyrus here *is* the new king of Serra," Kord said anyway.

Kord, you bastard.

Essandra's eyes widened as they darted to him. "You? King of Serra?"

Now it was Cyrus's turn to take a drink. A long one.

"You didn't even say anything," she said.

He slowly sat down his chalice. "Well, it just happened. Also, you're not talking to me... so..."

The daggers in her stare could have cut him.

"What does the council think?" she asked.

He shrugged. "I don't know. I haven't told them."

The table grew quiet again.

Corwin stood slowly. "I think I should leave for you to discuss this." He bowed. "Thank you, King Cyrus, again, for the invitation. It was an honor." Then he quietly made his way from the room.

Visa stood as well. "I'll check on dessert."

"I think we're all done here," Essandra said as she rose too. "It looks like someone needs to inform the council that we have two kingdoms now." She didn't give Cyrus another look as she swept out of the room.

Only Everan, Kord, and Hephain remained.

"What do you want us to do?" Everan asked.

Cyrus shook his head as he sighed and sank back in his chair. "Nothing for tonight. We'll figure it out tomorrow."

Everan nodded and followed after Visa.

Hephain cast a last glance back to Kord, then took his leave as well.

Kord watched him go, not rising from his chair.

"Kord," Cyrus called to him.

But Kord's gaze stayed on the empty doorway.

"Kord? Are you all right?"

Kord's attention snapped back, and he cut him a sharp glance. "When is anyone all right in this fucking place?" Then he rose and strode from the room, leaving Cyrus, once again, at a table by himself.

CHAPTER TWENTY-ONE

Two sets of identical eyes stared back at him. Varian and Martine. The Serran princes. Cyrus stood in the stateroom in the southern wing of the palace, where he held them, because keeping children in the dungeon felt... uncomfortable. So did visiting them, but here he was.

He glanced around the room. It was larger than his own—a grand sitting room turned boys' bedchamber. He wanted space for them, not that he kept them here all the time. They were permitted in various rooms under guard, and outside in the courtyard. He was satisfied with this, until he could figure out what to do with them long-term.

His eyes stopped on a series of charms above their beds. Moon-colored stones hung from intricate patterns of silver thread.

"What are those?" he asked.

"Moonweaves," Varian said. He was the more outspoken of the two. He'd been the one wielding the sword when Cyrus had taken them.

"Lady Essandra gave them to us to catch the night terrors and keep them away," Martine added quietly.

Cyrus tried to swallow the sourness in the back of his throat as guilt tugged at him. It wasn't his intention to give children night terrors.

"Lady Essandra visits you?" he asked.

They fell quiet.

"What does she say?"

"She tells us to be brave," Martine whispered.

Cyrus nodded. "I think that's very good advice."

"Are you going to kill us?" Varian asked.

Cyrus paused. "I don't want to," he said truthfully. "But my people demand justice. And I'm sure there are surviving Serran nobles who will do everything they can to restore you to power."

"I don't even want the throne," Martine said.

"But that's the thing, isn't it?" Cyrus told them. "You don't have to want something for it to be forced upon you."

Varian clasped his brother's hand. "We can be different from what our father was."

"The pressures of the crown will push you to do things you never thought you would do. I know these pressures."

"So, what are you going to do with us?"

"I don't know," Cyrus said. He paused, guilt still needling him. "But I don't want you to be afraid. I'll tell you this—mind yourselves, and you will be treated as wards of the crown. No harm will come to you here."

Martine glanced at his brother, then looked back to Cyrus, his brown eyes large and hopeful. "Do you promise?"

Cyrus nodded. "I promise."

The ink dried slowly, but he waited. He'd been careful with each sentence and didn't want to mess it up now. Cyrus did his best to write nicely for Miriel. She took such time with her letters, and he tried to do the same.

He wondered if Essandra had written her back as well. Probably. She sent Miriel things all the time. Cyrus and Essandra often talked about Miriel. Well, they did when Essandra was speaking to him, which she still wasn't. He rose from his desk and moved to the window.

Essandra's absence carried the weight of loss. And he didn't know how to fix it.

"Are you sulking again?" Visa called from behind him.

The dogs jumped to greet her.

Cyrus straightened and turned. "Why would I be sulking?"

She raised a brow. "Why won't you just go talk to her?"

He sighed and turned back to the window. "She doesn't want me to talk to her."

"She doesn't want you to control her. She absolutely wants you to talk to her."

"Wh-" He turned back to her. "What has she said?"

"No." She shook her head. "Don't ask me that."

"I know she's upset with me."

"Yes. And, again, that's typically remedied by talking."

Another sigh escaped him.

"No, you know what—I'm not going to keep watching you like this," she told him. She grabbed him and pulled him by the arm toward the door. "You're going to go right now."

He planted his feet. "I don't know what to say."

Visa moved behind him, pushing him. "Well, you'll figure it out on the way." She was quite strong for one so small, and she pushed him all the way through the door and out into the hall.

"I don't even know where to start."

"You can start by telling her you're sorry. Yes, you do stupid things, but they do come from a good place."

"Thanks?"

She took hold of his hands again. "She doesn't even know that you let go of an opportunity at your brother to bring her back when she was injured."

He froze, and his eyes locked with hers.

Visa bit the corner of her lip. "Everan told me."

"I don't want her to know that."

Her brows dipped. "Why not?"

He shook his head. "I guess... I don't want her to feel like I'm using that against her. She doesn't owe me."

Her hold on him softened, and she nodded. "I won't tell her. But, still, you need to talk to her."

"Fine."

She raised a brow.

"I will," he promised.

"Right now!" she pressed, shooing him.

"I'm going!" He started down the hall. As he looked back over his shoulder, Visa gave him another wave of her hand.

His footfalls echoed through the empty halls. He ran through the conversation in his head. He would say that he was sorry for not taking her to Serra.

Except he wasn't sorry. Serra had proven to be more challenging than he'd expected. It had been dangerous, not the best planned, as Orion would no doubt continue to remind him. He hadn't wanted her there. He'd been trying to protect her.

Because that was what one did when one felt—

As he rounded the corner, Cyrus stopped midstride as a man stepped from Essandra's workroom. His face was covered, with his gaze in the opposite direction as he closed the door behind him. His movements were quick. Stealthy.

"Hey!" Cyrus shouted at him.

The man jerked and turned and, upon seeing Cyrus, fled down the hall.

"Stop!" Cyrus demanded, and gave chase, but as he reached the end and hooked around the next corner, the man was gone.

Cyrus raced back and tore into Essandra's workroom. She whirled around from where she stood over her table.

"Who was that?" he demanded.

A flash of alarm lit her face, which she quickly hid. She pursed her lips. "Who was who?"

"Don't play games. There was a man in here."

Her eyes darkened and she cocked her head. "Are you jealous?"

"His face was covered." Cyrus stepped closer. "Was he an assassin?"

She turned back to the table, picking up the stem of an herb and pulling the small leaves from it.

"Are you freeing assassins?" he pressed.

She finished with the stem and started with another. "And what if I was?"

A storm rippled under his skin, and he grabbed her.

"Let go of me!" she hissed, but he didn't.

He pulled her closer. "Do you know the danger you call to yourself?"

She wrenched her hand away. "I already face a danger greater than anything you've ever seen. I don't care about the guild."

Cyrus hadn't forgotten about Soroya. Far from it. He thought often about the high witch who was hunting Essandra. But just because there was a greater danger out there didn't mean Essandra could ignore smaller ones. *Smaller.* He almost scoffed at himself. The danger from the assassins' guild was hardly small. And unlike Soroya, who seemed little more than a phantom in night terrors, the Jackals were here. They were reaching her with no one else around.

"Was he the only one?" he asked.

"The only one this week."

"How many?"

"Nine?" She shrugged. "Ten?" She finally turned to face him again. "Less if I'd have gone to Serra."

They'd come while he'd been gone. Rage rippled through him. Whether they timed their fortune like that or not, it didn't matter. "No more," he said.

"That's not your decision."

His skin grew even hotter. "I'll kill every assassin that steps foot in Rael."

Her eyes flashed. "Get out," she said.

They stood with their stares locked.

Her lips peeled back, showing her teeth. "Get. Out."

He snorted an angry breath but yielded, finally leaving her workroom. But now things were so much worse.

Talk to her, Visa had said.

Cyrus inhaled deeply, and the salty sea air filled his lungs. The ship bound for Pryam was almost ready and would be sailing soon. Cyrus had come to see it off. This wasn't a normal habit for him, but he needed something to occupy his mind.

He was supposed to be in Japheth right now, waiting for the Shadow King to arrive under Gregor's invitation to renegotiate their trade terms in person.

But the Shadow King had refused. Had he known Cyrus would be waiting for him? Waiting to confront him. Waiting to put the tip of his sword against the base of his neck, to look him in the eye as he pushed it through. How many times Cyrus had imagined it, had dreamed about it...

Had the Shadow King known? *No*, he couldn't have. But he had to have suspected something.

Cyrus should have known it wouldn't have been that easy, but he was disappointed nonetheless. Now he'd have to formulate another plan—a more direct plan. That also meant he couldn't ignore Aleon and Mercia.

He sent Jaem, with his talent for finding information, back to the Free Cities, which were always abuzz with the latest news and rumors. Not all of it was reliable, but most of it was directionally accurate and seemed to fill in what official letters and proclamations left out.

And not everything about the Shadow King's refusal to go to Japheth was a setback. In a hasty reaction driven by his insult and anger, Gregor had halted all trade between Japheth and the Shadowlands. It was obvious now that the alliance between them was crumbling, and Gregor was crumbling with it. His letters had become more and more erratic, more and more unreadable—Cyrus had stopped trying to make sense of them. The last four, he'd left unopened. The coward could no longer hide behind willful miscommunication and masked subversion.

Cyrus hoped the fracture was as obvious to the Shadow King. He gathered it was. Orion had returned from the Shadowlands, reporting a mass callback of Shadow warriors. What would be the reason to call back forces of that magnitude if not out of concern for a threat? Their influx through the Canyonlands had been so heavy that Orion had barely been able to make it out undetected. It had taken Cyrus every bird he could get his hands on to help get him out.

Orion had returned without his woman. She hadn't been in the Shadowlands. Well, she *had* been, but she wasn't there anymore. It was rumored that a freed slave from Elam, who Orion was convinced was Vitalia, was now in service to the queen.

It had been a while since Cyrus had thought about the Mercian queen. Regardless, she'd returned to Mercia, likely with Vitalia.

Orion had just missed her.

Cyrus wished he would have known sooner. He could have let Orion go sooner, although he'd needed him in the attack against Serra. He wouldn't have been able to kill the king and take the princes without him. And Orion's delayed trip to the Shadowlands had provided him with valuable information.

Still, the guilt ate at him. He toed at a loose board on the dock where he stood.

Footfalls came behind him, pulling him from his thoughts, and he turned to see Hephain.

The dogs had been sniffing around the dock nearby, and they trotted up to greet him. Hephain gave them a pat.

"Are you ready?" Cyrus asked him.

Hephain nodded with a small smile. "I am. I didn't expect a royal send-off back to Pryam, though."

Cyrus glanced around. Hephain was by himself. "Where's Corwin?" he asked. He hadn't seen the Pryamese man since the shitstorm dinner they'd had.

Hephain's smile faded. "He sailed back last week."

Last week. Right after the dinner.

"I'm sorry," Cyrus said.

"It's not your fault. I mean, dinner was an absolute disaster, but..." He shook his head. "I'd never told Corwin the history there. He figured it out pretty quickly, though. And it probably wouldn't have been an issue if I was over everything, and if I'd been honest with him." He swallowed. "But I'm not, and I wasn't."

A silence came between them again. Hephain's eyes teared, but he blinked them back as Ram trotted up along the dock to them.

"Hey!" Ram said with a grin. "I heard you were going, wanted to say goodbye."

They clasped arms and pulled each other close.

"Thank you, friend," Hephain said. "I won't be long in returning." He turned back to Cyrus. "I should go," he added. "You'd said you have a letter for Miriel?"

"Oh, right." Cyrus had almost forgotten. He pulled the letter and held it out.

"I'll be back in a few months," Hephain told him as he took it.

"I'm looking forward to it."

Cyrus watched as the gangways cleared the dock, and the ship pulled away.

The sun rose above the horizon, spilling light and nearly blinding him. But he didn't miss the large ship pulling into port as Hephain's departed.

"Who's that?" Cyrus asked.

Ram squinted across the harbor. "Green flags."

Green.

Gregor.

Fuck.

CHAPTER TWENTY-TWO

The dogs growled low, and Cyrus dropped a hand to settle them.

"You're here! Good!" The thin but potbellied king wobbled down the plank to the dock.

Cyrus almost wanted to see him fall. Gods, it was too early in the day to have to deal with this man.

"You got my bird!" Gregor shouted before he'd even reached the bottom. "I'd hoped you'd be ready and waiting."

What bird? Cyrus stared at him. "Ready? For what?"

Gregor gaped at him. "Did you not read my letters?"

No. "Of course I did."

"We have to go, then!"

Cyrus shook his head. "No, I didn't read them."

Gregor stared at him, wide-eyed and practically frothing at the mouth. "Phillip has moved forces to Bahoul! I knew Mikael would betray me. He's let Phillip position himself close with an army that rivals my own."

Any army rivaled Japheth's without the mercenaries. But Cyrus paused. Bahoul—the mountain stronghold that belonged to the Shadowlands—Phillip was there?

"We have to take action before he brings the rest of his army," Gregor said, "and before Mercia and Kharav join him!"

Cyrus wouldn't be so quick to act. His primary target was the Shadow King, not Aleon. "Let's go back to the palace," he told Gregor, "where we can think things through."

Despite Gregor's objections and incessant ranting, Cyrus did manage to make it back to the palace without harming him, although it was becoming increasingly harder to tolerate this man.

And he'd only just arrived.

"Gather the council," Cyrus told Ram as they strode toward the council room.

Summoning his council was rarely the first thing on his list in response to a situation, but he could use more people to shoulder the burden of listening to this wailing imbecile of a king. He stood in the council room as Gregor recounted the unfairness of life, having been hand-fed with a silver spoon but not getting the entirety of his inheritance.

"Tell me again how unfair life is," Cyrus quipped, his patience quickly evaporating.

The gaudy king's brows dipped in confusion. Finally, the council filed in. Cyrus had never been so happy to see them. Essandra was with them as well, with Orion escorting her to the door before leaving. Cyrus was happy to see him taking his charge seriously. He had meant it when he'd said he'd kill every assassin that came to Rael. Of course, Essandra was still livid, but if that was the price for her safety, so be it.

With the council assembled, Gregor ran through his updates once again, to an audience who did a much better job than Cyrus of appeasing his need for attention.

"So, we must act now," Gregor reiterated when he'd finished, "and strike before they come together."

"I'm not yet convinced Aleon, Mercia, and the Shadowlands are all allied," Cyrus said.

Gregor gaped at him. "You refuse the proof?"

Cyrus snorted. "What proof?"

"Mercia and Kharav are quite literally bound by a marriage alliance." There was a slight shake in his hand. "And Phillip is in Bahoul, the Kharavian stronghold!"

"The Shadow King wouldn't just *give* another king his stronghold. This feels *taken*."

"There can be no question about Mercia and Aleon, though," Gregor argued. "They have always been and will always be allies."

"But we don't know if the Shadowlands are with them."

"What did the Shadow King say when you confronted him?" Essandra asked Gregor directly, quieting everyone in the room.

Gregor leveled his beady eyes on her in surprise. "What?"

She said her words slower. "What did the Shadow King say when you confronted him? Did he tell you he gave the stronghold to Aleon? Or did he tell you Aleon moved against him?"

Gregor's thin lips thinned even more. "I didn't give him the opportunity to spew lies."

"So, you *didn't* confront him," she said.

Gregor's face twisted. "I don't need a wench telling me what I should or shouldn't do with my allies."

The room fell silent.

Cyrus's eyes snapped to Gregor. For a moment, he thought he hadn't heard right. "What did you say?" he asked.

"Time is of the essence! We must join our forces and strike before—"

"No." Cyrus stood. "What did you say?" he asked again. Fire rippled under his skin.

The knot in Gregor's throat bobbed. "I know Mikael very well, and I know how—"

"Apologize," Cyrus said, cutting him off.

Gregor paused, and his mouth fell open. His eyes traveled the room. "What?"

Cyrus stepped around the table toward him. "Apologize."

Gregor's eyes darted to Essandra and then widened. He looked at the council and then back to Cyrus. "You can't be serious."

"I'm rarely anything but. You'll apologize to Lady Essandra. Now."

Gregor's breaths came quicker and shorter. He looked back at Essandra, blinking rapidly. "I apologize if I—"

"No *if*," Cyrus cut him off again.

"I apologize—"

"On your knees," Cyrus added.

Gregor gaped at him. "To a *woman*? I am a *king*!"

"A king who's about to be a head shorter." Cyrus pulled his sword from its scabbard. The councilmen all pushed back in their seats. Some rose. But no one spoke.

Gregor took a step back. "She doesn't even look offended!"

"Because she's mastered the art of tolerating men for the greater good." Cyrus cocked his head. "I haven't."

"I am your ally!" Gregor shrieked as Cyrus stalked closer.

"On your knees, *ally*."

Gregor jerked up his hands, surrendering, gasping. Cyrus paused and gave him a moment. Slowly, Gregor sank to a knee and gave a stiff nod toward Essandra. "I apologize for my words and for the offense they've caused."

"And a proper address," Cyrus demanded.

"My lady," Gregor added. Then he scrambled to his feet.

Cyrus stepped to him and leaned close. "If you ever speak to her like that again, I'll cut your tongue from your mouth and feed it to you through the hole I rip in your throat." Cyrus stared at him through eyes that envisioned doing just that. "We're done for now."

Then Cyrus turned. "Lady Essandra," he said as he motioned toward the door, offering her to exit before him. He wasn't sure she would, but she surprised him and swept out of the room.

"What about Phillip?" Gregor called after him.

He didn't bother to look back. "I'll let you know what I decide." Then he followed after Essandra.

Out in the hall, Cyrus's blood still boiled. And more—he knew her chastisement was coming. She would remind him that she could take care of herself, that he'd imposed, crossed another line.

But her hand on his arm stopped him in his step. His anger suddenly evaporated. He forgot about Gregor.

She hadn't touched him since he'd returned from Serra.

"Thank you," she said.

He stared at her hand for a moment. He hadn't realized how much he'd wanted her touch—how much he'd needed it. He wanted to step even closer, but that wasn't how she meant this. So he simply said, "Of course."

She cast her gaze down, but she didn't take her hand from him. She hesitated for a moment before she said, "There's so much I need to say to you, but I'm in a bit of a whirlwind, quite honestly."

"It was a little shocking in there, I know."

"Not about that." She paused. "Orion told me. He told me that you brought me back, instead of taking an opportunity against your brother in Mercia."

He shifted back on his heel.

"Were you not going to tell me?" she asked.

"I was... I was waiting..." Then he shook his head. Why was he lying? "No. I wasn't."

"Cyrus," she whispered. "You should have killed him when you had the chance."

"But I couldn't."

Her brow dipped. "Why?"

He stared at her. "I had to make sure you got home. I had to make sure you got to Teron. I couldn't leave you."

"But you missed your opportunity."

"It was never an opportunity."

Her brows drew together. "What?"

"I can't kill him."

Her lips parted, then closed again. She shook her head. The line between her brows deepened.

"You need him," he said. He looked down at her hand still on his arm. "I can't kill him because you need him." His eyes met hers again. "And I'll find a way to get his blood."

Her eyes welled, and she clutched him tighter.

"I'm still angry with you," she whispered. "But I... I... Thank you." Her lip trembled. "For everything. For what happened in Mercia. For Alexander. For Gregor."

"Gregor," he scoffed.

She let him go and wiped her face. "That man is insufferable," she said. "Unfortunately, as much as I appreciated that, I'm not sure it was a wise idea."

Cyrus shrugged. "What's he going to do? He has no one else. His alliance with the Shadow King has crumbled."

"Which I'm sure he regrets now."

"If he doesn't, he will, when he finds out I can be so much worse."

Chapter Twenty-Three

Cyrus sat in his study, resting his weight on his elbows on the desk in front of him with his hands tented against his closed eyes.

He'd been wrong.

"Do we know how many?" he asked Jaem through the blood bond.

He'd asked Jaem to see what he could learn about anything going on between Aleon, Mercia, and the Shadowlands. Rumors and tavern talks were becoming surprisingly more reliable than official communications. It had taken a couple of weeks, but Jaem now reported that the combined forces of Mercia and Aleon had been sent to support the Shadowlands.

"In the thousands," Jaem replied, *"but I'm still trying to figure out if that means two thousand or forty thousand."*

Cyrus pushed a long breath out. It didn't matter if it was one thousand. It told Cyrus what he needed to know—that the three kingdoms *were* allied. He'd doubted it, but the proof was clear now.

"And there's more," Jaem said. *"They were led by the Mercian lord justice."*

His chest tightened, and he leaned back in his chair. *"My brother delivered reinforcements to the Shadow King?"*

He'd thought Alexander didn't have the power to inflict the hurt of betrayal anymore. But he found himself wrong again.

"*Is he still there?*" he asked.

"*I don't know,*" Jaem said. "*I'll use the blood to call to you when I find out more.*"

Cyrus heard the roar of his name in the hall even before Orion came barreling through the doorframe.

"Cyrus, we've got a problem," Orion said, not even bothering with a greeting. Orion always had a problem, which he then made Cyrus's problem.

Cyrus didn't have time for more problems. "What?" he said shortly, already annoyed.

"Joren went to the port two days ago. When he got back, he said he wasn't feeling well and started running a fever. I told him to take a rest. I didn't hear anything from him yesterday, and I sent Rev to check on him this morning."

Cyrus didn't know who either of those men were, nor did he care, and this story was already entirely too long. "So? He's still sick?"

"He's dead. I checked around—he'd taken a shared wagon back. Three others from that wagon have a fever now, and there's a second man dead."

Cyrus's annoyance was suddenly replaced by a sinking weight in his stomach. This was certainly a problem. A lethal fever could be devastating. The capital city was dense, especially with all the arrivals they'd taken in over the past year. Barracks were overrun, single homes occupied by multiple families, and even some market areas had been converted to temporary accommodations. It wasn't possible to separate people.

"There's someone else who caught a ride back on that wagon too," Orion said. "Your healer."

Cyrus's eyes darted to him, and he stood abruptly. "Teron?"

The assassin nodded. "I haven't checked on him," he added. "I just came straight here."

Cyrus didn't wait for him to say more. He nearly broke into a run out of the study and down the halls toward Teron's workroom, with Orion close behind. When he reached the workroom, he found it empty. He pivoted and quickened his steps even more toward Teron's bedchamber.

Essandra crossed them in the hall. She paused when she saw him. "What's wrong?" she asked.

He stopped only briefly. "There's a fever that appears to be spreading. I'm worried about Teron."

"Have you tried his workroom?"

"It's empty. I'm going to check his chamber."

"I'll come with you." They all picked up toward Teron's chamber, and when they reached it, Cyrus beat on the door.

"Teron!" he called. He beat again. "Teron!"

The healer didn't answer. Cyrus reached for the handle, but Orion caught him. "You can't go in there—if he has the fever, you could catch it."

Cyrus wasn't too concerned about himself, but he banged on the door again. "Teron!" he yelled.

Still, the old man didn't answer.

And Cyrus swung the door open. "Stay out here," he ordered Essandra and Orion.

Essandra grabbed him. "Cyrus—"

"Stay here," he told her again as he pulled away, and he stepped inside.

Teron's room was almost as large as Cyrus's, although he kept it quite sparse. A small writing desk sat against the far wall just under a tri-set window. Long draperies hung in the center of the room, serving as a partition separating his sleeping space.

Cyrus pulled back the drapery, and his heart stopped.

Teron lay in his bed, his face pale, his eyes closed.

Cyrus sprang to him, checking his neck for a pulse. "Teron!" Fever flushed the old man's skin, and Cyrus let out a breath of relief. *He was alive.* But the relief was short-lived.

"Teron?" He shook him gently.

Teron didn't respond.

"He's got the fever!" he called to Essandra in the doorway. "Is there anything you can do?"

She stepped inside just enough to see him, with a line trenched across her forehead. "I don't think so, but I'll go see what I can find in the books."

"Do it quickly!"

She slipped away in the direction of her workroom.

"Get Everan and Kord," Cyrus barked to Orion. "Have them check the army, and have our men start going through the people. We have to see if anyone else has caught it and do our best to separate them."

Orion left quickly to his task.

Cyrus sank to his knees next to Teron's bed. "Teron?" he called again. The old man still didn't respond. Cyrus clasped his hand. His eyes burned and blurred, and he blinked them clear.

This couldn't be happening. What had Teron even been doing at the ports? It wasn't unusual, he reminded himself. Teron had frequent shipments of books and supplies, and he didn't like other people handling them.

But why would he take a shared wagon? He could have used a palace carriage, although Teron never took a palace carriage.

Cyrus swore as he raked a rough hand over his face. He could argue *why* and *how* and *what if* all day, but the truth was, he was just angry. Out of all the people who actually deserved something like this, Teron was not one of them.

Or maybe it wasn't a curse against Teron.

Maybe the gods were punishing Cyrus. They knew what Teron meant to him.

"Don't take this man from me," he whispered to them. If he had to pray, he would pray. If he had to beg, he would beg. Teron had always taken care of him, saved him, loved him. Teron was his family, and Cyrus couldn't lose him. "I beg you, don't take him."

Essandra came bustling back in with jars of herbs and a bowl in her arms.

"Did you find anything?" he asked.

She shook her head. "No, but I—"

"You weren't even gone that long. Go through all the books, all the spells—"

"It doesn't matter," she said as she dropped down beside him and dumped the contents of her arms in front of her. "Witches don't have healing power. The only thing that I have is a warding spell. I thought I might be able to cast his fever away, but I found it won't work on those already infected or those without power in their blood."

"Teron has power!"

"But he's already infected," she said. "You're *not*, though, at least not yet. You have to let me ward your blood."

"We have to get his fever down."

"I brought some tanis extract for that." She picked up a jar with some yellow liquid. "Here—help me get this in him. We can also sponge him a bit."

Cyrus scooped his arm under Teron and lifted the old man slightly as Essandra poured the liquid down.

Teron coughed and sputtered.

"Essandra," Cyrus breathed shakily as his eyes caught on the blood that tinged Teron's lips. "Why's he bleeding?"

She shook her head. "I don't know. The sickness must be causing it. Cyrus, let me ward you."

"Where is some water? He needs some water."

She grabbed his arm. "I have to ward you first. Cyrus, if you get sick..."

He didn't care about himself. Teron's fever was dangerously high.

"It will only take a moment," she said. She quickly mixed the various herbs from her jars in the bowl. Then she made a swift cut on his arm, drawing off the beads of blood that swelled out.

He gritted his teeth.

She mixed his blood with the herbs in the bowl and breathed a spell over it, and a small green flame flared upward. When it died, she closed her eyes in relief. "It's done," she said.

"What about you?"

"Let me get some water for Teron, then I'll do mine."

Essandra retrieved a pitcher and basin and brought them beside the bed. She poured the water and dipped a clean linen cloth, but when she moved to sponge Teron's forehead, Cyrus took it from her.

"You ward yourself," he said. "I'll do this."

She let him take the linen to start on Teron while she worked to mix more herbs for her own spell.

Cyrus turned his attention to the old healer. He drew the wet cloth over the old man's face and down his neck, but as he pushed open the loose tunic to get his chest, he paused. He hadn't realized how frail Teron had become. His robes hid a lot. Very little flesh covered his frame.

He glanced at Essandra as she pricked her finger and added a droplet of blood to her mixture. She whispered the same spell she'd spoken for him, and again a green flame lit inside the bowl.

"What about Everan?" Cyrus asked. "And Kord and Ram and Orion. And the others?"

"They don't have power in their blood."

"What if you bonded them to me? Like you do when we pass through the portal. It's a physical bond. Would that cover them? I'm warded, so they'd be warded?"

She drew her bottom lip between her teeth. "Maybe? But you've only been able to tether three at a time before the bond starts to fall apart. Remember? You won't be able to cover everyone."

"What about the general blood bond?"

She hesitated. "That's a mind bond. I don't think that will work the same."

"We'll still do it. Have people consume it, not just put the blood on their skin."

"Okay. We can try it."

"Do the tether for Everan. And Kord and Orion and Ram—

"*Three*, Cyrus."

He stopped.

No. How could he pick only three? He didn't know if the blood bond would work—he didn't even know if the tether would work, but it seemed like it should.

Still... only three...

"Everan and Kord," he said finally. He stared at the ground as he swallowed. "And Visa." For Everan. "We'll use blood bonds on the others, as many as we can."

She nodded. "Okay," she said softly.

After they saw to Teron the best they could, and Cyrus felt like he could leave for a short while, they called Kord, Everan, and Visa to Essandra's workroom. Essandra made quick work of it, pricking their fingers and drawing their blood. Cyrus gripped Kord's shoulder as Essandra set the tether. She'd told him multiple times he didn't need to touch someone to tether them, but it felt more natural. He felt more sure of it this way, and right now he needed to be sure.

"So, this will protect us from getting the fever?" Kord asked as Cyrus moved to Everan.

"We think so," Cyrus said.

"We *hope* so," Essandra emphasized.

They moved to Visa. She smiled appreciatively as Cyrus put his hand on her shoulder.

Essandra breathed the spell, and it was done.

Kord glanced at Visa. "What about Leti?" he asked.

Cyrus paused. He'd forgotten about the girl Kord had been courting. "I can only tether three. Any more than that and the bond starts to break apart. But we're going to use the blood bond too. We'll have her take that."

Kord's brows drew down. "Will the blood bond work?"

"To be honest," Cyrus said, "we don't know if either of these will work."

"But the tether is the most likely?"

"The tether is a physical bond," Essandra replied. "It's stronger."

Kord shook his head. "You should have tethered Leti. Break mine and give it to her. I'll do the regular blood bond."

"No," Cyrus said. Kord was speaking out of obligation, and Cyrus wouldn't break his friend's best protection from the fever for a woman he didn't even love.

"I'm serious," Kord said firmly.

"I am too. She'll be fine with the blood bond."

"You don't know that!" He stepped closer, pleading. "Cyrus. Tether her."

But Cyrus couldn't do that. He needed Kord safe. "No," he whispered.

Kord's nostrils flared, and his lips thinned.

"She can have my tether," Visa said. "I'll do the blood bond."

"Visa," Everan objected, as Kord shook his head and said, "Absolutely not."

Kord set his steely glare back on Cyrus. "Use mine. Do it."

Still, Cyrus didn't relent, and after two more times pleading, Kord stormed from the room in a fury.

A quiet hung in the air.

"Visa," Essandra said softly, "will you help me prep wine for the blood bonds?"

"Of course," she said, and the women left Cyrus and Everan alone in the room.

Everan leaned back against Essandra's worktable with his arms crossed.

"Do you think I'm wrong?" Cyrus asked him.

His friend sighed. "No, but I would have wanted the same in his place. I probably even would have fought you for it."

Kord still might...

If Leti got sick, Kord would never forgive him. If she didn't get sick, he still might not forgive him. Still, Cyrus couldn't do it. He moved to leave, but Everan caught him.

"You could have given the third tether to so many others," Everan told him. "Others who you need." He swallowed. "I know you tethered Visa for me, and I'm eternally grateful, brother."

"Let's pray it works." Cyrus squeezed his shoulder, then headed back to Teron's chamber.

Cyrus stayed with Teron, leaving only to give Essandra blood to portion out with wine. He drained himself until he felt faint and had to sit before he lost his balance.

"That's enough," Essandra said, stopping him before he made another cut across his forearm.

"How many people can we cover with this?" He nodded to the two large bowls of blood on the table. He moved to stand.

"No—stay sitting," she told him. Then she looked at the bowls. "Maybe a hundred per bowl."

"That's all?" That seemed like hardly anything.

"I'm afraid to dilute it too much, which would render it ineffective and make this all for nothing." Her voice dropped lower. "We don't even know if this is going to work."

"How soon before I can give more?"

"A couple days at least," she said as she pulled some linen strips from a side cabinet.

It had to be sooner than that. "It could be too late by then."

"There's only so much you can do," she told him. She moved a stool in front of him and sat, holding out her hand for his arm. He complied, giving it to her.

"We also don't know how serious this is yet. It could pass over fairly graciously." Taking her time, she wrapped the linen around his arm, covering the cuts, and bound it securely.

He knew she was trying to keep him positive, especially in light of Teron. But the reality was that every report that came in to him told of more and more struck by the fever. There had been only a handful of deaths, and Cyrus prayed to the gods it wouldn't get worse.

"I have to get back to Teron," he said.

"Wait a moment." She stood and took a chalice from the cabinet, pouring an herb mixture from another bowl and then stirring in some water. She brought it to him. "Here. Drink this."

He took the chalice and eyed the green pulpy sludge. "What is it?"

"I know you're not eating, and your body needs sustenance," she said. "This will help."

It smelled something foul, and tasted even fouler, but Cyrus forced it down. If he hadn't been feeling well before, he certainly wasn't feeling well now.

She wrinkled up her face. "I know it doesn't taste that good. It has an earthiness to it."

"An earthiness?" He balked. "Is that how you describe shit?"

She tried to cover her smile by pursing her lips. "It's not that bad."

"No, it's worse." But enough play. "I need to get back to Teron."

She nodded. "I'll get the wine mixed and off to Everan to distribute, then I'll come by. I need to give Teron some more medicine for his fever."

He was glad Essandra didn't walk with him. Twice he needed to stop and just hold on to the wall until his lightheadedness passed enough for him to keep going.

When he reached Teron's chamber, he groaned in relief. He would pull up the chair beside Teron's bed and maybe just rest for a little while. Just until Essandra came by.

But as he stepped into the room, a gurgle caught his ear. Cyrus bolted to the bed to find Teron twitching and struggling for breath.

"Teron!" He quickly slipped an arm underneath the old man, pulling him up and leaning him forward, and hit his back with an open palm.

Teron's body shook as he coughed, and it wasn't just a little blood that tinged his lips this time. A thick rush spilled down his chin.

"Fuck, fuck, fuck," Cyrus said, panicked. He clambered onto the bed behind Teron, wrapping an arm around his front for a better hold, and struck his back a few more times. Teron heaved again, spilling more blood down his chin and chest and over Cyrus's arm.

Finally, the old man sucked in a breath. His body relaxed, and his tremble faded.

Cyrus didn't dare lay him back down. He gave himself a moment to let his own panic ebb. If he had come in a few moments later...

He wasn't leaving Teron again.

The door to the chamber opened. Essandra stepped in. "All right, I brought some more—"

She stopped abruptly when she saw Cyrus, and her eyes widened. Then she scrambled to him, shoving her jars onto the side table as she ran to the bed.

"What happened?" She gaped at the blood covering Teron's front.

"I don't know," he said. "I think blood's building in his lungs. He's getting worse."

"Keep him upright," she said. "Let me get him a new tunic." She shuffled into the side bath chamber and came back out with a clean linen top. Cyrus held Teron as she navigated the removal of the soiled top and redressed him. Then she brought a wet cloth and cleaned the old healer's face. When she was finished, she put her hand against his forehead.

"He's still burning up," she said.

Cyrus hadn't even noticed, but Teron did still feel like a fire.

Suddenly, a flood of chaos filled his mind, and he realized—the blood wine was being distributed. The blood bonds pulled at him all at once. He closed his eyes and tried to settle himself.

But one bond in particular thrummed in his mind. One of purpose. A stronger pull—a direct touch, not from the blood wine.

Bash.

Cyrus took a moment and closed his eyes, letting himself find his friend who was across the sea in Pryam.

"Cyrus! I've been trying to reach you all day."

That surprised him. He'd been so caught up in everything he hadn't even felt it. *"I'm sorry. There's a lot going on here."*

"Same here," Bash said. *"Cyrus, Pryam's wrecked with fever. It might be headed your way. You have to close the ports."*

Cyrus's heart stopped. He dropped his head against Teron and just tried to breathe.

"Cyrus?" Bash called.

"It's already here," he answered finally. He straightened. *"I'm going to send you some blood wine. Essandra's warded me against the fever, and we think it will help keep others safe as well. It will be on a ship today. Have everyone take it: Miriel and Brant and—"*

"Cyrus." Bash gave a heavy pause. *"Miriel's sick."*

Cyrus's breath caught. *"How sick?"*

"Bad."

His heart seized, and his chest tightened. Miriel was sick. *Miriel was sick.*

"Cyrus?"

His attention snapped back. *"You have to sit with her, hold her up."* Even in his mind, Cyrus could hear his own voice shaking.

"I am. I'm doing that now."

Fuck the gods.

"I'm scared, Cyrus," Bash said.

Cyrus was scared too. *"Don't be. Keep holding her. Help her breathe. I'm still sending you the blood wine. Have everyone take it, do you hear me?"*

"*Yeah.*"

"*Keep holding her,*" he said again. "*Talk to me again tonight, all right?*"

"*All right,*" Bash said quietly.

Cyrus opened his eyes back to Teron's chamber, where Essandra sat on the edge of the bed, staring at him.

"The fever's hit Pryam," he told her.

"Oh gods," she breathed.

"Miriel's sick."

She covered her mouth, and her eyes welled.

"Bash is with her."

She nodded.

"I need you to take some more blood," he told her. "Don't cut it with wine—ward it and send it straight."

"Cyrus, you can't give any more blood. Not yet. And if the fever's already hit there—"

"Take it," he demanded. "I want it on a ship within the hour." He held an open palm for her.

Reluctantly, Essandra drew another small bowl of blood, not as much as the previous ones, but enough to give to as many men as they could. Then she left to coordinate sending it.

Cyrus stayed sitting with Teron. He lost count of how many times he had to lean forward to help the old man purge the blood from his lungs. Each time, Teron grew weaker and weaker, struggling more and more to breathe. Cyrus held him tightly.

"Stay with me," he told him.

The chaos in his mind was nearly overwhelming now. And the more people who drank the blood wine, the more intense it became.

Teron's breathing grew more and more labored. A few times after he exhaled, he didn't draw in another breath. Cyrus leaned him forward and hit him on the back.

"Breathe, old man," he told him.

Blood already covered the front of his new linen tunic, and Cyrus's arms, and the bed. Cyrus ignored it. He knew he just had to keep him upright. He just had to keep sitting.

He could do that.

But his head hurt.

It throbbed with chaos.

He was getting better at shutting people out, but it took effort, and he was already physically and mentally exhausted. He just needed to stay awake and keep Teron upright.

Cyrus let his head fall back slightly.

He was so tired.

He just needed to keep Teron up.

He tried to keep his eyes open, but the chaos of his blood and his mind blended together, erasing the boundaries of reality and dream. His vision blurred as his eyes grew heavier, until even Teron's breathing seemed like a distant tide.

Chapter Twenty-Four

The silk sheets were soft against his skin. Cyrus stirred, letting himself enjoy the comfort before he had to...

Before he had to—

He pushed himself up on his elbows.

"Don't get up." Essandra stood from where she'd been sitting in a chair and stepped to the bed.

His bed.

In his chamber.

And it all came back to him.

He bolted upright. "Where's Teron?"

Her face was grave.

His stomach dropped, but she quickly said, "He's doing all right. His fever broke, and he's breathing easier. He's still resting, like you should be."

Cyrus could let himself breathe. *Teron was all right.* He glanced around. "How did I get back here?"

"Orion brought you. You walked, kind of, but you were quite out of it, so it doesn't surprise me you don't remember. You still need more rest, though. Everan and Kord and Visa are all resting too."

His pulse quickened. *Resting?* Why would they be resting? "What's wrong with them? What happened?"

"They're going to be fine." She kneaded her hands. "But they're suffering the effects of the tether."

He shook his head. "What effects? What does that mean?"

"It's a physical bond, Cyrus. What your body suffers, their bodies suffer."

He stilled and looked down at his linen-wrapped arms. His chest tightened as his stomach turned. "They felt it?" he asked. "I cut them?"

"They're going to be fine," she assured him.

"What about Visa?" The pulse of his heartbeat in his ears almost deafened him. *He'd hurt Visa...*

"She's going to be all right too, but Cyrus..." She paused. "I had to break her tether."

"Why? Why would you do that?"

She shook her head. "I wasn't sure if she'd make it. I broke it to keep her from killing you."

He didn't understand.

"Under the tether, if she died, you'd die," she explained. "And with all the blood loss, she was really close." Her lip trembled, and her voice pitched higher. "It's my fault. I should have known, I should have done the tether *after* taking your blood, but I... I was working too quickly. I wasn't thinking."

He pushed himself up and tried to rise from the bed. "I have to see them."

"No." She put her hand on his chest to stop him. "You need to rest."

He paused at her touch. She'd touched him yesterday as they'd worked, but it'd been in the flurry of things, and neither of them had been thinking. But now that they were alone…

Her eyes dropped to her hand, and she pulled it away. She obviously hadn't intended it to mean anything. He understood.

But he couldn't rest. He couldn't just lie here. He needed to get out of this room.

"I have to see them," he insisted. He stood, and a wave of lightheadedness hit him. He grabbed the edge of the bed to steady himself.

"Wait," she said.

"I can't."

"There's something else you need to know."

He paused. Could it get worse?

"The Serran princes." She paused. "They didn't make it."

The boys? *No.* "Both of them?"

She nodded. "It's taking children quickly."

Cyrus sank back down onto the edge of the bed. He wasn't sure why the loss hit him the way that it did. He shouldn't care at all. In fact, he should have killed the boys in Serra. He'd needed to eliminate the bloodline. It was his duty, his responsibility. But he'd told them they'd be safe here. Martine's whispered words still lingered. *Do you promise?*

He'd promised.

The gods had claimed them regardless.

A pain pierced his chest.

He'd fucking promised.

He couldn't think about this right now—it was too much. He tried to push it from his mind.

"I need to see Everan," he said, standing again.

"At least change the wraps on your arms before you go," she said.

"Later."

He left his chamber and hurried to the suite that Everan shared with Visa. His heart beat heavily in his throat as he knocked on the door.

Everan opened it.

Cyrus's gaze dropped to his friend's wrapped arms. Blood had seeped through, staining the linen crimson, like his own. His breath shook. "Visa?" he asked.

"She's sleeping." Everan opened the door wider, inviting him in.

Cyrus had always liked Everan and Visa's chamber. She'd adorned it with brightly colored tapestries that she'd woven herself, with patterns of flowers and animals and birds—all from her life as a child before she'd been stolen away. It was rich with a history not his own, but to Cyrus it still felt like home. Above their bed hung a tapestry of two trees, woven around each other. It represented their love, she'd explained to him after she'd woven it.

Now, to see her lying under it pained Cyrus all the more. Her arms, also wrapped and stained, lay crossed over her stomach.

"She'll be happy to know you came by," Everan said quietly.

And Cyrus couldn't hold himself any longer. He drew in a ragged breath as he sank to his knees in front of Everan. "I'm so sorry."

Everan grabbed him, pulling him up. "Get up. Get up!"

"I'm sorry," Cyrus said again. It was the only thing he could say. "Forgive me."

"You didn't know."

"Forgive me."

"There's nothing to forgive. You didn't know." Everan held him tightly. "She's going to be fine. And when Teron's recovered, he'll make it like it never happened."

But it *had* happened. A wave of emotion hit him, and suddenly, he couldn't breathe. He couldn't speak.

"Cyrus?" Everan said, gripping him tighter.

Cyrus shook his head. "I can't... I can't do it."

"You can't do what?"

He couldn't even get it out. "Everything... I can't do it."

"Sit down. Sit down." Everan pulled him to the bench at the foot of the bed, and they both sank down onto it. "Visa's going to be fine," he assured him.

It wasn't just Visa. It was everything. If the gods weren't wrecking it all, Cyrus was. *Everything.*

"Miriel's sick," he told Everan.

"I heard."

He couldn't swallow the knot in his throat. "And the Serran boys are dead."

Everan nodded gently. "I know."

Tears stung his eyes. "I promised them," he whispered. "I promised them they'd be safe here."

"This wasn't your doing."

"The gods are punishing me."

"You don't even believe in the fucking gods," Everan told him, clutching his arm. "So, fuck them."

"I've lost Essandra. I'm losing Kord."

"No, you're not. You're not. Essandra's helping you."

Cyrus shook his head. "But it's different between us now. I ruined everything."

"No, you didn't. It just... feels that way right now." Everan sighed. "And you're not losing Kord. He's upset, yes, but Kord is Kord. He'll come around. You should go talk to him. I bet he's thankful you didn't tether Leti now."

Everan was right. Now that Kord knew the effect of the tether—now that they all knew—he was probably relieved about Leti.

Cyrus nodded. He definitely needed his closest friends by his side, when everything was falling apart. "I'll go do that now."

"Good."

He looked at Everan. "Everan, I..." He wasn't sure exactly what to say. He wanted to tell him he was a good friend. A good brother. That he loved him and would do anything for him. That he needed him and couldn't imagine life without him. But for some reason, he could say none of these things, even though they were all true. "I..."

Everan clasped his shoulder. "I know. Go find Kord."

Cyrus left Everan's chamber with a little more spirit than he'd arrived with, but before he went to see Kord, he stopped by Teron's room.

He found the old healer sleeping peacefully, and Orion sitting in the chair beside the bed. The assassin stood abruptly as he entered.

"I didn't expect to see you here," Cyrus said in surprise.

Orion shrugged. "Essandra said if I left, she would... well... I just decided I should stay."

Cyrus nodded. "Wise." His gaze shifted to Teron, and he stepped to the bed. "How is he?"

"Sleeping like a babe. Occasionally snoring."

Cyrus snorted. "Thanks for looking after him."

"It's nothing. Hey, I, uh…" He bobbed his head from one side to the other. "Essandra said you'd wanted to do your tether-bond shit with me. I mean, I know you couldn't because you could only do a few, and I'm glad you couldn't because then I'd be looking like you right now."

Cyrus snorted again as he glanced down at his wrapped arms.

"But I just wanted to say that I appreciate you thinking about me," Orion continued. "I've really never had anyone do that before."

He gave a short nod. "Well, thanks for getting me back to my room earlier."

"Yeah, you're as heavy as a fucking horse, so I'll accept that."

Cyrus gave a small chuckle.

After checking on Teron, he set out to find Kord, which wasn't hard. He was in the field office, *not* resting like he should be.

Kord sat at the desk, working through a stack of parchments. His arms were wrapped like Everan's had been, and his cold gaze watched Cyrus as he stepped inside.

"I'm glad to see you're doing all right," Cyrus said, breaking the uneasy quiet.

"That's a relative term," Kord replied. "I'm not dead, so yes, I guess I'm all right." He was still angry with him.

Cyrus supposed he deserved that. "I just wanted to see how you were doing and tell you that I really am sorry."

Kord nodded, but it wasn't a nod of acceptance. "I *am* glad it was me instead of Leti. She's just a small thing—I'm not sure she would have survived."

He was probably right. That would have been worse.

"Will you forgive me?" Cyrus asked.

But Kord shook his head sadly. "No."

He wasn't sure why Kord's reply surprised him. He hadn't expected him to say yes, but perhaps *not yet*. However, a straight *no*...

Cyrus wet his cracked lips. "So where do we go from here?"

"We go back to work."

He wasn't sure what to say to that. Did this mean they just wouldn't talk about it again? Were they moving past it? Were they stuck here?

"We have over six thousand dead now," Kord told him, "and we don't have anywhere to put the bodies. I'm going to start piling them in the arena. We need to burn them."

Over six thousand dead.

"That's a lot of people dead."

Kord nodded somberly. "And it's just starting."

They couldn't clear the streets fast enough. They piled bodies in the arena and burned them to try to stop the spread of sickness, but they couldn't stop it.

Jaem still flitted between the Free Cities and the outer reaches of Mercia, soaking up information where he could find it. Miraculously, he managed to stay free of the fever himself, but he reported disastrous losses everywhere he went. The Free Cities, Mercia, Aleon, and beyond—no one seemed to have escaped the devastation of the fever.

And in Rael, death kept coming.

They worked to exhaustion. Every day. Every night. Over and over and over.

It became routine—Cyrus retiring to his chamber long after the sun had disappeared and sinking into the bathtub, where the water turned black with the ash of skin and bone.

All he could do was close his eyes and lie there. He was just so tired.

When would it end?

One light in the darkness—Miriel had recovered. No one who'd taken the blood wine had caught the fever. Cyrus wasn't sure how it was working, only that it was, but he simply didn't have enough blood to give. And his efforts felt so insignificant. What was saving a few hundred compared to the loss of thousands?

Tens of thousands.

The losses were catastrophic. By the time the fever had run its course, half of Rael was dead. Two months later, they were still finding bodies.

Cyrus stood in his study, leaning over his desk as he stared at the last letter that had come from Gregor. Japeth had been hit equally hard by the fever, although Gregor spoke of it with little concern. He was, instead, celebrating the devastation suffered by Aleon, as well as the complete loss of the island trading nation of Tarsus, which Aleon had overtaken earlier that year, effectively cutting the majority of Gregor's trade.

He seemed to be reveling as though this were a victory.

But Cyrus didn't care about Aleon or Tarsus. His eyes read over the sentence that had been only a mere mention—yet was the most important of all.

The Mercian queen had been overthrown.

If Cyrus found himself annoyed by Gregor before, it paled in comparison to what he felt now. Gregor offered no details—no indication of timing, no mention of whether she was alive or dead, no information about Mercia's alliance with the Shadowlands. *Nothing.*

The worthless piece of shit.

All the absolute fuckery that Gregor filled his letters with before, and now the one thing Cyrus was desperate to know more about...

Nothing.

He assumed the alliance was broken, which meant the Shadow King now stood alone. But Cyrus wasn't in a position to act. Anger rippled under his skin. He'd waited a long time for an opportunity, but now that opportunity was here and he couldn't take advantage of it. By the time he built his army up again, the Shadow King would likely have found another way to fortify himself.

He searched his mind for what he might be able to do now, but there was nothing.

A knock sounded at the door, and Orion and Kord stepped in.

"We have a problem," Orion said.

Cyrus closed his eyes and inhaled deeply through his nose. "What is it?"

"The farmers have brought their grievances to the throne room," Kord said.

Cyrus turned his head and stared at them. "Why are you both involved with farming grievances?" He looked at Orion. "Especially you."

"Because it's about the burn fields, and we're still burning," Orion said.

Cyrus sighed. They'd moved the burning of bodies to several fields outside the city. It had been too much to handle in the arena. Orion had led most of the work because Kord had been overwhelmed by the collapse of the army, and someone needed to do it. Orion had taken it over because he could, because Cyrus needed him to, and Cyrus was realizing just how often he did that.

"And Ruth is dead," Kord added.

Cyrus's shoulders slumped. He knew about his magistrate. She'd given her blood wine to her daughter, and before Cyrus had found out to be able to give her more, she'd caught the fever. She never recovered.

There weren't many grievances at the moment, probably because there weren't many people left to even have a grievance, or perhaps because death put things in perspective. The council had been temporarily managing them when they did arise.

"The council is divided," Kord told him. "The burning has lessened now, and we can move it back to the arena, but sowing the land that we burned half our people on so soon is disrespectful to the dead and their families."

"We need to start farming it again," Orion said.

"Eventually, but not yet," Kord argued. "Our population isn't anywhere close to what it was."

"But we still have refugees fleeing their kingdoms and arriving by the thousands," Orion countered. "We'll quickly be there again."

They both looked at Cyrus.

"Move the burning back to the arena," Cyrus told them. "Sow the land."

Orion gave a stiff bow and left the room.

Kord lingered.

Cyrus sighed. "I'm sorry you disagree."

"I don't care about the land, Cyrus. I was only voicing the opposing side of the council."

"Oh."

"But there's something else I wanted to tell you."

Cyrus waited.

"I'm going to wed Leti."

Cyrus gaped at him in surprise. He didn't know why he was surprised. This was what Kord had said he wanted—a life, a proper wife and family.

"I'm not asking for your permission," Kord said. "I'm telling you because I want you to be there as my friend. As my brother."

The fact that he would say that... Cyrus's chest grew tight with emotion. "Of course you don't need my permission," he said, "but if you did, I'd gladly give it. Congratulations, brother."

Kord's face softened. "Do you really mean that?"

"Yes. And of course I'll be there."

Kord glanced down at the floor, then back to Cyrus. "The wedding's in three weeks."

"I won't miss it."

A smile came to Kord's lips, and he nodded. Then he turned and left Cyrus to the quiet of his study again.

As the wedding drew closer, so, too, did the excitement around the palace. Cyrus found himself appreciating the fact that they had something to look forward to after everything that had happened. Visa in particular carried a broad smile on her face. After all the pain he'd caused her, Cyrus desperately wanted to see her well and happy, and this wedding seemed to do that. No doubt she felt she was gaining a sister. She was close with Essandra, but Everan had shared with Cyrus how she often felt alone. It would be good to have another woman around. Cyrus didn't know Leti well, but she seemed kind, although quiet. She let Visa drive much of the wedding planning, which Visa loved, as she'd never gotten to have a lavish wedding of her own. Everyone seemed happy, and that made Cyrus happy.

The day of the wedding, he stood in his chamber in front of the corner mirror. He pulled at the collar of the heavily embroidered shirt that Visa had selected for him. He didn't like things around his neck, but he supposed he could bear it for a short while. He unfastened the top button. That was a little better.

"There you are!" Visa said from behind him, and he glanced up in the mirror to see her step inside.

"Why do you say it like that?" he asked. "You told me to get ready in my chamber—I'm getting ready in my chamber."

"Well, you're never where you're supposed to be, so I was worried."

She spun him to face her, looking him over with a critical eye, then reached up and buttoned the top button on his shirt. He left it this time. She straightened the folds of his collar behind his neck and smoothed over the lines of his vest. Then she pulled his jacket from where it hung—a jacket that had no business being worn in Rael. She held it for him, and he let her slip it on.

"This is good," she said with a nod of approval after. "You look good."

Good. *Good.*

"Is Essandra going to be there?" he asked.

Her lips hinted at a smile. "Of course she is."

"Right." That was stupid. Why wouldn't she be? But he couldn't help himself. "Will we be seated near each other?"

Visa paused, and she lifted a brow. "Why do you ask?"

"I'm just curious."

"Mmm." Her eyes narrowed. "I might have put you beside each other."

Cyrus couldn't help a smile back. "Are you sure I look good?"

Her smile widened more. "Yes. You do." She patted the fold of his jacket along his chest. "All right," she said. "I told Leti I would help her finish getting ready. I'll see you down in the hall. *Don't be late.*"

"I won't," he promised.

She smiled again and left the room.

Cyrus looked back at his reflection in the mirror. It was amusing that this was probably the first time he actually looked like a king, and it wasn't even for any of his kingly duties. It was for Kord. For his brother, he was happy to do it.

He drew a deep breath and turned to head toward the great hall. He'd be slightly early. If he were honest with himself, he was a little excited. And it was nice to be excited about something.

But as he reached for the door, a pain rippled through him, stopping him in his step.

It was like nothing he'd ever felt before.

All the battles.

All the injuries.

This was different.

The next wave of pain dropped him to his knees. He clawed at his chest, but it wasn't in his chest; it was deeper. It wasn't a pain of the body but a pain of the soul—a ripping, splitting, breaking of his being.

It was tearing him apart.

A third wave came, and a cry escaped his lips just before he fell into darkness.

Chapter Twenty-Five

"Cyrus!"

Something was wrong. He knew it before his senses had even returned. He knew it before he could see. Before he even remembered where he was. Before he could understand who was calling his name.

"Cyrus!"

It was Essandra. However, he couldn't place her.

He blinked to clear his vision, but he still couldn't see.

Something was wrong.

So very wrong.

"Cyrus, what happened! What happened?"

He didn't know.

All he knew—

He was gone.

Cyrus clawed at his chest. He was gone.

He was gone.

A sob ripped from his lips. "He's gone..."

"Who's gone?"

He tore at his clothes. He couldn't breathe; he couldn't speak. "Get it off," he begged. He couldn't breathe.

Her fingers flew over him, furiously unfastening the buttons of his clothing. She stripped his shirt off, freeing him, but still, he couldn't breathe.

"Cyrus, look at me!"

He couldn't see. He clawed at his chest again.

"It's off! It's off!" she promised. "Cyrus, look at me!" Her hands grabbed him and pulled him still as her shadow hovered over him. "Cyrus!"

He made out the blur of her face through his tears.

"He's gone." They were the only words he could get out.

She held him tightly. "Who's gone?"

His breaths came fast and shallow, denying him the full fill of his lungs, denying him words.

And all the voices in his head—so many voices.

He tried to push them out, but he couldn't.

Essandra gripped him tighter. "Cyrus! Who's gone?"

He paused, shaking. "Alexander."

Cyrus sat cross-legged on the floor of his chamber, numb. Most of the clothes he'd donned for Kord's wedding lay strewn around him. His jacket was ripped.

He was wearing a tunic now. Essandra must have put it on him. She'd tried to get him to move to the bed, but he couldn't. He couldn't stand, he couldn't walk, he couldn't move at all. He could only sit. And stare into the void that surrounded him. The void that emptied him.

Alexander was gone.

Cyrus sat alone. Essandra had left to make sure the wedding continued, but she'd promised to return. He wasn't sure how long she'd been gone.

Was the wedding over now?

Had it even started?

He should go. He needed to be there for Kord.

But he couldn't bring himself to move.

Alexander was gone.

And he felt nothing and everything all at once.

Memories flashed around him—memories long forgotten. He tried to push them away. He didn't want to remember.

But he couldn't not look. He couldn't not return.

Cyrus clawed at his head. A sob shook him as he struggled against it.

He couldn't go back.

He couldn't go back...

He stared at his reflection in the metal. It shone like a mirror—polished as best as he could get it—and he smiled. He moved on to the next piece.

"Do you need another rag?" Alexander asked him.

"No." He flipped the rag he had over to use the other side. The linen had pilled, and the edges were frayed, but this made the best rag for polishing.

He set to work on the left vambrace. These were his favorite pieces, aside from the pauldron. He glanced up at the crown head of the great northern bear that hung on the wall. Their father wore it on his shoulder. They weren't allowed to touch that.

He focused his attention back on the piece in his lap. Alexander liked the breastplate, but it was the vambraces that came back with the stories.

A dark mark streaked the steel—evidence of a blow.

"Look at this one," he called to Alexander.

"Whoa!" Alexander reached out and ran his fingers along the strike. "What do you think it was? A sword?"

He shook his head. "An axe, I bet. A big one."

They polished their father's armor every evening, but their favorite was polishing it after battle. They'd marvel at the marks and dents.

"Boys." Their father leaned into the room. "Your mother has dinner ready. Wash up."

"How does it look?" Alexander asked him, standing and holding out a greave.

Their father looked at the armor piece, then smiled back at Alexander. "Good work. It's important you keep it up for when it's your own."

"Mine?" A smile lit across Alexander's face.

Their father ruffled Alexander's hair, then stepped out of the room.

Alexander turned, but when their eyes met, his smile fell. "He didn't mean me specifically," he said quickly.

But their father had said it to Alexander specifically.

"You're the eldest, Lucien. It'll be your armor." Alexander wrinkled his face. "Plus, I don't even want it. I want my own, with a reinam on the breastplate."

A reinam—a mythical sea serpent of the deep. "Reinams aren't real."

"Yes they are!" Alexander argued.

"Then how come no one's ever seen one?"

"They have; they just haven't lived to tell about it."

"Boys!" their father called again.

Alexander pulled him up and shoved him through the doorway toward the dining room.

Cyrus wiped his tear-stricken face.

He'd needed Alexander dead for so long, but now... he wasn't ready.

He wasn't ready to lose him.

He *couldn't* lose him.

Chaos still swarmed his mind—the pull of everyone that Alexander's blood had touched. Were they near him? Did they see him? Were they touching him?

He had to know.

Cyrus sucked in a ragged breath as he collapsed back and let himself follow the pull of his brother's blood.

There were fewer now—fewer voices, fewer trails—and a lot of fragments but with little clarity. Perhaps the blood had been wiped off, washed off. Cyrus followed what he could, reaching out, searching. There had been so many before, but now there were so little. His desperation grew, and he pushed further with his mind.

There had to be something.

He jumped from pull to pull, from mind to mind, not caring who it was, not caring if they felt him. It didn't matter.

Nothing mattered.

Only finding Alexander.

And then he did.

Alexander lay on a stone-slab table, his skin ashen, his lips tinged blue. Cyrus wasn't sure whose mind he was in, perhaps the keepers that tended the body, but he didn't care. He couldn't take his eyes from his brother.

It was the first time he'd seen his brother in their adult lives.

And he was dead.

His eyes stung, and he blinked back the blur.

Alexander was dead.

The loss in his chest was near unbearable. He needed him back. He needed—

Cyrus stopped.

His eyes traveled over Alexander's armor.

Their father's armor.

Alexander wore their father's armor.

The head of the Northern bear had been placed on the floor at the base of the table.

Alexander had worn the bear-head pauldron.

Cyrus trembled as the heat of anger licked his skin.

"*Alexander?*" a voice called, startling him.

He jerked up his gaze to a woman looking back at him.

And not just any woman.

The Mercian queen.

She was alive. And here. It was her mind he was in.

Cyrus took a step back toward the shadows. He'd been careless in his pursuit of Alexander, not bothering to mask his travel. And now they stood staring at each other. Blood stained her hands and her front—Alexander's blood, the blood that allowed him to travel the same as his own.

"*Is it really you?*" she whispered.

She thought he was Alexander.

She couldn't know.

He shouldn't be here.

He took another step back.

"*Wait!*" she cried. "*Don't go! Please.*"

He paused. He didn't want to go, not yet, but he couldn't be here. She couldn't know.

In her mind, she staggered up from her chair and drew around the table, closer to him.

"*How is this possible?*" she breathed. "*How are you here?*"

He had to go.

"*Do you not know me?*" she whispered.

Oh, he knew her…

She stepped closer, close enough to touch him now.

He had to go, but he still couldn't bring himself to. She brought her hand up, reaching for his face, and he pulled back.

"*It's me,*" she said through her tears. "*It's me, Norah.*"

He could feel the grief coming off her. He hadn't noticed it before, blinded by his own, but there was no missing it now. It pervaded every corner of her mind.

This woman grieved his brother.

Deeply.

Her eyes dropped to his neck, and her brow dipped.

Cyrus cursed himself. He knew exactly what she was looking at. He hadn't taken care to conceal himself at all, much less project something different, and she'd noticed his markings—markings Alexander didn't have. He should have left sooner. He pulled back into the shadows.

"*Wait!*" she called. "*Alexander!*"

But he couldn't wait. He wasn't Alexander.

Cyrus opened his eyes back in his chamber, panting heavily with a cold sweat across his brow. Darkness hung around him, driven back only by candlelight. It was night. How long—

"Cyrus!"

He startled as Essandra dropped down beside him and grabbed his arm

"It's me," she said quickly.

He waited a moment for his heart to slow. "How-how long have you been here?"

"A while." Her eyes darted over him. "I was afraid to pull you out from wherever you were. I wasn't sure what to do."

To be fair, *he* wasn't sure what to do.

"Where did you go?" she asked. "Where were you?"

It took a moment for him to be able to speak the words. Did speaking them make it real?

"He's dead," he whispered. He couldn't say it without shaking. "I saw him."

She crept closer. "Are you all right?"

He wasn't all right. Why did it hurt so much?

"Will you come off the floor?" she whispered.

Slowly, he let her pull him up. His body was stiff from not having moved all day.

"You also need to eat," she told him.

He wasn't hungry.

She moved to the side table and poured a glass of water, then pushed it into his hands. "Drink this."

He wasn't thirsty.

"I'm going to go get you some food and I'll be back."

He didn't want food.

"I'll be back, okay?" she repeated.

He nodded again.

She nodded back, giving him a small squeeze on his arm, and slipped out of the room.

Cyrus set the glass of water on the table. His mind was still in chaos. What had just happened? None of it felt possible, none of it felt real, yet all of it felt too real. He dropped his head to his hands, digging the tips of his fingers into his temples.

What was he to do now?

He had to pull himself together.

Cyrus forced himself calm. He needed to think and think clearly. He inhaled deeply, then let it out slowly.

The Mercian queen was still alive. Had she taken back the North? Was that how Alexander had died?

The emotion was too overwhelming. He had to think rationally about this. What was happening?

The queen had been in the Mercian castle.

His breath hitched.

Was the Shadow King with her?

His pulse quickened again—maybe he could find out.

He had a rare opportunity here.

Cyrus needed to go back. He needed to go back to her before she washed off the blood, before he lost this chance. She thought he was Alexander, a ruse he probably couldn't hold for long, but he might be able to hold it long enough to see what had happened and assess the current situation.

He could still feel her. He needed to pull himself together and go back *now*.

A knock sounded on his chamber door.

He paused.

Would Essandra really knock? No. She wouldn't. She'd just told him she'd be right back.

It came again, harder this time. It most certainly wasn't Essandra.

Cyrus moved to the door and opened it to find Kord. His chest tightened as guilt flooded him. The wedding...

"Kord—"

"Is this where you've been the whole time? In your chamber?"

"Kord, I'm sorry. I wanted to come."

"Yeah, I'm sure you did."

Cyrus couldn't do this right now. He needed to return to the Mercian queen. If she washed off the blood, he'd lose his chance.

"I waited for you."

Cyrus shook his head. "Kord—"

"I made Leti wait."

As if the dagger weren't deep enough. "I'm sorry."

"Are you? Are you really?"

More than he put into words, but... "Kord, I can't do this right now."

Kord scoffed. Pain etched across his brow.

And Cyrus hated himself. He tried to explain. "My brother is dead."

"Yeah, that's what Essandra said, but I don't fucking buy it. Your brother's dead—the brother you've wanted to kill your whole life? And now you're in here, fucking devastated."

This wasn't going well. And it was about to get worse.

"Tell me, Cyrus—when will the people you love get as much of your devotion as the people you hate?"

Cyrus wanted to argue; he wanted to deny him. But could he really? Even as Kord spoke to him, Cyrus was reaching his mind back out to the queen. He could still feel her, still return to her, but for how much longer?

Kord cocked his head. "Are you even going to ask me how the wedding was?"

A failure at every turn. Cyrus cursed himself again. "Of course—"

"It was the most beautiful fucking wedding this kingdom's ever seen."

Cyrus tried to swallow the lump building in his throat. It broke him that he hadn't been there. Just like it broke him to say his next words. "Kord, I have to go," he whispered.

Kord snorted, then gave a nod. He glanced down at the floor and then back up. "Fuck you, Cyrus." Then he turned and headed back toward the main hall.

Cyrus slumped against the doorframe. What was wrong with him? Why was he like this? But even his self-loathing couldn't stop him.

Essandra would be headed back soon. If he let her in, he'd miss his chance.

He closed the door, his hand hovering over the lock.

Gods, how he hated himself.

Then he turned it. The click shamed him like a confession, but he focused his mind on the Mercian queen.

Chapter Twenty-Six

The queen was still in the Mercian mortium with Alexander's body. It was easier than he'd expected to travel back into her mind. She was exhausted and weakened by grief, almost to the point of delirium. Still, Cyrus moved cautiously, taking care to shroud himself this time. He used to always slip into others' minds undetected. He used to have no power of presence at all. That was before Essandra had bonded their power. Now, he had to work to conceal himself.

He flipped through the queen's memories like pages in a book, from one, to the next, and to the next. He saw nothing of her youth, which was odd. He had very few memories of his own childhood—no doubt he'd suppressed them. He hardly remembered the queen at all. But she had *nothing*. He wanted to dig deeper, but then he saw Alexander, and nothing else mattered.

The number of memories the queen had of his brother was nearly overwhelming. So crisp. So clear.

And it was surprising how much he and Alexander truly looked alike. It was like looking in a mirror. They'd been indistinguishable as children, but Cyrus had assumed that as they'd aged, and been crafted more by experience and time, that perhaps they'd look not so similar anymore.

But time had done little to differentiate them, if anything at all. Alexander didn't have the stave markings, and his hair was better kept. Those were the only differences. He even had the same small crease in his brow above his right eye.

It was interesting—everything Cyrus saw of Alexander in the queen's mind was only what she'd noticed, what she remembered of him. For this level of clarity, she'd have to know every line of his face, every quirk of his countenance.

Movement jarred his mind. The queen was leaving the mortium now. He silently cursed himself. He'd gotten caught up in Alexander again, and now he was running out of time. When she washed off the blood, he'd lose the connection.

Cyrus worked quickly, flicking through the memories. He found the one of the Mercian insurrection and watched as the queen was attacked in her own castle and forced to flee. He slowed in seeing the man protecting her—not the Shadow King but most certainly a Shadowman. It could only be the commander. This was a formidable man. When the time came, Cyrus would need to be wary of him.

Back in the castle now, the queen stepped toward the bath chamber, and Cyrus raced through more memories.

He needed more time.

There was just so much. Too much. He'd never get through it.

Then he saw what he was looking for.

The Shadow King.

Cyrus slowed and watched as the Shadow army marched back to the North and helped the queen win back her throne.

He saw them storm the bridge. He saw them take the capital isle. He watched as the army claimed their victory.

And then he saw Alexander.

The shock of his death should have passed by now, as Cyrus had already seen his brother's body. But this sight was in the moment—the Mercian queen wept over him as blood puddled underneath them on the floor of the castle's keep.

His body would have still been warm here, his life perhaps not yet entirely gone. Had he felt the pain of separation as Cyrus had? Had he felt them being torn apart?

The queen sank down onto the bed in her chamber, just letting herself lie for a moment, and Cyrus thought he might have a little more time, but as her fingers worked loose the ties down her dress, he feared his opportunity quickly slipping away.

He pressed through the memories urgently, passing letters he didn't have time to read, maps he didn't have time to assess.

Cyrus jerked still at another vision of the Shadow King.

He stood in the mortium next to Alexander's body.

He was still in Mercia.

The Shadow King was still in Mercia.

Which meant he'd eventually travel back to the Shadowlands.

Cyrus needed more time. He needed to know when he'd leave. He needed to know how many men he'd take with him. He needed to know the route.

He ran quickly through options.

Any moment, she'd rise from the bed and strip the blood-soaked dress off. Any moment, she'd wash the blood from her skin...

His heart beat heavily in his chest.

The queen had seen him before.

She thought he was Alexander.

And she was delirious with exhaustion.

Before he could stop himself, he pulled back the veil that he hid behind.

And he knew she felt him the moment he did.

She opened her eyes in her mind.

Cyrus crafted a bed of flowers around her, reminiscent of a dream. Perhaps it would be easier if she thought this was a dream.

Slowly, she sat up and rose from the bed.

Then she saw him.

She smiled.

The mind was funny like that—stripping away pain sometimes, making one forget. But even in this dream of her mind, he watched as the memories came to her—as reality came to her.

Alexander was dead.

He watched as her face went from happiness to confusion to realization to devastation, then back to confusion as she stared at him.

As she walked toward him in disbelief, he pulled everything he'd seen of Alexander, every piece, every detail—the style of his hair, even his father's armor. The armor had been the hardest part—to put it on himself, to wear it. He couldn't stomach the head of the North bear and had to leave it off.

He waited as she drew near, his heart beating heavily in his chest. As she stepped even closer, he wavered. She'd know. She'd know he wasn't Alexander, and for a moment he almost withdrew, until she whispered, "*Please.*" She was shaking. "*Please don't leave,*" she begged.

He froze, and he let her come even nearer, ignoring everything telling him that he shouldn't.

Her eyes took him in, and he focused on projecting every detail of Alexander.

"*Am I a stranger to you now?*" she asked.

She knew something was different about him, and again, he cursed himself. He shouldn't have let her see him the first time. He should have taken more care.

"*Say something*," she told him. "*How are you here?*"

He almost spoke but stopped. While he looked the same as Alexander, he was certain he didn't sound like Alexander. He didn't even know what Alexander sounded like—and now more than ever, he wished to be able to hear memories and visions. But he could hear only when someone spoke to him in their mind like this.

"*Say something*," she begged.

He wanted to. But he didn't dare. And he didn't even know what he would say.

She reached out, and he shifted backward, having only a split moment to decide whether to let her feel him, or, rather, to make her *think* she felt him. He'd honed the ability to manipulate some of the senses, to a degree. Sight was the easiest. Touch was the hardest.

And in that split moment, he knew he couldn't let her feel him. He couldn't let it go that far. But she was already breaking, already believing, and if this got him what he needed...

As she reached for him, he didn't move away.

She sucked in a breath, her eyes tearing, as her fingers brushed him. Her lip trembled. She pressed her hand against his chest, still testing, still not believing. Then she spread her fingers wide.

That was enough.

He caught her hand and brought it down. He wasn't here just to give her one last connection with Alexander. He needed information, and once she washed the blood from her skin, he'd lose her. He needed her to let him back into her mind. More than that, he needed her to *invite* him back into her mind, use his blood and make the connection. So desperately, she wanted to believe he was Alexander—he could see it all over her face, feel it emanating from her.

He wasn't sure how he'd get her the blood—he'd figure that out later. First, he just needed to show her what to do to call him. He pulled a vial of blood from his pocket and opened her hand. Then he smeared a streak across her palm and closed her hand in his.

The skin between her brows dimpled.

It was frustrating to be in her mind but not know what she was actually thinking. Did she understand? She stared down at her hand in his, then looked back up at him. Cyrus reached up and brushed her eyes with his fingertips, bidding them closed.

She did.

His heart raced. If he could get her a vial, she might just call him.

Cyrus stared at the plate of untouched food in front of him. He wasn't hungry. He couldn't think about food at all as he waited for the pull from the Mercian queen.

If it would even come.

It had taken him a number of tries with the birds, each time leaving him with a crippling ache in his head. Simply looking through the animals' eyes and controlling them enough to carry a vial of blood were two very different things. He'd barely mastered the former and quickly found the latter a near impossible feat. If they made it over the Aged Sea, he'd lose them somewhere over the Tribelands. The few that did make it to the North were taken down by winterhawks.

Again, he tried. And again.

And then one bird *did* make it.

He'd lost connection shortly after it had plucked the string loose and left the small box with the vial on the queen's terrace. He wished he could have kept it to watch, but it was all right. The bird had done what it had needed to do.

And now he waited.

A day passed, then another.

Cyrus started to wonder if he'd left it on the right terrace.

No, it was the right one, he assured himself.

"Have you heard anything?" Essandra asked.

Her question snapped him from his thoughts. Her green eyes stared back at him.

How did she know? He hadn't told anyone about trying to get blood to the Mercian queen. He glanced around the dining table. Everan's brow quirked.

"Have you heard anything?" she asked again. "Anything more about your brother? Or about the North?"

Oh. His racing heart slowed. Cyrus shook his head. "No," he said, although that wasn't exactly true. Jaem had reported mass mourning for the fallen Mercian justice well beyond the Mercian outer reaches. Areas Alexander didn't even serve, Cyrus thought bitterly. Was anyone *not* mourning his brother?

He picked up his chalice but didn't take a drink. His mind wandered back to the queen.

When would she find the blood? Maybe she rarely went out on her terrace. She probably hadn't seen the vial yet. Or maybe she'd seen it and was trying to rationalize the physical reality with what she'd thought had been a dream.

He set the chalice back down.

She'd been so exhausted, maybe it had been more like a dream to her than he'd intended. Maybe she'd forgotten about it, only to then find a vial of blood on her terrace that she didn't recognize or understand.

His eyes drifted back to Essandra. She ate quietly.

Then the realization struck him. "You won't be able to use him to bring your sister back now. You won't be able to use Alexander."

Her eyes met his, and she swallowed.

"I'm sorry," he said.

She shook her head quickly. "No. Don't be sorry for me. This is a heavy blow to you. I don't want you to be sorry for me on top of it all."

"You needed him."

She drew in a deep breath and let it out slowly. "Who knows if it would have even worked."

"What are you going to do now?" he asked.

"I'll keep working on alternatives. The same as I have been."

"Dark magic."

She stiffened.

"I'm just asking," he added.

"I'll do whatever I need to."

Another day passed. The Mercian queen still hadn't touched the blood. Cyrus contemplated sending more birds to see if the vial was still on her terrace. But it would be a lot of energy with a strong likelihood of failure, and for what? What would he do if it was? What would he do if it wasn't?

Cyrus paced his chamber, feeling like a fool. For him to have thought that this had even the slightest possibility of working—he was such an idiot. He was glad he hadn't told anyone.

A knock sounded on his door. He crossed the room to open it and found Essandra waiting.

"I just came to check on you," she said.

"I'm a little late for dinner, I know. I'll come now."

"Late? Cyrus, you missed it entirely. Again."

"Again?" He shook his head. "I was there last night—"

"That was the day before."

No. Two days couldn't have passed. Could they?

Her eyes stared back at him.

"Are you worried for me?" he jested.

"I am," she said, not jesting.

He sobered. "I'm fine."

"You look awful."

Yes, he probably did. "Do you want to come in?" he asked her, opening the door wider.

She shook her head. "I can't."

Right. He wasn't even sure why he'd asked her. Not that he was inviting her for anything more than his company. But she didn't want his company. She was so careful around him now. So guarded.

The words came out before he could stop them. "I feel like you hate me now."

Her lips parted, and her gemmed eyes swept back and forth between his. "I don't hate you," she said softly.

"Well maybe not hate. Maybe dislike. I've messed things up, I know. But I don't want to be just another man for you to tolerate."

"Cyrus..." she whispered.

"I'm sorry," he told her. He was sorry for everything. For leaving her. For betraying her trust. For disappointing her. For not being able to give her what she needed. For forcing his decisions. It wasn't his desire to control her. He only wanted to keep her safe, to protect her, even if she didn't need it, even if she didn't want it. He couldn't not. He couldn't—

His heart stopped as he felt the pull—the pull that came when his blood touched a person's skin.

And not just any person.

The Mercian queen.

She'd found the blood. And had *used* it.

Essandra leaned closer. "Cyrus, I..." She glanced down at the ground.

She was sorry too? No—what would she be sorry for? He desperately wanted to know her next words, the words that sat on the tip of her tongue but wouldn't come.

And then he didn't.

He knew why she hesitated—because they were hard words to say. He'd ruined it. He'd ruined anything between them. And he didn't want to make her say it. He couldn't bear hearing it.

The blood still pulled at him. The Mercian queen. He could feel her. Despite the fact that he was about to be crushed by whatever Essandra had to say, he didn't want to leave. But the queen would wait only for so long. If nothing happened, she'd wipe away the blood and he'd lose the opportunity.

He couldn't let that happen. He wouldn't get the opportunity again. And he already knew Essandra's words would devastate him. He didn't need to make her say them.

Her eyes rose to meet his again, eyes that haunted him.

"I'm sorry," he whispered. He was sorry for all the things from before, but now even more—"I have to go."

"Oh," she breathed. "Okay."

And he closed the door between them.

Cyrus sank back against the wall beside the door and threw his mind toward the queen. His chest hurt from the conversation with Essandra, and the pit in his stomach threatened to swallow him from the inside, but he tried to cast that aside. If he let himself think about Essandra, he wouldn't be able to focus on the queen.

And he needed to focus on the queen.

He found her sitting at her vanity in her chamber and staring at the blood smeared across her hand.

She'd remembered how to use it...

But he couldn't come to her in person. She needed to meet him in the depths of her mind. Now to get her to do that...

As she glanced up from the vanity and into the mirror, he added himself to the reflection she saw, just behind her. It startled her, and she jumped up, overturning the chair.

She whirled to face him, but he wasn't behind her, not really. As she turned back to the mirror, shaking, her eyes met his in the reflection again. "*How is this possible?*" she whispered. She glanced behind her again, then back to the mirror. "*How are you here?*" Her breaths came quick and shallow. "*Is it really you?*"

If only she knew...

"*Does the blood bring you?*" she asked.

Did she really need him to answer that?

"*How? I didn't consume it; I only...*" She looked down at her palm again. "*Is this how you came to me in the mortium? Your blood on my skin?*"

Consume it? So, she did have experience with seers, although he was positive none of those experiences had been with someone quite like him.

"*I wasn't really dreaming then,*" she said, more to herself than to him. "*And I'm not dreaming now. Are you in my mind?*"

How else would he be here? Maybe she *didn't* have experience with seers.

Cyrus closed his eyes in the reflection, prompting her to do the same, and she did.

Finally, they stood in the depths of her mind, facing each other.

"*How are you here?*" she asked him, and she took a step closer. "*Is it really you?*"

His pulse quickened as she stared at him with her eyes wide and mouth open. Now was the test of whether he could really pass for

Alexander. He wore a light linen tunic and dark brown leathers, with even darker riding boots that stretched to his knee. This was the attire he'd seen Alexander wear, and Cyrus copied it exactly from the images in her mind.

"*Can you not speak?*" she asked.

He didn't dare. It was the one thing certain to give him away.

She reached out a hand toward him, and he fought every urge to pull away. He let her touch him, pooled his power to let her *think* she was touching him. Cyrus didn't understand this part of his ability, nor did he try very hard to. It didn't matter—the why or the how—only that he knew it worked this way.

Her breaths came broken and raw. "*How is this possible?*" Her hand spread wide across his chest, then clenched his tunic in a fist.

And suddenly, for a moment, he couldn't move. The way she looked at him. The way she touched him. The way she *grieved* him.

No. Not *him*. Alexander.

No one would grieve Cyrus this way. He'd never been on the receiving end of love so freely given, love so freely shown.

"*Is this what happens when you leave life?*" she whispered.

So, she did recognize a difference from the Alexander she knew. Her mind was frayed at the edges. Exhaustion still pervaded her, and he was thankful for it. If she were thinking clearly, she'd notice more differences. She'd know he wasn't Alexander. However, even in her state, she might figure it out.

He didn't want her to focus on him too intently, and he quickly pulled forward the vision of a tree-lined path, as he had the last time she'd seen him. He motioned toward it, and, slowly, she started forward.

"*Please, talk to me,*" she said as they walked.

He wished he could. He'd be able to ask her things directly, get more information, put their limited time together to better use. But he couldn't risk her discovering him.

"*I miss you, Alexander.*" She stopped, swaying, and clutched her chest. "*It hurts,*" she whispered.

Her eyes teared, and her breaths were short and clipped. He wasn't exactly sure what he should do, so he only stood.

"*I need you,*" she told him.

With Alexander as her lord justice, she would have depended on him.

She would have also trusted him...

Would she trust him still?

Cyrus reached out and took her hand. His heart raced in his chest. She stared at their hands a moment, her fingers clasped in his, then she lifted her eyes to him. A tear trailed down her cheek. "*I feel so lost,*" she said. "*And scared.*"

His heart beat faster, but he forced himself calm. He needed to keep her talking.

"*Mikael went back to Kharav. And, of course, he's made Soren stay with me. He's all alone.*"

Every muscle in Cyrus's body froze.

"*I'm worried for him,*" she continued. "*If Japheth and Rael attack before he makes it through the Canyonlands, it could be disastrous. He'll try to make it through the western pass. If he does, he'll be safe. But until then...*"

Cyrus's heart leapt to his throat. The Shadow King was traveling now. *Right now.* And *Soren.* He'd heard that name before—the name of his commander. He was here with the queen. The Shadow King was alone and vulnerable.

But only for a short time.

Cyrus had to go. He had to go *now*. The largest part of his army was in Japheth, ready to march. If he sailed from Rael without delay, he could reach Japheth and drive his army south in time to intercept the Shadow King.

The queen asked him something else, but he didn't hear it.

He had to go.

She caught his arm, snapping his attention back to her. "*Alexander.*"

He stiffened and leaned back, pulling away, and let the vision of the tree-lined path go.

"*Alexander,*" she said softly. "*I don't understand. Have you only returned to take silent walks with me? Why have you come?*"

A small pang of guilt stabbed at him for leaving her like this, but he wasn't sure why. She meant nothing to him. He stepped back into the shadows.

"*Are you leaving?*"

He had what he'd come for.

"*Wait!*" she called. She said something else, but he didn't hear it as he pulled himself from her mind.

As he opened his eyes to his own chamber again, his heart raced. This was it. Fire swelled within him. This was the opportunity he'd been waiting for.

It unsettled him to use the queen this way, to use her grief. But there was no room for guilt now, no time for regret. This was war. And fate had given him a blade.

CHAPTER TWENTY-SEVEN

Full sails blocked out the sky. Cyrus's ship carved the sea in half, sending sprays high along the bow.

Everan stood beside him. They didn't speak. The force of sea winds made talking near impossible anyway. When Cyrus had told him about the opportunity to intercept the Shadow King, Everan had asked how he knew.

"I just do," Cyrus had said, which Everan had accepted without pressing him further.

Kord didn't. But he'd still come.

So had Essandra.

Things were still strained between them. She'd pressed him about how he knew too, but he hadn't told her about the Mercian queen, which made things even more strained. He couldn't tell her. He couldn't tell anyone.

They would try to convince him it was madness to pursue the queen under the guise of Alexander. And perhaps it was. But it would take madness to get the Shadow King.

By the second day at sea, Cyrus's patience for travel was gone. He'd need to move his forces quickly once he made it to Japheth, but moving an army in excess of seventy thousand men would be anything but quick. He paced his cabin as his impatience grew. He wasn't sure if he'd need all his forces. He didn't know exactly how many men the Shadow King had—just that it was fewer than what Cyrus had. And he wasn't even sure what his plan was yet. He was just coming with everything he could. He'd had a larger army, but the fever had taken nearly half. However, he praised his obsessive past self for continuing to send Gregor men and building his strength on the mainland. He also had several legions from Serra.

Cyrus wondered how many of Japheth's forces Gregor would give him. He was prepared for it not to be many. Gregor's focus was on his brother, and he would hold forces for that opportunity. Cyrus expected he'd get maybe thirty thousand, if he was lucky. And he was fine with that. The Shadow King would be unaided by his allies, and with a hundred thousand men, Cyrus was certain he could take him. Cyrus's only concern was making it there in time.

As he paced his cabin, the pull from his blood came through.

He stopped.

His heart beat faster.

It was the Mercian queen.

She was calling him again. Why? Surely, the way he'd last left her had turned her from him. She couldn't possibly want to see him again.

Unless she did.

He shouldn't go. He'd gotten what he'd needed. But if she had something more...

Cyrus couldn't stop himself, and he pushed his mind to follow his blood.

He found her on a bench in a garden in her mind. He glanced around. She'd created this, imagined it, put herself here to meet him.

She was waiting for him.

Interesting.

He was glad not to disappoint.

She didn't turn to look at him, but her throat bobbed with a swallow. She knew he was there.

He sat down beside her.

The air was quiet between them. He really did wish he could speak to her.

"*Is it your power that allows you to come to me?*" she asked finally. "*The same power that kept the Wild from entering your mind and kept them from seeing you?*"

She spoke of Alexander's power. The Wild couldn't enter his mind? He'd heard of this place—a forest with creatures that could haunt the mind, take control of the body. While he had no intention of going there, this was good to know.

Her eyes were on him now, studying him.

"*How do you come through the blood?*" she asked. "*Are you a traveler?*"

So, she *did* know of seers, and that seers could travel. *Even more interesting.*

"*How did you get the vial to me?*"

Quite literally blood, sweat, a nauseating pain of the mind, his last scrap of sanity, and perhaps a few tears. He leaned back against the bench. He wished he could tell her, lest his efforts were vastly underappreciated. Still, he remained quiet.

"*Soren tells me this is a trick,*" she said.

She'd told the Shadow commander... A wariness pitted his stomach. He hadn't expected her to tell anyone. That might complicate things.

Her eyes caught on the small bracelet of tiny shells he wore around his wrist, and she sucked in a breath. Clearly it meant something to her. When he had more time, he'd search her mind for it. For now, he only knew Alexander wore it. So Cyrus did too.

"Are you here because I haven't sent you to the gods?" she asked. *"Do you want to go?"*

She hadn't sent Alexander's body to the pyre? If it helped her rationalize his presence, that worked in his favor. And he couldn't let her think he wanted to be released from her. He gave a faint shake of his head.

Her shoulders eased. *"I... I didn't know what you would have wanted. I feared I'd trapped you."* Her eyes welled, and for the first time, his heart actually hurt for her. To love someone so deeply, to care about someone so much...

"But this is the last time I can bring you back," she added. *"I don't have any more blood."*

What? What had happened to the rest? He brushed away the image of the garden and pulled forward her last memories.

The Shadow commander.

Cyrus watched as the beast of a man argued with the queen in her chamber and then ripped the vial from her hands and threw it into the fireplace.

He'd taken it from her.

He'd taken what Cyrus had worked so hard to give to her—he'd taken what didn't belong to him. And who did this man think he was, that he would treat his queen this way?

Cyrus forced a steady breath, but heat swelled inside him, a flame of anger growing hotter.

"*Don't be angry with him,*" she said. "*He cares for me. And worries.*"

That justified nothing. And how could the Shadow commander care about anyone?

"*He took your death hard,*" she said.

The commander? The Shadow commander had taken Alexander's death hard?

"*He won't admit it, but I see it in him. Adrian did too. He was devastated. Still is.*"

Whoever Adrian was, he didn't care. His mind was still on the commander.

"*Are you able to go to others—*"

Anger still burned under his skin, and he stood abruptly. How would he get her another vial?

"*All right,*" she said quickly, and she stood too. "*I just thought, at least Adrian.*"

His frustration flared at the thought of having to use the birds again, but now that she knew how the blood worked, now that she wanted to still see him, maybe he could try sending it a different way.

"*Do you not remember your brother Adrian?*" she asked him.

Cyrus froze.

What did she say?

"*He misses you. Terribly.*"

Alexander had another brother? Cyrus had another brother? That couldn't be right.

The queen reached out her hand to his arm. "*I'm sorry,*" she said softly. "*For everything. For any pain I've ever caused you, I'm sorry.*"

Her eyes welled. "*You deserved so much more, so much better than me, and so much better than what fate gave you.*"

He still couldn't move. His eyes stung. No one had ever said that to him before. No one had ever cared to say it. Cyrus never thought about what he did or didn't deserve. Maybe if he did, he'd think he *did* deserve what fate had dealt him. But for her to tell him otherwise...

"*Alexander,*" she whispered.

And suddenly, he felt very foolish. Of course she meant Alexander. Not Cyrus.

And what was she apologizing for? What more could fate have given Alexander? He'd had a privileged life, everything afforded to him: freedom, education, wealth, love, happiness, and in the end, a hero's death. She was right—Alexander hadn't deserved what fate had given him—but he'd enjoyed it nonetheless.

Cyrus pulled away from her.

"*Alexander,*" she said again, but he couldn't hear it anymore.

He wasn't Alexander, he didn't want to be Alexander, he didn't want to be here, he didn't want her to talk to him, or to look at him.

He needed out, to get away, and he ripped himself from her mind.

Cyrus sank to the floor of his cabin on the ship, panting. The conversation had rattled him in a way that few ever had. And now that he was alone, he could really absorb her words—

He had another brother.

Adrian, she'd called him.

Cyrus couldn't feel him, so he was fairly certain he didn't have power. Not that he cared about that, although it did tug at his heart that Essandra had lost the opportunity of fulfilling her spell with Alexander. Adrian couldn't replace him if he didn't have power.

Cyrus wondered what he was like, how old he was, what he looked like.

And he paused. He could find out some things...

He still felt a connection to the queen. She hadn't yet wiped off the blood. Perhaps he still had a few moments...

Before he could talk himself out of it, he followed the pull back to the queen. She sat on the floor of her chamber with her arms crossed around herself, staring into the empty fireplace.

Cyrus took care to shroud himself and quickly sifted through her memories. He wasn't entirely sure what he was looking for—a man who looked similar to himself, younger, but how young he didn't know. Fifteen? Twenty-five?

He flipped through the faces; he knew the ones that *weren't* him. And fuck the gods, how many blond men were there in Mercia? Everyone. Every fucking person. His frustration grew as he sifted faster. Where would he be? Cyrus assumed he and the queen would be close, so his image had to be close too.

And then he found him.

Cyrus knew the moment he saw him. And perhaps he'd seen him before, but he hadn't been looking for a brother before.

Adrian was fairly young, early twenties, but he was certainly a man, and a formidable one at that. He was slightly taller than Alexander, and thicker. He carried his sword across his back—unusual for a Mercian soldier.

But he looked like a fighter. Cyrus couldn't help a smile. He was probably a good fighter.

A sudden rush of emotion overwhelmed him, and he had to pull back out of the queen's mind. As he sat on the floor of his cabin, he choked back a cry building in his throat.

He had a brother.

A brother that still lived.

A brother that probably knew nothing of him.

Cyrus wiped his face and pushed himself off the floor.

After he took the Shadow King, he would find this brother.

CHAPTER TWENTY-EIGHT

"No."

Cyrus stared back at the coward fuck of a man who had suddenly found the poorly timed audacity to say that word to him. "No?" he repeated.

"We need to strike Phillip first," Gregor said.

This man was so incredibly stupid. "Aleon is *not* in a position of opportunity for us," Cyrus argued. "The Shadow King is. Their armies are separated, and he's alone and vulnerable."

"And how do you know this?"

"I have a reliable source."

Gregor scoffed. "Forgive me if that doesn't inspire confidence."

Cyrus felt his frustration growing. "If we go and he isn't there, then we'll simply return."

"And give away our intention."

"I'm fairly certain if Aleon and the Shadowlands have half a wit, they already know our intention." Much longer and he'd lose his patience altogether. "We take the Shadow King now, then the war is half won."

Gregor scoffed again, and Cyrus thought it was a similar noise to the one he might make if Cyrus choked him. Gregor pointed his finger at him. "You mean *you* get what *you* want, then leave me to face Phillip alone? Absolutely not."

Well, while an idiot, Gregor wasn't entirely wrong. That *was* an option. Cyrus didn't care about Aleon at all and had little intention of actually going to war with them.

Gregor pursed his lips as he sat back in his throne, feeling safe behind the line of guards at the bottom of the dais between them.

As if men could keep him safe.

"We strike Phillip first," Gregor said again.

"We don't have time for this. I have to leave now to catch the Shadow King before he reaches the pass. You don't even need to send your entire army."

"I'll send no one!"

Rage flamed through him, and Cyrus dropped his hand to the hilt of his sword, but Everan caught him discreetly from behind.

Cyrus quickly contemplated the consequences of killing Gregor right now, and he was pretty sure there were none. But Everan still held him. Regardless, he couldn't look at this man's face any longer. He turned and swept out of Gregor's throne room, not even bothering with parting words.

"Make sure the army is ready," he told Kord as they stepped outside. "We march within the hour."

"Are you serious?" Kord said. "We're going to march alone?"

"We have more men than the Shadow King."

"We have minimally trained soldiers."

"Don't sell them short—your training regimen is excellent."

"It doesn't matter how good the training is. Most of them have less than a year of experience."

"That's enough."

"Cyrus—"

Cyrus stopped, catching Kord. His grip was firm. "It's not up for discussion. Do it." He knew the whole thing sounded mad, but this was the only way to get the Shadow King. And he didn't have time for debate.

Kord glanced at Everan, who said nothing, then went to do as he was told.

Cyrus turned to find Everan and Essandra just watching him. "I don't even need Gregor," he told them. "I should have killed him in there."

"You need his money," Everan said. "You need him to feed our army, and you'll need his mercenaries if Aleon and Mercia retaliate for your attack on the Shadow King. You know his army will disappear as soon as the hand that pays them is dead."

"Gregor doesn't need to be alive for *me* to use his money. I can make sure they're paid."

"But you have neither the time *nor* the capacity to figure that out," Essandra countered. "Let alone the patience," she added. "Because you know what comes out of killing a king? Leading a kingdom."

"I wouldn't lead Japheth."

"Yes, you said that about Serra too." She raised a brow. "And Rael. Look where it's gotten you."

He couldn't argue with that.

"Forget Gregor," Everan said. "Let him do as he pleases. He'll join you against Aleon if you need it—that's the only thing that matters."

Cyrus gritted his teeth. "The Shadow King is the only thing that matters."

"Then let's go get him."

Cyrus paused. If Everan only knew what those words meant to him—the feeling of support and unity for his cause, his purpose.

"You have to tell me one thing, though," Everan said. "How do you know?"

He would give Everan whatever he asked, but on this, Cyrus hesitated.

"How do you know the Shadow King is traveling back?" Everan pressed. "And how do you know he'll be without allied forces?"

Essandra was silent, but her eyes asked the same. These were the people he trusted most in the world. He did owe them the truth, at least.

"The Mercian queen told me," he said finally. "I entered her mind when my brother's blood touched her skin."

Everan and Essandra both gaped at him.

"She thinks I'm him—his spirit—somehow."

They still stared at him, with their eyes wide and their mouths open.

"Four times now she's talked to me."

"Four times!" Everan exclaimed. "What the fuck, Cyrus? Why didn't you say anything?"

He shook his head. "I don't know. I figured you would try to stop me, I guess."

Essandra crossed her arms. "So, she uses your brother's blood to call you back to her?"

Now it was Cyrus's turn to stare.

That... would have been *so much easier* than getting a blood vial to her.

He wished he would have thought of that.

Of course, now it was too late. Whatever had been done to preserve Alexander's body, since he hadn't been sent to the pyre, would have drained him of his blood. And she'd already accepted receiving a vial. The only way to see her again would be to send her another.

"I sent her a vial for the last two times," he admitted.

Essandra's eyes grew even wider. "You did what? How did you get it to her?"

"A very laborious effort," he replied.

"What did you say to her?"

"I don't say anything to her. I don't speak at all—I know it will give me away."

"Then how did you show her how to use the blood?" Essandra's brow drew down sharply. "And if she thinks you're the spirit of your brother, where does she think the vials come from?" She scoffed. "Is she so easy to fool? Does she not have any sense at all?"

"Have you never been blinded by grief?" he snapped. "You—of all people—should know how the desperation of loss can make one believe the impossible!"

She quieted. Her mouth closed, but her throat tightened, and her eyes of surprise turned to eyes of anger. Eyes of hurt.

"I'm sorry," he told her, softer now. "I didn't mean it like that."

But she said nothing more.

Kord reappeared. "The army's ready."

Cyrus nodded. "Let's march."

The flame of the campfire lit the night.

He'd driven the army hard, until Everan and Kord insisted they stop to rest the men. Now Cyrus should be resting too, but he couldn't sleep, and so he sat staring into the fire. Everan, Kord, Orion, and Essandra sat with him. No one spoke.

He was glad. They'd only tell him this was madness, that they marched toward an ill-planned battle that they were unprepared for.

They'd tell him he'd lose his army. And... he likely would.

But he wouldn't need an army after this. Even if he couldn't defeat the Shadow army, he only needed to get to the Shadow King. If his men failed him in this, Essandra would help him. He knew she would. No matter how much she hated him right now. No matter that he'd hurt her, she'd still help him.

And the gods damn him because he would let her. In fact, he wouldn't just let her—he'd ask her to.

She should be back in Rael, safe and protected, regardless of whether she wanted to be. This was a much more dangerous endeavor than Serra had been. And if she was going to hate him, she should hate him from a place of safety. It was only a small comfort that he'd made Everan and Orion promise to get her back to Rael should things go poorly. That was their sole charge.

He watched her as they sat around the fire. The flames danced shadows across her face. She deserved so much better than him, so much more than he'd given her. He hadn't even given her honesty. Nor Everan. The guilt ate at him.

"I have another brother," he said abruptly, breaking the quiet.

They all stared at him.

"What?" Kord said.

"I have another brother," he said again.

Silence sat between them.

"Did she tell you that?" Essandra asked finally.

He nodded.

"Who?" Kord asked, glancing at Everan and Essandra. "Who told him?"

Everan filled him in. "The Mercian queen. Cyrus was able to enter her mind when his brother's blood touched her skin."

Kord gaped at Cyrus. "You've been talking to the queen? Is that how you knew about the Shadow King?" He turned to Everan and Essandra. "And you guys knew?"

"We just found out in Japheth," Everan said quietly.

"Is this brother in Mercia?" Essandra asked.

Cyrus nodded. "I saw him. I saw him in her mind." He paused and dropped his voice lower. "I can't feel him," he told her. "He doesn't have power."

"I..." She shook her head quickly. "I wasn't asking for—"

"I know. I just... I wanted you to know that I thought about it."

She softened in the firelight. "Thank you," she whispered.

Everan leaned forward. "What does he look like?"

"Like he could beat the shit out of me."

They both chuckled. Then Cyrus grew quiet again. "He's young. He's... beautiful. In every image, he wears a smile on his face." His whole life, Cyrus had hated the idea of Alexander being happy, but seeing Adrian was different.

"Are you going to try to meet him?" Everan asked.

"I'd like to. After all this is done."

"Why wait?" Kord asked. "We don't have to do this now. In fact, we're foolish to be doing it now, alone. Forget the Shadow King. Go meet your brother."

Cyrus refused to even acknowledge the idea with an answer. Kord knew he couldn't do that.

The quiet returned.

Finally, Everan said, "We march in a couple hours. We should all get some sleep."

Cyrus nodded. Then they all stayed around the fire until the dawn came.

The bird struggled in his hands as Cyrus marked its head with blood. They never liked this part. He estimated he was within a day's reach of the Shadow King. He'd know for sure within the hour. He released the bird into the sky and willed it west. Instantly, an ache creeped up into his head behind his eyes, but he ignored it. Nothing would stop him now.

"So today, then," Essandra said from behind him.

He turned.

She waved off he guard beside her, who had set a leather trunk at her feet. "Today you kill the Shadow King," she told Cyrus.

He nodded. "Today," he said. It didn't feel real. All the time he'd spent wanting and waiting, working and breaking himself and those around him over and over again, all the time consumed with the thought.

Now it was today.

Her lips were coldly pursed. No warmth came from her, not that he expected any. It was his own fault. He hadn't apologized to her for what he'd said about loss and desperation. Not really. Not the way he'd meant to. Not the way he should.

He needed to.

"Thank you for coming with me," he said. That was a stupid start. No, he needed—

"Get dressed," she told him flatly.

He paused and looked down at his leather armor. "I am dressed."

"No, you're not." She flicked her hand toward the trunk on the ground.

Cyrus stared at it for a moment, then moved to it and opened the latched top to find his armor inside. Not his old armor, but his armor made new.

He pulled the vambraces out in surprise. "When did you do this?"

"The day after you came back from Serra without it."

His eyes snapped up to her. "The day after?"

She didn't repeat herself.

He stared back at the impenetrable armor in his hands, armor that would likely keep him alive long enough to reach the Shadow King.

"Essandra, I need to tell you that I'm sorry for—"

"I don't want to hear it." She nodded back at the armor. "Put it on. And don't take it off this time."

Then she turned and left him to do as she'd said.

Donning his new armor, Cyrus checked the army. They looked good. He was impressed with how far they'd come. From slaves to free men to soldiers, fighting for a cause they believed in—a cause he believed in. Their spirits were high, and so were his.

"Cyrus!" He turned to see Everan and Kord striding toward him.

"Aleon moves to meet us," Kord said.

"They're on a path to intercept us, to aid the Shadow King," Everan added.

Now that was unexpected. The lift he'd felt just a little earlier evaporated. Was Phillip really coming to protect the Shadow King? Maybe Phillip moved his army with the expectation that Gregor was here. Maybe when he saw that Gregor wasn't, he'd withdraw.

But what if he didn't?

"Can we reach the Shadow King before Aleon reaches us?" Cyrus asked them.

"You can't be serious," Kord said. "Even if we could, once Aleon engages, it will all be over. The combined forces of Aleon and the Shadowlands will completely decimate our army." He stared at Cyrus, and his face changed. "You weren't planning on returning with the army." He shook his head. "Were you planning on returning at all?"

Cyrus didn't answer. He had expected to prevail. But if he didn't... Well, that would be his fate.

"How far is the Shadow King?" Everan asked him. "Can you see him?"

He shouldn't be able to yet, but still, Cyrus reached out his mind to the bird he'd sent west. And he stepped back in surprise.

His pulse quickened.

He *could* see.

He could see the Shadow army.

"I see them," he said to Everan and Kord, keeping his sight through the bird. His heart raced even faster. "He's closer than I thought. We can reach him. Today."

"How big is his army?" Everan asked.

It was hard to tell. "Fifty thousand, maybe."

Kord swore.

It was a massive army, although Cyrus's was larger—not significantly, but he had the advantage of numbers. And something more... The Shadow army moved slowly. It made sense: they were just coming off a battle to retake Mercia.

"They look tired," he told Everan and Kord. "It looks like—"

Cyrus froze.

His chest tightened and his blood ran cold.

"Cyrus?" Everan said.

No, this couldn't be right.

"Cyrus," Everan called him again.

He almost couldn't say the words. "My brother is with them."

"Adrian? Are you sure?"

He nodded. Adrian wore armor, the color black like the Shadows he rode with, but there was no mistaking his face. He looked exactly as he had in the queen's memories, only he wasn't smiling.

Cyrus pulled his mind back. He needed a moment to catch his breath.

"Why is he with them?" he snapped. "Why is he fucking there?" Everan and Kord stayed quiet. It wasn't a question for them. Cyrus paced a few steps, then turned back. "He should be in Mercia, protecting his queen! *Why is he fucking there?*"

Rage coursed through him.

This could ruin everything.

"Why is he there?" he bellowed, and then hurled the helm he held under his arm through the air, sending it far.

He paced another couple of steps, sucking in a deep inhale, and raked a rough hand over his face. He worked his mind for what to do now.

"Cyrus," Everan said quietly. "It's all right if you let this opportunity go. You won't have made a bad decision; you won't have failed. You'd simply be adjusting after new information—you had no way to know about Aleon, or your brother—and there will be another chance. We'll help you find it."

"But the chance is here, now," he insisted.

"And if you take it, you'll regret it."

He wasn't entirely convinced of that.

"You still mourn the brother you hated," Everan told him. "Imagine what you'll feel losing the brother you love."

Cyrus shook his head. "I don't love him. I don't even know him."

Everan shrugged. "It doesn't matter. You love the idea of him. You love the idea of family. We all do."

Cyrus had never thought about the idea of family. It was easier not to, because it hadn't been an idea that was possible before. But maybe it was possible now...

He threw his mind back out to the bird, finding Adrian again. Everything about him—his hair, his face, the way he sat on top of his horse. Cyrus couldn't take his sight from him.

"It's all right to make a change," Everan said.

Cyrus steeped on that for a moment, trying to think amid the tempest of emotion inside him. He was at a loss for what to do now.

But he did know one thing—he couldn't let harm come to Adrian. He couldn't march against his brother.

"Prepare the army to return to Japheth," he told Kord finally, although Cyrus wasn't looking forward to the next conversation with Gregor.

He turned to a nearby page, who was pretending not to notice the absolute breakdown he'd just had. "Go get that helm," Cyrus called to him, nodding in the direction he'd thrown it. If he lost it again, Essandra would kill him.

Chapter Twenty-Nine

"Cyrus, you can't just leave."

He absolutely could. He tried to drown out Kord's very persistent argument in his ear all the way from where they left the army, just north of Japheth's capital, to the port where his ship waited. Kord insisted Cyrus meet with Gregor before departing to smooth things between them. And his argument was convincing.

Just not convincing enough.

Cyrus couldn't talk to Gregor. He couldn't look at him. He knew he'd gloat at his failing, with his spittled smile, as he recounted how he'd told Cyrus not to march against the Shadow King.

He'd be smug. Unbearably smug.

Then Cyrus would have to peel that smug face from his skull and lay it across Gregor's lap like a dinner linen.

Orion shook his head as he walked beside Kord.

"What?" Cyrus asked him. "You think I should stay too?"

Orion snorted. "To talk to Gregor?" He snorted again. "Fuck that guy."

Cyrus almost belted a laugh.

"If you leave without speaking to him, he'll see it as a slight," Kord said, under the false hope that Cyrus might yet change his mind. "That will make things even worse."

Cyrus didn't care how Gregor saw it. In fact, despite Kord's incessant argument, he wasn't even thinking about Gregor.

His mind kept wandering back to Adrian.

Why had his brother been with the Shadow King when his queen was in Mercia? It wasn't uncommon for allies to share the talents of strategic men between them, but Adrian was barely past age twenty. He couldn't possibly be critical to war efforts.

Perhaps he was on an assignment for the queen. Surely, he held some position at court, being direct blood to the previous two lord justices.

Kord relented in his argument, finally, and split from Cyrus to prepare for departure. Orion followed, leaving only Essandra walking beside him. Everan had gone ahead to prepare the ship. The port was busy and crowded as they made their way through.

Cyrus wondered what kind of position Adrian would have—too young, too inexperienced to be an ambassador. A lower-ranking man of the army, perhaps. *No.* If that were the case, he wouldn't have been with the Shadow King without at least a Mercian legion with him.

A woman's voice rang above the crowd. "Sabine!"

Essandra stopped, and Cyrus stopped too. Not just because she did. He stopped in hearing the name Essandra had left behind so long ago.

"Sabine," called the woman's voice again.

Essandra and Cyrus both turned, and a woman in a dark cloak stared at them from only a few paces away. "Sabine Laveau."

Essandra's breaths shallowed, but when she answered, her voice was firm and steady. "You have me confused with someone else."

The woman's eyes narrowed for a moment, only a moment, then she gave a polite nod. "I apologize. You just look so much like someone I once knew."

Essandra papered on a smooth smile. "I hope it brings you warm memories. A pleasant day." She gave the woman a nod and then kept toward the ship. But her pace quickened as she went.

"Who was that?" Cyrus asked.

She didn't answer.

They reached the ship, and Essandra stopped only to look back over her shoulder before she swept on board. When they made it to the deck, Cyrus caught her by the elbow to pause.

"Who was that?" he asked again.

She pulled away and slipped behind a mast, taking cover in its shadow as she peered back out across the bustling port. Her fingers dug into the wood. "I don't know."

"She knows your old name—"

"Thank you for pointing that out," she snapped. She sidled closer to the mast, veiling herself deeper in its shadow.

He didn't react to her lashing out. She was afraid.

He moved into the shadow with her, just behind her, and scoured his gaze through the crowds as well. "You're sure you don't know her?"

She kept her eyes on the port streets. "I was very important to Soroya's coven. More people knew me than I knew them."

"What about people outside the coven? Could someone know you from somewhere else?"

She didn't answer, and he wasn't sure whether he was helping. "Don't let it bother you," he said. "You're safe now."

Her head jerked as she snapped around to face him. "There is *nowhere* I can go to be safe from Soroya. *Nowhere* I can hide." She turned back toward the port. "I've gotten too complacent."

Wait... "What does that mean?"

She moved to slip back toward her cabin, but he caught her.

"Are you thinking about leaving again?" he pressed. "Is that what you mean?"

Still, she didn't answer.

"Essandra—"

"Can we please just get out of here?" she begged.

He'd never seen her like this, and he didn't like it. He didn't like her afraid. He sighed as his shoulders dropped, then he nodded. Cyrus gave one last look toward the port before giving the command to cast off, back to Rael.

If Gregor was slighted by Cyrus leaving Japheth without so much as a goodbye, that seemed to have been forgotten the moment Gregor found something else to panic about, which he had.

Cyrus flipped the folded letter back and forth between his fingers as he sat at the desk in his study. Although it wasn't news that he was particularly concerned about, it *was* news he hadn't expected.

The king of Aleon was marrying the princess of Osan, or maybe he already had—the timing was unclear. Cyrus hadn't given any thought to Osan since King Tagasi had withdrawn his proposal for an alliance between Osan and Rael. He remembered his words, though:

Your court not only tolerates but elevates those who walk in the shadows—witches whose hands bend the laws of nature and corrupt the balance that holds kingdoms in peace. Osan does not bargain with darkness.

Aleon must not have witches.

Everan and Kord sat quietly as he mulled.

There was no news of whether Osan was joining the collective alliance between Mercia, Aleon, and the Shadowlands. Gregor tended to leave out all the important details when he sent his news, because who needed those? However, it was safe to assume the likelihood.

Cyrus flicked the letter across the desk to Everan, who opened and skimmed it before passing it to Kord. Cyrus should call his council together, but he wanted to organize his thoughts before that.

This news was, perhaps, of no consequence at all to him. If he wasn't going to fight against Aleon, he wasn't concerned about their allies, but it could become a problem if Gregor dragged him into a war against the combined kingdoms.

Essandra stepped into the study, and his attention shifted. He'd wondered if she'd come. She'd been withdrawn since returning from Japheth, and quiet. It was a different kind of quiet than the silence she gave him when she was upset with him. Cyrus didn't like her quiet at all, but he especially didn't like this kind of quiet. She'd said she was fine, but she was tense now, always alert. And she'd barely been eating.

Her words on the ship had worried him. She thought it was no longer enough just to hide from Soroya—she felt the increasing pressure to run. He'd asked her again if she was going to leave.

She hadn't given him an answer.

"How serious do you think it is?" Everan asked about the contents of the letter.

Cyrus didn't take his eyes from Essandra.

"How serious is what?" she asked. "What's happened?"

Kord held out the letter for her, and she took it, skimming over its words.

"I'm not overly concerned yet," Cyrus said, turning his attention back to the matter at hand. "But I need to eliminate the Shadow King before Gregor pulls us into a bigger war."

He didn't have long. Cyrus fisted his knuckles against his lips, thinking. "I need to see the queen again. She'll tell me if they're planning something."

Essandra's gaze snapped to him. "I don't think that's a good idea. She's past her grief now; she'll see right through you."

Cyrus leaned back in his chair. He wasn't so sure. The grief he'd felt from the queen wasn't something she'd overcome quickly. And she *wanted* to see him, or, rather, she wanted to see Alexander—to still believe he remained somehow.

Desperately.

"I need to get her another vial," he said, and he had to do it differently than he had before—following the previous approach would drive him to madness. He needed to get closer. He rubbed his temples, then straightened as a thought came to him. "I'll travel to the stone circle and send a bird from there."

"It's not safe," she argued.

"Why not? We've traveled to the stone circle many times."

Her eyes bore into him, but she didn't argue further.

Within the hour, Cyrus stood ready in Essandra's workroom, a bird tucked in his arm. Essandra invoked the tether spell, starting with the bird. This was the first time he'd been physically bonded to an animal to get it through the portal, and to his surprise, it felt like absolutely nothing at all. He didn't know what he'd expected—he felt nothing when tethered to Essandra or Kord, or anyone else he'd taken through, but it surprised him nonetheless.

Then Essandra whispered the tether spell between them. When she gave the nod, they stepped over the line she'd made on the floor. The cool air hit his face before his foot even touched the grass on the other side. He breathed it in. He'd come to like traveling to the stone circle. It was quiet here—peaceful, cool, a relief from Rael. He wasn't sure if it was a relief for Essandra, though, with so many memories here.

So many *bad* memories.

He wasn't sure why she still insisted on coming. He could portal himself. Well, he was pretty sure he could do it himself.

"You don't always have to come," he told her. "If you don't want to, I mean. If you have better things to do."

He went to release the bird, but she grabbed him. "Amana fasora," she whispered, breaking the tether with the animal.

Right—if the bird died while it was bonded to him, he would die too.

She pursed her lips. "This is why I have to come."

He supposed he deserved that, and he swallowed his pride as he released the bird into the sky.

It wasn't a long flight. What would have been a couple days' hard ride took just over an hour. The blood bond was strong without the burden of time for the animal to cross the Aged Sea, and he pushed it hard.

Cyrus wasn't sure why he'd expected success on the first try, but he had, which made it all the more frustrating when a winterhawk attacked, severing the bond abruptly. He'd been close. Very close—close enough to see the capital isle.

Then a flash of feathers and talons.

Then darkness.

Anger tore through him, and he stormed back through the portal into the workroom. Fucking winterhawks. He should have killed more while he was in Mercia, not that it would have made much of a difference.

"What are you doing?" Essandra asked breathlessly as she followed him.

"Getting another." He pulled a second bird from the keeping cage and hastily marked it with blood before attaching a prepped vial.

"Maybe you should take more than one this time," she told him.

"This one will make it." It had better make it. He didn't have the time or the patience. If he lost this one, he'd personally ride out and release another from the bank of the channel.

Cyrus tore through the portal again, back to the stone circle, just as Essandra yelled his name. On the other side, he paused, turning back to her.

"What?" he asked when she came through.

Her eyes were wide as she gaped at the bird and his arm.

"What?" he asked again.

"T-the bird," she stammered. "I didn't tether it to you."

He looked down at the animal, which struggled against the tightness of his hold but otherwise appeared to be all right.

"It's fine," he said.

She shook her head, her eyes still wide. "No, that's not possible."

He waved the perfectly fine bird in front of her, and she glared back at him. "It's fine," he said again.

Still not believing him, she reached out and touched it—testing, poking, prodding.

A thought came to him. "Maybe I never needed the tether."

"No, you definitely needed it. Remember how the Aether burned your men when you tried to take too many through and overwhelmed the bond?"

Yes, that had happened.

"Is it because it's small, then, or because it's an animal?"

She shook her head again. "I think your will alone brought it through."

"What does that mean?"

"I-I don't know. I think it means you're getting stronger. Your power is growing."

He couldn't read the expression on her face. Not fear... Worry, maybe. But he wasn't sure what would worry her about that. He still wasn't exactly sure what his power even was, let alone how it was getting stronger, but he'd think about that later. He turned his attention back to the bird and the task at hand.

The second try proved successful. The bird dropped its vial onto the Mercian queen's terrace, and Cyrus let it go.

Now he would wait.

The moment they crossed back into Essandra's workroom, she went straight to her wall of books. He paused as she pulled a large leather-bound book from the shelf and quickly flipped through the pages. Something was bothering her...

"What's wrong?" he asked. "Is this about my power growing?"

She ignored him and tossed the book aside as she quickly grabbed another.

"I don't know why that would be a bad thing," he added.

She tossed the second book and pulled another. "Power doesn't grow. When you come into your power, you come into all of it, all at once. That's why it's so dangerous to those who are young—those who don't know how to control it. But if your power is growing, it means you're different. Something about you is different."

He shrugged. "All right..." He still didn't see why this was a problem.

She snapped the book closed. "I need to know what I'm working with, or when I use our combined power, I could accidentally kill us both." Her voice was sharp and cold.

"Are you angry at me?" he asked.

Her icy gaze piecing him softened ever so slightly. She sighed. "No," she said. "No, I'm just—"

Her words dropped as her eyes caught on a small purple sachet on her center worktable.

"Where did that come from?" he asked.

"I don't know." She stepped closer and picked it up, opening it.

Then she froze as the color drained from her face.

Her breaths came short and clipped as she dropped its contents into her palm.

Cyrus moved nearer and saw it was a necklace with a round pendant. He leaned forward to make out its engraving: a complicated layering of triangles and circles.

"What is that?" he asked her.

Her breath shook as she raised her eyes to his. "It's a vinculum pendant—it bonds the wearer's power against their will."

His brow grew heavy. "Why would you put it on, then?"

"It's my pendant from when I belonged to Soroya's coven. She's found me. And she means for me to wear it again."

Chapter Thirty

"Slow down!" Cyrus called. "Wait!"

Essandra ignored him as she ripped through her bedchamber, stuffing clothing and essentials into her leather bag.

"Where will you even go?" he asked her.

"I don't know," she said as she balled up another riding dress and shoved it into her bag. "The coven will split up, then we'll come back together once I find somewhere safe."

"What place is safer than here?"

She snorted. "*Any* place that Soroya doesn't know where I am."

"And when she finds you again? Then what? You'll be on the run again. Is that the life you're choosing?"

"It's the life I chose when I left her." She fastened the bag.

"But it doesn't need to be the life you have now," he told her. "You have my protection."

She whirled to face him. "I don't know how many times I have to say this. Your power means *nothing*, even if it is growing."

"Not just my power. The strength of my crown and everything that comes with it—you'll have it."

She quieted as she stared at him.

"I have an army now, the strength of two kingdoms. Can this witch defeat that?" he asked her. "Because that's what she'd have to do to get to you."

Her lips parted, and she swallowed. "You'd use your army for me?" she asked, her voice hardly more than a whisper.

"Of course I would." He wasn't sure why that was even a question.

"But you need it for the Shadow King."

"I can always build another army, but I can't get…" He stopped himself.

"Another coven," she said, finishing for him. She nodded as she cast her eyes to the floor. "You could, actually. It would be difficult to find a bond witch, but not completely impossible."

That wasn't what he'd meant. Cyrus didn't care about a coven or a bond witch. He couldn't get another *her*. And he didn't know how to say that without sounding like he longed for something that no longer existed. Even if he did.

"You don't want to make an enemy of Soroya," she warned.

"I don't care about Soroya. I don't want you to go." They stood in the silence, their gazes locked. "And all this assumes she comes herself," he said. "How likely is that? If she's like any other head of state, head of anything, she'll send someone to claim you. But you're nothing like the person she knew before. You're stronger. You've built a coven, you have a bloodline bond through me that lets you draw endless power from the Aether, and you have one of the world's largest armies. If there was ever a time for you to stand against her, it would be now."

She said nothing to that.

"Stop running," he said.

Her eyes swept around the room again. He wished he could look in her mind, know what she was thinking. She was thinking *something*...

"You have enough to focus on," she said finally. "A war of witches is not something you can handle right now. It could take so much from you: time, energy, effort, men. You could miss opportunities at everything you've been working for—"

"Do you not believe that this is a price I'm willing to pay?"

She paused and sucked in a breath. "I want to believe you," she whispered.

"Then do. Stay."

Essandra didn't unpack her bag, but she also didn't leave. Each morning that Cyrus woke and went to her workroom, he worried that he'd find her gone, but each morning she was still there.

And each morning led to another day that the Mercian queen didn't call him through the blood bond. He'd felt nothing from her. Maybe Essandra had been right—maybe rational thought had prevailed, and she now suspected something was off. Maybe she wouldn't use it again.

Or maybe she hadn't found the new vial yet. He'd considered sending another bird to check if it was still on the terrace. But he waited.

Between Essandra and the Mercian queen, he found it hard to focus on anything else.

A letter had also arrived from Miriel. She was worried about the Etrean Union, which had been slowly fortifying their forces along

Pryam's border. Cyrus wasn't particularly concerned. With more Raelean people settling within Pryam, of course the Union would be on guard. They didn't know his agenda. But they had nothing to worry about, and he expected things to settle over time.

Several more days passed. And more.

With nothing from the Mercian queen.

And then came news from Jaem.

Apparently, Aleon's royal wedding with Osan had been a wedding to behold, with the Mercian queen in attendance. That would explain why she hadn't used the blood. She wasn't even in Mercia. And more interesting information: while the Shadow King hadn't gone, the Shadow commander had. If that didn't signify the unity of the four kingdoms...

Cyrus paced his study. The closer these kingdoms grew as allies, the harder it would be for him to get to the Shadow King. He was running out of time.

And then he felt her.

The Mercian queen. Finally.

"There you are," he said to himself, before pushing his mind down the bond that snapped into place.

The queen sat on the bed in her chamber, waiting for him, and when he showed himself in her mind, she rose. There was something different about her. Suspicion hung heavy in the air. She eyed him warily, and he realized this visit wouldn't be like the ones before.

She stepped to him.

He wondered what had happened. He wanted to search her mind, but he didn't dare do anything that might add to the doubt that pulsed off her.

She studied him, every line of his face, his hair, his body. And he focused—he focused on projecting every detail of Alexander, every mark on his skin, every scuff on his boots, down to the Mercian tunic stitching.

She stepped around him, moving slowly.

She knew. She knew something wasn't right.

But he didn't move. Despite his racing heart, he let her inspect him. He was sure it was what Alexander would have done. And so he waited.

The queen moved back around in front of him, with her eyes narrowed and her head cocked. Then she reached out and took his hand. He forced himself still. She pushed up the sleeve of his tunic. He knew what she was looking for—the staves. Still, he didn't move. She wouldn't find them. He'd hidden all his markings. Her eyes shifted to his neck, and she reached and tugged down the collar of his tunic.

As she pulled away, he couldn't read the expression on her face. He wasn't sure if her doubt was more or less now.

"*How are you here?*" she asked him.

Of course he didn't dare answer. He needed to maintain his stoic presence and simply let her do the talking. But he *wanted* to speak to her.

Her eyes narrowed even more. "*Can you come whenever you want?*"

It was a simple question, and he wanted to answer, but opening the door to any kind of reciprocal communication was dangerous. Yet he couldn't help himself, and he gave a single shake of his head. *No.*

His heart raced faster as he silently cursed himself. He shouldn't have done that. Why had he?

"*You need the blood,*" she said.

And now not answering was no longer an option. He gave a single nod in reply. *Yes.*

She stepped closer, and her breaths became shallower. *"But how did you send it to me? How can you... engage?"*

He cursed himself more. He couldn't let himself speak.

"Is it your blood?" she asked.

He was dangerously close to being discovered, and even if he could speak without consequence, there wasn't an answer that existed that sounded remotely reasonable for the situation.

She brought her hand to her forehead, clutching her temples.

He was losing her.

He was losing this opportunity. He racked his mind for how to keep the connection. What would Alexander do if he couldn't speak to her?

Cyrus reached out and took her hand, pulling her to look at him. Then he gave another nod.

Her lips parted, and her eyes grew larger. There it was—the hope. But her suspicion quickly overshadowed it. *"Yes, it's your blood?"* she asked.

He nodded again.

"That's not possible."

Of course it wasn't possible. But at the same time, he believed in many things that didn't seem possible. She could too. If she wanted to.

She shook her head. *"No,"* she insisted.

Yes. He nodded again. *Just believe*, he silently prayed.

Her eyes ran over his face again, and her lip trembled. *"Gods, why do I believe you?"* she whispered. *"But your body... How? How is that possible? I saw you sealed in the Hall of Souls."*

They'd put Alexander in the Hall of Souls?

Like royalty...

Anger flashed through him, but he quickly pushed it down.

She shook her head again. "*Your body is... There should be no blood to send. And even if there were...*" She rubbed her hand over her face as her heart battled her mind. He needed to give her something more, something else for her to focus on, something else to reconnect them.

And then it came to him.

"*Do you deceive me?*" she asked.

The question made him pause. He didn't *want* to deceive her. Surprisingly, he also didn't want to lie to her. It was a yes-or-no question, yet he couldn't bring himself to answer.

Instead, he reached behind him and pulled out a navy velvet box. Her face told him that she knew what it was the moment she saw it.

Her crown—the crown she'd lost when the Shadow King had first stolen her away.

Carefully, he placed the box in her hands. Like it was real. He made it real. She trembled as she took it and set it slowly on the vanity in front of her. She stared at it for a moment before glancing back at him in disbelief.

This crown meant something to her. It was important. He'd seen the memory of her grandmother giving it to her.

He gave her a nod of encouragement.

She turned back to the box and, shaking, opened it. She stilled. "*Where did you find this?*" she whispered.

He didn't feel pressure to answer that as she stared down at it.

And before he could react, she turned and threw her arms around him, embracing him tightly. "*Thank you,*" she breathed.

Cyrus wasn't prepared for her sudden rush of emotion toward him. He certainly wasn't prepared for the feeling it pulled from his chest. The way that she clung to him, the way that she loved him—so much so that she would accept whatever she could get from him, regardless of whether it made sense, regardless of whether it was possible.

She'd accept the scraps of death if only she could hold on to him.

And to be loved like that...

He couldn't help but let himself embrace her back.

Cyrus tore through another drawer in his study, scattering parchments to the floor. It was here somewhere. He turned and rifled through his shelves—through stacked books and boxes.

Nothing.

He moved to the trunk in the corner by the large side chair, even though he'd never opened the thing.

"What are you looking for?"

Orion's voice made him spin.

Cyrus paused. "Nothing," he said shortly.

Orion raised a brow as his gaze swept the wrecked room. "Doesn't look like nothing."

Cyrus pushed out an annoyed breath. "I have a Mercian crown. It's in a blue box. I'm trying to find it."

"That blue box?" The assassin nodded to the top of the shelf.

Cyrus turned.

And there it was.

He crossed the room and grabbed it, but he didn't open it. Not yet. "What do you need?" he asked.

"It's regarding Mercia, actually. I have to go. Vitalia's there—I know it. She has to be. I've chased every other trail, and this is the only one that's left."

"You still think she's in the court of the Mercian queen?"

"As a maid, I think."

"It's been a long time since you've seen her," Cyrus said. "What if she's moved on? What if she's loyal to the queen?"

Orion swallowed but nodded. "Then I'll know. But I can't not go. I can't not try."

That could prove risky. Not just because he could be discovered but because Orion's heart belonging to a woman who was loyal to Mercia, to Mercia's queen... If he did find her, what might he share with her? It could jeopardize everything. Cyrus couldn't let him go. Not yet.

He looked down at the dark blue box in his hands. Cyrus couldn't outright deny him. He'd given his word to help Orion get her back, and he had every intention of doing so, just... not at the expense of the mission. He could send Jaem, but he couldn't explain how that would be less of a risk than sending Orion. Still, he had to do something. If he could stall him, just for a little while... He sighed. "Get me her picture again," he said. He knew Orion had one. "When I'm in the queen's mind next, I'll look for her. Let me see what I can find first."

Orion quickly ruffled in his pocket and pulled a folded parchment. Not one. A couple. He held them for Cyrus. "This one shows her face best," he said, opening the first. "And this one is of her from the side," he added as he unfolded the second. "I can draw more. I can—"

"This is good," Cyrus assured him, taking both parchments. "I'll look for her."

"How long, do you think?"

Cyrus felt for him. He knew the agony of waiting. "I won't know until the queen calls me back through the blood bond."

"Right." Orion nodded, then he swallowed. "And you're sure she will?"

"She most certainly will." Cyrus had no doubt.

Orion nodded again. "And you'll tell me? Right after?"

"Right after," he promised.

"Thank you."

"Of course," Cyrus said. "I do want to help you." And he meant it.

Orion left, and Cyrus stood alone with the box in his hands. He set it on his desk and opened it. Norah had been overwhelmed when she'd seen the crown. He brushed his fingertips over the petaled design. It was beautiful, but he knew she didn't want it for its beauty.

He'd given it to her in a vision. He wished he could give her the real one.

Cyrus paused.

He *could* give it to her...

It was too heavy for a bird. Cyrus drew his bottom lip between his teeth, thinking. Then his gaze stopped on the dogs sleeping on their cushions by the window.

His pulse quickened.

"One," he called.

The big dog rose and followed Cyrus as he slipped silently out into the hall and toward the portal in Essandra's workroom.

CHAPTER THIRTY-ONE

The sound of metal against metal rang through the air as soldiers practiced their skills on the sparring field. Cyrus stood, leaning against the rail, watching.

But not really watching.

Three weeks. Three weeks had passed since he'd delivered the physical crown to Norah, following him giving it to her in her mind.

And he'd heard nothing from her.

Absolutely nothing.

Maybe she needed more blood...

No, there'd been enough in the last vial for four or five callings.

So why hadn't she used it?

Perhaps the Shadow commander had discovered her again; perhaps he'd taken it. That was a very practical explanation. He'd done it before. Rage simmered inside him. If that man had taken his blood away from her again, Cyrus would kill him.

It was the only logical thing that could have happened. Cyrus knew the crown was important to her. Norah would have been overjoyed to have it back.

She would have used the blood, because she would have had questions, like how he'd delivered it to her—questions he couldn't answer.

But still, he wanted her call to him, and every day he waited.

"I'd love to be able to get inside *your* mind once in a while," Essandra said as she suddenly appeared beside him.

He snorted. "What is it you want to know?" He'd tell her anything.

"Why you've been so quiet lately. What you're thinking about."

Well, *almost* anything.

Cyrus hadn't told her about the crown. He wasn't sure why. *That was a lie.* He knew exactly why. It was because he'd traveled to the stone circle without her. She hadn't been in her workroom when he went to take the crown to Norah, and so he'd gone alone.

He'd been careful, making sure to break the tether with One before sending the dog to his task. He didn't think Essandra would care so much about him delivering the crown, but she *would* care that he'd traveled deep into Mercia to do it, all the way to the channel.

One wasn't a bird, and Cyrus hadn't wanted to risk potentially losing the animal. The truth was, he'd become quite fond of the dogs, especially One. He'd gotten as close to the capital isle as he could before sending the hound.

It had been successful, as far as he could tell. Then he'd returned with the animal before anyone had realized he was even gone.

So why hadn't Norah called him to return?

"I take it you're not going to tell me," Essandra said.

Cyrus sighed. Was it really worth hiding? She'd find out eventually. "The Mercian queen hasn't called to me. She hasn't used the blood at all."

"That's not entirely unusual," she said. "It seems you're waiting on her more often than not."

"But I really expected her to. I gave her her crown back."

Essandra stiffened. "You did what?"

"I gave her her crown—"

"I heard you." She gaped at him. "Why would you do that?"

"Because it's important to her. I wanted her to have it."

Her eyes darkened slightly as they bore into him. "How did you get it to her?"

"I took it myself," he confessed. "Had One deliver it across the bridge to her."

Her mouth fell open. "You traveled to the stone circle without me?"

"I know you find this hard to believe," he said cheekily, "but I *am* capable."

She shook her head, her eyes darkening even more. "Do you know how risky that was? You won't even let Orion go to Mercia, but *you*—Rael's king, enemy of an empire—go completely alone to visit their allied queen that you're deceiving, and you told *no one*?! And for what?"

"Gregor is the enemy of the empire, not me."

"You're Gregor's ally!" she practically yelled. "Whether or not you want to be, whether or not you like him—it doesn't matter. Gods, Cyrus!"

"Norah deserved to have that crown back," he said.

She scoffed. "Norah? You're close enough now to be on a first-name basis?"

The heat of anger lit his skin. "Yes," he seethed as that anger grew hotter. "*So* close. Close enough that she calls me by my dead brother's name."

Essandra quieted.

"He's *dead*!" he snapped. "And still, it's all I hear. Alexander. Alexander! *Alexander!*"

She said nothing against his growing fury, and slowly, it started to fade. He hadn't meant to raise his voice to her. She had every reason to be frustrated with him, but he was frustrated too.

"There you go," he told her. "Now you know what's in my mind."

Cyrus left her at the railing and headed back toward the palace. The dogs trotted off the field to follow. When he reached the doors, he let himself slow. His shoulders ached. His legs were heavy. His arms were heavy. The air was heavy. He was tired, but the exhaustion that afflicted him couldn't be cured by sleep.

He stepped into a side hall and rested his weight against the wall. One nuzzled his hand, and he gave the dog a gentle scratch behind the ears. The animal leaned into his touch, and Cyrus couldn't help a small smile. Then he sighed. He'd go back and smooth things with Essandra.

As he rocked off the wall, a pull came, and he froze.

His blood called to him, and his pulse quickened.

But it wasn't Norah.

He pushed his mind down the bond under the cover of a veil.

Darkness surrounded him.

And he knew exactly where he was.

Cyrus took care not to reveal himself as he looked into the mind of the Shadow King.

How was Cyrus in his mind? How had the Shadow King gotten the blood? Had Norah given it to him? Cyrus shook off the latter idea. No. She wouldn't have done that. The Shadow King had to have taken it from her, like the commander had.

"*Show yourself!*" the Shadow King snarled at him. Blood trailed between his fingers from where he'd poured it across his palm.

Cyrus felt his own snarl rise in his throat, but he kept silent. Watching.

"*Show yourself, coward!*" the king challenged again. He pushed a smear up his arm, as if more blood would make Cyrus come. Then he let out another snarl and smeared a strip across his chest. "*Where are you?*" he raged.

Cyrus had no intention of revealing himself, but it hit him suddenly that he had a rare opportunity—an opportunity that would be gone when the king wiped off his blood.

He moved quickly. Only memories were here—not future plans, not intentions—but memories could be helpful nonetheless, if he focused. It was easy to find himself overwhelmed by the number of them. Through various images he passed, through sights of the Shadow castle, of marching armies, of older battles.

He paused at the Mercian queen's capture—a sight he hadn't found in Norah's mind, *because she hadn't seen it in its entirety.*

The Shadow King lined the Mercian soldiers up and forced them to their knees with their hands bound behind their backs. Then he watched as his commander slit their throats one by one. It wasn't unlike the executions Cyrus had done of Pyro's soldiers, and of the nobles of Rael, but Mercia wasn't Rael. They weren't guilty of the same crimes Rael had been.

Norah's mind was filled with memories of the Shadow King and his commander, but none like this. Even though this man was different from the one who'd ruled before, different from the man who had sold Cyrus into slavery, he was still the same. Norah might not see his nature, but Cyrus did.

And then Cyrus found what he was looking for: army records, as remembered by the king—numbers, provisions, weapons, maps—and they were good. This king was well informed.

The Shadow army was smaller than he'd thought. Just under sixty thousand. Fear always made things larger than they were, and the Shadow King certainly knew how to use fear.

But Cyrus wasn't afraid of this man.

The king raged more for Cyrus to show himself, but Cyrus ignored him and flashed through more memories, pushing himself faster. He didn't have much time. But one memory made him pause.

Another of Norah.

He watched through the Shadow King's eyes as he stripped her from her dress and laid her on a bed in the Shadow castle. Slow. Gentle. This was how the king was with her. This was the side that Norah saw.

But this wasn't who this man was.

Cyrus flipped through more memories, still searching for anything else useful. And he slowed again as he came upon the devastation of Mercia.

It hit him.

Hard.

He'd known about the coup and that Norah had re-won the throne, but he hadn't seen the aftermath, not like this. The dead were piled high, and nearly everything that wasn't stone had been burned.

He didn't know why it affected him. In his anger over the years, he'd fantasized about Mercia falling. So he didn't know why it hurt so much to see it.

His eyes shifted to a long line of soldiers with their hands bound—not Mercians but clearly the forces that were defeated to win back the Mercian throne, hired swords. They were led by the Shadowmen to cages on carts and shoved inside.

Cyrus knew these cages.

Slave cages. His blood ran cold. Yes—this was a different man from the previous Shadow King, but he was still the same.

And Cyrus would kill him.

CHAPTER THIRTY-TWO

He waited.

Again.

Norah was back in the Shadowlands. Although she was closer now, it was harder to get her a vial there. The Shadowmen were much more watchful. And some fucking girl with a bow was worse than the winterhawks had been at taking down his birds.

He had, however, managed to leave a vial on a garden bench that Norah frequented. He suspected she'd use the blood shortly after receiving it, and as he walked the hall toward his study, a small smile came to his lips as he felt the pull. He slipped into the chamber and closed the door behind him before letting himself chase the call.

As he entered her mind, he paused when he saw her. Cyrus couldn't *feel* emotion in another's mind, but he could read it. And, standing before him in her mind, she was very much on the verge of tears. Concern filled him, and he stepped closer.

"I wasn't sure you'd come, after Mikael..."

So, she knew the Shadow King had taken the blood. He discreetly flipped through her recent memories, looking for what had happened, and he found her showing the king the vial in what appeared to be a

336

temple. It didn't look purposeful, or malicious, more of a confession of sorts.

"*I'm sorry,*" she said. "*I didn't know he'd use it. I'm sure that was a surprise.*"

Not a terrible surprise, though.

She swallowed. "*I... I thought about it a lot, him calling you. At first I thought it would have helped him understand if he'd seen you.*" She paused again, looking down at her hands. "*But now*"—she shook her head—"*I think it would have made it worse, knowing you really are here. So, thank you. For not engaging.*"

But if she was thanking him, why did she look so sad? She stared at him, with her large blue sky of eyes traveling his face. "*But Soren says it's time for me to say goodbye.*"

Who cared what the fucking commander said?

"*And he's right,*" she whispered. She was crying now but forced a smile. "*He said you need to start doing your job looking over Mercia and stop haunting me.*"

This commander was really starting to annoy him...

Norah sniffed, then cleared her throat. She seemed so small.

"*I know you're not yourself,*" she said softly, "*at least not exactly, but I think it's what the old you would have wanted—for me to be able to move forward.*"

Wait—what was she saying? He shook his head as he stepped closer.

"*I want you to know that I'm all right,*" she told him. "*That I'm cared for and looked after.*"

She was leaving him. *No.* He couldn't let her. He reached up and clasped her cheek.

Her eyes welled. "*I'm all right, Alexander,*" she told him. And then she put her arms around him.

But he didn't want it; he didn't want this embrace—it meant she was leaving. She couldn't leave, but he didn't know how to stop her.

He had to say something...

A tear spilled down her cheek as she stepped up onto her toes and brought her lips to his cheek. "*Goodbye,*" she whispered.

He had to say something...

He had to—

The bond broke.

Cyrus opened his eyes to his study, gasping for breath.

Had she just severed them?

Was she letting him go?

Because of what the commander had said...

His blood burned in his veins. *No.* That wasn't going to happen. He shoved through his study door and stormed down the hall, his rage building with each step.

This Shadow commander thought he could get rid of him? As if Norah could simply say *goodbye,* and he'd be gone?

That wasn't how this worked.

He burst through the iron doors to the outside.

Who did this man think he was?

A large flock of birds foraged the grass for worms, filling the air with their merry chirps.

Cyrus ripped his blade across his palm and flung his arm wide, baring his teeth as he arced a spray of blood over them.

This commander thought he could send him a message. Well, Cyrus had a message for *him.* And the birds took off to deliver that message.

His footsteps echoed through the halls. Angry footsteps. The dogs trilled high-pitched whines as they followed.

Cyrus fisted his hand tightly as he pressed it against him, trying to stem the bleeding, but it didn't help much. In his anger, he'd cut himself deeply. Too deeply, and he needed to find Teron.

He also needed to send Norah another vial. She still had his blood, but she needed to know that he wanted her to use it again.

He'd send vials until she did.

"Cyrus!" Orion's voice sounded as he passed a side hall.

He slowed but stifled a groan. Guilt daggered him. He hadn't looked for Orion's woman when he'd been in Norah's mind. He hadn't even thought about her.

"Have you—"

Orion's words cut off when he saw Cyrus's hand, then his eyes followed the trail of blood down the hall. "What did you do?"

"Cut myself a little too deeply, that's all. I'm going to see Teron now."

Orion nodded. "Yeah, do that."

Cyrus moved to leave.

"Did you learn anything from the queen yet?"

Cyrus paused and shook his head. "Not yet," he said.

"She hasn't called you back to her?"

He shook his head again. "No."

Orion drew in a somber breath. "All right." He glanced down at the floor and then back to Cyrus. "I'll let you get to Teron."

Cyrus gave a stiff nod and continued on his way, but as he passed the throne room, he slowed again.

Kord stood in the center of the room, speaking to someone just out of view. His voice echoed firmly. "You can't just demand an audience with the king."

This wasn't an entirely unusual occurrence, but there was something unusual now.

Kord's hand rested on the hilt of his sword.

Cyrus stepped just inside the shadow of the alcove to see whom he was speaking to.

And his chest tightened.

It was a dark-haired man—tall and thin with a sharp jaw. Cyrus didn't recognize him, but he wore a black cloak, trimmed in dark purple, the same as the woman who had recognized Essandra in Japheth.

Cyrus stepped into the throne room. The man's gaze snapped to him, and a smile snaked across his lips. Immediately Cyrus didn't like him.

"King Cyrus," the man greeted him. "I bring a message from the high witch Soroya Fey."

Heat swelled inside him, but Cyrus calmly cocked his head. "Who?"

The man's eyes darkened. "Don't be coy. You know exactly who I'm talking about."

Now Cyrus really didn't like him. "Are you always a disrespectful guest?" *Guest* was a stretch. This man wasn't welcome here.

"Of course not, but you're harboring someone here who belongs to the high witch," the man told him.

Cyrus gave a dark chuckle. "If you think anyone here belongs to another person, you've done some very poor preparation for your visit to Rael."

"Where is Sabine Laveau?"

The man's question harrowed him, sowing seeds of violence along Cyrus's spine. "There is no Sabine Laveau here," he answered.

"What about Essandra Savoy?"

The mere mention of her name rippled fire under his skin. Cyrus stared at the man as fight flamed in his veins. "What is your message?" he asked. "I'll deliver it for you. If I like it."

"Oh, this message isn't for her. It's for you. Soroya gives you three days to return her." He smiled, then added, "Respectfully."

"Ah, respectfully." Cyrus nodded. "That's good." Cyrus moved closer, and the man's eyes dropped to his bleeding hand, noticing it for the first time. His brows drew down.

But Cyrus's hand was now the last thing on his mind. "Three days?" he asked.

The man was still caught on the stream of blood dripping to the floor. "Three days," he finally repeated.

Cyrus nodded. He turned and looked at his dogs. Reaching out his hand, he trailed a blood line across One's head. "Three is a good number, isn't it?"

The man glanced at Kord in confusion, then looked back at Cyrus. "What?"

Cyrus paused. "Three. It's a good number." He stepped casually to the second dog, doing the same—a smear of blood. Then the third.

The man swallowed. "I-I guess so."

Cyrus turned back to him and gave a thin smile. "One," he said. "Two." The man shifted back as his brow stitched deeper. "Three."

And the man was barely able to give a scream before teeth sank into his throat.

The dogs made short work of their kill. They were certainly efficient. They'd become companions around the palace. Cyrus had almost forgotten just how ferocious they were.

He leaned over the now dead pile of shredded flesh. "Your witch can fuck herself," he said. "Respectfully."

He felt Essandra's eyes on him, but Cyrus pretended he didn't as he took another bite of his food.

"Are you going to tell me what happened?" she asked.

He paused midlift of his chalice, and his eyes shifted to Kord.

Kord slowed his chewing, then swallowed, but didn't lift his fork again.

"Don't act like you didn't hear me," she pressed. "A number of people saw you hemorrhaging through the hall."

Cyrus's shoulders eased, and he took a drink. "A cut," he said casually. "A little deep, that was all." Not a lie, although Teron had had to work the better part of the afternoon healing it.

She eyed him suspiciously.

He flashed his healed palm at her. "Perfectly fine now."

Her eyes narrowed, and she shot a glare at Kord.

Kord took another bite of food.

She looked back at Cyrus. "What did you need the blood for?"

"Birds," he answered. Also not a lie.

Her suspicion lingered, but she didn't question him more, and Cyrus didn't offer more. After dinner, he retired to his chamber, not for sleep. Sleep wouldn't come. He needed to send another vial to Norah—a direct invitation for her to call him back to her.

If she would.

His body ached. He wasn't sure why. He hadn't done anything particularly laborious. General tiredness, maybe. He selected a clean vial and set it on the side table, but as he positioned a spouted catch over it, the bond called to him.

His pulse quickened. He knew immediately.

Norah.

This was a surprise. So was the anger in her voice as she called him.

"*Alexander!*" she seethed.

Cyrus hid himself behind the veil as he stepped into her mind. As much as he wanted to find out what had happened, there was something he needed to do first.

Something he'd promised.

He quickly sifted through her memories of the women around her, specifically for Orion's woman.

And he knew the moment he saw her.

Orion had a gift with the pen, creating portraits of Vitalia's exact likeness, and it appeared he was right in his assumption she was a maid. Perhaps she was even a friend. Orion would be happy to know she was taken care of, maybe it would even tide him over for a while. Cyrus would tell him she was well.

Until he found another memory of her in Norah's mind.

One of her not well.

Vitalia's green eyes stared back at him, dulled by death, as she lay on a stone floor. Spilled wine from an overturned chalice pooled and soaked the long blond hair around her head.

Orion's woman was dead.

He watched through Norah's memories as the Mercian castle descended into chaos. This must have been during the coup.

"*Where are you?*" Norah demanded, her anger echoing through every corner of her mind.

Cyrus swallowed back the dismay; he couldn't linger on Orion's woman for long. He'd have to make sense of it later and for now focus on the situation with Norah.

And why she was so upset.

He rifled through her most recent memories.

His blood ran cold.

His wrath of birds had reached the Shadowlands, and not just the ones that had been in his courtyard. They'd somehow pulled a whole flock with them. He hadn't been particularly sure what they'd do when his rage had sent them; he hadn't sent them with a specific directive. But now he watched her memory in horror as the small animals struck the tower of the Shadow castle by the hundreds, raining down their feathered deaths over the commander. *And over Norah*, who'd been with him.

No... Those hadn't been meant for her.

"*Alexander!*" she seethed again.

It wasn't just anger in her voice. It was hurt. She sank down into a chair at her vanity, her strength leaving her. "*Alexander.*"

This wasn't how he'd imagined himself returning to her.

"*I know you're there,*" she said.

Did she? He hadn't thought he'd revealed himself. But slowly, he stepped from behind the veil.

She didn't stand when she saw him. She only looked at him with a deep sadness in her eyes. "*Did you send the birds?*" she asked. Her voice cracked as she spoke. "*Did you do that?*"

He stepped closer. There was no way for him to explain what had happened, how he hadn't meant to, how he wished he hadn't.

Her lip trembled, and she shook her head. "*Why?*"

Cyrus stepped even closer.

"*Why would you do that to me?*" she whispered. "*How could you do that?*"

She grew even smaller in the chair as she sat. The pain in her eyes knifed him. She loved him. She'd trusted him.

He had to say something now. He had to tell her...

Slowly, he sank to his knees in front of her, dropping down eye to eye.

"*What happened to you?*" she whispered. A tear trailed her face as she brought her hand to his cheek. "*Is there anything left of the Alexander I knew?*"

He couldn't lie to her anymore. He couldn't deceive her anymore. Ever so slowly, he shook his head.

Her breath hitched as she pulled back. "*Then you're not Alexander. If you were, you aren't anymore. Not truly.*"

Again, he shook his head, and she sucked in a ragged breath.

Why did he always do this—hurt the people who cared? He took her hand and pulled it back to his cheek.

A sob escaped as more tears spilled from her eyes.

"*Grandmother's dying,*" she said.

Wait—the queen regent?

"Without her, I don't know what to do." She shook her head. *"And without you too."* Her voice was barely a whisper now. *"I'm trying not to hate you for leaving me, but I do. I do sometimes."* She pulled her hands from his and wiped her face. *"Mikael is taking me back to Mercia tomorrow."* She paused as she looked down. *"This is the last time I'll call you."*

No. No, no… He couldn't let her say goodbye again. He couldn't let her go. He shook his head.

She brought her fingers back to his face. She touched him like she held the world in her hands, and he couldn't speak.

"Goodbye, Alexander," she whispered.

And she broke the bond.

Cyrus sat quietly long after Norah had left him.

That was it. He knew that was it. She wouldn't call him back again.

It was his own fault. He'd ruined it, and he'd lost a valuable asset against the Shadow King.

And something more…

He hadn't thought he was particularly attached to Norah, but the way she looked at him, the way she spoke to him, the way she touched him…

He wanted to be looked at that way.

And spoken to that way.

Touched that way.

His whole life, he'd prided himself in not needing anyone or anything. It had been blissful ignorance. He hadn't known. He hadn't known how it *felt*.

But as his mind shifted back to the Shadow King, a thought came to him.

A thought of madness.

An opportunity. And he couldn't waste it.

He needed to talk to Everan.

Cyrus found him in the main hall with Kord and Orion.

"The queen is on her way back to Mercia," he told them as he hurried toward them. "And the Shadow King is with her."

"She called you again?" Everan asked in surprise.

Cyrus nodded. "Her grandmother is dying, and he's taking her back. If I travel to the stone circle, I can get ahead of him and be waiting when he passes through."

"You're going to kill her husband while her grandmother is dying?" Kord crossed his arms. "That's cold."

War was cold.

Everan's dark eyes were fixed on Cyrus. "Is that really what you're planning to do?"

Cyrus didn't feel like he even needed to answer that.

Everan shook his head. "Cyrus, if you march the army again, it will bring war with the empire, and we're not prepared for that."

"Are we not?" Wasn't this what they'd been working toward? Wasn't this what he'd suffered Gregor for? "Regardless, it doesn't matter. I'm not taking the army."

A line trenched Everan's forehead as he shifted back on his heel. "You can't go alone."

"He won't have his army with him—he's accompanying his queen, not marching to war."

Kord snorted. "He won't have a war army, maybe, but he will have *some* kind of army. He'd ensure his queen's protection."

"My point is that this should be a smaller strike—a targeted attack. I may have an opportunity at him directly, one that I'd never get facing him on a battlefield."

"I can go with you," Orion told him, "help get you in."

Cyrus nodded appreciatively. A swell of guilt weighted his stomach. Cyrus needed to tell him...

"Obviously, we're all going," Everan said.

"We're all going where?" Essandra asked from behind.

They turned.

"I'll give you one guess," Kord told her. "Because one guess is really all you need."

"The Shadow King is traveling to Mercia," Cyrus said. "If there's a chance at him... I have to take it."

Where he expected pushback, there was none. She simply asked, "When do we leave?"

"Today. We'll travel to the stone circle and wait for him just north."

She nodded. "I'll go prepare."

Kord and Everan followed her out, but Cyrus grabbed Orion to keep him back.

"Hey... I..."

Orion stilled. He didn't even breathe as his gray eyes locked on Cyrus with a desperate intensity. "Did you see something?"

"I looked through the queen's mind, and..." This would absolutely crush him. Orion had been looking for this woman for years.

He'd never find her.

He'd never see her again.

But what did a man have if he didn't have hope?

"It's not her," Cyrus said. "She's not there."

Orion's lips parted, and he let out a breath as his shoulders fell. He cast his gaze to the floor, gathering himself, then looked back at Cyrus. "Are you sure?" he asked.

"I'm sure."

Orion wiped a rough hand over his face. He swallowed and nodded. "Thank you for looking. For trying." He paused, and they stood in silence. Then an icy fire returned to Orion's eyes. "I will find her."

"Yeah," Cyrus said softly. "Of course you will."

Chapter Thirty-Three

Orion's steely eyes pierced through the slit in the wrap that covered his face. Cyrus had gotten used to seeing him uncovered—seeing him *not* as an assassin.

Things felt more serious now.

As they should.

Orion handed him another set of small blades that Cyrus slipped into the chevron concealments of his vest. He carried more weapons on his person than he ever had before, but aside from the short sword across his back, they were all completely hidden.

Essandra watched him silently.

Kord and Everan—*not* silently.

"Look, I get that it will be cleaner and faster with just two people," Kord argued, "but things are going to go to shit after you make your move, and you're going to need us."

"You're going to need help getting away," Everan added.

"That's why Orion's with me," Cyrus countered. Orion would actually be there to get him *in*, to help him get as close to the Shadow King as possible. Cyrus wasn't particularly concerned with the *getting away* part.

"We can be on standby, just a short way away," Kord said.

"No."

Kord's lips thinned. "I don't get what the issue is. If we're not needed, then we're not needed, but if something goes wrong—"

"I said *no*," Cyrus repeated firmly. It wasn't that he didn't think he'd need their help, but if something happened to him, which was likely, they wouldn't be able to get back through the portal. They wouldn't be able to get home. Worse—he'd get them killed with him. But Orion could get out, and he could find his way back.

Cyrus looked at Essandra, who surprisingly hadn't argued with him all morning since he'd shared he wanted them to stay behind. "I think we're ready," he said.

She stepped to him. "You need to be the one to create the tether with Orion so you can break it on the other side," she told him.

Cyrus reached to pull a blade.

"I'll get my own blood, thank you very much," Orion said quickly, stopping him. "I've seen how you cut yourself." He flicked his blade, and a bead of blood swelled from the faintest scratch on his forearm. Cyrus swiped it with his thumb and brought it to his lips.

"I know I've said this before," Orion told him, "but that's disgusting."

Cyrus almost smiled as he spoke the words that bonded them. There were plenty of other things he could think of that were more disgusting than blood.

"Now drink this," Essandra said as she put a small cup in his hand. Something mixed in wine.

Cyrus swallowed it down. "What's in that?"

"My blood," she answered, then whispered the words of the tether.

He jerked back. "What are you doing?" She wasn't coming with him through the portal.

"I have a feeling you're going to make some very poor decisions. Hopefully now you'll make better ones."

Heat rose across his skin. *She'd bonded her fate to his.* "Break it," he demanded.

"No."

He'd do it himself. Cyrus grabbed hold of her and hissed out the spell. Then he flipped a small blade from his vest and nicked it across the back of his hand to check.

Orion snarled as he grabbed his own hand. "Fuck the gods, Cyrus!"

Cyrus glanced down to Essandra's hand, which bore the same nick he'd just given himself. He gripped her tighter as he spat out the spell once more.

"How many times are you going to cut me?" she snapped just before he tested the knife against his skin a second time. "You know it won't work. Only the maker of the tether can break it."

"Then break it!" he demanded.

But again, she shook her head. "No."

He bared his teeth as his voice dropped to a whisper. "Why are you doing this? You'd take from me an opportunity to kill the Shadow King?"

"If it kills you too, then it's not an opportunity."

His hold softened, but he still held on to her. "Essandra," he pleaded. "I won't be able to do it like this. You have to break it."

"I won't," she said firmly, then she pushed him through the portal.

CHAPTER THIRTY-FOUR

Cyrus lay on his back on the ground with his arm resting over his face. It was easier to focus his sight through the birds this way. He could do it while standing, but melding his mind with the birds' often threatened his balance. He also found that this helped with the pulsing pressure in his head.

"Is the queen traveling with a maid at all?" Orion asked him.

Cyrus's stomach grew heavy. "No," he said. "No maid."

For two days he watched as the Shadow King and Norah made their way north. They traveled with a smaller legion of soldiers—a few thousand. And the Shadow commander. That man was probably going to be a problem. Cyrus would have to figure out what to do about him.

"So, what's your plan?" Orion asked on the third day, as Cyrus again lay watching.

Cyrus ignored him. He ignored the cold seeping through his layers from the hard earth underneath him; he ignored the wind. He pushed everything out—the crackling campfire, the animal chitter in the distance, the sound of Orion whittling a sharpened tip on a broken tree branch that he'd found.

Cyrus focused.

The Shadowmen traveled openly—an interesting choice. Their alliance with Aleon must've made them feel safe.

Good.

Feeling safe made one careless, although the king was still traveling with a legion, so he wasn't as careless as Cyrus would have liked.

"You do have a plan, right?" Orion asked.

Cyrus gave up the birds for a while and pushed himself up. He cut Orion a sharp eye but still didn't answer. He'd have a plan when it came to him.

Orion nodded with a frown. "Right." He cut another sliver from the tip of the branch he held.

"You planning on using that on the job?" Cyrus ribbed him.

Orion gave a slight smirk. "Feels like it fits the theme—two reluctant partners with no plan, care to the wind, against the famed Shadow King, the Destroyer, and a group of the most skilled warriors in the world." He butted his lopsided spear on the ground. "'Tis my valiant weapon."

Cyrus couldn't help a small chuckle at that. He liked this man. He was a lot like Kord—unafraid to speak the truth, brave, and skilled, with a good heart. He looked at Orion, growing more serious. "I would have called us friends, but I think the rest of it sounds about right."

Orion's smirk turned into a smile. A small one, but genuine nonetheless. The assassin nodded to himself, turning his gaze to his makeshift spear. "Can I ask you a personal question?" he said.

Cyrus gave a short nod.

"I get why you want to kill the Shadow King, but I've always wondered—what made you hate your own brother so much? Why did you want to kill him?"

Cyrus had never thought about it as a secret, but he'd only shared it with those closest to him. Maybe because it hurt. And that hurt carried shame. But he didn't mind telling Orion.

"He abandoned me," he said finally. "He was my brother, the one person I trusted most, and he left me." He paused as the familiar hurt returned. "Then he lived... a beautiful life, like I never even existed. Like I never even mattered."

His chest tightened. He hated that the memory could still feel so raw after so long. Alexander was dead, and it still hurt. He was gone, and Cyrus still couldn't get out from underneath it. And it was crushing...

"But look at all the people that you matter to now," Orion said.

Cyrus's eyes locked back on Orion, and the pain in his chest stalled.

The assassin gave another wayward look at his stick. "They're all waiting for you to come back, so it's probably best I use something better than this spear, yeah?"

And Cyrus couldn't help a smile.

The nearer he got to Mercia, the more Cyrus felt his chances slipping away, yet there was nothing he could do. The army kept their king well surrounded, well protected. Cyrus could only follow. And wait.

Until they reached the Free Cities.

The cities stretched along the southeastern border of Mercia, each blending into the next, so it was difficult to tell where one ended and another began. However, they were very different from one another, with their own unique primary trade. Farther north, Hanset held the world's largest fur trade outside of Tarsus; to the east, Borden dealt in rare gems. Cyrus had never been to any of these places, but these were known facts.

It was here that Jaem met them. He wouldn't be joining the attempt against the Shadow King, but Cyrus intended to return to Rael with him. Cyrus smiled when he saw his friend, and they locked arms with an embrace when they reached each other.

"Cyrus," Jaem greeted him with a grin.

"It's good to see you," Cyrus told him. Then he nodded to Orion. "You remember Orion."

Jaem gave him a friendly nod and extended his hand.

Orion took it. "Hey, um, I'm glad I can tell you this in person—I just wanted to thank you for what you did. Trying to find Vitalia."

"Of course," Jaem said. "And if there's anything else I can help with, let me know."

Orion gripped his hand in appreciation.

Cyrus's chest tightened. "All right, let's get moving."

The city of Redding sprawled as far as the eye could see. Cyrus's younger self would have loved to explore, to have taken in everything the diverse spread had to offer, but he was no longer his younger self, and that boyish curiosity had long died.

Now he was focused on one thing.

He hadn't expected the Shadow army to stop in the Free Cities or even pass directly through. Populous areas carried risks of ill-intentioned company—company like Cyrus. So when the

Shadowmen paused on the south end, and the king broke away and entered the city with a small group of men, Cyrus sprang into action.

A city never felt so big until one was trying to quickly make their way through it. Throngs of people knit tightly in between brightly colored market stalls slowed his pace. Orion slipped from shadow to shadow, as smooth as silk, while Jaem stealthily blended in with the masses. Cyrus gave up trying to copy them and resorted to simply pushing his way through. Merchants yelled words he didn't understand, likely telling him to slow down or be careful. He did neither of those things.

Finally, they made it to a narrow, hilled pocket street that had a broad view of the mainway. Cyrus sidled against the shadowed stone wall as he watched. And waited.

He didn't have to wait long, and he froze when he saw him.

The Shadow King.

Cyrus had been inside his mind, he'd seen him in visions and in the minds of others, but this was his first time actually seeing him in person. He was tall and broad-shouldered, a beast of a man. He stood like a wraith, like the toxic darkness he spread.

The promise of violence flooded Cyrus's veins.

The king looked like his ruthless father.

He was guilty like his father.

He'd die like his father.

But one thing stood between him and Cyrus: Norah.

She meandered freely through the streets, hidden in plain sight in the mix of travelers and merchants. Her hair hung loose around her. She made no effort to cover it. No one knew her here. Or she didn't *think* anyone knew her.

He hated that she was here. He hated that she'd see another person she loved die, even if it was the Shadow King. But, most of all, he hated that she'd find out about Cyrus this way. He slipped out from the alley and wove a path along the side of the mainway, careful to keep hidden behind the sellers and their wares. He waved Jaem to stay back, but Orion followed.

From merchant to merchant, they moved. Closer, and closer still.

"I count eleven with him," Orion said quietly. "Including the Destroyer."

Yes, Cyrus had seen the commander.

"They're too close," Orion added.

Norah paused at a stall where a portly man grilled meat over a pit fire. After a short exchange, she pointed to a plate of sausages, then dropped a coin in his hand before spearing one with her knife and taking it.

Closer still, he moved.

She turned back to the Shadow King. When she offered him part of the sausage, he bit the whole piece. That earned him an affectionate berating, at which the king chuckled.

Cyrus stiffened. Rage surged through him—this man could laugh, he could be happy. It was the cruelest injustice of the gods.

Promising her another sausage, the king lumbered back toward the meat market stall. Norah stayed where she was, watching him with a smile that he didn't deserve. Cyrus was only a few paces from her now.

Slowly, he pulled his sword from the scabbard. When the king returned to her...

"Not yet," Orion said in his ear.

This was the closest he'd ever come to being able to kill the Shadow King. The closest he might ever be. He could end it all.

Here.

Now.

Cyrus's body tightened—every fiber of his being coiling for launch. He focused like he focused in the bloodsport arena, and his body surged with fight. The air heated around him, and the cobblestone under his feet softened to sand. The blood-laden smell of the sport flooded his nose.

Time slowed.

The Shadow King wouldn't know what hit him. It would be over in moments.

"Not yet," Orion said again, firmer this time. "The Destroyer is still too close. You won't get out."

Cyrus glanced at the commander. He was a monster of a man, and he *was* close, but was he fast? Cyrus was pretty sure he was faster. "I can do it," he said.

"Are you really willing to take that gamble? You have your woman tethered to you."

"You don't think I know that?" he hissed. He looked back at the king. He could make it.

"If they're comfortable enough to stop and get sausages, they'll be lax the rest of the way through the cities," Orion told him. "They might even stay overnight in one. Another opportunity *will* come."

Cyrus shook his head. "You don't know that."

"I know you won't make this."

Cyrus clenched his jaw. He could. He was confident he could.

But was he confident enough to bet Essandra's life on it?

No.

As he let his blade slide back into its scabbard, his body threatened to rebel, to charge anyway. The muscles under his skin burned from the force of restraint. He gripped the corner of the stone fascia where they hid between two shops. His eyes blurred, as if to escape the torture it was to see an opportunity so close and not take it.

He couldn't even look at the king now, and he shifted his gaze to Norah.

She stood, smiling, still not knowing Cyrus was there. Not knowing how close to death her husband truly was.

Suddenly, her smile fell. She glanced around the market, searching, as if she could feel his eyes on her.

Cyrus stole himself back against the stone corner, out of sight.

"What's wrong?" Orion asked.

"If she sees me, she'll recognize me," he said.

Orion shifted, leaning past Cyrus to check. "I don't think she did," he said finally.

Slowly, Cyrus peered out again.

Norah had started back toward the main gates of the city, with the Shadow King and the commander with her. They were leaving.

Regret clawed at him as he watched his life's purpose walk away.

Orion's promise proved true. More than true. Not only did another opportunity come, but it was an opportunity even better than the one before.

As darkness came, the king broke away from his army again to stop overnight at a castle that had been converted into an inn. Cyrus guessed it was for Norah—a break from the discomforts of travel. The Shadow commander went with them, as well as a group of warriors, but Cyrus wasn't concerned about them this time. He didn't expect they'd be in the room with the king.

It did pose the challenge of how Cyrus would get in, though. He hid in the shadows outside, looking for options. The king wouldn't likely be on the same side of the castle as the adjoining pub, nor would he be on the ground floor. So somewhere on the west side—

"Hey," Orion said quietly beside him as they waited. "After this, I want you to grant me leave to go to Mercia."

Cyrus stalled in his thoughts. His throat grew dry. "Let's talk about it after."

"I know you didn't see Vitalia in the queen's mind, but that doesn't mean she's not there."

Cyrus had to tell him. But not now. "We have to focus on the Shadow King right now; we'll talk about this *after*."

"No. You told me to wait, and I've waited. But after this, I want to go."

"Orion—"

"I've been a loyal servant to your cause, and this is all I've asked in return."

"All right," Cyrus said finally. He couldn't argue this, not here, not now. "I'll give you leave to do whatever you want, go wherever you want." If he still wanted to go after he knew the truth. "I'll even give you whatever you need to get there, but right now, we have to focus on this."

Satisfied, Orion nodded.

Now they needed to find where the king was staying.

"You take the east side," Cyrus told him, "I'll take the west." He looked at Jaem. "You check out the pub. We'll all meet on the back side."

They split.

It was a solidly built castle, the stone stacked clean. Climbing wasn't an easy option. A few doors provided viable prospects, but he'd rather not come from the inside, to avoid the Shadow guards at their posts.

He paused as his eyes caught on a high window. The shutters were closed, but candlelight spilled from the cracks. He noted the room as a possibility.

Cyrus caught up with Orion and Jaem on the back side, and they crouched low in the darkness.

"The pub is full," Jaem said. "But I didn't see any Shadowmen."

"I took a quick look inside too," Orion added. Of course he had. "The pub might be full but there's practically no one staying at the inn. The king will be in the only occupied room, I think."

Well, that made things easier. "There's candlelight from a window on the west corner."

"That has to be him."

"How'd you get in?" Cyrus asked him.

"The front door."

Cyrus couldn't see Orion's face, but he still stared at his shadow. "That easy?"

"For me, not for you." The assassin gave a small chuckle. "Stealth isn't your strength, my friend. But there is a trellis on the pub side. You can climb that and take the roofline over, drop down to the wall walk, and climb through the corner merlons to this sort of... decorative mid-relief that runs all the way around. I think you could walk it if you're careful. How's your balance?"

"Good. I think." He hoped.

"You know," Orion said, "I should really be the one doing this."

Cyrus shook his head. "No. I need to do it."

Orion sighed. "Right. The Destroyer is tending the horses, so if we're going to go, I suggest we go now."

Cyrus shifted in surprise. "The commander? Tending the horses?"

"Look, I'm just telling you what I saw. The Destroyer is with the horses, so that means the king is alone in his room."

Alone with Norah.

Again, Cyrus hated this for her, but there was no getting around it. She'd see her husband die tonight.

"Wait for us on the south ridge," Cyrus told Jaem. "See if you can find some horses."

Cyrus didn't waste any more time. He and Orion made their way along the roofline from the tavern to the west side of the castle. Cyrus's balance wasn't as good as he'd remembered it being, but it was good enough to get him past the wall walk. He paused for a moment before he dropped down to the window ledge.

"Hey," he told Orion. "If this goes poorly, get yourself out. If I'm captured, you need to make Essandra break the tether." He'd already broken it for Orion.

"How would I even fucking do that?" Orion reached out and caught his arm. "I'm not leaving you."

Cyrus stilled. There were only a couple of people he would believe if they told him that. This man was one of them. And those words...

Whenever he heard them, those four words healed something ever so slightly more within him.

"So don't be an idiot," Orion added.

With a final nod, Cyrus dropped down to the window ledge while Orion waited on the roof.

He paused for a moment, drawing a deep breath. And waited.

Then came the calm—the calm of violent promise. He trusted this calm. It was what he'd relied on in the arena; it was what he relied on now.

His senses sharpened, and his skin prickled in anticipation. His heart beat heavily. Not nervous. Eager.

Slowly, he cracked the shutter and pushed open the hinged window. It complied silently, but the air snuffed the candle, and he froze.

He waited a little more.

All was quiet.

Cyrus slipped between the cracked windowpanes and sidled up into the shadows of the drapery.

His eyes searched the darkness.

The bitter taste of disappointment clawed up the back of his throat as he realized—the Shadow King wasn't there.

Cyrus combed the room—it didn't appear to be the *wrong* room. The queen was asleep on the bed. But where was the king? Perhaps he was in a different chamber, or perhaps he'd join her shortly.

Maybe Cyrus should wait.

Norah stirred and sat up. "Mikael?" she called.

Cyrus pressed back into the shadows. His heart beat in his chest. The last time he'd seen her as she slept, he'd been trying to kill her. The thought soured his stomach now.

He cursed himself. The king wasn't here; he couldn't stay. He needed to leave before she discovered him, but he didn't dare move.

"I know you're there," she said.

Well, shit.

At least she didn't know *who* was there.

His heart beat faster. Should he let her see him? Could he deceive her in the darkness the way he deceived her in her mind? The last they'd talked, she had told him she wouldn't call him back again. He'd come anyway. Would she be angry? Would she talk to him? He couldn't deny the *want* for her to talk to him again, and before he knew what he was doing, he stepped forward into the moonlight.

His hood covered him, not yet revealing his face.

She didn't startle. She didn't say anything. She only stared at him. Then, slowly, she rose to her knees and moved to the edge of the bed, stepping down onto the floor and putting the large piece of furniture between them.

He waited, unmoving.

"What do you want?" she asked. Her voice was low, but it wasn't weak. She moved slowly around to the foot of the bed as she spoke.

He didn't answer her. He wouldn't.

She moved closer. "Why are you here?" She cocked her head to the side. "I should tell you about the last time I woke to a strange man in my room." She paused. "I hate to spoil a good story, but it didn't end well for him. For any of them."

He remembered. If only she knew...

Norah drew closer. She was right in front of him now, but still, he made no move.

Then he felt the cold of a steel dagger as she whipped it to his throat.

"Final words?" she hissed.

Her speed surprised him. And he hadn't realized she'd had a dagger in her hand.

Impressive.

She hadn't been weak before, but she was even stronger now.

Cyrus held his hands up, showing her he meant her no harm, because he didn't. But she clearly didn't believe him, as she dug the tip of the dagger into his skin.

Did he dare to show himself to her? He couldn't. He couldn't explain now. It would jeopardize everything. He couldn't reveal himself. Yet... he couldn't not show himself.

Ever so slowly, he reached up and pulled back his hood.

Norah sucked in a ragged breath, and the knife in her hand dropped to the floor.

Still, he didn't move.

"What magic is this?" she whispered as she stumbled back. No doubt it was a shock for her—him appearing without the blood.

He stood, waiting, his heart pounding.

Norah reached out, her hand shaking, as she stepped forward again. Her fingertips touched him, and he felt her. He actually felt her this time.

She spread her hand flat against his chest. Her touch was warm and soft, and still filled with grief.

She gaped up at him. "How is this possible?"

But he couldn't tell her that. Not yet.

Her eyes glistened in the moonlight, stirring his own emotion. Never had someone looked at him like this. Touched him like this. It was the touch of longing. Of missing. Of loving.

He knew this already, he'd seen her love in her mind, but to be standing here in the flesh, truly feeling it from her—it was a power in itself, capturing him, holding him.

"How are you here?" she whispered.

He was desperate to tell her, but still, he said nothing.

Cyrus raised a hand to her cheek. She closed her eyes against his warmth. She wanted his touch, needed it even.

Then she threw her arms around him. She held him. Tightly. So tightly, like she couldn't let him go. There was a desperation, a need, and she clung to him.

And he let himself hold her back. He'd never been needed. In the arena—yes. In battle—yes. To build a kingdom—yes. But in love...

No.

And to feel that love now... He was at a loss for words. He couldn't speak even if he tried.

She stepped back for a moment but still held on to his hands. She held him like she was scared to let him go.

He didn't want her to let him go.

Slowly, he brought his hand up again and brushed the backs of his fingers against her cheek. She leaned into his touch.

And the pull toward her was like nothing he'd ever felt.

He couldn't help himself. Because he wasn't himself. He stepped forward and caught her mouth with his. He wasn't sure what made him kiss her. Maybe it was the way she looked at him. The way she needed him. The way she loved him.

Cyrus lost himself to logic and reason, and, suddenly, it wasn't Norah he was kissing.

His body moved on its own, walking her backward. She stumbled, and he caught her. He would never let her fall. But she spread her palms on his chest and pushed against him, breathing words against his mouth.

Cyrus wasn't sure what she said, yet he paused. Was she all right? He couldn't see her face in his shadow under the moonlight, but her touch still permeated through him. He brushed her cheek and dropped his head to hers again.

"No," she said, clearly this time, and pushed harder against him. Her voice sounded strange in his ears.

He stopped. Something was wrong.

"This isn't who you are," she said, "or who I am. This isn't what we were."

Confusion flooded him. She loved him. He could feel it radiating off her. He could see it even in the darkness.

"My heart belongs to another," she whispered. "You can't be here. Not like this."

He knew he couldn't be there. But he was.

"Alexander," she whispered.

His brother's name in his ear jarred him, and he stiffened. Suddenly, he felt very much like a fool. This was Norah. It was Alexander she loved. Had he really forgotten? No—he'd known. But there was a want inside him that played tricks on his mind. A want that pulled at him.

What was he even doing? He cursed himself.

He shouldn't even be here.

He never should have come.

She drew back from him, putting her hand over her face and drawing in a breath, and he seized his chance. Three silent steps to the window, and he slipped out and swung himself against the ledge. Quickly making his way back to the wall walk, he climbed to the rooftop where Orion was waiting.

"What happened?" Orion asked.

Cyrus shook his head. He couldn't talk about it.

"Is it done? Did you kill the Shadow King?"

Cyrus pushed out a breath in anger. Anger at himself. He couldn't speak. If he did, the shame would pool out of his throat and drown him. He could only shake his head again. No, he hadn't killed the Shadow King. He hadn't even seen him. He didn't know what had come over him, but he knew one thing—

He'd ruined his chance at the Shadow King.

He'd ruined everything.

CHAPTER THIRTY-FIVE

He'd lost his chance at the Shadow King. And for what? Anger pulsed through him, and Cyrus gritted his teeth so hard his jaw ached.

"Are you going to tell us what happened?" Orion asked him as they rested their mounts along a stream. Jaem had met them on the ridge with three stolen horses, and they'd pushed hard through the night until they were a safe distance from Hanset and the Shadow army.

Cyrus checked the leather saddlebags to see if they had anything helpful in them. They didn't. "I don't want to talk about it," he said.

Orion scoffed and threw his arms in the air. "What the fuck, Cyrus? I get you're upset about it, but you have to tell us what happened."

"I said I don't want to talk about it," he snapped. He *couldn't* talk about it. He'd lost his chance, and possibly worse—he'd kissed Norah. More than kissed her. He'd let himself get caught in a wave of... He didn't know what it was.

Infatuation? No.

Desire? No.

He craved a closeness—a closeness he'd been denied. No, not denied. It was a closeness he hadn't even been bold enough to ask for.

Not from the person he truly wanted it from. But Norah's touch had given that closeness. It had felt good in all the ways touch felt.

Although it hadn't felt *right*.

Still, he'd let himself get caught in it, and now the shame ate at him. Salt in the festering wound of failure.

"Are you still going to grant me leave to go to Mercia?" Orion asked.

Cyrus pushed out a long exhale. This was neither the time nor the place. "I can't have this conversation right now." He stepped back around his horse to remount.

Orion blocked him. "If not now, then when?"

Cyrus paused but shook his head. "We'll go back to Rael, then we'll talk about Mercia."

"I'm already here!" He pointed north. "I'm only days away. I'm going now."

"No, you're not."

Jaem watched them silently.

"You can't just keep dismissing me," Orion pressed.

"Don't," Cyrus warned.

But Orion wouldn't relent. "Don't what? Don't ask for what you promised me?"

He couldn't let him go to Mercia. Vitalia wasn't there. "Orion—"

"Is it because we weren't successful? Are you punishing me?"

Cyrus shook his head again. "Of course not."

"Then I'm going."

"You're not going," Cyrus snapped, his patience gone. "That's final. Get on your horse." He turned to his own mount.

"All you think about is yourself," Orion told him, "and what you want. And you don't care if it fucks over all the people that support you."

Cyrus spun back to him. "That's not true."

"Is it not? You, with your empty promises."

They weren't empty. "I've never made a promise I didn't intend to keep."

"The fuck you haven't!" Orion spat. "You promised to help me! You promised to help me find Vitalia!"

"Vitalia's dead!" Cyrus thundered. He regretted the words the instant they left his lips.

Orion's eyes of steel stared back at him, and his face paled. "You lie," he breathed.

He couldn't take it back now. Cyrus shook his head.

Orion burst forward and shoved him. "You lie!" he raged. "You're angry at your own failure."

Jaem moved to defend him, but Cyrus held up his hand.

"You lie," Orion seethed.

"No," Cyrus told him.

Orion shoved him again. "You lie!" His voice broke, and now it sounded more like a plea than an accusation. He shoved Cyrus yet again, this time pulling a knife.

Jaem stepped forward, but still, Cyrus motioned for him to hold.

Orion pressed the tip of the blade against Cyrus's neck. Cyrus made no move to stop him, no move to defend himself.

"Tell me that you're lying," Orion begged.

"I wish I could," Cyrus said softly.

Orion sucked in a weeping breath, and his hand trembled as he pressed the blade harder against Cyrus's throat. "Please," he begged again.

Still, Cyrus could give him nothing.

He bared his teeth and shoved Cyrus away from him. His chest heaved as he sucked in a silent sob.

Cyrus waited for his wrath. The only sound around them was the sound of the stream.

"How long have you known?" Orion asked finally, his voice hoarse.

"I saw it when I looked in Norah's mind."

Orion wiped his face and nodded, but he didn't sheath his knife.

Cyrus stepped toward him. "I wanted to tell you, but—"

Orion whipped his arm up with his knife pointed back at Cyrus. "Stay the fuck away from me."

He paused.

Orion had stopped shaking. He stood as still as stone. Calm. Cyrus knew that calm. The calm of hatred. The calm of contemplating violence. Orion tilted the blade ever so slightly. "When I get back to Rael, I'm going to collect my men, and we're leaving."

Cyrus nodded somberly. "Take whatever you need with you."

"I don't want anything else from you," he hissed.

And Cyrus understood.

This was how one lost a friend.

The two days it took to get back to the stone circle felt like two weeks. Orion rode ahead, not speaking. Jaem rode beside him, also quiet. When they reached the stones, Cyrus tethered them all. Orion couldn't even look at him as Cyrus took his blood.

And they stepped through the portal to Rael.

He'd let Essandra know they were coming, but she still startled as they stepped into her workroom, spinning around from where she'd been standing at the center table. Kord and Everan rose from where they'd been sitting near the window.

Essandra started. "What—"

But Orion grabbed Cyrus before he could even focus on them. "Break it," he seethed between his teeth.

The tether. Cyrus severed both bonds, and Orion leveled his cold eyes squarely at Cyrus.

"I'm bound to you no more," he said, then he strode from the room.

Jaem remained silent.

Essandra, Everan, and Kord all stared at Cyrus with their eyes wide and mouths open.

"What's going on?" Essandra asked.

"Did you kill him?" Kord asked. "The Shadow King?"

Cyrus shook his head. He sank into a corner chair and put his head in his hands. "I failed" was all he could say.

"What happened?" Everan asked.

He still couldn't say it. "I ruined it," he said finally. "I ruined my chance. I ruined everything."

"You'll get another one," Everan assured him.

"Stop saying that!" Cyrus snapped. "You don't know that! No one knows that!"

Everan didn't react to his burst of anger.

Cyrus pushed out a breath. Guilt gnawed at his chest, gnashing down into his stomach. There was no one to blame but himself. No one to be angry with but himself.

And it wasn't even the Shadow King he was angry about.

"Please," Cyrus said, calmer now. "I can't do this right now."

"Get some rest," Everan told him. "We'll figure everything out in the morning." He stepped from the room, and Kord and Jaem followed him out.

Silence hung heavy in the air. Essandra didn't ask him what happened again, she only stood by the table, watching him.

"Are you hungry?" she asked finally.

He shook his head.

"Okay, well..." She looked around the room, then cast her gaze down. "I guess tomorrow we can—"

"We followed the Shadow King to an inn in Hanset."

She grew quiet again.

"The opportunity was perfect. He'd split from his army. It was only him and the queen and a few of his men."

Cyrus stood. He walked to a pitcher of water that sat on the side table and poured a chalice full, but he didn't drink it. "I thought the king would be in his room, and I snuck in through a window. But only Norah was there."

She was quiet for a moment, then she asked, "What did you do?"

He set the chalice down and stared at it as the water settled—until it was as still as he was.

"I kissed her."

If the quiet could grow quieter...

He finally lifted his eyes to look at her.

She stood in deathly stillness.

"She thought I was him—Alexander," he continued. "She wanted to believe it so badly. And I let her."

Essandra showed nothing. Said nothing.

"She looks at me like I'm hers, she touches me like I'm hers, and I... I want that. Except—"

"Why are you telling me this?" she hissed bitterly. Her eyes were darker now, and the lines of her face sharper.

"Because it's not her touch I want, it's yours. I need that—with you. And I know that's not what you want, but—"

"Why do you say that?"

His words left him. "I thought..." He shook his head. "I thought..." He stared back at her.

"Cyrus, I love you."

The world stilled around him. He couldn't have heard her right. "You do?"

She gaped at him. "How can you be one of the most powerful seers in the world yet still be so incredibly blind?"

He couldn't answer. He couldn't speak.

"Of course I'm in love with you, you fool."

That couldn't be true. Slowly, he closed the gap between them. "That can't be true," he whispered.

"You're an idiot," she whispered back.

He drew closer, until they stood only a breath apart, and he dropped his head to hers.

"I've wanted to kiss you for so long," he told her.

"I've been waiting for you to." Her face tilted upward.

More than anything, he wanted to. He could almost feel her lips on his. But he didn't want to touch her when he was like this. Unclean. He didn't want to kiss her like this.

"I can't," he said.

Her face fell. "Oh," she breathed. Her lips closed, and she swallowed.

"I want to," he said. "But not when I'm like this."

"You've touched me before as a wild mess of a man."

Yes, he had, but... "That was different then."

Her eyes moved back and forth between his. "What's changed?"

"Everything." He glanced at the door, then back to her. "Will you come with me?"

Slowly, she nodded.

They walked side by side down the hall. He wanted to take her by the hand, lead her, but he didn't. He was careful not to touch her. Not yet.

It was dark inside his chamber. Essandra lit candles and, in the adjoining washroom, filled the tub with the connected pump as he pulled off his leathers and soiled clothing.

Naked, he stepped to the tub.

She leaned down and touched the water. It steamed.

A corner of his mouth turned upward. "You've found another fire witch, I see." He stepped into the tub and sank down into the water. The warmth lapped his sides. "Make it hotter."

She did.

"Hotter," he said. He wanted it to burn, to burn it all off—his failure, his sadness, Norah, the Shadow King, his hate. Everything.

The water heated to fire, to where he nearly couldn't stand it. Perfect. He let it flame his skin as he washed his hair and scoured his body, his face, his lips. Then he sank deeper into the inferno, rinsing himself free.

When he was finished, he stood.

Essandra only watched.

He let her look at him. Did her eyes crave the look of his body the way his did hers? He stepped out of the tub and dried himself with the towel that hung on the wall, but he didn't move to dress again. He only waited—a silent ask.

In silent reply, she unfastened the trail of buttons down the front of her gown and pulled it from her shoulders. It heaped to the floor, and she stepped from it. She moved to her chemise and the layers underneath.

He waited until everything was off, and they stood, looking at each other. He'd never been able to just appreciate the sight of her in her flesh before. She was beautiful. Her pale skin contrasted sharply with the dark locks that hung down over her shoulders.

Cyrus stepped closer, close enough to touch her now, but he didn't. He simply wanted to take her in, to etch her into his mind. Every piece of her, every detail—the smoothness of her skin, the high of her cheekbones, the way her emerald eyes sat large under her long dark lashes.

He saw it now—the look in her eyes. How had he not seen her love before? Perhaps because this was a woman hardened by hurt. She was a woman who guarded her heart.

And he wasn't a man to be trusted with a heart.

Cyrus was driven by blood and vengeance. But in this moment, it wasn't blood and vengeance he wanted.

It was only her.

He raised his hands to her face, brushing her cheeks with the backs of his folded fingers. Softly—so softly. He drew his thumb along her lips. The sweet warmth of her breath wrapped around his senses, pulling him closer, but still, he hesitated.

He'd wanted to kiss her for so long.

She leaned into his touch.

Closer still, he brought his lips, pulling her chin upward. But he stopped just short.

"Is something wrong?" she whispered.

"No," he said softly. Nothing was wrong. Everything was right. Everything was right, and he desperately wanted to keep it this way. Forever.

But he was afraid. He was afraid that he would kiss her, then it would be over, and she would be gone, and things would go back to how they were before, leaving him wanting and needing even more than he was now.

But she'd said she loved him.

His mouth was but a whisper away from hers.

She loved him.

"Kiss me, Cyrus," she breathed, dusting his lips with hers as she spoke the words.

The touch sent him over. He caught her mouth with his, and her taste was his undoing. They'd been together many times before, but never like this. This was different. She hadn't been his before. He'd never kissed her; he'd never touched her.

He touched her now.

Cyrus threaded his fingers into her hair, pulling her head back so he could drink deeper. And he did—drinking salvation from her lips. She was his Amoran Cup, bringing him back to life. A life he'd never thought he could have.

And he needed more. He pulled his mouth along the line of her jaw, grazing her skin with his teeth, and trailed down her neck, nipping gently.

"Cyrus," she breathed, and it drove him mad.

He used his frame to walk her backward, his fist still in her hair, his head buried in the nook of her shoulder. He pressed her out of the bath chamber and into the bedroom, and when the backs of her legs hit the bed, he released her so she could lie back onto it. Then he prowled over her. She opened her thighs and shifted to move him between them, but he didn't sink inside her.

Not yet.

He needed to kiss her. Again. And again. He needed to cover every inch of her skin, claim every part of her with his mouth. From her shoulder to the hollow of her neck and down between her breasts, he moved—kissing, nipping, licking. Prickles rose over her skin, and it fueled his need more. He swirled his tongue around a nipple before drawing it between his teeth. She writhed as a groan escaped her lips, triggering an obsession to get her to make that noise again. He moved to the other breast, and she shuddered. Her scent was intoxicating, and he breathed her in.

Cyrus trailed down her stomach, her body driving him more fervent, more feral. He paused at her hip, trying to regain control, but he had no more control with this woman.

He dropped his head between her thighs, teasing her with his breath. Ever so softly, he brushed his lips against her.

"Cyrus," she panted.

He needed her to say his name again—for her to yell it, to scream it. He slid his tongue over her.

"Oh gods," she said hoarsely as she met him with small thrusts of her hips.

He wanted more. He needed more. And more. And more. Outside of her, inside of her. As his tongue found her most sensitive part, she arched against him. Her taste brought a hunger within him that couldn't be sated.

It wasn't enough to kiss her.

He had to devour her.

She threaded her fingers into his hair, clutching him tightly, and rocked her hips against him. Cyrus felt her pleasure building, and it drove him even wilder.

"Don't stop," she panted. "Don't stop."

He had no intention of stopping. Her breaths came faster, and she clenched his hair in her fists. He was obsessed with her every sound, with every shudder of her body. She rocked her hips harder.

"Cyrus!" she cried as she fell apart. She twisted in climax, but he didn't let her escape him. He chased her pleasure through the peak until she crashed, falling back to soft kisses when she couldn't take it any longer.

And then he kissed her more.

She melted into the bed, her heavy eyelids falling closed, but he wasn't finished with her yet. He flipped her onto her stomach, garnering a small squeal. Gods, everything about this woman...

Slowly, he worked his way back up her body. Over the backs of her thighs and supple mounds of flesh to the curve of her lower back, he drew his lips. He moved up her spine—kissing, reveling, relishing, breathing in her being.

This woman was his. She loved him, protected him, made him stronger.

She loved him and she was his.

Cyrus wove his fingers into her thick mane, gripping her tightly. His body begged for his own pleasure, but he was still obsessed with hers. Pushing the hair from her nape, he razed his teeth down the back of her neck and along the tops of her shoulders, sending another wave of prickles across her skin.

She moaned.

He pushed her thighs apart with his knees and shifted between them. She submitted, dipping her back and lifting her hips. The primal urgency to take her quickly was overwhelming, but he forced himself slow as he sank into her.

Her gasp nearly sent him over the edge. Slowly still, he moved, controlling himself so that he could feel every wave of pleasure that rippled through her.

He caged her with his body.

She was his.

Essandra raised her hips more, on her knees now, pushing back against him and taking him deeper. He moved faster.

Cyrus shifted back on his knees, pulling her with him so she now sat on top of his thighs. He buried his face into the back of her neck and let her flood all his senses. Wrapping his arms around her, he ran his hands up her stomach. Up, up. He kneaded the smooth flesh of her breasts. She panted as another moan escaped her lips, and her head fell back.

She loved him, and she was his.

He splayed his hands wide across her chest, holding her to him, then ran them up and over her shoulders, gripping her and pulling her down on top of him even harder. Faster. And faster still.

Cyrus dropped a hand between her legs, stroking her as he thrust.

"I can't again," she panted.

But she could. And she did. Her climax pulsed around him, wave after wave racking her body as she cried out, and he lost himself. He drove deeper as his own release ripped through him. Together, they came in a tempest of want and need.

As the storm passed, the quiet returned with only the sound of their gasping breaths. She sank back against him, completely spent, and he cradled her to the bed. Cyrus pulled her body close, wrapping himself around her.

She loved him, and she was his.

But as he lay with her nestled in his arms, he knew—he loved her, and he was hers.

Chapter Thirty-Six

Cyrus slept. Deeply. More than deeply. For the first time in months, he actually felt rested. As sunlight poured through the windows, he reached out his arm for Essandra.

The bed was empty beside him.

He lifted his head. And he sighed. Of course it was empty. He should have known she wouldn't be here when he woke. No doubt she regretted what had happened between them, regretted what she'd confessed—regretted that she'd said she loved him.

And perhaps he regretted it too. She cared for him, yes, but Essandra wasn't a woman to let herself love, or let herself be loved. He'd pushed her too far with his need for her. He'd ruined it.

Like he ruined everything.

"I'm here," came her voice.

He pushed himself up onto his elbows with a start.

She rose from where she'd been sitting in the side chair, a long silk robe covering her. "Did you think I'd gone?"

"No," he said quickly.

She pursed her lips into a small smile and lifted a brow.

Cyrus held out his hand and she took it, and he laced his fingers between hers, pulling her closer. She *hadn't* left. She hadn't regretted what had happened between them.

And he didn't either. He brought her hands to his lips and kissed them.

A book lay spread page-side-down, where she'd been sitting. "Reading?" he asked. "This early?"

"It's not early anymore. And yes, I've just been working on some things."

"Where are the dogs?" he asked. He hadn't seen them since he'd been back.

"With Visa. She brought us some breakfast." She glanced back over her shoulder at a tray of food on the side table.

Breakfast could wait. Cyrus pulled her on top of him. "I already have a plan for breakfast," he said, and he rolled her underneath him.

She laughed as he nuzzled into her neck and kissed along her shoulder, but she put a hand on his chest. "Visa said Orion is leaving today."

Cyrus paused.

Her eyes shifted back and forth between his. "What happened?" she asked. "Why is he so angry at you?"

He drew in a long breath and let it out slowly as he brushed a lock of hair from her face. "The woman he's been searching for—she's dead."

Her eyes grew larger, and she put a hand over her mouth. "Vitalia?" she whispered.

He nodded.

"But why is he angry at you?"

"Because I knew and didn't tell him." He shook his head. "More than that. He asked me to look for her, and I lied to him about what I saw. But I couldn't tell him. I couldn't..." He paused. The hard part was knowing that if he were to do it all over again, he wasn't sure he'd choose differently. "What does a man have if he doesn't have hope?"

Essandra bit the corner of her lip as she reached up and traced the line trenched across his brow. "It might take a little time," she told him, "but he'll eventually see you were trying to protect him."

"I don't think so," he whispered.

She frowned. "Do you at least want to see him before he goes?"

"I do." It was likely the last time he'd ever see Orion again, and it tore at him. Orion was more than just a paid man. He was someone Cyrus could trust and rely on. He was a friend, even though Cyrus had lost that friendship.

She gave a sad smile. "Come on, then."

Dressed and finally presentable, Cyrus walked the main hall toward the east wing with Essandra beside him. He held her hand in his. Now that he'd won her touch, he couldn't be without it.

As they passed the throne room, a familiar face caught his eye. Cyrus grinned.

Ryman. He rarely saw the large man who used to be the lead fighter of House Lycus. Ryman oversaw their defensive forces across all of northern Rael, but lately he'd been responsible for moving legions to Japheth as they finished their training.

When he saw Cyrus, he broke from his men and crossed the room to meet him. "King Cyrus," he said with a warm smile.

They clasped arms.

"How are you, my friend?" Cyrus asked him.

Ryman gave a nod. "Good. Taking another two legions to Japheth today."

Essandra squeezed Cyrus's arm. "I'm going to go make sure Orion doesn't leave before you see him," she said. "Take your time, but don't be too long."

Cyrus nodded, then watched her go before turning his attention back to Ryman.

The man's grin broadened as he watched Essandra leave. "Took you long enough," he said.

Cyrus snorted, but he couldn't help his own smile.

"Hey," Ryman said, "I wanted to let you know that King Gregor has offered me a position. To lead his mercenary armies."

Cyrus shifted back. He wasn't sure why that surprised him. Gregor had asked him for a trusted man many times, and Ryman was among the best. He was smart and skilled, and his presence could be intimidating. Of course he'd catch Gregor's eye. And Cyrus had promised if there was a man who wanted the job, he could go with Cyrus's blessing.

Cyrus gave him a short nod. "Any king would be fortunate to have you lead his men."

"Oh, I'm not going to work for that fucking coward."

If Cyrus had had a mouthful of wine, he'd have spewed it all over the floor. He couldn't help a good laugh.

"I just wanted you to know that he did," Ryman added.

"He could make you a rich man."

"I already have everything I could ever want."

Suddenly, Ryman's smile fell. His face hardened as his gaze caught on something behind Cyrus.

Cyrus turned.

Essandra stood under the arch of the double doorway, with a hooded figure in a long dark cloak behind her. She was facing him, but she stood in a way that seemed not her own. Then he noticed the hand wrapped around her neck.

"Is this him?" asked the figure. A woman.

"Soroya, please," Essandra begged.

Soroya.

Soroya.

Cyrus's blood ran cold.

She'd come. She'd actually come.

Every muscle in his body coiled as the flame of fight sparked inside him.

Soroya pulled back the hood of her cloak. She was tall, almost as tall as Cyrus, but otherwise not much different from how he'd imagined: thin, with long dark hair, even darker than Essandra's. But her eyes... Her eyes were silver. Cold. Piercing.

Ryman stepped in front of Cyrus, pulling his sword. "You'll take your hands off the king's lady," he demanded. "Or I'll take them off for you."

Soroya leveled her steely gaze on the large fighter. Her voice held the same ice as her stare. "I don't have the patience to correct everything wrong in your words."

"And I don't have the fucking patience to tell you again." Ryman took another step forward, but as he did, his sword flashed red in his hands. He stared down at it in horror.

A scream ripped from his lips.

It took a moment for Cyrus to understand what was happening, but as smoke swirled up from Ryman's hands and wound around the blade, he shouted, "Drop it! Ryman, drop the sword!"

But he didn't. He couldn't. Ryman screamed louder as the sword grew hotter, and even louder as molten metal ran down the blade and over his hands.

Cyrus rushed forward, but before he could reach him, Ryman erupted into flame. Cyrus staggered back, shielding his face from the heat. Ryman's screams shook the hall as his flesh burned.

Cyrus had power over fire through his bond with Essandra's coven but lacked the mastery to control the flame. He didn't have the ability to extinguish it. There was nothing he could do as Ryman dropped to his knees and then collapsed forward in a smoldering heap on the stone floor.

The throne room grew quiet.

Ryman was dead.

Ryman was dead.

So quickly she'd killed him, so easily, and Cyrus couldn't even grieve him.

Soroya walked Essandra forward, and Cyrus noticed four more women with her, who all wore the same dark cloak lined in purple. She brought Essandra within ten paces in front of him and paused, her hand still around Essandra's neck. Her eyes mocked him as they traveled down his frame and back up. "This is the famed bloodsport fighter?" She laughed.

Essandra stood unnaturally, under an invisible hold.

Fury rippled under his skin. "Let her go," he commanded. His voice didn't sound like his own.

Soroya tightened her hold on Essandra. "You're in no position to make demands."

He ripped his sword from its scabbard and surged forward, but Soroya's power hit him with a blow unlike any he'd felt before, knocking him to the ground. His blade clanged to the marble beneath him. Pain vibrated through every bone in his body.

"Cyrus!" Essandra screamed.

The group of men who'd been with Ryman pulled their swords and rushed forward, but sharp spikes of stone tore up through the floor, impaling them midstep.

"You think mere men stand a chance against two hundred years of power?" Soroya snapped. Her hand tightened, and Essandra writhed in her clutch.

Cyrus shook with rage.

"Stupid girl," Soroya hissed against Essandra's ear. "Did you think I wouldn't find you?"

"Soroya, please," Essandra whimpered.

"You almost had a chance. You'd seemed to have completely disappeared from this world. Then I heard from the Jackals that there was a witch breaking the guild bonds of their assassins. And I thought: Who could that be? There's only one person strong enough." She smiled as she brought her lips to Essandra's ear again. "My little bond maker, my little bond breaker," she sang.

Essandra struggled against her, but the invisible force still held her. "Let him go," she begged, "and I'll send them back. I can reverse it."

Even Cyrus knew she couldn't do that.

"The assassins?" Soroya said. "Oh, I've already taken care of them. My gift to the guild."

Orion. The pit in Cyrus's stomach grew. "What have you done?" he seethed shakily.

"Soroya," Essandra begged again. "Please. I'll go with you willingly."

"You think I want you back now?" Her fingers tightened, and Essandra clawed at them, powerless and struggling for breath. "I loved you, Sabine," Soroya hissed between her teeth. "I loved you like my own daughter. Trusted you more than any other. And you betrayed me."

"Don't hurt him," Essandra pleaded. "I'll do whatever you want."

"I want you to die."

Essandra's eyes met Cyrus's, and they teared. Her lips mouthed a silent spell. He didn't need to hear it to know what it was.

The spell to break the tether.

She hadn't broken it when he'd returned the day before, and there was only one reason she'd be breaking it right now—to protect him. She knew she was going to die.

"No!" Cyrus shouted. "Essandra!"

Her lip trembled.

"No!" Cyrus pushed through the pain, grabbing his sword, and staggered back to his feet. But Soroya only hit him with another burst of power, this one somehow even harder than the first. It flung him backward.

She hit him with another blow, then another. His head cracked against stone. Every bone in his body felt like it was breaking.

"Cyrus!" Essandra screamed.

More of his men came charging into the throne room, but Soroya flicked her wrist, obliterating the massive grand columns and sending the ceiling above them crashing to the ground. Sunlight poured through the plumes of dust and debris from above.

"I am not a silly man with a sword," she spat at Cyrus. "I am Soroya Fey, descendant of the Nocturn, high witch of the Moon Coven, and scepter of the Spirit."

Cyrus tried to push himself up, but his broken arm buckled underneath him. Something trickled down the back of his neck from his head. Blood.

"Sabine is mine," Soroya said. "Her life is mine, and I've come to claim it."

"Don't hurt him," Essandra begged again.

"Oh, I'm definitely going to hurt him."

Witch fire flamed in Soroya's hand, and she leveled her eyes back on Cyrus. The flame grew brighter.

He braced for the burn.

Just then, a figure moved in front of him. A man with blades drawn. His head and face were covered, but Cyrus knew immediately who it was.

Orion.

Soroya shifted back for a moment. Her eyes narrowed. "Another assassin? I thought I'd gotten all of you. You should have escaped while you had the chance."

Orion backed up slowly, keeping himself firmly between Cyrus and the witch. "No fun in that," he said. His body coiled, ready to fight. "I'm the only one allowed to kill this man. If you want him, you're going to have to go through me."

Soroya's eyes flashed, then she smiled. "I've never had anyone ask before." She cast Essandra aside, pinning her against the wall with the invisible force. Then she balled witch fire in her hand again.

"Orion!" Cyrus warned.

The flame tore through the air, but Orion was faster. He moved with lethal grace, twisting out of the way, while in a single motion, he flung a handful of bladed darts at the witch.

Soroya whipped up her hand and shielded herself merely with air, but one of the witches beside her stumbled and sank to the floor, hit. Soroya's face twisted as she realized. Her eyes blazed back on Orion.

"That was a foolish thing to do," she hissed. She flicked her wrist, and the partially collapsed ceiling cracked even more. Orion spun and darted again, just as a thunder of stone fell from above him. He narrowly escaped from underneath. Another plume of dust and debris flooded the hall, blinding them all for a moment.

Orion scrambled to Cyrus. "Get Essandra out of here!" he snapped as he pulled Cyrus up. "My ship is set to sail. Get to the harbor and go!"

Pain racked his body, and Cyrus wasn't sure his legs would hold him, but he forced himself forward. He had to get to Essandra.

"Is that all you've got?" Orion goaded Soroya as he stepped out of the dust. "I have to admit, for someone touting so much power, I was expecting something more... extraordinary."

Soroya's eyes found him, and her mouth popped with a small scoff. "More extraordinary?"

Orion's eyes traveled over the broken throne room, and he shrugged. "I've just seen this all before."

Cyrus skirted the edge of the throne room through the haze. Or maybe there was no haze, maybe it was his own eyes clouding.

Soroya laughed at Orion's challenge. The stained-glass windows high above lining the throne room shattered, raining down shards of glass. Orion darted again. Away from Cyrus, away from Essandra. The destruction followed him. So did Soroya's attention.

Cyrus pushed himself faster. He could see Essandra fighting against the force that still pinned her against the wall. He was almost to her.

Then, one of Soroya's witches called out. She shouted in foreign words, but Cyrus knew exactly what she'd said—she'd revealed him. And Soroya's wave of destruction shifted after him. Another blow of power struck him, and another, crashing him against the remains of a marble column with a force that broke bone and knocked the wind from his lungs. He crumpled to the ground.

Pain coursed through him—excruciating pain—but he had no breath to cry out. He rolled to his side, struggling for air. Suffocating. Both Orion and Essandra yelled his name. His lungs finally filled, but it wasn't the relief he needed. With each inhale, each pulse of his heart, came a deep pain in his chest. His ribs cracked as he moved. Each breath was war.

"Fool," Soroya hissed.

Cyrus sucked in another breath, but it was wet and raspy. He couldn't escape the feeling of drowning.

Soroya shaped a ball of fire in her hand again, stalking toward him. "Did you really think you could—"

Her words cut with a gasp, and she whirled. A small throwing dagger protruded from the back of her shoulder.

She ripped it out. "You'll die for that," she seethed at Orion, and she hurled the fire in her palm at him.

Orion careened out of the way again, but as he pulled two more blades to throw, he froze.

Soroya stretched her arm out and, with her invisible force, dragged him toward her. He flailed, his knives still in hand.

"Tell me," she called to him. "Is this extraordinary enough for you?"

She lifted him into the air with nothing but her power. His face slacked and his eyes widened. He twisted against the force that held him. Then his eyes jumped wildly to the blades in his hands—the blades that now turned inward toward his own body. He struggled violently, but he couldn't stop them. The knives closed slowly in toward him.

"Orion!" Cyrus choked out.

Orion struggled, more frantic now, as the blades closed in on his chest.

Essandra's voice pleaded for him.

The assassin struggled more. The tips of the blades reached his body. He fought with everything he had. But he didn't call out, he didn't beg for mercy.

Cyrus tried to crawl toward him.

Orion's eyes met his as the blades slowly pierced him.

A cry burst from Cyrus. "No!"

The knives sank deeper.

Orion's struggle lessened. Slowly, he stilled.

Slowly, he died.

His gray eyes stayed locked on Cyrus until the life ran out of them. Then Soroya dropped his body to the floor.

Cyrus tried to call out to Orion, but that only pulled a cough from the wreck of his lungs. Blood poured from his mouth, hot and thick with foam.

Soroya's gaze flicked to him, to his blood spattered on the stone in front of him. Her eyes grew wide before flashing back to Essandra. "You found yourself a seer." She tilted her head ever so slightly. "Did you use his blood?"

She stalked back to Essandra and curled her hand around her throat again. "It doesn't matter. It won't be enough to save you."

He tried to stand again, but more pain erupted inside him—scraping, clawing, biting, dropping him back to the floor. He groaned in agony, then heaved another burst of blood from his lungs.

"No!" Essandra cried. She begged Soroya. "Please don't kill him."

But already, Cyrus felt the life in him fading.

"It's too late, darling," Soroya said. "He's already dying."

He could barely move now.

Soroya grabbed Essandra again. "This next part needs an audience." And she dragged her from the room.

Cyrus lay broken and bleeding. Orion's dead eyes stared back at him. But Cyrus could do nothing. Even his silent cry drew an ungodly pain.

From outside, the earth shook again with the power of Soroya's destruction. She wasn't just bringing down the palace, she was bringing down his whole kingdom. And there was nothing he could do to stop her.

Then he heard Essandra scream.

A piercing, guttural scream.

That scream tore something open.

A storm roared through him—feral and vicious—every muscle, every fiber of his being. It filled him with fire. And he moved. He didn't feel his body, only the pulse of rage. He rose not by strength but by will.

The ground shook again with Soroya's thunder, nearly dropping him, but he forced himself through the rubble of the throne room. Through the destroyed main hall that now had only open sky. Through the fractured palace doors and into the courtyard. Through the gates of the palace that had been ripped from their hinges.

In the center of the mainway that ran from the palace through the capital, Soroya held Essandra in the air. The wind surged around them. Bodies lay crumpled on the ground—two witches from Essandra's coven. Dead.

People were running. Some were frozen in horror. Palace guards swept toward them with their swords drawn, but they were thrown back.

"I gave you everything," Soroya seethed at Essandra. "You were *nothing* when I took you in. Now you'll die like nothing. And nothing is all you'll ever be."

No.

No, she didn't get to decide that.

Cyrus pushed himself forward. Each step was war. His ribs grated, his lungs burned.

Soroya caught him in the corner of her eye, and she turned. Her eyes widened slightly before they narrowed. "You," she hissed. "Kill him," she told her witches.

They started toward him, and Cyrus pulled the dagger from the belt around his waist. One of the witches laughed. She balled a flame in each of her hands.

"You bring a knife to a fire fight," she jeered.

His breaths were raw and ragged. He waited, although he barely had the strength to keep standing.

As the witches stalked toward him, he brought up his hand, his arm outstretched. He opened his fingers, letting the dagger lay flat across his palm.

The witch's brow quirked. "Giving up so soon?" she asked with a cruel smile.

He didn't answer her. It didn't matter. *She* didn't matter.

She shifted her eyes to the dagger.

To the blade.

To the crack that now snaked up the metal.

She didn't even have time to react as it shattered, hurling its hundreds of sharp fragments into the three witches. Into their faces. Into their throats.

They screamed as they fell back, writhing on the ground. The fragments buried themselves deeper. Through flesh. Through bone. Cyrus willed them even deeper, until the witches stilled.

Soroya's eyes flashed darker. "You've bonded your power." She looked at Essandra. "It won't be enough." She balled her fist, then spread her fingers wide.

He braced for the blow.

But it didn't come.

Instead, there was a ripping, a tearing from his body, and his legs buckled as his strength left him. Essandra had warned him. Soroya couldn't use the power, but she could take it. She could strip him of everything he had to fight.

Cyrus gritted his teeth. He tried to pull it back, tried to resist. But there was nothing he could do. She was too strong.

Then he realized—

His power wasn't a bucket to be emptied. It was a river from the Aether. A river of power.

Unlimited power.

Cyrus opened himself, drawing from the Aether as quickly as she ripped it from him. More power he drew. And more.

He used it to straighten. More power he pulled from the Aether. Blood trickled from his nose, but he opened himself more.

More power still, he pulled.

Soroya hissed as she saw her attempts to drain him failing. She dropped Essandra and surged toward him.

He moved to meet her.

The ground split, and jagged rock surged upward to stop him, but Soroya wasn't the only one with access to a geomancer. Cyrus pulled from the bloodline bond—his bond with Essandra, his bond with her coven. He broke through the rock with bursts of his own power, hurling pieces back at Soroya with a force that could crumble a stronghold. The witch shielded herself.

He pulled more from the Aether, melding it with the power of Essandra's coven. *His coven.* He let his rage fuel him—the rage that came from this woman daring to think she could take Essandra from him.

Cyrus released a burst of fury. The force billowed out from around him. He'd bring his whole kingdom to the ground if he had to. Every last stone.

Soroya stumbled backward with a jolt. Her magic flared, wild and chaotic. And then he saw it in her eyes—fear.

She desperately clawed the power from him, but she couldn't take it fast enough. The heavens cracked. Not with thunder. With power. Birds fell from the sky.

Cyrus pulled even more power, letting it build. He would have no mercy. He would destroy this woman.

He broke the ground beneath her feet.

"Stop!" Soroya cried. "That's enough!"

But it wasn't enough. Nothing would be enough. The hand that she'd wrapped around Essandra's throat cracked as it distorted, and she screamed.

But he wasn't finished. He reached for her.

In one last frenzied defense, Soroya cast flame across his palms and up his arms. He ignored the burn and clasped her face in his blistering hands.

"What *are you*?" she whispered in horror.

"Vengeance," he said. *And he broke her.* Her screams filled the air. Crack after crack, scream upon scream.

Blood pulsed from her nose and mouth and out her ears.

She fought—clawing, screeching curses in a language as old as the earth. She slammed power into him, tearing muscle and tendon.

But he would not let go.

When her screams had died, when all life had left her, he dropped her body to the ground, just as she'd done with Orion.

Cyrus didn't have the strength to hold himself any longer, and he buckled to the ground. He sucked in another rattled breath as his eyes searched for Essandra.

She lay a few paces away, weakly pushing herself up. When she saw him, she struggled to her feet.

With his last bit of strength, he pulled himself across the ground toward her. She stumbled to him, dropping down and throwing her arms around him. He buried his head into her neck as he held her tightly.

It didn't matter that everything in his body rived with pain. It didn't matter that he was dying. Nothing else mattered. Only her.

CHAPTER THIRTY-SEVEN

It took Teron four days to heal him. Cyrus drifted in and out of consciousness. Every time he woke, Kord and Everan were there. Sometimes others were there—Jaem, Sergen, Ram, and more. But always Kord and Everan. They paced his room, racked with guilt that they hadn't been with him in the fight against Soroya. Cyrus was glad they hadn't been. They'd have been killed like Orion.

Orion.

Teron could heal wounds, but he couldn't heal the pain of loss. Cyrus couldn't even think about Orion without his eyes burning.

Another letter arrived from Miriel, but he couldn't bring himself to read it. She'd tell him all the things she was working on that made her happy, which always made Cyrus happy. Then she'd tell him how she missed him, how she loved him, how she couldn't wait to see him again.

But Cyrus didn't have a right to be happy. He wasn't worthy of being missed. He wasn't worthy of being loved.

He should have let Orion go to Mercia when he'd asked. He should have let him leave sooner. If he would have just let him go...

Orion didn't deserve this. He didn't deserve anything that fate had given him.

But he *did* deserve vengeance.

"I'm going to destroy them," Cyrus said. His throat was raw, his voice hoarse.

"What?" Kord asked, and both he and Everan moved to the bed.

"The Jackals. The guild. The Shadow King. I'm going to destroy them all."

Kord stared at him, wild-eyed. "This is literally the first thing you say after coming back from the brink of death?"

The bed shifted as Essandra sat down beside him. "Cyrus," she said softly, "the Shadow King isn't responsible for this."

"He is. This is the world he builds. The Shadowlands sell men to the Jackals—*children*—to be made into assassins. He's responsible for *all* of this!" He dropped his voice to a whisper. "I'm going to kill them all," he promised.

Her brow dipped and her mouth parted.

"When does it end?" Kord asked.

He shook his head. "It doesn't."

Kord looked at Everan.

Essandra squeezed Cyrus's arm. "Rest now. We'll talk about all this later." She nodded at Kord and Everan. They cast a wary glance at Cyrus before stepping out.

"Rest," she told him again. She picked up a book on the side table and moved to the corner chair.

No part of him could rest. Rest only served to trap him in the confines of his mind, leaving him to wallow in the trenches of failure and regret. The only thing that kept him from collapsing in on himself was his vow of vengeance.

He'd killed Soroya—the person truly responsible for Orion's death. And he knew taking on the guild was impossible. But whether something was possible or not didn't matter. Focusing on what was possible didn't bring any relief from the guilt and the rage. It didn't mend what was broken.

Vengeance would. So vengeance he'd have.

Vengeance against the guild.

Vengeance against the Shadow King.

And for that, he had to plan.

"I'm going to tell her who I am," he said.

Essandra lowered her book. "What?"

"Norah," he said. "I'm going to tell her who I am."

She set the book down. "Why would you do that?"

"If I'm to keep any trust at all, *I* need to be the one to tell her. The closer I stay to her, the closer I stay to the Shadow King."

"She's already pushed you away."

"No." He shook his head. "She pushed Alexander away. I need to come as myself now, as Cyrus. I'll meet her as king of Rael."

She rose from the chair, her mouth slightly open with unspoken questions and her brow stitched in worry. "You're going to be honest with her?"

"How else is there to be?"

Essandra scoffed. "Once she finds out your intention against her husband, there will be no saving any trust with her. And the Shadow King won't trust you either."

Cyrus pushed himself up to sit. "Norah doesn't know the man she married. She doesn't know what he's capable of. But she cares about people—I need to show her who he is."

Essandra paused. Her gaze fell to the floor for a moment. "A woman overlooks a great deal when she loves a man."

"The Shadow King is going to lose everything," he said. "Norah will too, if she stays loyal to him."

Her brow dipped further, and her voice dropped lower. "Why do you care?"

Cyrus paused. He reached out his arm for her. She stepped to him and slipped her hand into his, and he pulled her to him. "You don't have to worry about her," he promised. "Only you have my heart."

She sighed and gave a small shake of her head. "I don't know why I said that. I'm not actually worried about her. I trust you. I just don't like it. What happens when the Shadow King finds out it's been *you* haunting his queen? That it was *you* who first tried to kill her?"

"He's going to find out eventually anyway. So will Norah. If I'm to keep any connection with her at all, I need to be the one to tell her." His eyes moved to the stacks of books and parchments piled on the sideboard. More sat on the floor, and even more by the chair she'd been sitting in. "Have you been working in here? That can't be convenient."

"It's no trouble."

His eyes traveled his room, and for the first time, he noticed jars of herbs, more parchments, more books, practically her whole workroom.

"Well, I couldn't leave you by yourself." She glanced down again. "And I..."

"Essandra," he said softly.

"I guess I don't want to be alone." She shook her head. "I just… I still can't believe it. I can't believe she's actually gone."

Soroya.

"All this time, I've been running; all these years, I've been hiding." She pushed out a breath. "I keep expecting her to suddenly appear, saying something like, *did you really think you could kill me?*"

"I did," he told her. "*We* did."

"I've been trying to make sure. I've been searching for any remnant of her power that still lives."

"Have you found anything?"

She shook her head again.

He clasped her hands. "Hey," he said softly. "Look at me."

Her eyes met his.

"She's dead," he assured her. "You're free."

She still shuffled uneasily, glancing back at her books.

"Why can't you believe it?" he asked.

"I just don't know how you did it. No one in the coven has power like the power you used. You literally crushed her from the inside. The closest I can guess is that you somehow manipulated the geomancer power."

He shrugged. "I used the power of the Aether."

"That's not how it works." She rubbed her temples. "The Aether is a channel, an amplifier; it doesn't grant new power of its own. What you did shouldn't have been possible."

"Essandra," he said softly, and he pulled her close again. "She's dead. Even if you can't explain it, she's dead. She's not coming back."

Her green eyes shifted nervously.

"She's not coming back," he said again. "Do you hear me?"

Slowly, she nodded.

"So now we move forward," he told her. He brushed a lock of hair behind her shoulder. "Will you come with me to meet Norah?"

She closed her eyes and let out a long breath. Then she nodded again.

Traveling to the stone circle was easier after so many times, or perhaps it was from his growing power. Cyrus could now take a group of men at a time. He still didn't risk trying it without the bond. It might work with birds, but he wasn't willing to gamble with lives.

They set up camp half a day's ride outside the Mercian outer reaches. Sergen and Jaem secured horses, while Ram, Everan, and Kord ensured a safe perimeter.

Essandra watched as Cyrus penned the last of his words on the parchment before folding it and stamping his royal red seal of a sword. He held it out to Sergen. "Directly to the queen's hand," he said.

Sergen gave a short bow of his head. "Directly to her hand," he repeated.

Cyrus held out a vial of his blood. "And let me know once you do."

Sergen nodded again. "I will." He mounted, tucking the letter safely into his jacket, and urged his horse north, toward Mercia.

Cyrus watched until he was out of sight. Then he turned to Essandra. "Now we wait," he said.

Waiting was the hardest part. It had been a day and a half since Sergen had called him through the blood and told him he'd delivered the letter. He'd been treated kindly, but they hadn't let him leave. Was Norah going to send him back with a letter?

Cyrus waited longer.

"What if she asks for peace?" Kord said as they sat around the campfire. The cold smoked their breath in the air. Essandra had used the power of her fire witch to warm them, but the heat from the flame still felt good against the skin.

"Mercia can have peace," Cyrus replied.

"You know what I mean," Kord said. "What if she wants that peace to include the Shadowlands?"

Cyrus frowned. "That's not something I can give."

"So, you're going to ask her to side with you instead of her husband?"

"I think that when I show her who he is, I won't have to."

Kord ran a hand through his hair. "Cyrus, this is a different man from the one who took you. You'd be showing her things that have already changed."

"Nothing's changed!" Cyrus snapped. "Do you know what he did with the captured mercenaries after they retook the North?" He glanced at Essandra, then Everan, then back to Kord. "He sold them to Elam," he told them. "*He is his father's son.*"

"He won back her kingdom for her," Kord countered.

"He won it back for himself. He needs Mercia beside him, because with Mercia comes Aleon."

Kord sighed. But this was an argument Cyrus wouldn't yield on.

By the second day, Sergen still hadn't been released. He was still held in the castle.

Cyrus tapped another sealed letter he'd penned against the palm of his hand as he sat and mulled. What was taking her so long? Perhaps she was uncertain.

Essandra ducked into the tent and paused when she saw him. "You're going to send another letter? We haven't even received a reply yet."

Cyrus straightened. "I'm going to offer to meet her in the outer reaches."

Her mouth dropped open. "Absolutely not! It's too dangerous. If she agrees to meet you, the Shadow King will be with her, *with an army*. You have to meet her somewhere safe, somewhere you can get away. Have her come to the stone circle."

Orion would have told him it was a poor idea too. Cyrus brushed the strap across his chest that Orion had given him to stow a few hidden throwing blades. The feel of them brought back the ache of loss. He tried to push it down and focus back on the task at hand.

If he wanted to talk to Norah again, he'd have to compromise. And he did trust her, for the most part. "If she comes, she'll come in good faith, army or no."

"You don't know that."

"Don't I?" He stood. "Sergen's been treated well and shown comfortable quarters. And I like to think I know Norah, at least a little."

"Still, meeting in the outer reaches is too dangerous."

"I need to offer something too hard to refuse before she decides against it."

"I don't like it." She crossed her arms.

Cyrus didn't particularly like it either, but he didn't know what other choice he had. And it could be a moot point; she might not be willing to meet at all.

He sent Ram with the second letter, then he waited again.

If Orion had been with him, they could have found a way into Mercia, catching the queen alone.

His chest tightened, and he sank back down onto the stump next to the fire.

No. If he had Orion... he'd never ask anything from him again, not even this. He'd give him lands to live freely, ships to leave, money to explore the world. Orion wouldn't have accepted it from him, but it would've been his nonetheless.

Cyrus only wanted one thing from his friend now—for him to come back. For him to be alive.

He felt Essandra behind him, and she wrapped her arms around him. "What are you thinking about?" she whispered. "I can feel your sadness."

But he couldn't say it. If he spoke it, the emotion would come, emotion he couldn't control. He only squeezed her arms in return.

She was warm, and he leaned back against her. He traced the lines of the markings on her skin from her wrist toward her elbow and stopped at a new one.

"What is this?" he asked.

"Why do you ask me questions you already know the answer to?"

"You're still using dark magic."

She said nothing.

"It's dangerous," he said.

She stepped around to face him eye to eye. "You're the last person to be lecturing me on using dangerous power. At least I know what I'm doing, and I take measures to protect myself."

He sighed. "Are you making progress?"

She hadn't talked about her efforts to bring back her family in a while. Essandra was an extremely private person, and he had felt he'd lost privileges to that private life quite a while ago. But now... Now that they were together, now that they were one, it felt like his life too. He just wasn't sure if she saw it the same.

He worried that her silence answered that for him, until she finally said, "I think so." She tucked a lock of hair behind her ear. "I'm still chasing proxy alternatives, but I think I'm close."

He wasn't sure exactly what that meant, but *close* sounded...

"Good," he said with a nod. "That's good."

"Yes."

He reached out and took her hand and pulled her fingers to his lips. "Would you tell me if you needed anything from me? If there was anything I could do?"

She drew in a long breath.

He stood and pulled her closer, tipping her chin up to him. "You would tell me?"

She nodded.

He smiled and lowered his lips to hers.

Then came the reply Cyrus had been waiting for.

"*We're on our way back to you,*" Ram told him through the blood bond. "*Sergen and I both. And we have a letter from the queen.*"

"*What does it say?*"

"*I haven't opened—*"

"*Open it,*" he said impatiently.

It took a moment for Ram to break the seal and read its contents. It was all Cyrus could do to keep from pushing into his mind and reading it himself.

"*She wants to meet,*" Ram said. "*In the western valley.*"

She wanted to meet. Cyrus let himself revel for a moment in the relief. Just for a moment. Then he nodded. "*Write her this—*"

"*I don't have anything for a letter. Or a seal.*"

Cyrus swore. "*Then go back and tell her two days' time. I'll meet her in the valley in two days.*"

Two days was a good amount of time, but to prepare an army, it was nothing at all, which was the point. Still, Cyrus worked hastily to leave camp. He'd reach the valley before the queen. This would let him assess the terrain better, as well as watch her approach.

As he saddled his horse, Essandra moved beside him. "I have your armor," she said.

He snorted. "I'm not wearing armor for this. It's not necessary."

"Mmm." She pursed her lips into a smile.

Cyrus tightened the girth of the saddle and looped the strap.

"Cyrus," she said, making him pause. "I know you're inclined to show Mercia grace, and you think this queen will come in good faith. But let me be very clear..." She put her hand on his arm, and her eyes flashed darker. "If she doesn't, if she tries to move against you and take advantage of your goodwill, I'll kill her."

He pulled her closer. As he clasped the side of her neck, he thumbed her chin up. She complied, dropping her head back and offering her lips, but her compliance wasn't weakness, and under his palm, he felt the pulse of power. There were few people in the world more powerful than Essandra, and, like him, she was a protective creature.

"I'd expect nothing less." And he kissed her.

CHAPTER THIRTY-EIGHT

Cyrus shifted uncomfortably in his armor from where they waited on top of the ridge overlooking the western valley. He wanted to pull it off, but he was pretty sure Essandra would only fuse it to his body. The helm was the worst—a full-face cover with a daggered crown on top. Cyrus didn't like a simple crown on a normal day; he especially didn't like a nonsimple one affixed to a suffocating face shield of metal.

Heaviness weighted his stomach. Norah thought she was meeting the king of Rael, but when he pulled off the helm...

"*Where is she?*" Essandra asked through the blood bond, even though she sat on her horse right beside him. He'd had her, Everan, and Kord all take the blood to be able to keep communication.

He closed his eyes and let himself drift back to the birds in the distant sky, ignoring the dull ache in his head. "*She's almost here.*"

Norah came with an army. He wasn't surprised. The Shadow King wouldn't have allowed her to come alone. Cyrus wouldn't have if it had been Essandra.

His heart thrummed heavily as he sat, waiting. This would be his first time meeting Norah as himself. As King Cyrus. He wondered if she would be angry when she discovered him. It was likely. No one appreciated being deceived.

But just how angry would she be?

When she finally appeared on the ridge, Cyrus felt more anxious than he did before battle. She glanced back over her shoulder, where her army waited just out of sight.

"*Is that the Shadow King?*" Everan asked of the large, mounted man that accompanied Norah.

A wrap covered his face.

"*It's the commander,*" Cyrus answered. He didn't like that she'd brought him, but, again, he hadn't expected her to come with no protection at all.

Essandra shifted in her saddle.

"*Leave him,*" he told her. Had it been the king, he would have taken the risk, but he didn't want to lose Norah over a mere army commander. "*Just keep an eye on him.*"

"Cyrus," Essandra said aloud. He paused and looked at her, and she held out her hand to him. "Take this."

In her palm was a firestone necklace. Its surface was veined with molten threads of red and orange, as if capturing flame itself inside. It was beautiful, but...

"What's it for?"

"Is it not appropriate to bring a gift when meeting a queen? And you can't let the commander see the blood. Use the necklace to hide it."

Cunning woman. He couldn't help but smile under his helm as he took it.

Cyrus advanced his horse with Essandra beside him, down the hill and into the valley, toward Norah and the commander. Everan and the rest of their small group stayed on the ridge.

Norah and the commander did the same, advancing too.

As they drew closer to each other, Norah's stare stayed locked on Cyrus. She wore a silver-spun riding dress and a dark navy cloak. No armor. Her hair hung long around her shoulders.

Essandra dropped an illusion over them all, an extra level of precaution against the watching eyes of the Shadow King and his army. The illusion witch in Essandra's coven wasn't strong, but she was strong enough to shield anyone from seeing what was really happening. Cyrus could take the queen and be gone with her before the Shadow King even knew, although he had no intention of doing that. Not yet, anyway.

Cyrus and Norah stopped a few lengths from each other.

"King Cyrus," she greeted him with a respectful nod of her head. Her voice was firm yet kind. Melodic.

She couldn't see his face yet.

His heart beat heavier in his chest. He didn't like surprising her this way, but it was too late to change course now. He was committed.

Slowly, he reached up and pulled the helm from his head.

As Norah's eyes met his face, she gasped. She stared at him with the shock of surprise, then her lip trembled.

"Alexander?" she breathed. Gods how he hated that name, but now she'd know him for who he truly was.

Disbelief filled her eyes. Yes, he'd come to her before, but as a ghost of her grief. Now, to be before her in the light, for everyone else to see, under the banner of an enemy... he couldn't ignore the pang of guilt that needled him. He should have done this privately.

It was the slightest of movements, but Cyrus still caught it, and he jerked up his shield just as the commander loosed two bolts from his crossbow.

He gaped at the arrows protruding from his shield. This man had actually tried to kill him... *here... now...*

Then the commander charged.

"No!" Norah cried.

Anger flashed through Cyrus. So much for a goodwill meeting. Had she planned this? He hadn't exactly considered Norah a friend, but it still felt like betrayal.

She'd had his trust.

Essandra countered with a holding spell, stopping the commander and his destrier midstride. Her words echoed in Cyrus's mind as she summoned the power of fire.

She'd burn them where they stood.

"Stop!" Norah cried out, and it seemed to be directed at the commander just as much as at Cyrus.

"*Wait*," Cyrus told Essandra through the blood bond.

"Stop!" Norah yelled again. She frantically looked back over her shoulder to where her army waited. Did she think they'd save her?

"The Shadow King cannot see," Cyrus called to her. "Nothing looks amiss for him."

The commander snarled as he fought against his hold—no doubt Essandra was making it as painful as she could for him.

Good.

"Please," Norah called. "Stop. You're hurting him."

That was the point.

But Cyrus cast Essandra an eye that asked for restraint. *"I want to hear what she has to say."*

Essandra relented on the pain but still held the commander in place.

Norah stared at Cyrus, her breaths short and clipped. "Who are you?"

"Perhaps the name Lucien may be more familiar to you," he said. As he gave her his childhood name, he had to force his voice steady. He hadn't spoken it in a very long time. Did she know Alexander had had a twin?

Her eyes grew larger, and she sucked in another breath. "Alexander's brother?"

So, she did know... He watched as she started piecing everything together.

"You're his exact likeness," she whispered.

"As many twins are."

She swallowed as she shook her head. "You're supposed to be dead."

It was strange to think about this life that he'd had before. Strange to speak about it. He'd made himself forget for so long, but now to remember...

You're supposed to be dead.

"Yes, I am," he said finally. "At least that was the intent of my mother."

Mother. Another word he hadn't spoken in quite some time. His chest hurt.

Her eyes traveled his face, still not believing. "But now you're king of Rael?"

"Now I'm king of Rael and Serra," he said. His words didn't feel like his own, his voice didn't feel like his own.

Norah swayed slightly, and she gripped the mane of her horse near the pommel of the saddle. He almost feared she'd fall, but when he stared back into her eyes, it wasn't weakness he saw. And it wasn't fear.

"I did *not* come here for blood," she said firmly.

Cyrus glanced at the Shadow commander, who still struggled against Essandra's hold. "He seems to have other intentions," he said.

"He doesn't respond well to deception," she said sharply. "Neither do I."

There was the anger he'd expected.

"But I *have* come to talk," she added.

That held a faint air of promise, but... He cast his gaze to the ridge behind her. "With an army?" he asked. Then he shifted to her commander. "And the *Destroyer*."

Norah pursed her lips. "Well, you didn't come alone either, with your..." She looked at Essandra and paused.

"Witch?" Essandra finished for her. The corners of her mouth drew up ever so slightly in amusement. "You can say it," she taunted.

But Norah didn't engage with Essandra. She simply looked back to Cyrus. "Can we take a walk?" she asked him. "Just you and me?"

"Salara!" the commander snarled, clearly not liking the idea.

Cyrus almost smiled. "I would love a walk," he told her.

She glanced back at the ridge. "Will he see?"

He. The Shadow King.

Cyrus could let him see. He could let this king see as he took his commander. As he took his queen from him.

Cyrus could make him hurt.

Badly.

But that wasn't what he was here to do—he wasn't prepared to take on the Shadow King and his army.

And he didn't actually want to hurt Norah.

So, he simply shook his head. "No."

Norah slid down from her mare, and Cyrus did the same. The commander fought Essandra's hold harder, but it didn't matter. He couldn't get free.

"You won't hurt him?" Norah asked him.

The corners of Essandra's mouth curved darkly. "Not too much," she said.

"She won't hurt him," Cyrus assured her, and that seemed to settle her.

The commander growled out to his queen again, but she ignored him. She kept her eyes on Cyrus.

He held his hands out and open at his sides, showing her he carried no weapons. He had no intention of harming her—he hoped she saw that.

Slowly, she stepped toward him, and he motioned them forward, away from the commander.

As they walked, the air calmed between them. He was grateful—it had been a rocky start, but if he could just talk to her...

"It was you," she said, breaking the quiet between them. "It was you who came to me."

He said nothing; he only waited for her reaction.

"All this time," she said. "The visions, the dreams, it was all you."

Was she angry?

"You're a seer?" she asked. Then she paused. "No, not just a seer, a traveler."

A small smile came to his lips. She was smart, and obviously much more knowledgeable than he'd thought. "You continue to surprise me, Norah."

Her brow caught, as if his words hit her strangely.

Her eyes dropped to his neck. She'd spotted his markings. He didn't try to hide them now. He only stood, letting her look at him and string the details together in her mind.

"It was your blood," she said.

She was doing quite well—how much could she figure out?

"But in the Free Cities," she continued, "in the inn, that wasn't a vision."

He wasn't quite prepared to explain what he'd done in the Free Cities. He wasn't sure he could. It hadn't been his finest hour, and he'd rather they move past it.

"You really were there," she said.

Yes, he had been.

"You came to my bed," she whispered. Pain etched across her brow. Was she looking at him, or was she looking at his brother? It was hard to tell. "I let you close," she said. "An enemy of the North and Kharav, you could have killed me then. Why didn't you?"

Because he didn't want to.

Anger eddied in the depths of her eyes. "Is this all you wanted?" she asked sharply. "We came all this way to meet only so that I could see your face?"

"No," he said, finally finding his voice. Well, no and yes. He pulled out a blood vial and held it for her. "I came to give you this, in person this time."

She gaped at him. "What's that?"

"You know what it is. Invite me back, and I'll tell you everything."

She scoffed. "You've told me nothing!"

Not for lack of want. "I will," he promised. "I need more time, time we don't have here. Let me come to you."

"Absolutely not." She shook her head.

"Did you really think we'd settle things so quickly?" he asked. "With your army on the ridge and only a few fleeting moments?"

Her face slacked.

"Take it," he said, holding the vial out nearer to her. "And then decide."

Norah glanced back at her commander. Worry scored her brow.

"*Give her the necklace with it,*" came Essandra's voice in his mind.

Cyrus revealed the firestone necklace in his palm, then pushed both items into her hands.

"What's this for?" she asked of the necklace.

He glanced back at the Shadow commander. "A small gift. To use."

"*The illusion is weakening,*" Essandra said. "*We have to go.*"

He was out of time, and there was nothing more he could do in the moment anyway. He'd made his offer, and now the choice was hers.

Cyrus turned back toward his horse, passing the commander, who snarled at him in the Shadow tongue—a slew of curses no doubt.

"*Give him a gift from me too,*" he told Essandra.

The commander jerked in pain against her hold as another snarl ripped from his lips.

Cyrus smiled as he mounted. Then he glanced back at Norah, who still stood where he left her. *"Do you think she'll use the blood?"* he asked Essandra.

"The way she still looks at you—yes, she'll use it."

Then they turned their horses and urged them back up the ridge to where Everan and the others were waiting.

Chapter Thirty-Nine

Cyrus gripped his temples and leaned his head in his hand with his elbows on the edge of his desk. The dogs whined at his feet. He dropped his hand to One's head, but that did little to ease the weight within him.

If he'd have helped Orion find Vitalia sooner, would she still be alive? Would she have gone to Mercia? Perhaps Orion would have brought her back to Rael.

Or maybe he would have taken her to travel the world.

Free.

Happy.

Maybe he'd still be alive.

"It will take her some time to get back, and time to think about things," Essandra said, breaking him from his thoughts. She sat in the wingback chair across from him.

"What?" *Norah.* "Oh, right." He nodded. It had been three days since he'd met her in the valley and given her his blood, but she hadn't yet used it.

And he'd hardly thought of it.

Coming back to Rael brought the overwhelming weight of loss. Not just Orion and Ryman, but old loss.

Kieve.

Manus.

Even Alexander.

The sadness, the anger, the shame that came with failure—he tried to push it down, but it plagued him. It threatened to consume him.

Cyrus reached his hand out for Essandra. She stepped around the desk and over the dogs, and he pulled her onto his lap, wrapping his arms around her and burying his face into her warmth. She was still grieving too, not just the loss of Orion but also the loss of two members of her coven. She hid it well. But he didn't have the strength to hide anything from her. He held her tightly until the wave of emotion passed, then he tried to focus his mind back on Norah.

"Do you think she's told the Shadow King?" he asked.

"About you or about the blood?"

"Both."

She drew soft fingers through his hair. "She would have had to have told him something, so undoubtedly he knows you exist. As for the blood—it depends on whether she intends to use it."

Cyrus agreed. "If she does call me with it, it'll mean she's keeping it from him."

"Unless he convinces her to use it against you."

He shook his head. "No. He loves her. He doesn't know what my blood does. He won't let her use it."

"What if *he* uses it again?"

"It will only be to his disadvantage. I'll be able to look inside his mind again, as I did before."

He froze when the pull hit him, and his eyes darted to Essandra. Slowly, she stood. "What is it?" she asked.

His pulse quickened. "It's her."

"She's calling you? Now?"

He nodded.

Essandra swallowed.

He pulled her hands to his lips. "Don't worry," he said softly, and he kissed them. "Will you stay with me?"

She nodded.

Cyrus closed his eyes and let his head drop. He entered Norah's mind quietly, not letting her know he was there yet. He watched as she replayed the memories in her mind of when she'd thought he was Alexander. The images were tattered and unclear as she fired through them—she was angry. More than angry. He didn't fault her for that. There was a lot to overcome between them now. He'd betrayed her trust. He needed to fix it. If he could.

Cyrus called a vision around them that he found the most peaceful—the cliffs overlooking the Aged Sea. Then he sat on a rock near the edge, looking out over the water, and waited for her.

When she finally came, he didn't move.

"*This is my favorite place,*" he said, not turning as she approached.

"*You speak?*" she said coldly. She didn't even try to hide her anger. "*Have you been able to speak this entire time?*"

It was a question he'd fully expected.

"*Why?*" she demanded. "*Why didn't you?*"

"*I didn't know his sound. Only his image.*" He plucked a long blade of grass from in front of him. Unease pooled in his stomach. Now that he had to explain himself, the deception felt so much worse than it had before. "*I didn't know his voice,*" he said. "*Or his words. I couldn't speak as he did.*"

She snorted. "*So, to keep up your charade, you said nothing?*"

He shot a look over his shoulder at her. "*I didn't intend to deceive you.*"

"*Yes, you did,*" she snapped back. "*Otherwise, you would have told me exactly who you were.*"

He stood and turned to her. "*You asked me if I was Alexander, and I told you no.*"

"*You knew my context! I thought death had changed you!*"

"*I never lied to you.*"

"*That's all you've done! Deception is a lie, whether you spoke the words directly or not. And you*"—she sucked in a breath—"*you made yourself him. You showed yourself as Alexander.*"

The worst lie of all.

She didn't speak that last part, but he heard it nonetheless. And it shamed him, because it had hurt her. He'd taken advantage of her grief. Guilt weighted his chest.

He called forward a different view, and a sun-filled forest rose around them. Perhaps a change in scene would help soften the edges between them.

"*I'm sorry,*" he said. He genuinely was. Not that he expected acceptance of his apology. He could see she wasn't prepared to give it.

"*You're sorry you tried to kill me?*" she said flatly.

He shifted his weight back. She knew...

"*That's right, I know. I know it was you who sent the assassins. It was you who spoke through them.*"

He had more to recover from than he'd thought. *"I've done many terrible things I should probably be sorry for. Many I'm not, but... that has become one."*

"Why did you do it?" she asked.

To break the Shadow King from his alliance with Mercia—that was the strategic answer. But this was a conversation of truth, and the truth was... *"Because you were the wife of the Shadow King. And Alexander's queen—I knew it would destroy him."*

"You did it to hurt Alexander?"

"I did it to hurt them both," he snapped in a sudden blaze of anger. He'd done it to take something from them, the way they had taken from him.

She shook her head, still not understanding. *"Why?"*

Her little heart of peace would never understand a heart of vengeance. He drew in a long breath and let it out slowly. He hadn't realized he'd darkened the forest around them, and he called back the sun.

"You said you would explain everything," she told him.

He had said that.

"Explain," she demanded.

He didn't even know where to begin to get her to understand. He eyed her. *"Where do you want me to start?"*

Norah sat on one end of a fallen tree and crossed her arms. *"From the beginning,"* she said. *"What are you?"*

She'd already guessed it, but he supposed she wanted acknowledgment. He took a seat on the other end of the tree. *What was he...* He rubbed a hand over his face.

All right, then. From the beginning...

"The Evil is what my mother called it. I didn't know how I was able to do it, get inside her mind, but I could. Not Alexander's, but I could hers."

Norah waited, not saying a word.

"I would have dreams," he told her. *"Some were... terrible things. The worst was when I was scared. I just wanted to be near her, but she cast me out. I tried to show her."*

He hadn't meant to share that, but... it had come out anyway.

And then the memory came like it was yesterday: the falling snow, trees stripped of their leaves like bones of the earth. *"I was so young,"* he said, *"but I remember. I remember how she took me away. And left me in the forest."* The bite of winter seeped through his clothes, as it had all those years ago. *"I ran after her as she rode away. I ran until my legs wouldn't work and I couldn't feel my face for the cold."* It had stung. Even now, it stung. *"I fell, and I lay there, looking up at the tops of the trees, calling out for her. For my father. Calling out for Alexander. And that's how I was found."*

He'd never told that story. Not like that. All the years he'd pushed the memory out, covered it, tried to forget it. Now to speak it... He turned his head as his eyes stung.

She sat as stiff as stone, but he caught the subtle shift in her posture—the way her arms wrapped tighter around herself, the way her jaw tensed, as if she were biting back everything she wanted to scream.

Her voice, when it finally came, wasn't the sharp blade it had been earlier. *"Who found you?"* she asked.

She said it like it was the end, but this story was just the beginning...

"By fate or by luck, the man who came upon me had a wife. They had for a long time tried to conceive a child but couldn't. And they raised me as their own."

Norah exhaled a breath of relief, and she gave a small smile.

How naive she was to this world.

"No. That's not what happened," he said. He wasn't even sure why he'd said that. *"It's what I imagined had happened many times over in my life. How... different... things would have been. But that's not what happened."*

Her smile fell, and he stood.

He'd show her.

The forest twisted under their feet, and he pulled the darkness over them.

"I was found by a demon in the night," he said, *"and he took me to his hell."*

Cages clanged down around them—the same cages he'd been held in. Norah stifled a scream. Men surrounded them inside, half naked in the cold of winter, some dead, more dying. They hadn't eaten in days and were plagued by sickness and exposure. A man sat hunched in a corner, his uncovered toes as black as death. Cyrus had stared at those toes for six days before he'd made it to the docks where ships would carry him across the sea to a land forsaken by the gods.

"This isn't real," Norah whispered.

She had no idea.

"Oh, it's real," he told her. *"It's very real."*

He showed her the men dragged from the cages. The ones that had perished were piled high to be transported to a mass grave. The ones still alive were shuffled to holding pens along the docks.

And he showed her his captors.

Ink marked their skin, and dark wraps covered their faces.

She gasped.

Now she'd see.

A shadow loomed over her, and she jerked her head up. Horror filled her eyes as she stared at the beast of a man cloaked in black with a horned helm. Then came the recognition. He saw it. She knew exactly who this monster was, and she watched as he spoke to a tall man with a shaved head.

"*Who's he talking to?*" she whispered. "*What are they saying?*"

Cyrus remembered their every word. "*A Serran slaver,*" he told her. "*And he's deciding whether a small boy is worth any price at all, or if I should just be killed.*"

Did she understand now?

"*Everyone I loved abandoned me,*" Cyrus said, "*including Alexander.*" Especially Alexander.

Her head jerked back to him, her eyes wide. "*He didn't abandon you! Your brother loved you.*"

Cyrus swept away the image of the cages and men in chains, and they stood again in the winter forest. He shook his head. "*No. If he loved me, he would have looked for me. He would have tried to find me.*"

"*He was only a boy! He thought you were dead.*"

"*He would have felt me!*" he raged in a sudden burst of anger. "*The way I have felt him all these years.*" He would have felt the pull, the weight, the burden.

"*He didn't have your gift!*" she insisted.

"*He did.*" Cyrus knew he had. "*He had a shield. I couldn't see him.*"

"*No.*" She shook her head. "*It wasn't the same. It was... different.*"

He paused. What else did she know? "*How?*"

She shook her head again. "*I... We don't know. He was only starting to uncover it when he died. But I swear to you, he didn't know you were alive. He would have gone to the ends of the world to find you.*"

Cyrus didn't believe that.

"*I mean it,*" she said. "*If he had any idea you were still alive, he would have come for you.*"

She spoke with such surety—it was... almost convincing.

"*He would have come,*" she told him, "*as soon as he was able.*"

But he didn't believe her, or rather, he didn't want to believe her. He couldn't let himself believe her, because that would make the loss of Alexander worse than it already was. And he couldn't handle *worse*. Yet even as he told himself not to believe it, his strength left him.

His voice dropped to a whisper. "*I spent my entire life hating him. I followed the news of his rise, planning how I'd kill him too.*"

She wavered for a moment. Then her eyes narrowed. "*What happened to your mother?*"

His eyes locked with hers. He hadn't meant to share that deeply.

Her wide eyes stared at him. "*Did you make her take her life?*"

How did she know his mother had taken her life? Maybe Alexander had told her. Regardless, that wasn't something he was willing to talk about. "*I told you. I've done terrible things.*" If she were smart, she'd let that be the end of it.

But she stepped closer to him. "*Lucien, your brother loved you. Family was so important to him. And to Adrian—do you know what it would mean to him to learn that you're alive?*"

For the first time, his childhood name didn't claw at his ears. And to hear her mention Adrian...

"*I never knew I had another brother*," he said quietly. "*Not until you told me.*"

She smiled, but it was a sad smile. "*He's such a beautiful person.*"

"*Is he... like... us?*" He brought his hand to his chest. "*Alexander and me?*" He already knew Adrian didn't have power, but he wanted to be sure.

"*No, there's nothing weird about him,*" she said with another shake of her head. "*He's perfectly normal.*" She frowned. "*That didn't come out right,*" she added quickly.

He couldn't help a smile. Norah was much easier to talk to than he'd imagined. He should have known. He *had* gotten to know her over these past few months. He should have told her about himself sooner—

Then came the rupture.

The trees blurred, and the sky cracked. His breath caught in his throat—his vision shredded into white. The blow almost felt physical as he was abruptly forced from her mind.

And then...

Silence.

Cyrus's eyes shot open to find himself back in his study.

Essandra was already at his side. "What happened?"

"I—I don't know." He wasn't sure exactly. "We were talking, but then... the bond broke."

"Is she angry?"

He shook his head, still reeling. "I don't think so. She was, but not now."

"What did she say? Do you think she'll call you back?"

"I don't know."

She was firing questions at him faster than he could think.

The bond was gone. Something had severed it. Abruptly. Violently. What if she'd been harmed… No, she was safe in Mercia.

Essandra sighed and rose. "Well, let's wait to see if she calls you back." She picked up a letter on the edge of the desk. "This came for you while you were with Norah. It's from Miriel. She didn't send me one, and I was worried. I hope you don't mind that I opened it."

"Of course not," he said, his mind still on Norah.

"She's worried about Etreus," she told him. "They've fortified their borders with more forces than she's ever seen before, and they're adding more Union soldiers each day."

Etreus—Pryam's neighbor and the primary power of the collective Union with four other kingdoms. They'd expelled Pryam the year before, stripping it of all its protections. They feared Miriel's power.

Cyrus rubbed his temples. He couldn't think about this right now. Plus, Hephain would have told him if there were a problem.

"I'm sure they're reacting to us sending waves of people to Pryam." Cyrus had been moving refugees by the shipload, as well as building out Miriel's army. "They're probably just being cautious," he added.

"What if they plan to move against her?"

"That would be stupid of them."

Essandra held the letter in her hands, biting the corner of her lip.

He stood and pulled her close. "Miriel's fine," he promised. She wrapped her arms around him, and he dropped his head into the crook of her neck, breathing her in.

It was so much easier when she was here.

She calmed him, and he could focus.

He focused now.

Cyrus threw out his mind, reaching, searching for any birds still wearing his blood that he could redirect.

He found one. Then another.

And he willed them to Mercia. To Norah.

Chapter Forty

Chaos.

That was all Cyrus felt now. He'd been too free with his blood, sharing it with his men who simply left it on their skin or who did a piss-poor job of wiping it off. And now his mind was always filled with chaos.

Cyrus focused on shutting everything out, save for one voice in particular—Norah's. But he wasn't sure she'd use the blood again. Something had happened, and he had to find out what.

He'd sent two birds—one he'd lost over the Aged Sea, but the other was still on its way. He held control of them longer now, most likely due to his growing power. He still didn't know what this growing power meant, which was frustrating, but he just added it to his growing list of frustrations.

Another letter had arrived from Gregor. He added it to the stack that he hadn't yet opened. It would only enrage him. It was probably a request for more legions, as if Cyrus hadn't already given him a hundred thousand men.

Then there was the matter of war, which Gregor so openly declared. There would be no avoiding it now, and in truth, Cyrus didn't want to avoid it. War was good—but it was imperative for him to be able to focus on the Shadowlands and make Gregor deal with Aleon, although Aleon could still cause Cyrus problems. They had an advantage in their new alliance with Osan, which boasted the world's mightiest naval fleet and also gave Aleon spying eyes up and down the coast. No doubt they were reporting Cyrus's every move. It made the connection with Norah all the more important.

And now, as he sat at his desk, Cyrus wondered if a second letter in front of him that bore a yellow seal would be his sanity's breaking point. It was a letter from Serra. He groaned as he opened it and read the words from his viceroy, Vin Atari. It was regarding disputes in land distribution. These were the same challenges Rael had dealt with when its slaves had become citizens, and Vin should be able to make the proper judgments.

What was the point of having a viceroy if Cyrus had to deal with these issues himself?

He wouldn't.

They could fucking fight it out.

He tossed the letter onto the desk and pinched the bridge of his nose. An ache was forming behind his eyes. He needed sleep, but there was no time for that.

Cyrus reached out his mind to check on the bird.

His pulse quickened. He could see the Mercian capital isle. *Finally.*

He pushed the bird through the mainland city and over the channel, up and around the turrets to the north side, where he found the queen's balcony, and he willed the animal to the railing. It was exhausted and weak, but he held it. He waited until he saw movement in her chamber. And he waited longer.

He wasn't exactly sure what he was going to do; he couldn't communicate through the bird, and it carried no blood and no message.

Still, he waited, looking to see if everything was all right, trying to surmise what had happened—

Suddenly, the bird startled as Norah practically ripped the doors open on the balcony.

She stared at him, her lips pursed into a thin line, anger flaming off her.

Did she know it was him?

She said something to the bird. To him. But he didn't catch it. His heart beat faster. She definitely knew it was him.

And he didn't need to hear her to read the next words on her lips.

"I need more blood," she said.

More blood. She was asking him for more blood.

Cyrus released his hold on the bird, and it flew off into the sky—only for a moment, before dropping to the ground in exhaustion. But he didn't care about the bird. He'd gotten what he needed, and he'd get Norah what she needed too.

Within three days, Cyrus had delivered another vial to her, and Norah called him through the blood bond as soon as she received it. She drew him to a dark tunnel in her mind, where she sat in a stairwell. He assumed this was where she was currently, somewhere under the castle.

"An interesting place to call me to," he said when he arrived.

She gave an apologetic smile. "*We won't be interrupted here.*" She didn't seem to grasp the concept that one could mentally be somewhere completely different from where they were physically, and it amused him. But he didn't care *where* she called him, just that she *did* call him.

He lit up the tunnel around them, and her eyes were on his face.

"*I take it that's what happened before?*" he asked her. "*Why you left so suddenly?*" He covertly searched her memories, and he found exactly what had happened. She'd been found and pulled from their conversation by the Shadow King, with the commander, who'd pried open her hand and wiped Cyrus's blood away.

Fucking commander. He always seemed to be getting in the way. Cyrus should have killed that man when he'd had the chance.

"*I'm sorry about that,*" she told him, pulling his attention back. "*But there's still so much more to talk about. I wanted to see you again. I hope you don't mind.*"

"*I don't mind.*" He didn't mind at all. The previous worry he'd had about the break in their last conversation fell away. She didn't hold the same anger she'd had when they last spoke. And more, she *wanted* to talk to him. This was good.

But now... he stumbled for where to start again. "*Will you walk with me?*"

She nodded.

Good. That was good.

He pulled light around them, weaving a vision of a forest path with vining flowers overhead. She liked flowers, from what he'd gathered, and they were easy to give to her.

"*Shall we?*" he asked, motioning toward the path. The invitation felt too formal on his lips, but he did want to show her some air of refinement beyond the harsh reality of their circumstance.

She picked up beside him. She walked close, as if at ease. He hoped she *was* at ease.

"*I've been thinking, a lot, just about everything,*" she said.

In a good way, he hoped. "*I have too,*" he replied.

She walked calmly, but the way she clasped her hands and dug a thumb into her palm betrayed her anxiousness. "*I still have questions.*"

"*Ask them.*" He'd answer whatever he could.

"*Why didn't you try to kill me again? Why only come after me once?*"

"*I came twice, actually.*" As soon as the words came out, he cursed himself. Why did he have to say that?

She stopped. "*What?*"

He might as well tell her. "*I came once before, when you traveled to marry the king of Aleon. But by the time I arrived, someone had beaten me to you.*"

He dropped the vision of vining flowers and brought forward his own memory of when he'd first gone to the Mercian outer reaches. He showed her the remains of her army—how he'd found them—dead, with their throats slit.

Her breath caught and she grimaced. Cyrus didn't shield her from the sight. This was what the Shadow King did. This was who he was. Her men had been executed on their knees, and the Shadow King had left them where they'd fallen.

"*It's when I found this,*" he said, conjuring the image of her crown in his hand.

She gaped back at him. "*You had my crown all that time?*"

He nodded. "*Then came news of your marriage to the Shadow King,*" he continued. "*That... was a surprise.*"

He dropped his hand and let the image of the crown disappear. "*It was never really about you, though, Norah. I wanted Alexander. I thought he'd accompany you to Aleon, and he didn't. But, when his blood touched your skin in the Shadowlands, I knew he was there with you. He was so close; I couldn't not come.*"

"*So, it was never about me, but you came to kill me?*"

"*I came to kill the both of you.*" He couldn't hold back now. Despite his mind screaming at him to soften his words, he couldn't.

She shook her head. "*But why me?*"

To break Mercia's alliance with the Shadowlands—that was the political answer. But he was already on a warpath of truth and couldn't stop himself now. "*Because Alexander was sworn to protect you, and I wanted to show him he had no power to do so. And you weren't innocent—you so willingly allied yourself with a monster, the Shadow King.*" His words were tinged in venom. "*To turn a blind eye to everything he's done, that makes you complicit!*"

She grew quiet, and her throat moved with a strained swallow.

"*And the Shadow King loved you,*" he added.

Silence sat heavy between them. "*Why didn't you try again?*" she asked finally.

His anger simmered and cooled. He'd told himself it hadn't been practical to try again, but, really, he'd learned more about her—most entertainingly from Gregor. "*Because... you weren't as I'd expected,*" he confessed. "*And... I didn't want to, after that.*"

Her eyes were piercing. They studied him. "*How did you get into Kharav?*" she asked.

"*You ask me my secrets?*" A warning flagged in the back of his mind. Perhaps he was being too honest with her. There was danger in sharing too much, and right now, he feared he might tell her whatever she wanted to know.

"*Do they really still need to be secrets?*" she asked.

She already knew about some of his power; she'd seen a little of the birds. He supposed revealing a little more wouldn't hurt.

Cyrus pushed away the image of where she'd been captured on the way to Aleon, and he brought back the daylight. He projected a flock of birds overhead.

"*They show me,*" he said.

She followed his gaze up.

"*They show me the landscape,*" he explained, "*how to get through, if danger is near. They are my eyes.*"

"*You control them with your blood?*"

He smiled.

A line trenched between her brows. "*So, you just go around dripping blood on creatures, having them do your will?*"

He chuckled. "*Something like that.*"

Exactly like that, actually.

She frowned. "*Does it hurt? You have to... cut yourself?*"

It was a simple question, but a thoughtful one. "*It did,*" he said, "*but I'm used to it now.*" In fact, now he never even thought about it.

"*I'm sorry,*" she said, her voice soft. "*That still sounds terrible.*"

"*You don't need to feel sorry for me.*" He didn't need her pity. Pity was for people who opposed him. Cyrus pulled his dagger from his belt and drew the blade across his palm, opening the skin and spilling his blood to the floor.

She gasped.

Then he showed her how the wound closed, healing as if it had never existed.

She gaped at him. "*You can heal yourself?*"

He wished he could do that. "*No. I have a healer. A true healer.*" He wasn't sure why he was being so open. Perhaps he should have told her he *could* heal himself, but he didn't want to lie to her. Not anymore.

"*Your witch?*" she asked.

"*No. Another, not a witch.*"

Her face was full of intrigue, her eyes full of questions. He liked her eager curiosity.

"*How do you control someone's mind?*" she asked him.

Cyrus hesitated as the warnings flashed again inside his head. He shouldn't talk about his weaknesses, his limits, but he liked this trust building between them. "*I can't,*" he admitted. "*Humans are too intelligent, too strong.*"

"*But the men you sent to kill me—*"

The assassins.

"*They willingly yielded their minds to me.*"

"*And died for you,*" she added.

A pang of guilt ate at him. Orion had lost quite a few good men that day, but they'd been there of their own free will. "*They're all willing to die for me, for our cause.*"

"*And what cause is that?*"

That was the question he didn't dare answer. She had a lot of patience for him right now, a lot of kindness, but he didn't think he'd keep that kindness if he so blatantly shared his intention of killing her husband, someone she clearly loved. He didn't understand how someone like her, someone filled with compassion and light, could love a man like that. Surely, she couldn't for long.

She sighed. "*I should return, before I'm missed,*" she said.

Cyrus didn't want to make trouble for her. He wanted it to be easy for her to talk to him, easy to share her own secrets. He brought back the vision of a forest path with its woven greenery overhead and walked her back to the stairs where he'd first arrived.

"*I'd like to talk again,*" she said.

Good. "*I'd like that too.*"

She gave him a soft smile. "*Goodbye, Lucien.*"

He let her call him that. She'd been speaking to a person she thought was like herself—someone that maybe he used to be or could have been—a person filled with compassion and light and the desire to bring good to the world.

He didn't correct her, but he was sad for how wrong she was.

Chapter Forty-One

A pounding on his chamber door woke him abruptly, and Cyrus bolted up in bed. The sun hadn't yet risen.

"Cyrus!" Everan called through the door, and he pounded again.

"I'm here," he answered as he stumbled out of bed. Beside him, Essandra had woken too and was quickly pulling her robe around her.

Cyrus swung the door open, and torchlight spilled in from the hall. Everan stood in the doorway. "Etreus has taken Pryam."

It took a moment for Everan's words to register, then Cyrus's stomach dropped. *Miriel.* "What about Miriel?" he asked as he jerked on his clothes in the darkness. "Where is she?"

"She escaped. Her ship just arrived in the harbor."

Cyrus stopped for a moment to let himself breathe. She'd gotten away. And she was here.

Wait, she was *here*?

Essandra rattled off questions before Cyrus could ask them himself. "Is she all right? Was she injured? Did we lose anyone?"

"I think she's fine," Everan said, "although I haven't seen her myself. I came here as soon as I heard the news. I don't know anything else yet."

Essandra lit a candle on the table, then turned to Cyrus. "Get the horses. I'll meet you in the courtyard in a few moments, and we'll head to the port."

Cyrus pulled his sword from where it hung beside the bed and fastened the belt around his waist. Ready, he gave Essandra a soft brush on her arm before following Everan out.

By the time they reached the docks, Miriel's ship was already anchored and moored. Cyrus strode quickly with Essandra, followed closely by Everan, Kord, Ram, and Jaem.

The torchlit harbor walks were overflowing with men. Cyrus stared at the masses in surprise. They couldn't have all come on one ship.

"Cyrus!" a voice called out over the chaos.

He looked to find Bash on a mainway, and beside him—Miriel.

"Cyrus!" she cried as she ran to him and flung her arms around him.

He held her tightly for a moment, then pushed her back slightly to look at her under the torchlight. His eyes darted over her—her neck, her arms, her body, the way that she stood—looking for injury. He clasped her face in his hands. "Are you hurt?"

She shook her head. "No, but it was awful. They attacked the capital in the night, killing anyone they found as they went. Everyone fell back to the palace, where we could fight as one together, but the Union army was too big. We had to make a run for the ships." She looked back at Bash. "Bash got me out. We came straight here."

"Why didn't you use the blood?" Cyrus asked angrily. He should have been informed the moment this happened.

"I did!" Bash insisted. "You never answered me."

Surprise stole his words. *Well, fuck.* He had been pushing voices out. That was his own fault, and Miriel had needed him. Guilt pooled in his stomach.

Kord interjected. "Are these all the men that came with you?" he asked Bash.

"We have four ships," another voice said, and Brant appeared. Cyrus was relieved to see him. "There was a fifth one, the last ship," Brant added, "but it didn't make it out of the harbor."

"Where's Hephain?" Kord asked, his tone urgent now.

Brant hesitated. Then he said, "On the last ship."

They all grew quiet, but especially Kord.

Cyrus's chest tightened. Hephain. That loss was beyond hurt.

Miriel's eyes caught something behind him. "Essandra!" she cried and ran toward her.

Essandra hugged her tightly. "Thank the gods you're safe." She looked her over as well. "Are you all right?"

"Yes, but I've been so sick about what's happened."

Essandra nodded. "Well, you're safe now." She looked at Cyrus.

"Take her back to the palace," he told her. "Get her settled in and taken care of."

"Of course." She gave Miriel another hug and took her hand. "Come on, let's get you inside."

Cyrus watched as they disappeared toward the waiting horses, then he turned back to Bash and Brant.

Brant bowed his head. "I'm sorry," he said. "I couldn't hold the capital. There were too many."

Cyrus clasped his shoulder and squeezed it firmly. "You did exactly what you were supposed to do. Miriel is safe because of you." He looked at Bash. "Both of you. Well done."

"I'll settle everyone into the army barracks on the south side until we can figure out what to do with them all," Brant said.

Everan stepped forward. "I can see to that. You need rest."

Cyrus let his gaze travel over Brant and Bash. Blood crusted their clothing, and tiredness lined their faces. "You two come back with me," he said. "We'll get you food and some beds so you can get a few hours' sleep." He turned to Everan, leaving Kord to his silent grief. "Let Ram and Jaem manage the men. Wake the council. We need to have a plan by morning."

Everan nodded.

But by morning, they did not have a plan.

The air in the council chamber was thick with the heat of spent arguments. Cyrus stood at the head of the table, his hands braced against its surface, while members of his council slouched in exhaustion behind their quiet, stubborn resolve.

"So, we're agreed," Turin said, his voice hoarse. "We send a delegation to Etreus. Begin talks. Attempt to negotiate for Pryam's return."

They most certainly weren't agreed. Cyrus laughed under his breath—a laugh fueled by rage and the need for blood. "Etreus refused all discussions with Miriel in the past. You think they give a fuck about negotiation now?"

Etreus saw Miriel as evil, which was ironic given that Etreus was a kingdom that still enslaved people. They weren't interested in negotiating with her or about her. They'd wanted her gone, and they'd done it. The possibility of anything amicable had been destroyed the moment they tried to kill her.

There would be no negotiating.

"But the reality is, we can't manage two wars," Everan said.

"They came in the night and butchered people while they slept."

"Then what do you propose?" Verin, his merchant councillor, asked. "That we pull men from Serra? Recall legions back from Japheth? What would Gregor do then? And what would you tell the people?"

They weren't wrong. Not politically. Not strategically. Cyrus was barely holding Rael together while barreling toward a war with the Shadow King and his allies—Aleon and Mercia. He didn't have a dependable alliance with Japheth, and Serra was still unstable.

Taking back Pryam would mean he'd have to reprioritize. He'd have to let go of the Shadow King, deny Japheth a move against Aleon, and risk losing Gregor, who he needed—as much as Cyrus despised him.

Cyrus could do none of these things.

He could do nothing against Etreus.

It was yet one more thing lost: Orion. Pryam. Hephain.

When would it end?

But he knew the answer.

It wouldn't.

"No one goes to Etreus," Cyrus said coldly. "No negotiation."

The room fell silent.

Then he turned and strode out of the council room before they could argue. If he stayed, he'd do something worse.

Like declare war anyway.

The afternoon brought a heavy heat, and Cyrus contemplated traveling to the stone circle just to be free of it. But he wanted to be free of more than just the heat. He was tired. Tired of failure, tired of having to be strong, tired of the unrelenting pressures of the crown. Pressures of duty and responsibility. And in the wake of it all, to have to shoulder the loss—the unrelenting, unforgiving loss…

He wasn't sure how much more he could take.

Shouting sounded through the courtyard, and the dogs tore off and outside. Cyrus followed to see the commotion. He swore to himself as he went. One more fucking thing and he'd seriously lose every—

As the crowd parted, he stopped.

A wave of emotion flooded him.

Soldiers filtered in, weary and worn, but leading them—Hephain.

He'd made it home. He'd fucking made it home.

The dogs jumped around him in excitement, but Hephain didn't look at them. His eyes searched for Cyrus, and when he saw him, he came immediately. Dropping his head in defeat, he said, "I'm sorry. I—"

Cyrus didn't even let him finish before he reached out and pulled him close. He held him tightly.

One less loss. Cyrus needed one less loss right now. He gripped Hephain even tighter. There was nothing he could say because words weren't enough.

Finally, Cyrus pushed him back to look at him, clasping his shoulders. It still took him another moment before he could speak. "I'm glad you're home, brother," he finally managed to say.

An emotional smile came to Hephain's lips, and he nodded. "It's good to be home."

"Come inside," Cyrus told him, and he pulled him back toward the palace.

It didn't take long for news to spread. Despite everything that had happened, the air was lighter now. Everyone seemed in higher spirits. Even Miriel, who'd been in tears since her arrival. That was what one godsend could do.

As the day faded into night, Cyrus caught Kord alone in the hall. He didn't have anything really to discuss, but he felt compelled to check in. "How are you?" he asked.

"Good," Kord answered. "Yeah, good."

"Good," Cyrus said back.

They both stood in the hall, nodding silently.

"I'm happy... about... that." Cyrus cursed under his breath. He didn't even know what he was saying anymore. "Did you see Hephain?"

Kord's gaze dropped to the ground, but a relieved smile came to his lips. "I did." Then his brow quirked as he looked back up at Cyrus. "It makes me feel like I can actually be happy about other good news I have to share."

Cyrus smiled back. He'd take all the good news he could get.

But suddenly, a pull came in the back of his mind.

Kord's brows dipped. "Is something wrong?" he asked.

This was terrible timing. "I'm so sorry," Cyrus told him. "It's Norah. She's calling to me."

Kord nodded. "Oh. Yeah, you should go."

"I really want to hear—"

"It's fine," Kord assured him. "Really. Go. I'll find you later."

"Are you sure?"

"Yes." He nodded again. "That's important. Go. We'll talk after."

So, Cyrus went. It *was* important. He couldn't lose his progress with Norah. He hoped to gain more information on the Shadow army—where they were now, what they had planned, but he needed to be careful. Things were fragile, and he could quickly lose this opportunity.

Norah called him to the dimly lit stairwell again, where she sat, waiting.

He should just tell her she could imagine herself wherever she'd like to be, but really, it didn't matter. He could take her places she couldn't even dream of.

As he approached her in her mind, he brought with him summertime. He waved away the dark stairs where she sat and replaced them with a garden bench surrounded by roses. In front of her, he placed a fountain with a small bird in the air. She watched it with fascination as Cyrus took his seat on the bench beside her, just beyond arm's reach.

Norah kept her eyes on the bird, not looking at him directly, but she knew he was there. The bird swooped around the fountain and flew away. She watched until it was out of sight before pulling a vial of his blood from her pocket. *"So, your birds bring me these?"* she asked.

Her gaze finally shifted to him, and he nodded.

"And my crown?"

"I have larger friends." He called forward the images of One and Two.

When she saw the dogs, she withdrew slightly against the back of the bench and folded her hands against her stomach. *"Did you do that to them?"*

It took him a moment to understand her aversion, but then it occurred to him that she wasn't familiar with arena dogs. She'd have no understanding of why their ears and tails had been removed; she knew nothing of the hell of the bloodsport.

He shook his head. *"No. With me, they have very different lives from what they had before."*

Cyrus waved the image of the dogs away, and she turned her attention back on him. Her lips parted as though to say something else, but she didn't.

"You have more questions?" he asked.

She pulled her bottom lip between her teeth, studying him. *"You said something, before, both the last time we spoke and when you came as the assassins. You knew Alexander's blood had touched my skin in Kharav. How?"*

More questions about his abilities. This one seemed harmless enough, though. Alexander was dead—this wasn't something he could use anymore. *"His blood allowed me to travel the same as my own. When it touched your skin, I saw you. And I knew he was with you."*

"And that's how you came to me in the mortium after he died," she said. She was putting it all together.

He hadn't wanted to talk about Alexander, but now he found himself doing just that. The words just came.

"I knew something had happened," he told her. *"A searing pain came to me, greater than I'd ever felt before."* He remembered it: falling to his knees, everything going dark, Essandra crying out his name. *"When I*

woke, his weight—the weight I'd carried inside for my entire life—it was just gone." He sat, numb, still feeling the void.

"*And his blood touched so many,*" he said. "*So many minds, so loud—his blood was on all their skin. And I knew.*" He swallowed the knot in his throat that threatened to choke him. "*All those years, I wanted him dead,*" he continued, "*and then for him to be snuffed from me in an instant... I wasn't ready. I couldn't believe it.*" He still couldn't believe it.

"*I wanted him back,*" he said. "*And so, I searched, but the weight was gone. I sought his blood, reaching out to everyone it had touched. And it brought me to the mortium. To you.*" His eyes stayed on her, but he wasn't looking at her anymore. "*I saw him,*" he whispered, more to himself than to her, "*in your mind, for the first time in our adult lives.*"

It had to have been a shock to her when he'd first come; it had certainly been a shock to *him*. He swallowed. "*You saw me as I am, before I realized where I was, before I realized I was in your mind. It was too late to change my projection.*"

"*The markings on your neck,*" she said.

He didn't bother to hide them anymore.

She sat with her arms crossed and a fist resting against her lips. "*And then you came back; you came as Alexander.*"

He nodded. He hated that he'd done that, although he wouldn't have done it differently if given the chance again. "*I wanted you to let me back in,*" he confessed. "*You still had his blood on your skin, and so I returned. I could project everything: his dress, his hair*"—he paused—"*everything but his voice and his words.*"

"*So, you came back for my secrets.*"

He would have been a fool not to. "*I saw it as an opportunity against my enemy, yes.*" He hesitated for a moment, then said, "*But as I got to know you*"—he paused again—"*it didn't make me happy to deceive you.*" That was the truth.

Quiet fell over them.

"*And now?*" she asked. "*Now that you know things are different, that things have changed—*"

"*Nothing's changed,*" he said.

Her brow twitched. "*How can you say that? You would still move against Mercia?*"

"*Norah, Mercia was never the target of my wrath. Only those who've oppressed my people.*" Those who had wronged his people. Those who'd wronged *him*. He sighed. "*For Alexander I felt a personal vengeance, yes, but you and I have never truly been enemies. And I'm sorry you've been caught in the middle.*"

"*No one wants this war,*" she said.

Anger flashed through him. "*I want this war.*" His people wanted this war. They demanded it.

Her expression faltered for the briefest moment. "*What? No—why?*"

Did she really still not get it? Did she truly not see? "*Because that's what change requires,*" he said. "*And that's the price owed.*"

"*Lucien, thousands of people will die, your own people included.*"

"*All of us are willing to sacrifice.*" Especially Cyrus.

Norah's hands tensed in her lap. "*For what?*"

"*For justice! The Shadowlands must pay.*" Gods, did she really think they would make nice, and he would walk away?

"*Kharav is not the only kingdom who has slaves,*" she argued.

"The Shadowlands fuel it. They sell the spoils of their wars; the slavers use Shadow rice to support their trade. There are others, it's true—Etreus, Persus, Elam, Lorys—and they will all pay. Every single one of them. But I'll take the Shadowlands first."

She stared at him, her breaths quick and shallow now. She swallowed. *"I think we're both tired and have a lot to think on."* Her voice was careful now. Too careful. *"Can we talk more later?"*

He'd scared her. The situation with Miriel was still affecting him, everything was affecting him, and he'd let his anger go too far. Cyrus rose from the bench and tried to calm the air between them. He nodded, letting the garden fall away, and he brought her back to the stairwell.

"You'll return to me?" she asked.

"When you call me," he promised. *If* she called him. He didn't want to let her go like this. There was a high chance she wouldn't call him again now. He needed to fix this.

"Good night, Lucien," she said.

He couldn't let her go.

But he feared anything he tried would only make it worse. There was nothing he could do. He gave a stiff nod. *"Good night."*

Cyrus opened his eyes to his study, and he rose to his feet.

He'd fucked it up again. Anger flashed through him, and he swept his arm across his desk, knocking everything to the floor. He pinched the bridge between his eyes. Threatening the Shadow King was *not* going to get him anywhere with Norah. What was the matter with him? He needed some air.

Cyrus strode from his study, through the halls, and out into the courtyard. He headed toward the sparring fields. He needed to get out some anger—anger at the situation, but mostly anger at himself. If he lost the connection with Norah, it would be difficult to get information on the Shadow King.

And he wouldn't be able to save her.

He almost didn't notice Kord falling in step beside him.

"Did you speak to her again?" Kord asked.

Kord knew he had. Cyrus didn't slow his stride. He didn't want to talk about this right now.

"What did she say?" Kord asked.

"It's complicated," he answered shortly.

"Complicated because she wants peace?"

Cyrus paused in his step. He couldn't avoid it, which grated on him further.

Kord's eyes searched him for answers. "She does, doesn't she?"

"You know that's not an option."

Kord shook his head. "No, why isn't it an option? It's literally what everyone needs. Look at what's happening in Serra, and we're scrambling to figure out how to deal with Pryam."

"This is what the people want."

"They don't know what they want. They need you to rally them." He sighed. "If you take us to war with the Shadowlands, right now, with all this going on, then you do this for yourself."

"I do it for all of us!" Cyrus snapped. "And everyone we've lost. For Orion, and Manus, and Kieve—"

"Who are all dead! Kieve's dead! You think he gives a fuck about vengeance anymore? Gods, Cyrus, you don't even see it—you never did. Kieve was broken! And he didn't need Pyro's blood; he needed his brothers. He needed me. He needed you!"

Cyrus stood, his fists clenched, his breaths shaking. "Is there anything else?" He was done with this conversation.

His words stung Kord; he saw it—the grimace of hurt.

"Yeah," Kord said. He wiped a hand over his face. "I didn't get a chance to tell you earlier, but you should know—Leti's with child."

Cyrus stared at him in disbelief. "You'd bring a child into this world just as we march to war?"

"You want me to give up life to have a war." Kord shook his head. "Why can't you give up war to have a life?"

"This is beyond me!" Cyrus argued. "The people want justice!"

"This isn't justice!" Kord shook his head. "You have the power to change things," he pressed. "Cyrus! You inspire people. All you have to do is take this dream of war and replace it with something else. Give them a new dream—a new life. They'll follow. People will follow." Kord threw his hands into the air. "I don't even know why I keep trying to argue this." He shook his head. "I didn't come to argue with you. I just wanted to tell you about Leti." Then he gave a disgusted snort. "You know what the fucked-up thing is? I actually thought you'd be happy for me."

Cyrus quieted. "Kord—"

His friend shook his head again. Then he turned and walked away.

"Kord!" Cyrus called after him. But he didn't stop.

Cyrus swore as he pushed out a sharp breath.

"What was that?" came Essandra's voice from behind him. He turned.

She wore a long purple dress, and her hair was swept back behind her. Gods, he needed her right now. He reached out and pulled her close. Her touch calmed him, and he let out a long sigh.

"Leti's with child," he told her.

She gasped in surprise and smiled. "That's wonderful news."

His brow stitched. "No, it's not." How could this be wonderful news? "We're going to war. It's not the time for children."

"Leti's not going to war."

"But Kord is, and I can't have him distracted. None of us can afford to be distracted." His stare caught hers. "Are *you* continuing to take precautions?"

She snuffed as her mouth dropped open. Then her eyes narrowed. "Of course I am."

"I can't stray from this path."

She pursed her lips and pulled her hand from his. "Then don't let me *distract* you." And she turned and walked away.

Chapter Forty-Two

Cyrus paced his chamber. Norah still hadn't used the blood again. She wouldn't call him back the same day, he told himself, or at this point—in the middle of the night. The sun had long since set. The earliest would be tomorrow. Despite this practicality, each passing hour brought more and more concern, more and more doubt.

He swore under his breath. He shouldn't have been so direct with his intentions. His connection with Norah was fragile, and he was managing it poorly.

And that wasn't the only thing he was managing poorly.

His gaze landed on his empty bed. It had been over a month since Essandra had confessed her love for him, and they hadn't spent a night apart since. But apparently she had no intention of staying in his chamber this evening.

Essandra. Norah. Kord. Was there anyone *not* unhappy with him?

He wouldn't be able to sleep until he remedied one specifically. He needed Essandra by his side; he couldn't face everything alone. And so, he found himself at her chamber door.

Cyrus rapped softly on the wood. He should have come sooner. She hadn't said a word to him since their conversation. Simply giving her some time to calm down did *not* seem to be working.

She didn't answer, and he knocked again. Heavy. Too heavy.

He'd just made a simple comment, and she already knew he didn't want a child. But the more he thought about it, the more uneasy he became. Maybe she was starting to change her mind.

Essandra needed a blood relation to Cyrus to complete her spell for the Amoran Cup. That was supposed to have been Alexander. Now Alexander was gone. There was Adrian, but Adrian didn't have power.

However, a child would fill that need. A child born of a witch and a seer. A child born of Cyrus.

Was she considering that now? She hadn't before, but failure changed things. And Essandra had suffered a lot of failure.

He had to find out. Just as he turned to start toward her workroom, she opened the door, and he spun back around. She stood with her hand on her hip. Her nightgown hung long to the floor, and an open silk robe covered her shoulders.

He forgot what he'd planned to say. "I-I almost thought you weren't here." The words sounded stupid as he said them.

"I was deciding whether I wanted to talk to you," she said.

So, she was still angry.

"I came to apologize." Although he wasn't sure exactly what for.

She crossed her arms but didn't say anything. This wasn't going well.

"Are you upset that I don't want a child with you?" he asked.

Her green eyes flashed with something he couldn't read.

"We've talked about this before," he said. "You know what's coming. You know the path ahead of me."

She just stood, shaking her head in disbelief, although none of this should be surprising to her.

He hadn't even given her the protection of marriage. Wouldn't she want that first?

"We're not even wed," he said.

She gave a small snort, and before he could say anything else, she closed the door in his face.

He stood, staring at it.

She ripped the door back open. "Nice apology," she said. Then she slammed it closed again.

By the end of the second day, Norah still hadn't called him through the blood. Cyrus told himself it was for the best. He hadn't slept since Miriel had arrived, and he needed to be at his best when he talked to Norah again.

Yet he still didn't sleep.

Instead, he found himself at Miriel's door. She seemed to be the least angry with him, although she probably had the most reason to be. When he'd told her he couldn't move against Etreus, she'd taken the news quietly, but with tears in her eyes. She'd told him she understood, which—somehow—had made him feel even worse.

She opened the door to his knock, and he could see she'd been crying.

His chest tightened. He'd done what he needed to do, but he hated himself for it.

"I came to check on you," he said.

"I'm fine." But she didn't look fine.

"I know this is hard, but I—"

"I told you I understand why you can't do anything." She wiped her cheek as another tear spilled down it.

It gutted him. "Understand this too, though," he said. "I will get Pryam back for you. I just need time. It's not that I can't do anything at all, it's just that I can't do anything *right now*."

She nodded, but he wasn't sure she believed him.

He'd hoped to feel better after talking to Miriel again.

He didn't.

Now he found himself in the doorway of Essandra's workroom, prepared to feel even less better.

Essandra stood against the shelf on the far wall, leafing through a large leather-bound book. She stopped when he entered, but she didn't look up at him.

"I'm back for a second attempt," he said.

She pursed her lips as she finally turned her eyes on him. "A second attempt at what?"

"An apology." He drew closer to her. "I'm sorry. I didn't mean to upset you, but clearly I did."

Her eyes grew more shadowed. She slipped the book she was holding back into its space on the shelf. "You can see that the problem isn't the fact that you don't want a child, right?" she asked. "Because I *also* don't want a child."

Perfect. He'd upset her with something they agreed on. That confused him even more.

"But it felt like you were implying that I would do something like this without your consent," she said. "And if that's really what you think of me—"

"It's not," he said quickly.

"I would never—"

"I know." He desperately needed her to believe him. "It was a poor choice of words. But it was something I wanted to talk to you about, because it's something that we've been of like mind on, but I also understand how things can change. If you keep failing at alternatives for your spell—"

"If I choose to have a child, it will be because I *want* it, not because of what it can do for me. And I already have an alternative."

He stopped. "You do?"

"Let me show you something." She led him to the other side of the room, to a corner where a tall, lidded basket sat. Pulling off the lid, she reached inside. As she straightened again, he took a sudden step back.

She held a large black serpent wrapped around her arm, its dark scales slick and gleaming.

"What is that?" he asked, his voice sharp as it coiled toward her neck.

"Exactly what it looks like," she said. "Don't worry, it won't harm me—I created it. Nor will it harm you—it's borne of your blood, which means I should be able to use it for the Amoran Cup spell."

He stared, trying to process. "You think this... creature... can replace a person?"

"The script says it needs to be a bloodline bond with power. Nowhere does it say that an anchor needs to be a person."

"That should be a given. Usually something with a bloodline bond to a person... is also another person."

She looked at him sharply. "It was borne of your blood, and it holds enough of your essence to create the bloodline tether."

"It has no soul."

"The cup doesn't need a soul. It needs a vessel that can anchor the magic. This will work."

He still stared at the serpent, his mind reeling. "How did you even make it?"

She drew her lip between her teeth, not answering.

And he realized... "Dark magic. It's why you have the new marks on your skin." He shook his head.

"After this, I don't need to use it anymore."

"What about for the Amoran Cup spell?"

"That's not dark magic."

"Essandra," he said, drawing closer. "I don't like this. We can find another way."

She put the serpent back into the basket and returned the lid. "It's already done. And I don't need dark magic for anything else."

He wasn't sure he believed that.

"And hopefully this puts your mind at ease about my needs and intentions with a child," she added.

It certainly didn't put him at ease, but he did believe her about the child. "I'm sorry," he said softly.

Finally, she nodded. "I accept your apology."

His voice came softer. "Are we better?" He needed them to be better. He couldn't go another day without her.

She slowly lifted her eyes to meet his. "There is something more."

He stepped closer to her.

"I don't want to feel like a distraction to you." She drew a breath in. "I mean, I do want to be able to distract you from your obsessions, but... I want to feel like I'm an obsession too." She dropped her gaze to the floor. "That probably sounds ridiculous."

He reached out and tipped up her chin, forcing her to look at him again. "If you don't think you're an obsession, then I've done a very poor job of showing you how I feel."

He leaned into her, dropping his head to the curve of her neck and bringing his lips to her ear. "I'm obsessed with having you by my side," he whispered. He nipped softly at her skin, and she shuddered. "Near me, with me, all the time. I can't eat without you, I can't sleep without you."

Slowly, he sank to his knees in front of her, holding her hands and bringing her fingers to his lips. He trailed kisses around and across her palms.

"Do you really think you're not an obsession?" he asked, staring up at her.

Her heady eyes stared back at him.

"I'm obsessed with your touch," he told her. Lifting her skirts, he curved his hand behind her knee, bringing it up so he could dip his head and brush his lips across her milky skin. "The way you feel."

He hooked her leg over his shoulder, looking up at her. She clutched him tightly to keep her balance.

He smiled as he kissed the inside of her knee again.

"I'm obsessed with the way you smell," he whispered, working his way higher. "The way you taste."

A soft sigh escaped her as her head fell back.

"But most of all, I'm obsessed with the way you scream my name," he said.

And he pushed his head between her thighs.

Chapter Forty-Three

Cyrus walked with Essandra through the stone gardens. They'd spent the morning in bed, tangled in each other. She'd run her fingers through his hair as he talked. And he'd talked about everything—Etreus and Miriel, Gregor, Kord, Serra, Rael. He'd talked about Norah. There was nothing he left out. Not that he'd been keeping secrets, he just hadn't shared the smaller details before. He certainly hadn't shared his worries, his fears.

He shared them now.

Cyrus didn't like to talk, but now he couldn't stop. And she'd only listened.

They'd eaten a late breakfast in the morning sun. Then he talked some more.

"She still hasn't called me to return to her," he said as they passed the center fountain. "I fear she won't."

Essandra walked with her arm looped through his. "Do you want my thoughts?" she asked finally.

"Of course I do."

"I think she will call. I don't think she'll give up on you so easily, and you have to show her you're worth not giving up on. You have to show her you can be civil, amicable, gentlemanly even."

He snorted. "I'm none of those things."

"You are when you want to be." She pulled him to a stop and faced him. "What if..." She paused and pulled her bottom lip between her teeth. "What if you just entertained the idea of peace? It's so obvious she wants it."

He pulled back. "I'll never have peace with the Shadow King."

"Peace with *her*. She's queen of the Shadowlands. She could influence change. Of course, I'm sure that would come with the requisite that you stop trying to kill her husband, but not killing someone is not the same as having a friendship with them."

"Peace with her *is* the same as peace with the Shadow King," he argued.

"Not exactly. And, Cyrus, this isn't even the same king."

"He's the same as his father!" he snapped.

She quieted.

He sighed as he stared down at her. "Are you saying I'm wrong?" She was the only one he would hear it from right now.

"I'm saying everyone around you is *not* wrong. I don't think Norah is wrong."

The pull came so unexpectedly that it almost startled him, and he stilled.

Essandra's brow creased, and her lips parted. "Cyrus?"

"She's calling me."

"Norah?"

He nodded.

"Now?"

He nodded again.

"Well... go!"

Yes, he had to go. Wait... He had to sit. He found a bench. "Will you stay with me?"

"Of course," she promised. "I'll be here. Go." But then she gripped him. "Just... remember—civil, amicable, gentle. *Gentlemanly*. Don't even talk about the Shadow King this time."

Don't even talk about the Shadow King.

He clutched her hand as he closed his eyes, letting his head drop, and traveled where his blood called him.

Norah sat in the stairwell again, but her mind wasn't as it usually was. It was jagged and frayed.

Broken.

Cyrus knew grief when he saw it. He silently shifted through her mind and immediately saw what had happened.

Her grandmother had passed, the old queen regent.

This was what had kept her from calling him, and he eased. The worry he'd had faded.

Gentle, Essandra had told him.

"*I thought you might not invite me again.*" He spoke quietly in the darkness, simply letting her know he was there. "*I thought you might be angry,*" he confessed. "*But now... I see. I see your sorrow.*"

He drew down soft light around him and stepped in front of her at the bottom of the stairs. "*I'm sorry for your loss,*" he said.

Gentle. Cyrus offered her his hand. She stared at it for a moment, surprised, but she took it and stepped down off the stairs to his side.

Gentle. Gentlemanly. He pulled her hand into the fold of his arm and led her to walk with him. It seemed like a gentlemanly thing to do, and she let him.

She walked solemnly, but he could tell she was trying. The fact she was so dedicated to this cause to still talk to him again despite her grief, and despite his last interaction with her, made him think he owed a little more effort himself. He brought forward a field under the dark of night and filled it with fireflies.

She didn't seem impressed, not that he was trying to impress her; he was trying only to lessen her sadness. He wasn't sure why he thought fireflies would do that.

Perhaps they could just sit awhile.

Cyrus led her to a bench—the same bench that was in the stone gardens in Rael near the fountain, but beside it, he created a bubbling stream and pulled in the soft light of early morning.

Letting go of his arm, she sat, and he sat beside her.

"*I can't believe she's gone,*" she whispered.

Her words struck something within him that he hadn't expected. He knew that disbelief.

"*How cruel death is.*" Her voice shook. "*I spoke harshly to her before, over something... so stupid, and I didn't even get a chance to make it right.*" She wiped her nose. "*Death took the chance to tell her I was sorry, the chance to tell her goodbye.*"

Cyrus's chest tightened. He knew that pain as well.

A tear spilled down her cheek. "*She looked so fragile in her bed,*" she told him. "*I tried to remember her as she was before, but even that seems to be taken from me.*"

That sparked a thought.

"I can show her to you," he said softly. *"As she was. I can help you remember."*

She shook her head. *"No. I would know it would be you under her face."*

"And if I stay right here?" he asked. *"I can simply show her to you."*

The corners of her eyes tightened. *"Like a vision, or a memory?"*

"Something like that, yes."

She wanted to see her grandmother—the desperation was written all over her face, but he'd hurt her with the vision of Alexander. No doubt that was in her mind now. She needed this to be different. He hoped she'd let him give this to her. He wanted to give her something.

Finally, she nodded.

Cyrus called more light around them. He pulled every detail he could find from her mind. He didn't remember much of the queen regent from when he was a child, but Norah knew every part of her, every line of her face. So Cyrus did too.

He brought the vision of the old woman just behind her. Norah turned to follow his gaze, and when she saw her grandmother, her breath caught. She glanced at Cyrus with her eyes wide, then back to her grandmother.

Cyrus pulled more power, and the vision of the old woman smiled warmly and held out her arms to Norah.

Norah glanced back at him, her breaths coming faster. *"It's not a memory, it's..."* She looked back to her grandmother. *"It's like she's there."*

Cyrus would make her there. He'd done it before for Essandra. He could do it again. He willed her there. He summoned more power, pouring it into the vision. *"You can touch her,"* he said.

She reached out and gripped him tightly, like she didn't dare to let herself believe it.

He gave her a reassuring nod. It was all the encouragement she needed. Norah staggered up from the bench and rushed to the old woman. She cried as her grandmother's arms swept around her.

Warmth. He needed to give her warmth. Cyrus pulled more power, focusing. This—something so small—drained him almost as much as Soroya had when she'd fought him for Essandra. He opened himself to the Aether and drew even more power.

Norah clung to her grandmother.

He felt himself fading. He couldn't hold the vision much longer. Cyrus pulled the old woman back and had her wipe a tear from Norah's face. He drew the image forward to give her a kiss on her cheek, then, slowly, he released the vision back into the light.

Essandra's worried voice cut through. "Cyrus!" She was calling him to come back, but he couldn't leave yet.

Norah wept, smiling through her tears, still looking into the light long after her grandmother was gone. Finally, she turned back to him, but as her eyes landed on him, she gasped.

"*Lucien!*" she cried, and she ran to him. She dropped down onto the bench beside him and pulled him to look at her. "*Lucien, are you all right?*"

"Cyrus!" Essandra's voice called again.

He had to focus to keep from slipping out of Norah's mind. "*I don't have the strength to stay with you much longer,*" he said weakly. "*It's the seemingly simplest things that are sometimes the hardest.*" He gave a weak smile and squeezed her hand. He couldn't keep the vision of the garden around them any longer, and he let it fall away.

"Lucien! Whatever you're doing, you have to stop! Go. Rest."

"Cyrus!" Essandra called him, her voice sharper now, more urgent.

"Will you call me back, Norah?" he asked. He could barely get the words out, but he needed to make sure she'd call him back.

"Yes, but go," she told him. *"You're hurting yourself."*

His vision began to unravel—white threads unspooling into black. A buzzing filled his ears. His hands felt distant, foreign.

"I—" he tried, but the words slipped from his lips before they formed.

Still, he managed the faintest smile before he let himself fall from her mind.

He woke with a jolt in the stone garden back in Rael.

Essandra clutched him, panic etched across her face. "Cyrus, look at me. Look at me."

Blood ran freely from his nose, hot and thick. He tried to speak, but his throat was tight.

"I'm all right," he rasped. He wiped the blood that ran into his mouth. "I'm all right," he said again, but as he moved to stand, the world dipped sideways. His legs gave out underneath him.

Essandra tried to catch him. "Help me!" she cried out over her shoulder. Her voice broke in desperation.

But Cyrus didn't see who she was yelling to. Darkness had already taken him.

Chapter Forty-Four

A hand brushed his hair from his forehead.

Cyrus knew her touch before he even opened his eyes. As he blinked back the blur of grogginess, he found Essandra's worried eyes looking back at him.

She squeezed his arm. "There you are," she whispered.

Sunlight spilled through the window. Cyrus pushed himself up and looked around. He was in his chamber, in his bed.

"What happened?" he asked.

"I was hoping you would tell me," she said. "One moment, you were sitting in the garden, the next you were bleeding everywhere and blacking out."

And it all came rushing back. *Norah.* He rubbed his head where an ache pulsed heavily in his temples.

"Kord carried you back."

He snapped his head up. "Kord?" They hadn't spoken since their argument.

"He's been by to check on you every so often. And Everan. And the others. They're worried, although I've been trying to reassure them you've just overexerted yourself." Her face grew more serious. "You did just overexert yourself, right?"

"What do you think I did?"

"Cyrus." She clutched him nervously.

As tempting as it was to mess with her, he wasn't in the jesting spirit. "Her grandmother passed away," he told her. "It's why she hasn't used the blood. They'd parted on bad terms, and she was devastated."

"Oh," she said softly.

"I wanted to give her the gift of a goodbye, of seeing her one last time."

"Like you did for me."

He nodded.

Essandra let out a small breath of relief, closing her eyes briefly. "I'm sorry to hear that. I'm sad for her." She clasped his hand. "But I'm glad it wasn't something more serious. I racked my mind for what you could've done. We've all been holding our breaths."

"Did you think I'd launched some kind of attack? Started a war?"

"We thought that was the most likely scenario," she confessed, although her lips held a smile now.

He couldn't help a smile himself. "How would I have done that?"

She shook her head. "I was coming up with all kinds of weird things in my mind."

"Tell me these weird things, so I can try them."

She laughed. "Absolutely not." Then she quieted and grew serious again. "I'm glad you're all right."

He put his hand over hers. "I'm all right." He glanced around again. "How long have I been asleep?"

"Three days."

He jerked. "Three days?"

"You clearly needed it."

"What if she tried to call me back?"

"Then she'll call you again."

He hoped so. Norah had known something was wrong with him. She'd call again.

A knock sounded, and his chamber door opened. Kord stood in the doorway. His brows shifted up when he saw Cyrus. "You're awake." He stepped inside.

Essandra squeezed Cyrus's arm. "I have some things I have to see to. I'll be back later." She stood and gave Kord a small smile, then slipped out of the room.

Kord stood, looking at him warily.

"Checking to see if I've done something stupid?" Cyrus asked him.

Kord snorted. "Checking to see if you're all right. And yes, if you've done something stupid."

Cyrus swung his legs over the edge of the bed but stayed sitting. His whole body ached. He waved to the chair by the bed. "Please."

Kord moved to the chair and slowly lowered himself into it.

"I gave Norah a gift," Cyrus told him. "Probably almost killed myself in the process. It needed a lot of power, but everything is fine. I'm fine. She's fine. The Shadow King is... fine. Unfortunately."

Kord's shoulders relaxed. His head dropped with a nod as he rested his weight forward. "Good."

"I *did* do something stupid, though. When you and I last spoke."

Kord's eyes darted back up and locked with his.

"I'm sorry," Cyrus said. "When you told me about Leti, what I should have said is—I'm happy for you. If a child is what you want,

I want that for you. I want a life for you. The gods know you deserve it. You've been one of my most loyal friends. My brother. I want you to be happy."

Kord's eyes welled. "Thank you for saying that," he whispered.

A quiet sat between them, but the air was lighter now.

"Will you eat breakfast with me?" Cyrus asked.

Kord snorted. "It's midday."

He smiled. "Midday meal, then. I'm starved."

Kord smiled back.

Having washed and eaten, Cyrus finally felt like he'd rejoined the land of the living. The ache in his head had subsided, although his body still protested each movement. He was getting soft not fighting in the arena anymore. Or maybe just old.

He took the main hall outside and strode through the courtyard. He wanted to check on how everyone who'd escaped from Pryam was faring. They'd been temporarily set up in the army barracks, although many had already been placed in more suitable long-term accommodations. Most of them had been refugees that Cyrus had sent from Rael to begin with, but there were also some Pryamese who'd been loyal to Miriel.

Everan joined him as he walked, holding out a letter.

Cyrus didn't need to look to guess who it was from. "Gregor?"

"Yes."

Cyrus snorted and kept walking.

"Are you not going to read it?" Everan asked.

"You can."

"I already have."

"Good."

Everan stopped. "Do you not want to know what it says?"

No. Cyrus sighed. "What does it say?"

"Phillip has moved his forces to Eilor."

Eilor. That was the southernmost kingdom of the Aleon Empire—closest to Japheth. Closest to Gregor. Of course Gregor was nervous. But this wasn't new news.

"Isn't that exactly what his last letter said?" he asked.

"It was just Aleon's forces before. Now Phillip has gone himself. He's there—in Eilor."

So, the king of Aleon was positioning himself for a move against Japheth. Or he could be anticipating Cyrus again. Phillip was now in a position to come with full force if Cyrus marched his army from Japheth to the Shadowlands. Perhaps it was for both reasons.

"Gregor urges us to move against Aleon before the Shadowlands and Mercia can join him," Everan said.

Of course he did.

Everan folded the letter back. "What are you going to do?"

Cyrus shrugged. "Nothing. I have no intention of marching against Aleon."

"Then what will you say to Gregor?"

Cyrus paused, then shrugged again. "Nothing."

Then came the pull in his mind. *Norah.*

"You can't just say nothing—"

"I have to go," Cyrus said, and abruptly turned back toward the palace.

"Cyrus," Everan called after him.

He waved him off. "I'll find you later."

As soon as he reached his study, he sank to his knees, closing his eyes, and let his head drop as his mind traveled to where it was called.

Norah sat in the stairwell. They really needed to stop meeting here—such an unpleasant place.

"*I was worried for you,*" she said, surprising him. He didn't think she knew he was there yet. Perhaps he was getting sloppy with his entrances.

He showed himself in front of her and lit the tunnel around them. Even more surprising—"*You were worried?*"

Her brows drew together. "*Of course. Two times I called you and you didn't come. I thought something might have happened.*"

A smile tugged at his lips. She'd been worried about him. "*My last visit pulled a lot of strength,*" he explained. "*My healer can only repair the flesh, so I had to recover the old-fashioned way—sleep.*"

She smiled. "*Thank you,*" she said softly, understanding his gift came at a cost.

He nodded. He was happy to have given it to her.

"*What happened to you?*" she asked.

"*Walk with me,*" he said. He offered her his arm, as he had the last time he'd seen her, which she'd responded well to.

She slipped her arm underneath his, and they started down the tunnel. *This fucking tunnel.* He pushed it away and brought forward the cliffs overlooking the sea. He loved this place in Rael.

"*How did you show me my grandmother like that?*" she asked. "*That wasn't a memory, or a vision. I know it wasn't real, but how could I feel her warmth?*"

He smiled. "*Don't break the magic.*"

"*But it was difficult for you.*"

"*It's the most difficult. More than anything else. As I said, it's the seemingly smallest of things.*"

"*Well, thank you,*" she said again. "*For that.*"

He felt her eyes on him as they walked.

"*You're a very powerful traveler, aren't you?*" she asked.

"*I suppose.*" He never really felt powerful.

"*Are those staves on your neck?*"

He paused. "*How do you know about staves?*" Hardly anyone aside from Essandra knew anything about seers at all.

"*All travelers use them.*"

All travelers? He stared at her.

"*Are they staves?*" she asked again.

Slowly, he nodded. What else did she know?

"*Can I see them?*" she asked, pushing herself up on her toes as her eyes dropped to the markings on his neck.

She wanted to see his markings? Her face held a deep curiosity. He knew she had no ill intention, and what harm was there in her seeing them?

There wasn't.

He reached back between his shoulders and pulled his tunic over his head. More markings covered his lower back and legs, and he stripped down to his braies.

Her eyes widened. "*Oh... uh... I didn't mean—*"

Pink flushed her cheeks, but he wasn't quite sure why. She'd asked to see them, and he wasn't naked. He'd worn less than this when he'd fought in the arena.

But she quieted when her eyes landed on the markings.

They were impressive, he knew. Essandra had given him more than protection—she'd given him art. He held his arms open, letting her study him. Then he turned and showed her his back. He didn't mind showing them off, especially after what he'd had to endure to get them.

She stepped closer, her eyes large and her lips parted. No one cared about the markings back in Rael. He was almost happy someone appreciated them now. She reached out her hand toward his skin but then stopped herself.

"*You can touch them,*" he said. They wouldn't... burn her... or whatever she feared they might do.

But she didn't touch them.

"*What do you know of staves?*" he asked her.

"*Not much,*" she said. "*Only that they protect your body from the strain of your power. And that the more power you have, the more staves you need.*" She quieted for a moment. "*You have more than I've ever seen.*"

Her words made him pause. "*Alexander didn't have them?*"

She shook her head. "*He didn't... use power like you do. It was more like... he was immune to others', or something. He didn't really need staves.*"

Her gaze moved over him, no longer on the markings, but on his face. A deep sadness filled her eyes. She was thinking about Alexander. She loved him. His death still hurt her. Cyrus could still feel her grief.

"*I could give him to you, Norah,*" he said. "*I could give you Alexander.*"

The flicker across her face told him that was something she wanted more than almost anything. Her eyes welled, and her lip trembled. But she shook her head. "*It wouldn't be real,*" she whispered.

"*You could let it be real.*"

She smiled sadly. "*No, Lucien.*"

He sighed. If she ever changed her mind, he would give him to her. She only needed to ask.

His mind shifted.

He did have something to ask of her. His pulse quickened.

"*Would you let me see Adrian?*" He stepped closer to her. "*Will you let him come to me? I've looked at him in your mind, but... to see him in his person, in life. I'd like that.*"

Her lips parted, but no words came out. She shifted her gaze to the ground, then back to him. "*Things are... complicated,*" she said. She swallowed. "*I haven't even told him you're alive.*"

Surprise caught him, although as soon as she said it, it made sense. Adrian had lived his entire life thinking Cyrus was dead. To now discover he was alive, and the enemy...

"*I understand,*" he told her. Still, he couldn't deny the wave of disappointment.

Norah bit the corner of her lip. "*Can I think about things?*"

"*Yes, of course,*" he said. If she could find a way... He had a blood brother, and the thought of meeting him... His pulse leapt to his throat.

Her gaze moved back over his markings. "*Thank you for sharing this with me,*" she said. "*For sharing everything with me.*"

Perhaps it had been too much, but he didn't care.

She gave him a small smile. "*I should go.*"

"Do you have enough blood to call me back?"

She nodded.

"Goodbye, Norah," he said.

"Goodbye," she told him, and he opened his eyes back to his study.

His heart still beat heavily.

Norah was going to think about him meeting Adrian.

He needed to tell Essandra.

He walked quickly through the halls, to the places she usually was—her workroom, her chamber, and Teron's room. But she was nowhere to be found. The sun had reached its peak, which meant the heat had reached its peak—she wouldn't be in the gardens, but he walked there anyway.

Still, he didn't find her.

Cyrus checked his own bedchamber, which was empty. He checked the dining hall, the council room, and the library. Still nothing.

He went back to her workroom. On the center table lay her spell book and loose pages of notes. Various bowls of crushed herbs and mixes sat about. It wasn't like her to leave everything out like this. His gaze landed on the Amoran Cup.

She definitely wouldn't have left *that* out.

His chest tightened. Something wasn't right.

But nothing was spilled or broken. There was no sign of a foul engagement.

His eyes traveled the room.

And he stilled.

The lid to the serpent's basket was off.

He stepped toward it.

As he drew closer, his eyes found the bottom.

It was empty.

Cyrus tore back out of the workroom and down the hall.

This could be a good thing, he tried to tell himself. She could have brought her sister back.

Or it could be a very bad thing.

Something could have gone wrong.

He wished she would have told him that she was going to do the spell. Had she used dark magic again? She'd said she didn't need to anymore.

Unless something hadn't worked and she *had* needed it again...

Cyrus quickened his pace. He barked orders to find her at everyone he passed.

He'd tear this kingdom apart.

Outside again, he stormed the grounds. His footsteps fell heavy on the cracked earth. He'd find Everan and Kord. But as he passed the side fields, he paused as something in the corner of his eye drew his attention.

It was Essandra. Alone.

He hurried toward her. She sat on the ground, leaning back against a stone well. He wasn't sure why she'd be there. It was a dry well.

Her black dress was dusted with sand, and her hair had blown loose from the clip that held it.

"Essandra," he called to her.

But she only sat, unmoving.

"Essandra!" He reached her and dropped down beside her. Only then did she raise her face. She looked up at him, and her eyes focused.

"What's the matter?" he asked. "Are you all right?" He looked around. "What are you doing here? Are you hurt?"

"I was just walking, and I... I needed to sit down." Her face was blank, her voice barely more than a whisper.

"Are you hurt?" he asked again. He anxiously checked her over. She didn't appear injured.

"It didn't work," she said.

He paused. *The spell.*

"What happened?"

"Nothing. Absolutely nothing." She shook her head. "The spell wouldn't catch."

He sighed, feeling the disappointment for her.

"The blood from the serpent should have worked," she said. "It should have worked."

"We'll figure out what happened," he promised.

"But I can't." Her fingers tightened in the fabric of his tunic. "I can't figure it out."

"You will."

She shook her head. "I can't." Her eyes welled, and her lips trembled. "Nothing I do works."

"Hey. Look at me." He lifted her chin to him. "Finding out what doesn't work is still progress."

A tear skimmed down her cheek, leaving a trail in the dust on her skin.

"It's still progress," he told her again. "All right?"

Ever so faintly, she nodded.

Then her expression shifted, as if she were just seeing him for the first time. "Did you need me for something?" she asked.

"It doesn't matter," he said. "Come here. Let's get you inside." And he pulled her into his arms and carried her back to the palace.

They sat quietly at the dining table, just the two of them.

Essandra had barely touched her breakfast. She only moved it around her plate with her fork as Cyrus watched her.

When she glanced up, she caught his stare. "I'm fine," she said for the hundredth time.

"I know." But he still didn't believe her. She hid her weakness behind walls thicker than a castle stronghold. From everyone. Even him.

She took a drink of her tea. "It's the same disappointment I've been managing for years. It just hit a little harder yesterday, that's all."

He'd been trying to figure out why. It was possibly because she'd truly believed it would work, more than she had the previous times. Or perhaps it was because it had been the closest she'd come yet, and to still have it slip through her fingers...

She carried every failure on her shoulders. Heavier and heavier. It was going to eventually crush her. Perhaps it already was.

"Essandra," he said softly. "You can't keep—"

"Do you think Norah will call you today?" she interrupted.

He didn't want to change the subject; there was still more he had to say. Maybe it would be better to let her calm a little more first. And he did need to tell her about his visit.

"I spoke to her yesterday," he said.

She straightened in her chair. "I'm sorry. I didn't realize. I should have asked—"

"How would you have known to ask?" He didn't blame her at all. "It's perfectly fine. It went well."

She let out a relieved breath and nodded. "Good. I'm glad to hear that. What did you talk about?"

"I asked to meet Adrian. She's going to think about it."

She stilled, with her eyes fixed on him. "How would you meet him? Would she give him your blood?"

That hadn't occurred to him, but even if it had, it wasn't what he wanted. "I want to meet him in person."

"So, you would go to Mercia again?"

"Most likely, yes."

She set her fork down. "Cyrus, I desperately want you to meet your brother, but I don't think that's a good idea. The Shadow commander had no hesitation in trying to kill you the last time, and you have *not* improved your position with him or the Shadow King since then. Quite the opposite, actually."

He didn't care about the Shadow commander. "I think I have a good relationship with Norah."

"Which she's kept a secret!"

"She'll keep this too. Most likely."

She shifted in her chair and shook her head. "I don't like it."

"I'll make sure it's safe," he promised.

They finished breakfast and left the dining room, walking slowly. It was strange they were talking about him when really it was her he was worried about. Finding her sitting by the well had been the worst he'd ever seen her.

"I still want to talk about yesterday," he said.

"I don't," she said firmly.

He took her hand and pulled her to stop. "Essandra."

She pulled free. "I said I don't want to talk about it."

"You can't keep—"

"I can't keep doing this?" she snapped. "I can't keep failing and failing and failing over and over again? Is that it? You want me to come to terms with the fact that they're gone? That I can't keep wanting? I can't keep trying?"

He sighed and took her hand again, pulling her closer. "I was going to say you can't keep doing this alone. You can't keep me at a distance. Before, it was just you trying to bring them back. Now it's us. When you do the next spell, I have to be there."

The spiked emotional armor she wore so often faded as her eyes softened.

"It's you and me now," he said again.

"Cyrus," a voice called, and he turned to see Everan walking quickly toward them. He held a letter in his hand.

"Another one?" Fuck the gods. *Gregor.* "He didn't even give me time to respond to the last letter."

"An Osani ship has been spotted off the coast of Japheth."

So Aleon had wasted no time engaging their new alliance with Osan. The king of Osan had once offered Cyrus an alliance but then quickly withdrew it once he learned about the coven. He should have been less concerned with making alliances and more concerned with making enemies. Osan was on the wrong side now.

"Gregor presses us to move against Aleon," Everan added.

Cyrus pushed out an annoyed breath.

Everan held out the letter for him, but Cyrus didn't need to read it.

"Would you like me to respond?" Everan asked.

Cyrus shook his head. "Not yet."

"Cyrus—"

"I said *not yet.*"

Everan sighed. Essandra only watched him.

Cyrus just needed to think. A moment of quiet. He kissed Essandra on the head, then struck out alone toward his study.

However, as he passed a small side room, he paused at the sound of hushed voices. Silently, he stepped to the cracked door and peered inside.

Kord and Hephain.

They stood close. Too close.

Cyrus couldn't understand what they were saying, but Hephain was upset. Kord reached up and curled his hand along the side of Hephain's neck, pulling him closer. Then he kissed him. Long. Deep.

Cyrus stepped back, into the center of the hall. He wasn't meant to see that.

Just then, Kord came through the door, leaving, and when he saw Cyrus, he paused. "Were you looking for me?" he asked. "Did you need something?"

Cyrus stared at him for a moment, then shook his head. "No."

Kord's expression changed, ever so slightly, as he stared back. Was he wondering if Cyrus had seen? If he was, he didn't ask. Instead, he just nodded and departed down the hall.

Cyrus watched him leave. He stood for another moment, until Hephain, too, came out.

When he locked eyes with Cyrus, he froze.

"What are you doing?" Cyrus asked him.

Hephain shook his head. "Nothing."

"Kord is married. He has a child on the way."

"Please don't," Hephain begged hoarsely as he turned away.

Cyrus quieted, just watching him.

Hephain reached out and leaned against the wall, sucking in a breath. When he turned back to Cyrus, his eyes were rimmed red. "You can't make me feel any more shame than I already do." His lip trembled. "But I can't help it. I love him." He sucked in another ragged inhale as he glanced down at the floor, then back to Cyrus. "I love him. And I'll do anything to keep him. Even if it's only pieces of him."

Cyrus's heart broke for them both.

The sun had long dipped below the horizon.

Cyrus sat on his knees on the floor in his study, his head reeling, his pulse racing. He couldn't get up. He couldn't even bring himself to move the few paces to the chair.

He hadn't been prepared for Norah's call.

The news had come too soon; the opportunity was too soon.

He'd wanted it, more than anything, *but this was all happening too soon.*

The door to the study opened, but he didn't move. His heart beat heavily, and he felt it everywhere except his chest—his ears, his head, his hands.

Essandra stepped in front of him. She said something, but it didn't register.

"Cyrus?" She dropped down beside him and put a hand on his arm. "What's wrong? Is it Gregor?"

Slowly, he lifted his eyes to meet hers.

He hadn't even thought about Gregor. He swallowed. "It's Norah," he whispered. "I just spoke to her."

He swallowed again.

"She's going to bring me my brother." His eyes stung. "I'm going to meet my brother."

CHAPTER FORTY-FIVE

Cyrus waited, his breaths shallow, his heart racing. He watched through the birds as Norah and Adrian made the journey to the valley.

They came alone, which meant they came in secret.

Cyrus was alone as well, with the exception of the dogs. Kord, Everan, and Jaem had helped him make camp, and Essandra had warmed the tent. They'd waited with him, but as Adrian drew closer, Cyrus wanted to wait alone.

He wore no armor. He hadn't even taken his sword, only a dagger at his waist. He waited in the tent, but he didn't want to be inside when they arrived, so he stepped outside.

Except it was fucking cold outside.

He stepped back in.

His palms were sweaty, his mouth dry. He wondered what Adrian would think of him. By now, Norah would have told him everything.

Would she have told him everything?

They were here.

His pulse beat heavily in his ears.

He ducked outside to meet them.

Adrian wasn't wearing armor either. Cyrus had seen it before in Norah's mind. It wasn't the silver armor with the bear-head pauldron of their father—the armor that Alexander had worn. Adrian's armor was black with a winterhawk on the breastplate, and he'd left it behind.

Adrian slid down from his horse, and Norah followed.

Cyrus couldn't help a smile.

Adrian was taller than he'd expected. Taller than he was. And larger. But his face...

Slowly, Cyrus stepped in front of his brother, whose stare was locked on him in return. Cyrus recognized so many of his own features: the blue eyes, the line of his jaw, the shape of his nose. All like Cyrus's. There was no doubt in his mind they were blood.

Adrian stared back at him. His eyes traveled over his face and down his body, and back up again. Then they welled. Slowly, Adrian lifted a trembling hand and touched Cyrus's cheek as a tear trailed down his own.

Cyrus couldn't move. He couldn't speak. He couldn't breathe.

Adrian drew his hand down and gripped Cyrus's shoulder. He was probably thinking the same thing Cyrus was—was this a dream?

If it was, Cyrus didn't want to know.

He didn't want to wake.

He didn't want to ruin it, like he ruined everything.

Suddenly, Adrian pulled him into an embrace.

This embrace wasn't meant for Cyrus. He knew. It was for Alexander, but he still gave himself to it. And he needed it too. This was the only blood family he had in this world.

When Adrian pulled back, his blue eyes were rimmed red.

Cyrus clasped him on the shoulder. "Come inside," he said, although his voice didn't sound like his own. He led them to the tent.

As they entered, Adrian was the first to speak. "Mother told me you had died."

Mother. A name he spoke only in his nightmares. He glanced at Norah.

She swallowed and wrung her hands tightly as her eyes bore into him, silently begging him to keep quiet. Adrian had loved their mother.

Cyrus would let him keep that. He said simply, "She thought I did. I was taken away."

The faintest breath of relief passed her lips.

"Norah told me," Adrian said.

Cyrus glanced at her again, then shifted back to Adrian. "Then you know my story."

Adrian nodded. "You were taken as a slave, led a rebellion. And now you're a king."

"And now I'm a king," he echoed, more to himself. The concept didn't seem so strange to him anymore, and he wondered when that had changed.

His brother still stared at him, wide-eyed in disbelief.

Cyrus couldn't help a small smile. "Do you want to see?" he asked. "I can show you."

Adrian leaned back slightly on his heel, not immediately warm to the idea. Cyrus wondered if he'd ever known a seer. Norah had told him that Alexander hadn't exhibited any indication of power; they hadn't even known he'd had it until just before his death. Regardless, Adrian would have never experienced a seer like Cyrus.

Despite his initial hesitation, Adrian nodded.

Cyrus pulled his dagger, running his thumb down the edge, and blood beaded along the cut. "Close your eyes," he told him.

Adrian glanced at Norah, and she gave him a nod of reassurance. He closed his eyes. Cyrus took Adrian's hand and pressed his blood to his skin. Then he closed his own eyes.

His brother's mind was not like his own. There was no torment; there were no terrors, no sharp memories signifying that they haunted him. There were, however, memories frayed around the edges.

Memories filled with grief.

Memories of Alexander.

Cyrus couldn't idle long; Adrian was waiting and unaware of his prying. He pushed himself on. He pulled forward images of Rael: the capital around the palace, from his favorite viewpoint—overhead, in the air.

"*Where is this?*" Adrian asked, as he and Cyrus looked down on the golden city.

"*Rael.*" Most of the capital had been rebuilt, and Cyrus took a moment just to appreciate how far they'd come. Progress always seemed so slow in the moment, but looking at the city now, glowing in the rays of the sun—it really was beautiful.

He let Adrian continue to be riveted by the sight as he broke away for a moment to offer his hand to Norah to share the image with her as well.

She took it, letting him touch his blood to her skin, and closed her eyes. He let his own eyes close again and fell back into the vision.

Adrian still looked on, enthralled. "*You can fly?*" he asked.

Cyrus chuckled. "*No. Now* that *would be power.*" He pulled them down to the cobblestone street and shifted the vision to show a flock of birds overhead. "*I see it through them,*" he said.

"*You control them?*" Adrian asked.

"*I can.*"

"*Can you control all animals?*"

"*Most, I can. With blood.*"

Adrian quieted for a moment, then asked, "*Did Alexander have power?*"

Cyrus dropped the vision and brought them all back to the tent. As they opened their eyes, his gaze bore into Norah. She hadn't told him everything.

"He had power, yes," Cyrus said, "but it was different. What it was—I don't know."

Adrian's eyes were still on him. "You—" His voice hitched, and he swallowed. "You look just like him." His breaths came short and shallow. "Just like him."

Cyrus could feel Adrian's loss, the grief he still held. "Norah said you two were close."

Adrian nodded, and his eyes filled with emotion again.

"I like to think we would have been close." Cyrus had many brothers—all brothers the arena had given him—brothers he would die for, and who would die for him. But to have a brother like Adrian... They would have been inseparable.

"We could be," Adrian said.

But they couldn't. His brother was so naive to this world. Perhaps Cyrus should be happy about that. "If I had known... about you...

things might have been very different. I'm sorry, Adrian." He wasn't sure how they would've been different, but they would have been.

"Things don't have to be this way," Norah said, finally speaking. "Mercia's not your enemy."

"I don't see Mercia as an enemy."

"And Kharav isn't the same kingdom as it was," she added.

He took a step back. How could she say that? It was exactly the same kingdom it had always been.

"The king you knew is dead," she said. "Everything has changed."

"Does the Shadowlands still force people into slavery?" he cut back. "Still buy them? Still sell them?"

She didn't have a reply to that. Of course. She couldn't deny the truth.

"Then nothing has changed," he said. The fact that she was even trying to convince him things were different was insulting.

"Lucien." She stepped closer. "Change takes time. Mikael is a good king."

"A good king?" he snarled as his anger flared. "I've been in his mind, seen his memories. You think he's innocent?" She had no idea the monster she'd married.

She stilled as her eyes widened. "He said you didn't come." She knew the Shadow King had called him with the blood.

"I didn't show myself to him. That doesn't mean I didn't see."

"Then you would have seen the good as well," Adrian said, stepping forward, "unless you chose not to."

His brother's position surprised him. Cyrus shook his head, confusion flooding him. "You defend the Shadow King?"

Pain flickered in his brother's eyes—the pain of betrayal. Did Adrian really think the betrayal was Cyrus's?

The youth fell from Adrian's face. He squared his shoulders. "I defend *my* king." His voice had a sharpness to it.

Cyrus took another step back. For Adrian to not only defend the Shadow King but anger over his honor, champion him...

Adrian extended his hand. "Brother, things aren't as they were, and they can be different still."

Why did they keep saying that when nothing had changed? Cyrus's eyes shifted to his brother's outstretched hand, and to the black marking that extended out from under the cuff of his sleeve.

Cyrus's chest tightened.

A mark of the Shadows.

It was arms that bore these same marks that had taken him so long ago. While over twenty years had passed, he hadn't forgotten. He would never forget.

A fire lit over his skin. "You're one of them?" he breathed.

Norah stepped closer to him. "Mercia and Kharav are united," she said.

His gaze jerked to her. If this was her decision... "Then Mercia will share the same fate."

"Lucien," she pleaded. "Change doesn't always require war. Mikael works for things to be different; he just needs time. Even as king, he has people that he's accountable to."

"I do too!" He had people he'd promised, people who'd sacrificed. People who'd died.

She trembled slightly, and he forced himself calm.

"Even if I didn't want to take the Shadowlands, I have no choice," he told her.

She shook her head. "There is always a choice."

He was done arguing this. "Then you'll just have to accept the fact that I want to."

Norah reached out and clasped his arm. "Lucien, please. I beg you. Help me change fate. I can't lose him. I can't."

Her words made him still.

Lose him.

Fate.

Did she know something? The realization came to him—she'd seen something...

"The Shadow King falls?" he asked.

"By your hand," Adrian said.

Cyrus jerked his head toward him. "What?"

"All this time, we thought it was Alexander," Adrian said, "but it's you who will kill Salar."

"Me?"

Adrian's eyes narrowed. "You're a seer, and you haven't seen this?"

"I can't see myself." He searched Norah's face, desperate to see if it was true. "I kill the Shadow King?" His next words stalled as another thought came. "Wait, you saw me?" That couldn't be right. "I can be seen?"

She nodded.

Cyrus's mind spun. That couldn't be right. "You're not supposed to see me. I'm not supposed to be seen." Seers couldn't be seen. He pulled his arm from her grasp and ran a hand over his face. "I can be seen?"

What did this mean? What had they seen? Everything? His plans, his strategy?

He looked back at Norah. "So, you can see me in the visions. And I succeed?"

"Lucien," she whispered, "I'm begging you to help me create a different future. You're the only one who can." She reached out again and took his hand. "Lucien. Please." Her touch was soft and earnest.

He wished he could give her what she wanted. If it was anything else, he would. "I'm sorry, Norah. I can't."

Her fingers tightened around his, pleading.

Still, he shook his head. "It's fate, Norah. If it's been seen, there's nothing you can do. And that means this is my fate too."

"No." She grabbed his other arm, clutching him tighter. "No. We can change it."

He shook his head again. "I don't want to change it. It's my fate. I have to do it."

"No," she gripped him even tighter. "I won't let you."

Let him? "There's nothing you can do," he said again.

Her eyes welled as they darted back and forth between his own. Despite the exhilaration of this news, he did feel sad for her. He really had come to care for Norah, and he'd do anything in his power to help her with whatever she needed, but he couldn't give her this.

This was fate.

A tear spilled down her cheek. Perhaps after her tears, after the emotion passed, she would see.

Her hands shook as they gripped him, her desperation cracking through. Desperation always came before acceptance.

Except she didn't reach acceptance.

He almost didn't catch her hand in time as she grabbed her dagger and tried to plunge it between his ribs. *Of course she would fight him.* She was fast. Almost too fast. He grabbed her wrist and twisted it away, making her drop the blade.

At the same time, Adrian pulled his sword and lunged toward them, but, drawing from the coven's power, Cyrus threw out a bolt of pain. The blood bond still between them made it hit even harder. Adrian dropped to his knees as his hands flew to his head.

Norah struck with a hard kick to his inside thigh, nearly bringing him down, but he didn't let her go. He snarled as anger flashed through him. Did she really think she could fight fate? Did she think she could fight *him*? She clawed at his eyes. As he shielded himself, her hand dropped and flicked toward his own dagger at his waist.

She was good. But she wasn't a bloodsport fighter. Not trained to kill. Not like he was.

He delivered a sharp blow across her cheek with his elbow, stunning her and making her stumble backward. But he grabbed her again, pulling her up and holding her by the neck.

"I don't want to hurt you," he said between his teeth. If she would only stop fighting...

"Then don't do this," she hissed.

"I don't have a choice. Fate is fate, Norah."

"I won't let you!" She said it like he wasn't the one holding *her* by the throat.

"How will you stop me?" Certainly not by herself. "With the Destroyer?" He could possibly be a problem, but... then his eyes dropped to the blood on her lips.

Blood that could tether.

"No," he told her. "He'll do nothing. Neither will your king."

And he brought his lips to hers. As her blood touched his tongue, he willed the tether between them. He didn't even need the spell, but he spoke it anyway, just to be sure.

Then he released her.

Adrian, partially recovered now, staggered to his feet and picked up his sword.

"You don't want to do that," Cyrus said.

Adrian bared his teeth. "Brother or not, I think I do."

Cyrus pulled his dagger and ripped it across his palm.

Norah cried out as she clasped her own hand, her eyes widening in horror at the wound that matched his.

"We're bound now, you and I," he told her. "Tethered through blood. What happens to me also happens to you."

She gaped at him in horror, then her eyes darted to Adrian, who stopped in his step. Her horror turned to anger. She snapped her gaze back to Cyrus.

"I won't tell them," she hissed. "So, all you've done is made me share your fate."

She was a fighter. He'd give her that.

"You might not," Cyrus said. Then he turned his eyes on Adrian. "But he will." He knew that look of duty. Adrian wouldn't let Norah be harmed—he wouldn't keep this a secret if it allowed her to die.

Alexander. Cyrus. Adrian. They were all nothing if not committed to their duty. It was in their blood.

"Do your duty, brother," Cyrus told him. "Protect your queen."

Adrian trembled in rage, because he would protect Norah, which meant there was nothing he could do to Cyrus.

Cyrus glanced back at Norah. While it brought satisfaction to have the upper hand, it didn't bring him satisfaction to hurt her. He hadn't wanted it to be at her expense. "I'm sorry, Norah," he said.

Whether she believed him, he didn't know, but he really did mean it.

And now he had to go.

Cyrus didn't remember leaving the tent, or pushing his horse hard to meet Essandra, Everan, and Kord back at the stone circle.

Only when he reached them did his senses seem to return.

Everan's eyes traveled Cyrus's lathered mount as he pulled it to a halt. "What happened?" he asked.

Cyrus slid down, panting as heavily as the horse.

"Cyrus?"

There was no turning back now.

"What happened?" Everan asked again.

"Write Gregor," he said. "Tell him to prepare for war."

Chapter Forty-Six

Glass shattered across the floor.

"Cyrus!" Essandra gasped. She'd followed him from the main hall and into his study.

He flung another chair across the room, and it splintered against the wall.

"What's going on?" Her voice was high and laced with worry.

But he couldn't speak. He was furious—furious at the Shadow King, furious at Norah and his brother. But mostly, he was furious at himself.

He threw open the side double doors and strode out onto the balcony, sucking the air into his lungs and trying to calm himself.

Essandra came behind him. "What happened?"

He still couldn't answer her.

She put her hand on his arm, but he pulled away. "Cyrus, what happened?" she asked again.

It took a while for him to be able to get it out. "I lost it," he finally managed.

"Lost what?"

"I hurt Adrian. And I struck her." He clawed at his head. "Why did I do that?"

"You struck Norah?"

He nodded. "And I tethered us."

Her eyes widened. "What?" Alarm rang through her voice. "Why?"

"War is inevitable now."

"Why did you tether her?"

He gripped the stone railing as he leaned against it.

"You have to break it," she told him.

He shook his head. "No. They won't let harm come to her. If we're marching to war, then I need it."

"Cyrus," she pleaded. "She's trying to help you."

"She's trying to help herself! Because I succeed. I kill the Shadow King." He drew in a deep breath and let it out slowly. "She saw me. She saw me in a vision."

The line between her brows trenched deeper. "That's not possible."

"Somehow it is."

"Seers are shielded from visions. You're covered by a shield."

"Am I?" he cut back. He ripped open his tunic. "By the same shield that's supposed to protect me so that I don't need so many of these gods-damned markings?"

"You need a lot of markings because you have a lot of power," she countered.

"Or maybe I need a lot of markings because I don't have a shield." He paced back into his study, and she followed.

"You're the most powerful seer I've ever known," she said.

"It doesn't matter. If they can see me, they can see what I'm doing, what I *will* do."

"Whatever there is to see, there's a high probability that it's already been seen," she argued.

"I need to stop them from seeing more. How can I do that?"

She shook her head. "I don't think it works like that."

"How *does* it work, then?" he snapped.

She quieted.

He pushed out a long breath and drew in another. "I'm sorry. I don't mean to take this out on you." He reached out and pulled her close to him, cupping her face in his hand. "Leave me for a while, until I'm better company." He was angry and frustrated, and she didn't deserve that.

"No, it's fine—"

"Just a little while," he said. "It's not fine."

She sighed, staring back up at him. "Just a little while," she echoed.

He bent to kiss her softly on the lips, then she slipped out of the room.

Cyrus sank into the wingback chair in the corner. He should be happy—fate intended for him to kill the Shadow King.

But he could lose this opportunity if he wasn't careful.

He'd told Norah that fate couldn't be changed, but he didn't entirely believe that. Part of him feared he'd manifested this destiny, that he'd forced it into existence with his relentless compulsion, and that he was hanging on to it by a thread. Or perhaps fate had just taken pity on him.

But it was foolish to think that once fate revealed her intention, all work was finished.

No.

He would need to strategize and plan. Meticulously. Commit. Then execute. He would need to give everything, perhaps even his own life. And this vision would be his reward.

Cyrus sat, thinking. Then he sat longer.

It wasn't until his study door opened that he realized the rays of the sun had given way to darkness. It was night.

Essandra stood in the doorway.

"I fear I'm not better company yet," he said softly. He had several solid war strategies against the Shadow King, but they all required the element of surprise. A single vision could bring them all down.

"You will be," she said. "I have a solution."

He straightened in the chair. "You can stop them from seeing me?"

She smiled. "Possibly something even better."

Something better... He stood slowly. That was when he noticed the bowl she held in her hand. She swept into the room and set it down on the desk.

"I can't stop the Eye from seeing you," she said. "But I can stop it from showing anything to anyone."

The Eye in the Aether. That was what gave seers their visions.

"You can stop it from showing me to other seers? From showing them what I'm going to do?"

She nodded.

He narrowed his eyes. "How?"

"If seers can't enter the Aether, they can't access the Eye. If they can't access the Eye, they can't get the visions. Any of them."

He still wasn't sure he understood the *how*.

"This would also keep seers from going into the minds of others," she added. "They need the Aether to do that. That means even for the visions they've already seen, they can't reshow them to anyone or go back and study them."

Cyrus still didn't quite get it, but he didn't care about the *how* anymore. He understood the result—no one would be able to see him, and not just him. They wouldn't be able to see anything. He could only stare at her, speechless.

"I know it's not perfect," she said.

He stepped to her and took her face in his hands. "What are you talking about? It's absolutely perfect." And he kissed her. "Don't you see? A shield would have only hidden me. This will hide our army, hide our plan of attack. From the Shadow King. From Gregor. From everyone." This woman could do anything. He was so fucking proud of her. He kissed her again. "Do it."

"I thought you would say that." She pulled at his tunic. "Take this off."

He pulled it off over his head and smiled.

"Don't get too excited," she told him. "This isn't going to be pleasant." She picked up the bowl and brought it up between them. "If you don't mind," she said, flashing her dagger.

Cyrus knew what she required. He held his palm open over the bowl.

Her brow creased. "I'm sorry. I need a lot for this."

He offered his other palm as well, but as she moved to slice his flesh, something caught his eye. He grabbed her wrist, pushing back her sleeve to find a new set of markings on her arm.

"You're using dark magic," he said.

She pulled her wrist from him but didn't reply.

Cyrus shook his head. "No. We'll use something else."

"I've already cast the spell and paid the debt," she said.

Dark magic was corrosive and destructive to the one who wielded it, and she'd committed to not using it anymore. His eyes bore into her.

"It's already done," she added. "Use it for your benefit or everything I've already given is for nothing."

He still didn't like it, but he needed this spell, and what was done was already done. He offered up his palms again, but angrily this time.

"No more after this," he told her.

"No more," she promised.

When Essandra had said she needed a lot of blood, he hadn't realized she'd nearly drain him dry. When the flow from his left hand slowed, she moved to his right.

An unsteadiness hit him as the bowl brimmed. "Are you sure this isn't the part where I die?" he jested.

She cut him a smirk. "You'll live." She stirred the blood in the bowl with the mixture of herbs that she'd already prepared.

Tendrils of smoke rose into the air.

For a moment, her face paled, and she wavered.

"Are you all right?" he said, stepping forward. "Is it the dark magic?"

"I'm fine," she told him.

"Essandra—"

"I'm fine. Really." She pushed his bloody hands away and focused her attention on him. Carefully, she lifted the bowl above him, stretching up on her toes, and poured it over the top of his head. She dipped her thumb and lined a mark between his brows and on his chin, which felt completely unnecessary given the warmth trickling down his back and the sides of his face.

But he stayed silent and let her carry on.

Essandra knelt down and poured the rest of the blood from the bowl onto the floor, creating a large puddle.

He shuffled back to avoid it.

"No, step into it," she told him.

This was getting weirder, but he complied.

"Now, this is very important," she said as she set the bowl on the desk and then stepped into the puddle with him. "You can't leave the blood through this next part."

He glanced down at that crimson pool that had now spread wide all around them. That shouldn't be a problem.

Essandra moved close again with blood-coated fingers and drew a line down his chest. When she reached his stomach, she drew a triangle inside a circle.

"This next part is going to hurt," she warned. She held up her dagger, and he watched as a black flame lit across the blade.

He paused. "Will Norah feel this?" He'd still do it, but he hated the idea of Norah feeling pain. Cutting his palms was bad enough.

"No. Not this. You will, though."

"Do it," he said.

But he instantly regretted those words as she plunged the searing dagger into his stomach. A growl ripped from his throat. That hadn't been what he'd expected, and he gaped down at the hilt protruding from the center of the blood-encircled triangle.

"I'm so sorry," she gasped as she pulled it free.

He stared down at it, panting heavily, then looked back at her. "What did you do?" She'd stabbed him. *She'd stabbed him.* He stepped backward, but she caught him.

"Stay inside the pool!"

Then his eyes widened as a black serpent slipped out from her sleeve, winding itself around her arm. It was the same one he'd seen before. It grew larger, and larger still. Its black scales changed to red, and a hood opened wide around its head. It slithered upward, rising off her arm, as if to strike him.

He tried to step back again, but she clung to him. "Stay inside the pool!" She gripped him tightly. "Close your eyes," she begged him.

But there was no way he was closing his eyes.

The snake struck. Only it didn't bite. Instead, it buried its head into the wound in his stomach.

Cyrus bellowed and writhed, instinctively trying to grab at it, but she seized his hands. He threw her off, but as he clawed at his stomach, the last of the snake disappeared inside him, the wound vanishing as well.

He staggered back, panting and gaping down at his stomach. "It's inside me?" He tore at his flesh. "Get it out!"

She grabbed him again. "It's in the Aether!"

"Get it out!"

"It's not in you; it's in the Aether!"

"Get it out!"

She caught his face. "Cyrus!" She held him tightly. "It's not in you. It's in the Aether."

He gripped her, steadying himself as her words sank in. "In the Aether?" he asked hoarsely.

"It's not inside you," she assured him.

Slowly, he sank to his knees as panic still rippled through him, his chest heaving. The violation still lingered.

She sank down with him.

"Is that it? Is it done?" he asked shakily.

She nodded. "It's done."

He gave himself another moment to calm, but calm wouldn't come. "How long will it last?" he asked. Fuck if he had to do this again...

"It's made of your bloodline power. So as long as that remains, so does the serpent."

"So, as long as I'm alive."

She nodded.

Thank the fucking gods.

"Are you all right?" she asked him.

"No," he panted. "I'm not."

CHAPTER FORTY-SEVEN

Teron tended to Cyrus's cut palms as Essandra cleaned the blood from the floor, despite Cyrus's objections. Visa helped her, but that didn't make it better. He didn't like seeing them do that, but by the time Teron was finished, they were done.

The hour was late—well into the night.

"Thank you," Cyrus told Teron and Visa before they took their leave.

Alone with Essandra again, he was finally starting to feel a little better. But Essandra's face was pale. He held out his hand for her to come to him, and he pulled her close.

"Are you all right?" he asked her.

She nodded.

"It's the dark magic, isn't it?"

"I'm fine," she insisted.

A pang of guilt ate at him. She'd done this for him.

"Let's get you something to eat," he said, and he led her down the hall toward the kitchens.

The kitchen staff was asleep, but how hard could it be to find something to eat? He sat her in a small chair before rummaging through the shelves and pantry. So much food, but none of it really in a state that he was used to eating it. Raw vegetables—carrots, celery, asparagus. Unpalatable. He kept looking. Finally, he found some dried fish—a personal favorite—and he smiled.

"Here," he said, bringing it to her.

She stared at it for a moment, and her brows dipped down. "Actually," she said, "I'm not hungry. I think I just need to rest."

"Are you sure?" he asked, holding it closer. If she just smelled it, it would probably trigger her appetite.

But she pulled away with a grimace. "I'm sure," she said quickly.

He set the fish on the center worktable. "All right," he said softly. She looked worse than before. *No more dark magic*, he swore to himself.

She stood but held his arm tightly. He didn't like this at all.

"I got you," he said, and he scooped her into his arms.

Cyrus carried her back to his chamber and laid her gently in his bed. By the time he'd pulled off his clothes and climbed in beside her, she was already asleep.

He pulled her close. Her warmth calmed him—the feel of body against body, skin against skin. Soul against soul. He closed his eyes as he breathed her in, then let sleep take him too.

He fell into the colors of his mind, into the world of dreams, where a vision of a woman came. He'd seen this woman before—a woman on a white horse. Her dark hair blew wild in the wind around her, with long braids and feathers woven in. She wore paint on her face, as she had when he last saw her, but it was different this time. She'd marked her eyes in black, running the ink wide from temple to temple, with red lines down her cheeks.

It wasn't often he had recurring dreams, but a couple of times now, he'd seen her. He still didn't know who she was, although he didn't particularly care. She meant nothing, she was no one to him. But she was easier to watch than dreams of blood.

When Cyrus woke, Essandra was gone, probably off doing witchy things. He stretched and rose quickly. The morning was still early, and despite not getting very much sleep, he felt rested and well and in high spirits, all things considering.

It was the start of a good day—a day of planning war.

He was ready. He was glad he'd left Jaem in Mercia again, to resume his feed of information. Cyrus had also settled on a strategy, and now that he was confident he could maintain the element of surprise, he was even more sure of it. He just needed to convince his council. He wouldn't spend too much energy on that, though. He would move forward with or without their support.

It was Everan and Kord he cared about more. They were the ones who would be with him on the battlefield. And the rest of his men.

And Miriel. But Bash would be a challenge, once he heard what Cyrus planned to ask of her.

"Absolutely not," Bash snapped as they all sat around the table in the council room. He reacted just as Cyrus had expected.

As did his council, although Cyrus didn't care about them.

Cyrus looked at Miriel. "You only have to hold the illusion of our army there in Japheth until I reach the Shadow King." All he needed was for her to distract Phillip and keep him focused on Japheth until Cyrus could launch an attack against the Shadowlands.

"Gregor will figure it out pretty quickly," Bash said. He gave the king of Japheth too much credit.

Cyrus didn't actually think he would. "Miriel's illusions are exceptional. He won't have a clue."

"And the more distance we keep between the illusion of our army and his actual army, the easier it will be to maintain the ruse," Everan added.

"Putting pressure on Aleon by making Phillip believe our army is in Japheth will keep him from moving his forces to the Shadowlands," Cyrus said.

"So, you'll send her to fight with Gregor?" Bash asked bitterly.

"There won't be a fight," Cyrus insisted. "As soon as I launch my attack against the Shadow King, you'll pull Miriel out."

"Gregor isn't going to react well to that," Kord said.

Cyrus shook his head. "It doesn't matter. Once Phillip sees Gregor is alone, he'll take care of him."

"I don't like it," Bash said.

But it wasn't Bash's decision. Cyrus focused on Miriel. "You'd only be there to put up the illusion," he told her. "Then I'll pull you out. I promise."

"What about Mercia and Osan?" Bash asked.

"Let me worry about Osan. As for Mercia, if they think the main threat is in Japheth, they'll send their forces to join Aleon."

"Great—exactly where Miriel will be," Bash said sharply.

"You'll be out before they even get there," Cyrus told her.

Miriel bit her bottom lip. "And this will let you take the Shadow King by surprise?"

Cyrus nodded. "And it will distract his allies and leave him without their support."

Miriel glanced at Bash, then back to Cyrus. "I'll do it."

Feeling one step closer to victory, Cyrus made his way back to his chamber. It was fucking hot. He'd already sweat through his tunic. He'd change and go find Essandra. She hadn't been at the meeting, which was odd. Well, not too odd. Sometimes, she was wrapped up in something she was working on.

He pulled a fresh tunic from the side dressing room but stopped as the crash of glass sounded from the bath chamber.

He stepped back into the main bedchamber. "Essandra?"

There was no answer, but a shuffle came from behind the closed door.

He quickly moved to it. "Essandra?"

"A moment!" she called from inside.

"Are you all right?" he asked.

"Y-yes." But she didn't sound all right.

"Can I come in?"

Another shuffle came, and the sound of something falling. A stool, perhaps.

"Essandra?" He tried the handle, and it wasn't locked.

"No!" she cried as he pushed the door open.

She was on her knees on the floor, frantically trying to wipe up blood from the marble.

"Essandra!" He swept inside and dropped down to her. "What happened?"

Tears streaked her face. Her eyes were full of terror. "I'm so sorry! It was an accident!"

"What?" He shook his head in confusion. "What was an accident?"

She clawed up the towels on the floor, still desperately trying to wipe up the blood. "I didn't mean for this to happen."

He grabbed her arm. "Stop! Leave that! Are you hurt?"

"I couldn't do it!" she said through her sobs. "I was going to get rid of it, but I couldn't do it. And now I think I'm losing it!"

"Losing what?"

Her whole body shook. She couldn't get the words out. She was a mess of blood.

And he froze.

The blood was coming from between her thighs. It soaked her dress to her feet.

"I didn't mean to," she cried. "It was an accident. I swear to you."

His breaths quickened and shallowed as his heart raced faster. "What was an accident?"

Another sob escaped her lips. "I'm so sorry."

He gripped her shoulders and pulled her still. "What was an accident?" he asked again.

"The child," she whispered through her tears.

His pulse thrummed so heavily in his throat he could barely pull in a breath. He almost couldn't ask. "You're with child?"

Another sob escaped her.

Confusion flooded him. "I thought you could prevent that."

"I was! I mean, I've been doing the spells, but I don't know—I messed up." Her sobs racked her body. "I didn't do it on purpose. Please don't think I did it on purpose!"

"Stop," he said, still holding her to try to calm her. "Stop, stop. I don't think you did it on purpose."

Sobs still shook her. "I'm so sorry!"

He gripped her tighter. "You don't have to be sorry. Don't be sorry."

"I didn't mean for it to happen! I know you don't want it. I didn't mean to. I was going to get rid of it," she cried. "But then I couldn't go through with it."

"That's not..." He shook his head. This couldn't be happening. "Don't even think about that," he said. "If you're with child—"

"I went too far, though," she sobbed. "I think I'm losing it now."

He glanced around her and noticed her spell circles and candles. His eyes raked over her in horror. "You did this to yourself?"

Another tremble rippled through her. "I started but I couldn't go through with it. I don't want to lose it!"

He pulled her close to him, trying to quiet her. "It's all right. You don't have to get rid of it. Everything's going to be all right."

"There's so much blood," she cried.

"I know." He scooped her up in his arms and carried her to the bath. "We'll get you cleaned up," he said as he set her gently on the floor beside the tub. "I'm going to go get Teron, and I'll be right back. He'll fix all of this."

She nodded through her tears.

Cyrus tore out of his chamber and through the halls. "Get Teron!" he thundered. He barked out orders to anyone who could hear him. "Water! Hot! And linens! Now!" He didn't care who they were. They all scurried to help. When he reached the chamber again, Visa was there, helping Essandra peel off her dress. Her deft fingers quickly worked through the layers, and Cyrus was grateful.

Two more women came with hot water, filling the tub. Essandra stood shakily, but Cyrus was there in an instant, picking her up and lifting her in.

Teron came running. Cyrus moved to give him room but kept hold of Essandra's hand. Teron reached out and put a hand on her shoulder.

The water was now red with Essandra's blood. She winced as she doubled forward.

"Take the pain away," Cyrus demanded.

"I'm trying," the old healer said.

"I'm so sorry," Essandra said through her cries.

"Stop saying that," Cyrus told her. He was out of breath now, his sole focus on Essandra. "You don't need to be sorry. It's all right. You'll be all right."

Tears still streaked her face. "I don't want to lose it."

"You're not going to lose it."

But Teron paused, his face grave.

And Cyrus realized. *They already had.* He shook his head, stopping the old man from saying the words. "Heal her," he said between his teeth.

Teron leaned forward again, reaching out, and put his hand on Essandra's stomach.

Slowly, her body relaxed, save only the tremble of her sobs.

As the old healer finished, he pulled back and gave Cyrus a small nod. "She'll be all right," he said. "But she should rest now."

"Thank you," Cyrus told him.

Teron left the bath chamber and Cyrus brushed Essandra's hair from her face. "Let's get you to the bed," he told her.

Visa grabbed some towels and draped them around Essandra as Cyrus helped her stand. Then he picked her up and carried her to the bed.

Climbing in beside her, he pulled her close, wrapping his arms around her. He placed gentle kisses on her eyelids as her tears still came.

"Rest, my love," he whispered.

He'd thought he'd do anything to keep from having a child. Now he'd do anything to get it back.

Chapter Forty-Eight

Cyrus lay awake in the dark.

She'd been with child.

The guilt tore him from the inside out—she'd thought she couldn't come to him. She'd thought she had to get rid of it and shoulder that burden alone.

A child would give her what she needed to bring her family back. Yet he didn't think for a moment that she'd done it on purpose. Her desperation haunted him.

And she'd kept apologizing.

Like he would be angry with her.

He *was* angry.

But only at himself.

He was angry that she couldn't tell him, that she couldn't trust him, that she couldn't depend on him when she'd needed him most.

And it was all his fault.

Cyrus pulled her closer.

It was true he hadn't wanted a child, and all the reasons he'd given were true—he couldn't be distracted from his duty, and he simply didn't want one. But more, he didn't want a child if he couldn't give it his everything. If he couldn't love it wholly, if he couldn't raise it, if he couldn't be there for it. And he hadn't expected to live to do any of that.

He'd expected his vengeance against the Shadow King would come at a cost—his life—and he'd been at peace with this. He'd accepted what fate might demand of him. So, he'd never allowed himself to want or to dream.

But here, now, with Essandra in his arms, for the first time, he let himself dream. He could imagine a future with her. For the first time, he wanted to live. And now that he knew he'd prevail...

Cyrus pulled her even closer, and she stirred. Her eyes fluttered open, and she stared back at him.

"How do you feel?" he asked. He brushed the side of her cheek with the backs of his fingers.

Her eyelids fell in a slow blink. "It's gone," she whispered.

Cyrus knew. He pushed her hair from her brow.

"Have you slept?" she asked.

He shook his head. "No. It's all right, though. It's nice to just lie here with you. And think."

"What were you thinking about?"

He studied her face. Her brow, her nose, her lips. "How wonderful it would be to have a life with you." His voice dropped to a whisper. "I would be a good husband. And a good father."

Her eyes welled, and he kissed the tears as they fell.

"I don't know if that's what you want," he told her, "but if it is, then I want that too. I want it with you. We'll have the most beautiful wedding this kingdom has ever seen."

She nodded. "I want that with you," she whispered. "But I don't want a wedding. I just want to be your wife."

"It's done, then." He kissed her. "Wife." He kissed her again.

She clung to him. "I want to leave all this behind," she said. "Let us leave it all. Just you and me."

"When all this is over," he promised, "and whether or not I am king, you will be my queen. And I will love you. I will love you all the days of my life."

She cupped her hand against the nape of his neck and pulled him even closer. "Love me now," she pleaded. "Let it be over now."

"Soon, my love. Soon."

Cyrus pulled her to his chest and kissed the top of her head. He held her tight as she cried herself back to sleep.

Cyrus watched the ship slowly sail from the harbor. Miriel waved from the back deck. It would only take her two days to reach Japheth, giving Cyrus two days to think on if he'd made the right decision.

He was starting to doubt.

It wasn't that he was worried about Gregor discovering his ruse. With Essandra's guidance over the past year, Miriel had become a master of her craft. Cyrus had sent her with his blood to give her even more power, but she didn't need it. She could project an illusion of an army greater than the world had ever seen, completely on her own.

Still, a heaviness weighted his chest.

Essandra had asked him to be done. She'd asked him to be done with it all.

Never had that been something he'd even thought of entertaining before. When Kord had pressed him to stop, even when Norah had pleaded with him, he'd felt such a visceral rejection to the notion.

But now that Essandra had asked him...

Now that she'd asked to be his future...

He wanted to give that to her.

"Are you all right?" Everan's question snapped his attention.

"Of course," Cyrus said quickly. He glanced out across the water to find Miriel's ship gone.

They turned back toward the palace, and his mind shifted back to Essandra.

When this is all over, he'd told her. But when would it be over? After he killed the Shadow King, he still needed to take down the assassins' guild. He needed to win back Pryam for Miriel. He needed to bring down Etreus, the Union, and all those who supported the slave trade. That was what he'd promised.

If he gave everything up for Essandra, not only would he be giving up the Shadow King, but he'd be giving up everything he'd committed to, everything he'd promised.

He could still call Miriel back before she reached Japheth.

If he did, she would know it would all be over, that he wouldn't win Pryam back for her. She would never forgive him, but she'd be safe in Rael. She could join Essandra's coven, if that was what she wanted.

The thought of letting her down turned his stomach.

His army was ready. When he pulled his legions from Japheth and replaced them with Miriel's ruse, he'd be a hundred and seventy-five thousand strong. The largest army in the world.

But he could hold them.

He could stop.

He could stop for Essandra. His wife. His queen. His future.

He *would* stop.

They reached the palace, and Cyrus strode through the heavy doors and down the main hall. Everan said something else to him, but he didn't catch it as his mind turned. He would do it. He would do it for her. He would recall his army home—

A sudden searing pain ripped through his mind, nearly dropping him to the floor, but Everan caught hold of him.

"Cyrus!"

Cyrus gripped his head. Burning talons clawed the inside of his skull—ripping, mauling, lighting flames of agony behind his eyes.

It took him a moment to understand, a moment to push through the pain to realize...

Something was tearing at the tether—the tether with Norah.

Not something.

Someone.

They were trying to break the bond. *She was trying to break it.*

"Cyrus!" Everan called to him. "What's happening?"

But he couldn't answer. He couldn't speak. The pain was crippling—stabbing, piercing, gnashing at his hold on her.

Anger surged through him. Who dared to think they could break the tether that he himself had created?

And did she think it would be that easy?

Cyrus fought back with a burst of power through the bond. If another mind was joined with hers, he would crush it.

He'd crack it open and disintegrate it.

He chased the pain to the source, pushing through with a counterattack, but just as he nearly wrapped his own mental talons around the intruder, they withdrew.

The pain abated, and he fell forward onto his hands and knees, panting.

"Cyrus!" Everan shouted again.

It took a moment for him to finally be able to speak.

"It's Norah," he said through labored breaths. "She's trying to break the tether."

"Can she do that?"

"She's found someone who thinks they can." And whoever or whatever was helping her was powerful. Very powerful.

He didn't think she could break the tether, but if she did, he'd lose his advantage.

He couldn't take that risk.

He needed to move *now*.

The current plan was for Miriel to hold the illusion of an army in Japheth, distracting Aleon, while Cyrus's real army sailed to launch a surprise attack against the Shadowlands from the west. With the rocky coast of the Shadowlands giving no grace for ships to land, sailing up the inlet and cutting through the northeastern corner of Osan was the only way to do this.

Cyrus had planned for the army to stop in Rael on the way from Japheth, to gather supplies, but they didn't have time for that now.

"Prepare a vessel," he told Everan. "When our ships start arriving, they won't be stopping. I'll lead them straight through to Osan."

He was going.

He was going to kill the Shadow King.

Chapter Forty-Nine

Cyrus's ship carved the sea as he drove a blistering pace for his army to follow. He had the coast of Osan in his sight, and he led his fleet up the inlet between Osan and the Shadowlands, toward the Osani capital port.

He'd contemplated landing farther down, on the southeast shoreline, but sailing straight to the capital was shorter and faster, and time was against him. Initially, he'd hated that he had to march his army through Osan. They were a kingdom with a rich history of peace and freedom. But now they were allied with the Shadow King, and they'd share his fate.

In all, Cyrus had two hundred and twenty vessels carrying almost two hundred thousand men. The challenge was keeping them all close enough to stay concealed under Essandra's illusion. The illusion witch in the coven wasn't as strong as Miriel, but amplified with his power, she was strong enough to cover their ships, strong enough to project the simple open sea, and that was all he needed.

Cyrus had hoped Essandra would stay in Rael, after everything that had happened. It felt too soon, but she'd wanted to come. She'd wanted to be by his side, and he was proud to have her there. He'd brought Teron too. He'd debated it heavily in his mind, but he needed to make sure when he reached the Shadow King, he had every advantage possible. He couldn't risk an injury before the final battle. But Cyrus would make sure Teron stayed safe. He'd surrounded the old healer with a small army of his own, and he'd brought the dogs.

"You still haven't told us the plan for when we meet the Osani fleet," Everan said to him as they made their way up the inlet. The Osani fleet was one of the most revered across both the Emerald and Andan Oceans. Osan had a naval force that was one of the strongest in the world.

They stood on the bow of the ship with Kord and Sergen.

"They won't be a problem," Cyrus told him. He kept his eyes on the coastline. Any moment now, he'd see the capital; any moment now, he'd know if what he'd just said was true.

Kord shifted uneasily. "How are they not going to be a problem? They're not just going to let us sail into their capital. And with their numbers and their cannons, they have the strength to eliminate us from the water—every single ship, every single man."

"*Viceroy*," Cyrus called down the blood bond.

"*We're in position, Sire*," came the reply.

"*How many ships do they have?*" Cyrus asked.

"*Too many to count.*"

When Cyrus had first had the blood delivered to Serra, the viceroy had been reluctant to use it. It was easy to forget sometimes that communicating through a blood bond wasn't a common thing, and that people not accustomed were quite put off by it. Orion had thought it was disgusting.

Orion...

His chest tightened.

"Should we advance, Sire?"

His mind snapped back. *"No,"* he replied. *"Hold until my command."*

"Cyrus," Kord pressed him. "What's the plan? What are we going to do about Osan?"

"I said they won't be a problem."

Please, fucking gods, don't let them be a problem. If Osan had split their fleet, they'd be a problem. *Don't let them have split their fleet.*

"Cyrus, how much longer?" Bash's voice cracked through the bond like a whip, sudden and jarring. *"Gregor's going to realize. I need to get Miriel out."*

The timing couldn't be worse. Between the Serran viceroy and his shipmasters in his head, and Kord and Everan at his side, there were entirely too many voices.

Bash was still worried for Miriel—worried that Gregor would discover that Cyrus's army had left and that only an illusion remained. But Cyrus needed her to keep the ruse, to keep Aleon's attention on Japheth. Just until he reached the Shadow King...

"Cyrus," Kord pushed.

He ignored him. *"Not much longer,"* he told Bash. *"As soon as I have the Shadow King in sight, you can pull her out."*

"Where are you now?"

He hesitated. *"We're almost to Osan."*

"You haven't even made land? Fuck, Cyrus."

"Cyrus," Kord pushed.

"It will be fine!" he snapped, both to Kord and back down the bond to Bash.

He prayed to the gods it would be fine.

It had to be fine.

It had to work.

"Cyrus."

"What?!" he stormed in reply.

It was Jaem. *"Mercia is marching to join Aleon."*

Cyrus stilled.

"The Shadow King is headed to the mountain stronghold alone," Jaem told him.

Surely he hadn't heard that right. *"Mercia is marching to join Aleon?"*

"Yes, and the Shadow King is headed to the mountain stronghold," Jaem repeated.

But it was still sinking in. Mercia was going to join Aleon, leaving the Shadow King completely alone.

Favor of the gods...

"Cyrus, there's more," Jaem said. *"The Shadow King has with him only about a quarter of his army."*

Cyrus's heart beat faster. It was more than just favor from the gods. It was a sign from fate. Fate was handing him this victory.

He looked up to find all eyes staring back at him. "Mercia marches to join Aleon," he told Everan and Kord. "The Shadow King is headed to the mountain stronghold alone, with only a partial army."

Everan and Kord glanced at each other.

"It's fate," Cyrus said, almost a whisper to himself. Did they see it now?

The Osani capital came into view, and his pulse thrummed heavily in his ears.

Kord leaned over the railing, as if it would give him better visibility. "Where's their fleet?" Only two ships sat in the harbor. He whirled back to Cyrus. "Where's the rest of their fleet?" he asked again.

"Engaged with a threat on their west bank," Cyrus said.

His brows stitched. "What threat?"

Cyrus spoke the words aloud as he sent them through the blood bond. "*Viceroy.*"

"*Yes, Sire,*" came the reply.

"*Attack.*"

Kord's eyes flashed in alarm as he realized. "You sent the Serran fleet to bait them?"

"We had to draw them out of the inlet somehow."

Kord shook his head. "Those men don't stand a chance."

"They don't need to."

Kord glanced at Everan, then took a step back. "You sacrificed them?"

"They went willingly," Cyrus said.

"Do they know they'll die? All of them. *All of them.* They'll *all* die."

That wasn't necessarily true, but even if it was... "It's the price to pay to land our ships." *The price to pay to kill the Shadow King.*

He heard his own words echo back at him. A younger version of himself might have railed against a man who said something like that.

Orion would have hated this. Kieve would have hated this.

But Orion and Kieve were dead. And this was the cost of winning.

Kord shook his head again, his mouth agape.

"These are the decisions that need to be made to win this war," Cyrus told him.

"Who are you?" Kord took another step back. "I don't even recognize you anymore." He lingered for a heartbeat, the shock in his eyes hardening into something colder. He turned without waiting for a reply and left Cyrus on the bow. Sergen cast his eyes to the deck, then followed after.

Everan leaned heavily against the railing.

"There was no other option," Cyrus told him.

His friend sighed wearily. "Except the option not to come at all."

"That *wasn't* an option."

Everan said nothing.

The two Osani ships that had remained in the port put up a good fight, but even with their cannons, they were no match for Cyrus's numbers, and they were quickly overwhelmed.

As his ships moored and his men landed, they were met by the Osani king. He came with only a couple hundred men and now stood between Cyrus and the capital—in a single line, swords drawn. Their iron-plated armor reflected the sun, and their red-and-yellow banners rippled with the wind. These were royal guards, and now Osan's last defense.

There was something majestic about men staring down their inevitable fate, bold and unafraid—something that pulled at the heart.

"Cyrus," Everan said quietly. "Entreat him to let us pass. Leave him unharmed. Osan isn't our enemy."

"He's allied with our enemy."

"No, he's not. He's an ally of an ally of an ally. There *is* a difference."

Cyrus's horse threw its head impatiently. Cyrus didn't blame the animal—Cyrus was impatient too.

"Tell him we'll simply pass through," Everan urged him again.

Cyrus looked at Essandra, who sat quietly on her own mount, and she gave him a nod.

"Fine." Cyrus slid down from his horse. As he approached, the king broke from his meager line of men and walked to meet him.

They stopped two paces from each other.

The king pulled off his helm.

Cyrus eyed him. He was older, perhaps thirty years Cyrus's senior. His long dark hair had been grayed by time and was tied neatly behind him.

"Let us pass, and I'll let you live," Cyrus told him.

"Turn around and leave, and I'll let you go," the king replied.

This king was fearless, Cyrus would give him that. It was a shame Osan had invested so much into their naval fleet rather than a real army.

"Stand aside," Cyrus warned again. "My sword is sharpened for the Shadow King. I don't need your blood."

"My blood will curse you."

Cyrus gave a dark chuckle. "I am already cursed." He was also running out of patience.

"Evil will not prevail here."

The word cut a trail down his spine, and Cyrus paused. "Evil?" The irony, given this man's ally.

The king pointed his sword at Essandra. "You bring that wickedness here and expect passage? With her darkness and destruction? I won't allow it. Not your army nor your witch whore. Leave these lands," the king commanded.

Cyrus stepped closer so that their faces were no more than a hand's width apart. "That's not my witch whore," he said, his voice low and calm. "That's my witch wife."

And faster than the king could move, Cyrus sank the blade of his dagger into the old man's throat. He held him, blood running down his arm, as he leaned into his ear. "This world has no idea what destruction is," he whispered. "But I am happy to show them."

He released the king, who dropped to his knees, sputtering as blood pulsed down the front of his armor before falling forward onto the ground.

Cyrus watched the blood pool toward his feet as chaos erupted around him. He let his men respond to the charging Osani guard, and simply turned and walked back to where Essandra, Kord, and Everan waited.

He reached for Essandra's hand and planted a kiss on her fingers. Then he swung up onto his horse.

Kord and Everan gaped at him.

"He said *no*," he told them.

Cyrus raised his sword. "Forward!" he thundered to his army.

Chapter Fifty

"I'm getting nervous, Cyrus." Even through the blood bond, Bash's voice betrayed his worry. *"Aleon's army is massive. Where are you now?"*

"Settle," Cyrus told him. *"I've got good news. The Mercian army is marching to join Aleon."*

"How is that good news?"

"Aleon won't act until the Mercian army arrives. It buys us time. All you have to worry about is Gregor, which shouldn't be any worry at all so long as you keep distance between you."

"He's pushing for us to launch an attack."

"Let Ram handle Gregor." More like let Ram ignore Gregor.

"Aleon's army is scouting us."

"Let them. Like I said, they won't act until Mercia arrives."

Bash's silence betrayed his uncertainty.

"How is Miriel?" Cyrus asked.

"She's good," Bash said. *"But she's pushing hard—too hard. She won't rest. She's obsessed with holding every detail. For you. Did Ram show you the army? It's incredible."*

Ram had shown him in his mind—Miriel's illusion of a vast army spread across the horizon, staring down the Aleon line. Had they been a real army, any attack against them would've been suicide.

"*He did,*" Cyrus said. "*Tell her I'm impressed.*"

"*She said you would be.*"

Cyrus smiled.

"*Where are you?*" Bash asked again.

"*We're passing the ruins of Aviron. As soon as I reach the Shadow stronghold, I'll pull you.*"

"*Hurry, Cyrus. Please.*"

Bash's fear tugged at his heart. "*I'm going as fast as I can,*" he said. "*Miriel will be all right. You'll all be all right. I promise.*"

Despite this promise and his belief in it, Cyrus pushed his army harder.

"The men are tired," Kord said as they made camp late the following night.

"Oksana is growing weary as well," Essandra added, taking a seat beside Cyrus by the fire. Oksana was her illusion witch. "I don't know how much longer her power will hold," she said.

"I'll give her my blood."

"Your blood doesn't solve for exhaustion. You should be worrying about Miriel too."

"Miriel's strong. She held her own army's illusion for weeks after her father died." He *was* worried about Miriel, though—all the more reason for them to move faster.

"But this is so much more."

He knew that.

"We have another problem," Everan said as he joined them. "We have some deserters."

Cyrus straightened in surprise. "Men are leaving?"

"They're upset about Osan."

"Why?"

"Because Osan wasn't our enemy," Kord said.

"We gave them the option to let us pass, yet every man stood and fought." So every man died.

"Osan was a place we would have taken refuge," Everan said, "back when we were bloodsport fighters, if we'd ever gotten the chance to escape."

"Well, they don't offer us refuge now."

"They fear what we're becoming," Kord argued. His voice lowered. "What you're becoming."

"I am what I've always been."

Everan and Kord conceded, offering no more argument, and ate around the campfire in silence.

Cyrus looked at Essandra.

She only put her hand on his knee.

By the end of the following day, mountains loomed in the distance, and Cyrus's pulse raced faster. His blood ran hot through his veins.

He was close now.

So close.

"Oksana can't hold the illusion any longer," Essandra told him.

"She can drop it. It doesn't matter anymore. The Shadow King can do nothing. We're here."

Shouts rang out as a man approached on horseback, and Cyrus smiled as he got closer.

Jaem.

It had been a while since Cyrus had seen him, and he was happy to have his friend with him once again.

Jaem pulled his lathered mount to a stop and slid down with a grin on his face. "Having an army appear like that will give a man a fucking heart attack," he said as he held out an arm for Cyrus. "Cyrus," he greeted him warmly.

Cyrus clasped it and pulled him close. "Good to see you, brother." He cuffed him on the shoulder. "What are we looking at?"

Jaem had been scouting the stronghold for the past several days.

"The main entry is on the west side, but there's no getting through that—the gates are Mercian steel, I'd wager. Mercia held this stronghold for the past several years before giving it back to the Shadowlands, and unfortunately, I think they made a lot of improvements."

"We brought Necross." The coven's geomancer. If Cyrus couldn't get through the gates, he'd bring down their walls.

Jaem nodded. "Most of the walls are built into the mountain, so destroying them won't necessarily make our task easier. But there are a few places on the north side where we might be able to breach more easily."

"Find them," Cyrus told him.

"Will we hold until then?" Everan asked.

"No." He couldn't wait. He nodded to a dip in the valley just before the mountains. "When we reach that syncline, we'll send the first wave."

"I'll lead them," Everan told him.

"No," Cyrus said again. "I want all of our men from the arena to wait."

"For what?"

"For the end, when the real fight begins."

Cyrus pushed them to advance as Jaem and Necross broke away to continue scouting opportunities to breach the stronghold.

Suddenly, Ram's voice broke through in his mind. *"He's attacking!"*

Wait, Ram was with Miriel. Cyrus didn't understand. *"What? What's happening?"*

"He's attacking!"

"Aleon?" Phillip was attacking?

"The Shadow commander—he leads them!"

Wait... the Shadow commander wasn't in the stronghold?

"Cyrus!"

"Is the Mercian army there?" Cyrus asked.

"No!"

None of this made any sense. Aleon would wait for Mercia to join them before launching an attack against Gregor, and against an army the size that Miriel was projecting.

"Cyrus!" Bash's voice joined the panic. *"Aleon's attacking!"*

"Get out of there!" Cyrus ordered both of them. He ripped his sword from its scabbard, but there was nothing he could fight himself, nothing he could do. His heart pounded in his chest.

"What's going on?" Everan asked, alarmed.

"Aleon's attacking!"

Essandra gasped. "Is Miriel still there?"

"We're falling back!" Ram shouted down the bond.

"Fall back behind Gregor's army," Cyrus told both Ram and Bash. *"Then make a retreat to the coast. Get Miriel out of there!"*

"We've put too much distance between us and Gregor's army," Ram said. *"They're too far."*

"Then just retreat."

"Miriel's trying to stop them!" Bash called.

Cyrus was going to lose his fucking mind. *"With what? It's a fucking illusion! Just get out of there!"*

"Can they get out?" Everan asked.

He couldn't process it. He blocked Everan out. *"Drop the illusion—run!"* he bellowed at Ram and Bash. If it came between a few men of Rael and the whole of Japheth, he was pretty sure Aleon would focus on Japheth.

"Cyrus, we're surrounded!" Bash said frantically.

"Ram, do you see Bash and Miriel?"

Ram didn't answer.

"Ram!"

Still no answer.

"Get her out!" Cyrus barked at Bash.

"I don't see Ram."

"Get Miriel out!"

"I'm not sure I can."

The bond broke.

His mind went quiet.

"Bash?"

Bash didn't answer.

"Ram?"

Kord and Everan stood, gripping their swords. Essandra covered her mouth with her hand.

Cyrus waited, his heart pounding. "*Bash?*"

There was nothing but quiet.

He bellowed into the air as he set his raging eyes on the mountain. He'd kill this king. He'd kill this commander. He'd kill every last one of them. "Charge!" he thundered to his army.

Chapter Fifty-One

Cyrus drove a ruthless assault, trying to breach the walls of the Shadow stronghold, wave after wave, but the Shadow King held, despite having a fraction of an army.

He'd called out to Bash and Ram again, over and over, but they still hadn't answered. He'd even searched the bonds for Miriel, although he knew she hadn't taken the blood. He prayed to the gods he'd previously cursed that she'd made it out.

Cyrus had two birds left in the air, and he pushed them both to Japheth. It would take time for them to reach the battlefield in the southernmost kingdom of Aleon. He'd have to wait to see.

Fuck the gods, he hated waiting, *but not fuck the gods entirely*—he needed Miriel safe.

Hephain pushed a waterskin into his hand. "Drink. You need your strength."

Cyrus wasn't sure when he'd last had something—water or food. He wasn't thirsty, but he drank it anyway. When the water touched his tongue, it was good, and he gulped it down.

"Have you eaten anything?" Hephain asked.

"I'm not hungry."

"Just bring something," Essandra said, coming up behind him. "He'll eat it."

Cyrus didn't care about food right now. He turned his mind to Brant, who was with the geomancer Necross, searching for a weakness in the stronghold walls. "*What have you found?*" he asked through the blood bond.

"*Not much yet,*" Brant told him. "*Everywhere we've tested is reinforced with Mercian steel. These walls aren't coming down.*"

Cyrus growled out in frustration. Then he paused.

He had a forge witch.

"I need Mal," he said to Essandra. "There's Mercian steel reinforcing the walls. Necross needs help to bring them down."

A line trenched her brow. "A forge witch won't have power over Mercian steel," she told him.

"That's not true."

"That's *absolutely* true," she argued.

"I'll give him my blood."

The line in her brow deepened. "You act like that solves everything. I'm telling you—he won't be able to manipulate it."

"Send him anyway."

"Cyrus—"

"Please."

She sighed and finally nodded, relenting.

"*The forge witch is on his way,*" Cyrus sent back to Brant.

"Let me take a legion to the east side," Everan told him. "I'll see if there's an opportunity there."

"Not you. Not yet." Not until he knew more.

Cyrus looked back at the western walls of the stronghold under siege.

"Another wave!" he ordered.

Cyrus was relentless. He hammered the west wall with men. Bodies lay so thick that one couldn't see the ground underneath. These were heavy losses to his army, but the Shadowmen had shifted to hand-to-hand defense against his men that reached the top. They were out of arrows or saving what few they had left. They'd run out of men eventually too. Cyrus had enough to batter them for days.

"*Cyrus,*" Brant called in his mind. He was still looking for a way to breach the stronghold with the witches.

"*What do you have?*" Cyrus asked him.

"*The witches can't do anything against Mercian steel, and this stronghold is full of it.*"

Cyrus swore under his breath.

"*But the north barbican isn't reinforced,*" he continued. "*They probably imagined it strong enough on its own because it's a secondary wall and it has banded iron. And it's fucking massive. But if we get past that, the second wall is just stone, no steel.*"

Cyrus's patience was waning. He didn't need an architecture lesson, he needed a breach in the wall. "*Can the witches bring it down?*"

"*They say they can.*"

Good. "*Have them do it. Tell me when they're close.*"

"*Cyrus,*" Jaem's voice broke through. He'd continued to sleuth the stronghold with a small group of men, looking for additional opportunities. *"A Shadow army—forty thousand maybe—is gathered just beyond the southern ridge."*

So, the rest of the Shadow King's army had arrived. Cyrus needed to hold them off until he could get into the stronghold. *"Brant found a weakness in the wall,"* he relayed.

"I'll do you one better," Jaem replied. *"I found a tunnel inside."*

Cyrus froze. His heart beat faster.

"It's not a large one—we can't get our army through."

Damn.

"But if we can get a few men in, we might be able to open the gates from the inside."

"Do you think you can do it?" Cyrus asked him. Jaem was no Orion. But he was good.

Jaem's chuckle echoed in his mind. *"Of course I can."*

Cyrus felt confident about breaching the north wall, but nothing was certain. And, if Jaem and his men could get through the tunnel, they could open another path for the army. *"Do it."*

"I'll go now."

"Jaem," Cyrus said, *"good work. And stay clear of the north wall. We're going to bring it down."*

Cyrus strode back to where Kord and Everan were waiting with Essandra. The dogs rose from where they'd been lying by Teron, who sat in a wheeled chair that Cyrus had made for him. Cyrus wasn't thrilled about the old healer being here, but Teron had insisted on coming, and Cyrus had needed him as he kept drawing blood. And it was a low risk, keeping him in the back of the army. If things went poorly, there were men committed to getting him back to the safety of Rael.

"It's time," Cyrus told everyone. "Brant and the witches will have the north wall down soon, and Jaem found a tunnel into the stronghold."

Kord and Everan snapped up.

"But the rest of the Shadow army has arrived," Cyrus added. "They're waiting just past the southern ridge."

"What are they waiting for?" Kord asked.

"Likely nightfall. They don't have the numbers to take us directly in broad daylight." He looked at Sergen. "Take forty thousand men to the south. You won't be able to stop the Shadow army, but you can delay them until we breach the north side."

"I'll go with him," Everan said.

Cyrus didn't like that idea at all.

"Forty thousand is a lot, Cyrus," Everan added, seeing his objection. "He'll need help positioning them. And I want to get eyes on the Shadow army. Once they engage, I'll join you on the north side."

Reluctantly, Cyrus nodded. He looked at Kord. "You'll take a legion to the tunnel. Once Jaem makes it in, just keep feeding men through." Jaem had said he couldn't fit an army, but that wouldn't keep him from fucking trying. "I'll take the rest of the army to the north wall." He nodded to Hephain. "You're with me." Then he nodded to them all. "This is it."

Teron stood wearily and put on his cloak, and Cyrus stepped to him.

He put a hand on the healer's shoulder. "You stay here."

"You'll need me."

Cyrus shook his head. "Not this time." He smiled. "You got me all the way through to the end, my friend." He pulled him into an embrace. "I'll see you on the other side."

Cyrus turned to Essandra. "Will you help me get ready?"

She nodded and followed him into the tent they shared. Without a word, she started putting on his armor and fastening the buckles.

She stopped at his shoulder. "You..." She sucked in a breath. "You..." Her lips trembled, and she started to cry.

"Hey. Hey, what's wrong?" He reached out and clasped the nape of her neck. "Look at me."

She shook her head. "Something's not right. I don't feel good about it."

He pulled up her chin to lift her eyes to his. "I kill the Shadow King. It's been foreseen," he assured her. "I prevail."

"At what cost?" she whispered.

"I've paid the cost. It's everything I've done to get here."

She shook her head again, and another tear spilled down her cheek. "Don't do this. Cyrus, please don't do this. We have everything we need; we have each other."

"I have to do this. For our people."

"Our people are free."

He caressed her cheek, then drew his thumb across her bottom lip. "But I'm not free," he said hoarsely.

"You can be. You have Rael and Serra. Those most guilty have paid. And the Shadowlands—this isn't even the same king. Let's just go back to Rael."

Cyrus held her face in his hands. "If he deserved to live, fate would have had mercy. But it's fate who has sent me."

She quieted again. He pulled her close, holding her tightly.

"I prevail," he assured her again. "You'll see."

She pulled away and attached his breastplate. When it was fastened, she spread her fingers wide against the steel. "Don't take it off," she said.

"I won't."

Her breaths came shorter, and another tear fell. "Don't. Don't take it off," she said again. "I know you'll want to. But do *not* take it off. No spear, no arrow can pierce it, but you *cannot* take it off."

He put his hands over hers. "I won't take it off."

She kissed him, and kissed him again, and again. "Don't," she begged.

"I won't." He pulled her hand up to his cheek and nuzzled her palm.

"After this, you have to be done," she begged. "Please be done. I want to be done."

"After this, we'll be done," he promised.

Back outside the tent, Hephain was waiting. Everan, Kord, and Sergen had already left.

Cyrus mounted his horse and Essandra mounted beside him, still quiet. He reached out and squeezed her hand. He whistled for the dogs to follow, then he led his army out toward the north wall.

Cyrus pushed them quickly. It was almost nightfall, and he needed to breach the wall before the waiting Shadow army made its move. But he wasn't overly concerned. Everything was coming together.

He reached the north side and could already see a mountain of rubble, with the geomancer pulling down rock, piece by piece. As he drew nearer, he felt Jaem calling to him from where he was trying to get through the tunnel.

"Are you in?" he asked him.

"Cyrus, we've run into Shadowmen."

"Can you get through?"

"I think so. I—"

Cyrus's heart skipped a beat. *"Jaem?"*

Essandra reached out and clasped his arm. "What is it?"

"Jaem?"

Cyrus's horse shifted under him, feeling its rider's fear.

"Jaem?"

Jaem's panicked voice came back. *"They're collapsing the tunnel!"*

"Get out of there."

Jaem's voice pitched higher. *"We're too deep!"*

"Turn around and get out!"

"It's coming down! It's—"

Cyrus's mind went quiet.

"Jaem?"

But all he heard was his army around him.

"Jaem?"

Cyrus let out a roar and slammed his helm down to the ground.

"What's wrong?" Essandra asked.

But he couldn't even say it. "Bring down that wall!" he raged at the witches.

"Kord," he sent down the blood bond. *"Turn around. Come back north. The Shadowmen collapsed the tunnel—you can't get through."*

"What about Jaem?" Kord asked.

Cyrus paused, cursing. *"Just turn around."*

Everan's voice came through the bond now. *"Cyrus, the Shadow army is attacking."*

No—already?

Suddenly, the north wall crumbled, sending plumes of dust high into the air. Cheers of victory rang out from Cyrus's army, then they rushed to meet the Shadowmen who'd started pouring out in defense.

They'd done it. They'd breached the wall.

It was fine.

Everything was going to be fine.

"*Tell Sergen to hold them as long as he can,*" he commanded Everan. "*Meet me on the north side. The wall is down.*"

But Cyrus quickly found that bringing down the wall was the least challenging thing. The Shadowmen fought with skill he hadn't seen outside of the arena. They slaughtered his men like his army was standing still.

All Cyrus could do was try to overwhelm them with numbers—send wave after wave of men. And he did. Well into the night.

Essandra refused to leave his side, ripping destruction through the enemy like a goddess of war. Cyrus felt like a god beside her.

Brant and Hephain barked orders to fill holes as they lost men, helping Cyrus maintain the onslaught. Kord brought the legions he'd redirected from the tunnels, and Cyrus used those as well.

Kord fought at his side, and for a moment, they were brothers of the bloodsport again. They moved as one, their rhythm forged through trust and years. Cyrus could almost smell the dust of the arena, hear the roar of the crowd. He could feel the savage pride of surviving side by side.

Back then, it had been simpler. Fight, bleed, win. There had been no kingdoms, no armies, no gods whispering in their ears.

And for a heartbeat, it was like that again.

As morning neared, Everan still hadn't reached him. Cyrus had checked in on him multiple times over the hours, and each time, he'd said he was coming. Yet he still hadn't.

"*Everan?*" Cyrus reached out again.

"*I've lost Sergen; I can't find him,*" Everan called back. "*It's bad, Cyrus. We're down to about a quarter of our men left on this side. Maybe less. It's hard to tell.*"

The sun rose over the horizon with the start of a new day, and it spread its rays across a sea of bodies.

"*Get to the north wall,*" Cyrus told him. Again.

"*What about the rest of the men?*"

"*Bring what you can with you but get here. Now!*"

"*I'm on my way.*"

"Cyrus!" Hephain called. "Mercia and Aleon are here!"

Cyrus whirled to see a sea of white and blue crashing against the red of his own army in the distance.

No. *No!*

"Push them back!" he ordered.

Kord and Brant sent several legions to meet them. They were using their reserve forces now, but Cyrus wasn't concerned yet. Even with the current losses, he still held the numbers advantage.

He charged forward with Essandra just behind him. She formed a protective cover, taking down anyone who came close to him. Fire, rock, pain—she used it all.

And he felt invincible.

With her, he was.

"*Cyrus!*" Everan said in his mind.

If he had to tell Everan one more time—

"*I see the Shadow commander,*" Everan told him.

Cyrus paused. The Shadow commander—likely trying to reach the Shadow King.

He wouldn't.

"*Kill him,*" Cyrus said. He only regretted that he couldn't do it himself. All that man did was cause him problems. He would have gotten a lot of satisfaction pushing a sword through him.

The flow of Shadowmen out of the stronghold had lessened now, and Cyrus's men were finally able to break through to the inside.

They were in.

The stronghold was his.

He could almost taste victory.

Four kingdoms littered the battlefield, and Cyrus took down anything black, white, or blue.

"Slow down!" Essandra called to him. She was trying to take down every man before Cyrus could even reach them, but he didn't want her to. The fact that they thought they could stand against him was laughable. It fueled him, and he fought harder, faster, cutting them down with a vengeance.

But it wasn't enough. He needed more.

Harder still, he fought. He couldn't swing his blade fast enough. Cyrus paused and gripped the hilt of his sword. He willed one blade to become two—then fought with double the fury.

Hephain appeared on his left. "We're pushing them back! Mercia and Aleon are falling back!"

Good. *Good.*

Cyrus cut down another Shadowman.

They were actually doing this. *He* was actually doing this. He was bringing them all to their knees—the Shadowlands, Aleon, Mercia.

He'd have this day.

"Everan!"

He took another head and kicked the body back.

"Everan! Where are you?"

No answer came.

Cyrus froze.

"Everan!"

Essandra was by his side in an instant. "What's wrong?"

"I can't hear Everan."

"It's absolute chaos right now," she told him.

It didn't matter. *"Everan!"*

Still nothing came.

He felt like his chest would cave in. He couldn't breathe. He immediately lowered his swords and combed the battle.

"Cyrus!" Hephain yelled as he blocked an attacking Shadowman.

Essandra jerked him back.

Another Shadowman charged them, and she dropped him with a burst of power.

"Everan!" Cyrus desperately looked for him, his gaze traveling over the battlefield.

"Look out!" Essandra yelled at him, dropping another Shadowman. "You're going to get yourself killed!"

"I need to find Everan!"

Hephain thwarted another attack.

She grabbed Cyrus. "I'll find him!"

No. *No.* She wasn't leaving his side. *"Everan!"*

"Look at me!" she yelled as she snapped him to focus on her. "I'll find him," she promised. "He's fine, and I'll find him."

He shook his head. He couldn't let her go.

"I can handle myself." She grabbed the sides of his face. "Look at me. You're here for the Shadow King. He's here. This is your time. Everan is fine. I'll find him. You focus on staying alive. You focus on what you're here to do."

The chaos around him grew silent.

He was here for the Shadow King.

This was his time.

"I'll find Everan," she said again.

Finally, he nodded.

She glanced at Hephain.

"I've got him," Hephain told her.

Essandra pushed Cyrus's helm back into his hands. "Put this back on."

He did.

"Don't take it off," she begged, gripping him tightly. "Cyrus, please."

"I won't take it off," he promised.

She mounted her horse and urged the animal forward to go find Everan. Cyrus let out a low whistle, calling the dogs and sending them with her.

"Cyrus!" Kord bellowed. "The Shadow King! I see him!"

Cyrus whirled. Time slowed. The mountain of a man fought on the west wall of the stronghold, trying to hold back Cyrus's army.

Trying and failing.

They had him.

Cyrus had him.

His eyes traveled the battlefield around him. The enemy was falling. The day would be his. Essandra would find Everan. He'd have the Shadow King's head. Cyrus started toward him.

This man was his.

This war was his.

This world was his.

Then that world exploded.

A thunder of violence struck from behind. He hit the ground with a force that nearly knocked the wind from his lungs. His vision pitched black. A shrill ring pierced his ears.

For a moment, he was no longer in battle. His thoughts fractured. He couldn't move.

Pain bloomed, and his senses flooded back.

He blinked against the sun as chaos rushed in.

Hooves flashed past him. The ground shook beneath him.

His hearing sharpened over the ringing. Screams filled the air.

Cyrus staggered to his feet, reeling, and clawed for his sword again. A clash of horses had hit them like a tidal wave.

What—

And he stopped.

The woman on a white horse. The woman from his dreams. From his visions.

Her dark hair was wild with long braids and feathers. Black color striped her face from temple to temple, with red lines like blood tears down her cheeks.

War paint.

And she screamed a war cry.

The horsemen swept through his army like a wildfire.

No! Cyrus spun back to find the Shadow King again, but he didn't see him.

He snarled as he cut ruthlessly through. Where was he?

Where was he?

"Cyrus!" Kord clapped his arm. "We have to fall back!"

Fall back? "I have to find the Shadow King!"

"The horsemen have joined against us! We have to fall back!"

No. He hadn't come this far to fall back. Not after everything he'd sacrificed to get here.

"Hold!" Cyrus ordered. "Our men need to hold until I get the Shadow King."

"Cyrus!" Kord grabbed him. "Did you hear me? We're falling!"

"And I said *hold*!"

Kord still gaped at him. "We're losing men by the thousands. They're either being slaughtered or fleeing."

Hephain appeared beside him, panting heavily. "Cyrus, we have to fall back."

"We're not falling back!" This was for everything they'd lost. For everything they'd suffered.

This was for everything Cyrus had promised—

"Cyrus!" Kord clasped him tighter.

He ripped his arm free. "I said *no*! Hold them!"

Kord stood in the chaos as battle swarmed around them. He shook his head. "You're never going to stop, are you?"

"Why would I stop now?" Cyrus bellowed. "I'm so close!" He grabbed his second sword, which had fallen to the ground, but when he straightened, Kord had his crossbow raised.

Orion's crossbow.

Fixed on Cyrus.

Chapter Fifty-Two

Cyrus's eyes locked on the arrow—its barbed tip, pointed at his chest. They traveled the length of the barrel to the end, then moved to Kord's hand on the lever.

"Kord, what are you doing?" Hephain shouted.

"We're all going to die here," Kord told him. "He's going to kill us all. He's never going to stop, and we're all going to die." He didn't take his eyes off Cyrus.

Cyrus shifted and squared in front of him. "Do it, then," he challenged. Orion's bow could pierce armor. Not Cyrus's armor, but Kord didn't know that. It hardly mattered, though. Kord wouldn't shoot him.

Kord held the crossbow tightly. "Why can't you just stop?"

"Do it," Cyrus challenged again.

"Kord, put it down," Hephain said, moving closer to Cyrus's right.

Brant drew closer on his left. "Kord," he warned. "Don't."

But Cyrus still stared him down. "Do it."

Kord shook his head. "Cyrus."

Cyrus stepped closer. "Do it. *Brother*."

Kord's eyes welled. "Cyrus," he begged.

"Do it!" Cyrus raged.

The arrow flew from the crossbow.

And hit Hephain as he stepped in front of Cyrus.

"Hephain!" Cyrus caught him as he fell.

Kord staggered back in horror.

"Hephain!" Cyrus yelled again. He shot his gaze back to Kord. "What have you done?!" he raged. Hephain couldn't stand on his own, and Cyrus lowered him down onto his back. The short bolt had pierced his breastplate and buried itself deep, halfway through the fletching feathers.

Brant dropped down beside him.

"Get Teron!" Cyrus bellowed at him.

Hephain struggled for breath, but he couldn't draw it in.

Cyrus's hands shook over the arrow. He couldn't pull it out. He ripped at Hephain's breastplate, but he couldn't take it off without moving the bolt. And there wasn't any blood. Where was the blood? Hephain coughed and it sputtered from his lips.

"Get Teron!" Cyrus shouted again. He clung to him.

Brant dashed off toward the back of the army, where Teron was safely positioned.

He wouldn't make it in time.

Cyrus swore as his eyes burned.

Hephain tried to speak, but no sound came.

"I've got you," Cyrus told him. "I've got you. Teron's coming."

A wild fear grew in Hephain's eyes as his body became heavier, and his breaths slowed. Blood was in his teeth and on his lips.

Cyrus clutched him. "Hang on! Teron's coming."

Hephain's breath rattled as he inhaled.

He didn't breathe it out. His body stilled.

"Hephain?"

His eyes were still open.

"Hephain?"

Cyrus sucked in a ragged breath. "Hephain?" A cry shook him as he drew his hand over Hephain's eyes, brushing them closed. He couldn't move. He couldn't do anything. He could only hold him as an overwhelming fury built in his core.

Cyrus's men created a defensive circle, struggling to keep back the attacking Shadowmen. Cyrus jerked his gaze around him to find Kord, but he'd disappeared.

Brant burst through with Teron, but it was too late. There was nothing that could be done.

Hephain was dead.

Slowly, Cyrus rose. His rageful eyes searched for Kord again. "Where is he?" he shouted. "*Where are you?!*" he snarled down the bond to Kord.

He let out a roar as he launched himself into the attacking Shadowmen. He killed with savage indifference—he didn't care if it was clean, he didn't care if they suffered.

No, he *did* care.

He *wanted* them to suffer.

And they would.

And Kord would suffer when Cyrus found him.

"Cyrus!" Brant yelled in a panic, stopping him in his tracks. He jerked back to see a Shadow warrior holding Teron with a knife against his throat.

"Kiran, do it!" another Shadow warrior called to the one who held Teron.

And the warrior didn't hesitate.

"No!" Cyrus bellowed as the warrior dragged his dagger across Teron's throat.

The old healer fell to the ground.

Cyrus flung both his swords, striking the warriors in their chests and dropping them where they stood.

He scrambled forward and fell on his knees beside Teron. The old man clutched Cyrus's arms as he sputtered and gurgled.

"No, no, no," Cyrus sobbed. He pulled Teron's hands to his bleeding throat. "Heal yourself, heal yourself!"

But he knew it didn't work that way. The old man weakened.

"Heal yourself!" Cyrus practically screamed at him. He clutched Teron's neck in his hands, trying to stem the bleeding. He willed the power of healing. With everything he had, he willed for Teron to be healed. *Heal.* He pulled power from the Aether—more and more and more. *Bind the flesh, stop the bleeding*, he commanded. *Heal!*

The old man stilled under his hands.

No. Cyrus wouldn't accept it. He pulled more power, opening himself, pulling everything he could into Teron.

Heal!

But he was gone.

Teron was gone.

Hephain was gone.

Jaem was gone.

Bash.

Ram.

Tears streamed down his face.

Miriel. He'd lost the birds he'd sent to find her. He couldn't feel them, but he didn't need to see to know she was gone too.

And then Cyrus saw him.

The Shadow King. He fought from on top of his horse, surrounded by his warriors as Cyrus's men swarmed around him.

Cyrus stood slowly as an all-consuming fire lit through him. He would end this now. He stepped to the dead Shadowman and pulled his sword. He wouldn't let this all be in vain. Seizing Orion's crossbow that Kord had dropped, he leapt onto his horse and spurred the animal forward through the sea of bodies.

As he reined up just short of the king, a calm washed over him—the calm before a kill. The calm of promised vengeance. Fate had sent him here. For this purpose. For this moment. He nocked an arrow and pulled the crossbow to his shoulder.

Cyrus aimed for the king.

With the steadiest hand.

He loosed the bolt.

And it hit true.

The Shadow King jerked in his saddle. He clasped his side where the arrow had pierced him. Through the armor. Through the flesh. He wavered slightly. Then he fell from his horse.

Cyrus dropped down from his own mount, pulling off his helm. He tugged at his breastplate, but as his fingers reached for the clasps, he stopped.

He'd promised.

He left the breastplate on.

The Shadow King paused when he saw Cyrus. Their stares locked. The arrow still protruded from his side. He tried to drag himself backward, but there was no escaping.

Cyrus stalked toward him.

The king held his sword in his hand, but he made no effort to lift it. He made no effort to fight.

Cyrus struck it from his grasp.

Still, he didn't resist.

Did he accept his fate?

Pathetic man.

Cyrus swung his sword above his head. How he'd waited for this moment. How he'd dreamed of it. This was what he'd come for. This is what he'd warred for. He held the sword high.

Justice.

Vengeance.

Freedom.

Peace.

He'd have it all.

And he'd have it now.

But before he could sweep the blade down, a pain pierced his chest.

Deep.

Deep.

His arms went numb.

He couldn't breathe.

Cyrus wavered. Then he stumbled sideways, swaying. His hands couldn't hold his sword, and it slipped from his fingers, dropping to the ground behind him.

His chest was on fire. He clawed at the armor, but he couldn't get it off. Blood poured from underneath his ribbed breastplate. He didn't understand—nothing had pierced it, nothing had struck him. He looked around wildly.

Then he saw her.

Norah stood with her hand wrapped around a dagger in her own chest. Their eyes met.

She was here.

And he realized.

The tether. She'd done this.

His strength left him, and, slowly, Cyrus fell to his knees.

She'd stabbed him.

He sank to the ground.

Why would she do this, at the cost of her own life?

He rolled onto his back, looking up at the sky. He never looked at the sky. It was so blue, so beautiful. He'd never seen it like this before.

Perhaps it was fate's consolation.

But he didn't understand. Fate had sent him here. He was supposed to kill the Shadow King. He'd been willing to die for it. But Norah was willing to die too. And she was the one fate had answered.

There was a flurry across the field toward her. Cyrus blinked back the blur in his eyes to see the Shadow commander crouched over her.

And the Shadow King crawled. The crawl of desperation.

Both men held her. They held her like her breaths were their breaths, like her life was their lives.

And suddenly, Cyrus was sad that he'd only scraped the surface of knowing this woman—this woman who'd changed fate. His whole life he'd fought injustice, so why did her death feel like the biggest injustice of all?

"*Essandra,*" he called through the bond.

"*Cyrus?*"

"*She's dying.*"

"*Who's dying?*"

"*Norah. Can you help her?*"

Her voice came more urgently now. "*Cyrus, where are you?*"

"*I'm fine, I... I broke the tether.*"

He could hear her relief.

"*But I need you to help her,*" he said.

"*I'm not a healer.*"

"*You're the most cunning witch this world has ever seen, the most resourceful person I know. If there's a way, I know you'll find it.*"

She was quiet for a moment. "*I might have a bond that can help, if there's someone with her.*"

He struggled to focus his vision and barely made out the wounded king lifting her onto a horse. "*She's with the Shadow King.*"

"*He lives?*"

Breathing was getting harder. "*Fate spared him.*"

Her breath hitched. "*Did fate spare you?*" she whispered.

He felt his heart slow. "*Fate freed me,*" he said. "*Did you find Everan?*"

She was silent again. "*No,*" she said finally.

A tear spilled from his eye. She'd never been good at lying to him, but she didn't need to tell him—he already knew. Everan was gone. Cyrus had always thought they'd die together. It was all right. Cyrus would follow him soon enough.

"Will you help Norah?" he asked her. *"The Shadow King is headed east with her."*

"I'll do what I can. Where are you?"

"Help Norah first."

"I will, but where are you?"

"The northeast side."

"Stay there."

"I will." He wasn't going anywhere. He hated that Essandra would find him this way. He hated that he was leaving her alone in this world. He hated that he couldn't stay to love her longer.

As his mind quieted, he broke the tether with Norah. It gave her the best chance at whatever Essandra might be able to do for her, not letting his battle-worn body draw what life was left from her.

Cyrus struggled to focus his eyes around him. Brant lay not far—loyal until the end.

He looked back up at the sky. So blue. Had it always been that blue?

Footfalls drew near, or maybe he was just imagining them. A shadow loomed over him, and a face came into focus.

A face he knew.

"Adrian," he whispered.

No, it couldn't be Adrian.

But the eyes staring back at him...

Gods, let it be Adrian.

It was, and Cyrus wept.

Adrian knelt beside him.

Cyrus stretched out his bloodstained hand. If he could just touch his skin... He struggled to speak; his strength was gone. "Adrian," he whispered again, begging. If he could just touch him, he could come to him in his mind...

For a moment, he thought Adrian would just watch him slip away, but then he felt the warmth of his hand.

Cyrus let his body relax, and he chased the blood trail with his mind. He didn't entirely let go of the physical world. He didn't want to let go of the feel of Adrian's hand.

"*Brother*," Cyrus said as they stood in the battlefield in his mind. There were no bodies, no blood, no death. It was only him and Adrian by the mountain stronghold with a low fog rolling in.

Adrian eyed him warily.

It was deserved.

"*I broke the tether*," Cyrus told him.

"*But it won't help her now, will it?*"

It could, but he didn't say that. He wasn't looking for grace or appreciation. He did want to give him hope, though. Cyrus still had hope. "*I've sent someone to help her. A friend.*"

If Adrian saw Essandra, Cyrus didn't want him to see her as the enemy.

"*A healer?*"

A pain daggered Cyrus's heart. "*I lost my healer.*"

"*Will this friend save her?*"

"*I don't know if she can.*" Gods, he prayed that she could. "*I didn't mean to hurt Norah. I didn't think she'd sacrifice herself.*"

"*Because you don't know her at all,*" Adrian said angrily.

Cyrus didn't fault him. He had a right to be angry. He only hoped that one day Adrian might understand. "*I don't have much time,*" Cyrus said, "*but I wanted you to know that I wish things could have been different between us. I like to think they could have been, if we'd lived in a different world, in a different time."* He had to stop as his eyes welled. How he wished now more than ever that he'd been able to have known Adrian. To have loved him.

He *did* love him.

"I don't dare ask your forgiveness," Cyrus told him, *"but I do want to give you something."*

Cyrus drew all the power he could, everything he had left, and he focused it toward the light. Adrian followed his gaze to see Alexander walking toward them.

Adrian's breath quaked, and he trembled. *"Is it really him?"*

He nodded.

"I don't understand. You can link with the dead?"

Cyrus nodded again. *"Something like that."*

Adrian stumbled toward Alexander and fell into his arms with a sob. He clung to him.

Cyrus wanted to hold Adrian; he wanted to feel him. In the physical world, he squeezed his hand tighter.

Adrian pulled back from Alexander. *"How are you here?"* he asked, still in disbelief.

But Cyrus couldn't give him that...

Adrian looked back at Cyrus. *"Can he not speak?"*

"I don't have enough power to let him speak, but he wants you to know that he loves you."

I love you, Cyrus wanted to say. *"He's proud of you, and the man you've become. He says our father is proud."* Cyrus was proud.

"I love you, Alec," Adrian said through his tears. *"I'll hold everything you taught me. I'll honor our family. I love you."*

Cyrus couldn't hold the image any longer, and he let it go. *"Our time's come."*

Adrian stared back at him.

"Goodbye, brother," Cyrus said softly.

He couldn't feel his arms anymore. He wasn't sure if he was still holding Adrian's hand.

Cyrus didn't fear the other side. He was looking forward to seeing his brothers again. Kieve. Jaem. Orion.

Everan.

He wondered if he'd see Alexander.

He longed for Essandra one last time. To hear her. Feel her. Breathe her. He would wait for her.

As the darkness came, he didn't fight it.

Finally, he would sleep. He was free.

EPILOGUE

He felt pain before anything else.

Searing heat rippled over his skin. Scorching. Blistering. The pain—it was too much. He wanted to scream, but he had no voice. He couldn't move.

He was burning—burning and he couldn't move.

Burning.

Dying.

No. Not dying. He was already dead.

He remembered dying.

Yes—he was already dead.

Except now, he wasn't.

How was he not dead? But he couldn't think. The pain—the pain made him want to die all over again.

A woman's voice was chanting words, words he didn't understand. Did he know this voice? Other voices chanted with her, but it was her voice in his ear. He couldn't focus with the pain.

Did he know this voice?

He couldn't think for the burning. His skin was on fire.

A boom sounded to his right—a door slamming, maybe? But he couldn't turn his head, he couldn't see. He didn't care—the pain...

"Stop this!" another woman's voice called out.

Yes, stop! Please, stop. He couldn't speak, but he begged with every fiber of his being.

But the voice beside him replied, "I have *not* come this far to stop now."

His lungs screamed for air, but he couldn't draw a breath. He was suffocating.

The chanting wavered.

"Do not stop!"

They picked back up again. The burn lit a trail across his chest.

"You're dealing with a force unnatural."

"I am a force unnatural!" she snapped. "And I will have him back!"

The pain...

"It's working," she cried. "Louder!"

The voices rose.

His chest tightened. It tightened until he thought he would burst. He couldn't bear it.

Then everything stopped.

The voices fell quiet.

The pain stopped.

And he sucked in a breath.

"Cyrus," she whispered. "Cyrus. Wake."

Wake.

Slowly, he opened his eyes.

Silence lay all around him. The air smelled of earth and ash. Candles flickered. He lay on a table, or perhaps an altar.

He pushed himself up to see a dark-haired woman staring back at him. Then he glanced around. Twenty—maybe thirty—people stood in a circle around him with their hands joined. On each of their foreheads was a smear of something—blood?

He looked back at the dark-haired woman.

But as she stared at him, her expression changed.

"You're not Cyrus," she said, her voice as cold as steel. "Where is he?"

Alexander glanced around him again. "Who is Cyrus?" he asked.

Books by Nicola

NORTH QUEEN   SHADOW QUEEN   WAR QUEEN

BLOOD KING I   BLOOD KING II

AUTHOR'S NOTE

I know in the first *Blood King* book, I dedicated the duology to myself, because that felt right at the time. But since then, something happened that reframed everything.

Our writing group nearly lost a very close friend. It feels nothing short of a miracle that she's still here. While the road to recovery is long, she's still with us, and for that, I'm so incredibly thankful.

Kaylin has been part of this story from the very beginning. She helped shape the *Crowns* series into what it is today and continues to pour her insight and heart into everything I write. She was one of the first people to ever read *North Queen*, and now she's always the first person to read anything new. Her belief in me and my stories has never wavered.

It's only fitting that I dedicate the best book I've ever written to her.

So, Kaylin—this one's for you.

About the Author

Nicola Tyche (TIE-kee) is a romantic fantasy author, weaving stories full of twisty suspense, fierce heroines, and villains you can't help but root for.

She lives in the Pacific Northwest with her husband and three daughters. When she isn't writing, she enjoys tacos, traveling, gardening, exploring the great outdoors, and other creative projects.

To stay connected, visit her website at www.nicolatyche.com, join her reader communities on Facebook or Discord, and find her on your favorite social platforms through the link below!

www.ingramcontent.com/pod-product-compliance
Lightning Source LLC
Chambersburg PA
CBHW061030310726
48969CB00004B/907